MEREDITH DURAN

WITHDRAWN

LUCK BE A LADY

POCKET BOOKS

New York   London   Toronto   Sydney   New Delhi

Pocket Books
An Imprint of Simon & Schuster, Inc.
1230 Avenue of the Americas
New York, NY 10020

This book is a work of fiction. Any references to historical events, real people, or real places are used fictitiously. Other names, characters, places, and events are products of the author's imagination, and any resemblance to actual events or places or persons, living or dead, is entirely coincidental.

Copyright © 2015 by Meredith Duran

First Pocket Books paperback edition September 2015

POCKET and colophon are registered trademarks of Simon & Schuster, Inc.

For information about special discounts for bulk purchases, please contact Simon & Schuster Special Sales at 1-866-506-1949 or business@simonandschuster.com.

The Simon & Schuster Speakers Bureau can bring authors to your live event. For more information or to book an event, contact the Simon & Schuster Speakers Bureau at 1-866-248-3049 or visit our website at www.simonspeakers.com.

Manufactured in the United States of America

10 9 8 7 6 5 4 3 2 1

ISBN 978-1-4767-4136-9
ISBN 978-1-4767-4139-0 (ebook)

This book is dedicated to Lauren McKenna, a marvelous editor who also moonlights as muse, confidante, cheerleader, international strategist, and raconteur nonpareil. Working with you is a privilege in countless ways, and an absolute pleasure, always.

ACKNOWLEDGMENTS

A novel is not truly born until it has been read. And so, in addition to the usual suspects (you know who you are), I gratefully acknowledge those who read my books. Your letters, emails, Facebook posts, tweets, and our rare and wonderful encounters offline never fail to move and inspire me.

PROLOGUE

London, 1866

Across the street, in the little park they called No-Man's Land, two girls were skipping rope. It was a wonderful day to be playing out of doors, Catherine could tell. The sun was very bright on the green grass, and the girls looked happy. When one tripped and fell down, the other pretended to fall, too, collapsing in a laughing heap beside her friend.

Catherine pressed her finger on the windowpane, blocking out the spot where the skipping rope had fallen. Mama said that at the age of seven, she should know better than to skip rope in public. But those girls looked nine at least. Even from three stories above, Catherine could see how they giggled.

It made her feel queer. She had no friend like that.

She didn't need one. She got to come to her father's auction rooms. No other children were allowed at Everleigh's. Being here made her special.

"What are you looking at, dear?"

Catherine turned. Her father was standing before an easel, on which sat a handsome drawing that might be by Mr. Raphael, or might not. He was trying to tell. "Nothing," she said, feeling guilty.

Papa smiled at her. "Come here. Tell me what you think."

She wiped her sweaty hands on her pinafore before reaching into her pocket for her loupe. Papa had given it to her for her seventh birthday. It looked just like the loupe Papa always carried in his own pocket. It had come with a velvet-lined box for safekeeping, but Catherine carried it at all hours. It was, Papa said, the "tool of the trade," and no true auctioneer ever let his loupe go far from him.

As she put it to her eye, it did a magic thing, calling out the woolly edges of the ink, revealing the way the artist had drawn his strokes from top to bottom.

"Steady now." Papa's hand closed around her wrist, holding her hand steady. "Now, what do you say? Raphael's, or no?"

Anxiety tightened her throat. It was a very important thing to decide. This drawing could be worth a fortune, but if it was a forgery, putting it to auction would bring shame upon the company. Nobody would trust an auctioneer who sold forgeries.

As she squinted into the loupe, she answered the questions he had taught her to ask of an old Italian drawing. "Mr. Raphael used iron-gall ink," she said. "It gets darker with time. This ink is very dark, which is good."

"Yes," he murmured. "What else?"

She had never confessed to him that she cheated on these tests. She listened to his voice as carefully as she looked at the drawing, to know what *he* had decided.

His opinion was the most important thing in the world.

But maybe he had guessed at her cheating, for she could tell nothing from his voice as he prodded her. "Go on, Cate. Speak your thoughts aloud, so I might hear them."

She frowned. She could do this. She was very smart for her age—smarter even than her brother, who was three years her elder. So Papa had told her. "The old masters drew very quickly, without lifting their quills from the page. But some of these lines are broken, and their edges are fuzzy. Feathered," she corrected quickly. That was the grown-up word.

He made a happy noise. She lowered the loupe and found him beaming at her.

"What does that tell you?" he asked.

"It is not Mr. Raphael's work."

He grinned. "Shall we toss it into the rubbish, then?"

Once before, she had fallen into this trap. She remembered how he had corrected her. Simply because an artist was not famous did not mean his work was rubbish. Sometimes it was the role of an auctioneer to steer public interest to items worth admiring.

She tucked her loupe back into her pocket and pulled out her gloves, which she drew on very quickly before turning the drawing upside down on the easel. Papa said this view freed the eye from "the tyranny of the whole," allowing one to spot imperfections.

Even inverted, the figure looked very fine. His hands and feet were handsomely drawn, and the shadows of his robe were crosshatched in a careless way that reminded her of Mr. Raphael's work.

"Maybe it was one of his students," she said. "I think we should sell it."

"What a fine eye you have!" Papa rubbed her head. "Now tell me, dear—how would we list this in the catalog?"

"By Mr. Raphael's surname only," she said. "That suggests it belongs to his period and style, but shows we make no claim that he drew it himself."

He picked her up by the waist and lifted her into the wing chair in front of his desk. This was where the dealers and private clients sat when meeting with him. As he sat across from her, he smiled. "You're my diamond, Cate. Do you know that?"

Her spirits rose like confetti lifted by the wind. She nodded, buoyantly pleased.

But his smile faded as he continued to look at her. She wondered if she'd made a mistake, after all. "Is something wrong, Papa?"

"No, no. I'm pleased as punch with you," he said softly. "I'm only thinking—you've got your mother's face, my love. A true beauty, you'll be."

She bit her lip. She would rather take after Papa.

"You'll have your pick of gentlemen to marry," Papa went on. "But I hope you won't ever forget the auction rooms."

Horrified, she sat forward. "I would *never*. Papa, I wouldn't!"

He chuckled. "Your husband will want you at home."

"Then I won't marry!" She saw no fun in it anyway. Even when Mama was well, she was full of complaints.

"Don't say that, Cate." Papa reached across the desk for her hand. "Better to say—we'll find you a man of discerning tastes, who knows brilliance when he sees it, and knows to treasure it, too."

She hesitated. "Gentlemen don't want a lady who knows more than them."

"Your mother told you that?" When she nodded, he pulled a face. "Well, that isn't quite true. Some men reckon it a very fine thing, to have a wife with a brain." His eyes narrowed. "And you've got one, Cate. A very clever brain, and I won't let it go to waste. What do you say to this? One day, my love, this place will be yours."

Her breath caught. *Hers?* The thought dazzled her. Nowhere was more magical than Everleigh's, with its corners and shadows filled with treasures, and important people in jewels and silks parading through the halls at all hours.

But . . . "Mama said that Peter must have it." Her older brother was at school now in Hampshire. Mama said he was learning important things there. But he could not be learning *so* much. Catherine could look at a painting and tell whether it was real or fake. Peter could not do that. He was as thickheaded as a wall when it came to art.

"Yes," Papa said. "Peter will share Everleigh's with you. Ladies, I'm afraid, cannot be auctioneers. But you, my love, will be the soul of this place. Peter will manage the sales—but *you* will manage the art. Never forget, we Everleighs are not merely tradesmen. Art is our calling, and a true auctioneer must understand it better than even the artist himself. You will help Peter to do that, won't you?"

She did not want to help Peter do anything. When he came home on holidays, he pinched her until she bruised. But it seemed a small price to pay, to be given the auction rooms as her own. "The artist creates," she recited dutifully. "*We* give his work value."

"Precisely." He lifted her hand and kissed her knuckles, as though she were a proper grown-up. "My beauty," he said softly. "You make me proud. Do you know that?" The grandfather clock chimed, causing Papa to drop her hand and cast a startled glance toward the time. "Ah, we've missed dinner again. Your mother won't be pleased."

Catherine struggled out of the chair. Mama hated when they did not arrive for dinner. Sometimes, as a punishment, she kept Catherine home the next day. "I want to come tomorrow, too," she said. "Please, will you bring me?" It was so boring at home. Mama was well, right now, which meant she spent the afternoons visiting friends, who talked of nothing but dresses and troublesome servants.

Papa had risen to put on his coat. "Of course," he said over his shoulder. "If you are to inherit this place, there's no time to waste. You must come daily, and learn everything there is to know."

Perfect happiness felt like the heat from a fire on a cold winter's night. "I will learn everything," she promised. She would make him prouder than he imagined.

Saturdays were the best days. Provided you found a room, the single night's rent would purchase you two days of rest, for no landlord came calling on Sundays. What a glorious thing it was to settle under a roof for the weekend! Ma had laid down some blankets for his bed, and Nick had slept Saturday through, and most of Sunday besides. When he'd woken at last, the vespers had been tolling from Christ Church, and a feast had been waiting on the floor beside his bed.

His fever had finally broken. He'd known it by the hunger he felt. Hardest thing he'd ever done, to sit there, stomach growling, for another two hours till Ma appeared again. She gave him sass for having waited, but he would not eat a bite till she agreed to take half for herself.

That feast would keep his stomach busy for days. Cheese, an entire crusty loaf of bread, and two kinds of meat, sheep's head and pork together—the Lord's last supper hadn't been so grand. Nick relished every bite, trying not to think on what Ma had sold to get it. This week had pinched. Usually he found work at the docks, but the ganger had seen the fever in his face on Thursday, and turned him away two days running. That cost seven shillings, with most of the rest going to the week's rent. What pennies remained would not have paid for a quarter of this ham.

It seemed Ma tasted what she'd done for it. The meat turned her sour. She started in on him again. Lately she'd taken it into her head to send him to his older sister in Whitechapel. Seemed she could talk of nothing else. Oona would take him in; she'd agreed to it already, Ma said.

But Whitechapel might as well be the moon, as far as Nick cared. He'd grown up in Spitalfields. His father had died here, killed in a street brawl just outside Lyell's public house. He had friends in these streets; everyone knew his face. Did Ma want him in pieces? For the boys in Whitechapel didn't care for nobody but their own, nor should they. It would make no difference to them that Oona's husband was boss of those parts. To be related through a sister was barely to be related at all. Ma knew that as well as Nick did.

It frightened him a little that she had started pretending otherwise. It seemed a measure of desperation, as though things had gotten worse, though in his view, nothing had changed. Now the fever was gone, he'd find work again, easy. He was strong, and tall for his nearly eleven years. With food in his stomach, he'd be sure to impress the ganger. Maybe one day soon he'd move into the "Royals," that rank of men who were always called first to work when a ship docked for unloading.

He went to sleep on Sunday with these hopes in mind. Yet when he woke on Monday, he did so with a pit in his stomach. Mondays were the worst days of all. On Mondays, the landlord resumed his circuit. Nick could already hear him on the other side of the curtain, having it out with Ma.

"Just an hour more," she was saying to Mr. Bell. "He's been sick, you see."

Nick hated that wheedling note in her voice. She never used it with anybody else. On the street, in rough company, she sounded tough as a boxer. But with Mr. Bell, she said, there was no choice but to snivel. That was what he wanted, even more than the rent, and as long as he owned most of Spitalfields, snivel she would. *Know when to box, and when to bow,* she liked to tell Nick. *And don't feel no shame for either. It's the way of the world, if you mean to survive.*

Easy for her to say. Women could grovel without any loss of face.

Usually Mr. Bell was easily won over. Nick didn't like to think why. But today he sounded hard, pissy as a wench whose lad had gone roving. "I know what you're about," he said. "Who's sick here? You, or the boy? For it's clear as day you're breeding."

Behind the curtain, Nick caught his breath, and waited for his mother to deny it.

But all she said was, "Well, and if I am, you've cause to know why."

Shock exploded through him. So *this* was why she'd changed her tune, and grown so eager to ditch Nick in Whitechapel! Why, what would she do with a baby to look after? How could they afford it? And by God, who was the pervert father? Ma was already a grandmother twice over!

You've cause to know why.

No. It couldn't be!

Red rage drove him to rip aside the curtain. Bell skittered backward as a chunk of ceiling came down. "I'll kill you," Nick choked.

"No!" His mother caught him around the waist, hauling him back. She was stronger than she looked, and he didn't fight, for he didn't want to hurt her.

But how could she not see it? Bell was the cause of all their problems. "Filthy bastard. Somebody needs to teach him to keep his hands to hisself!"

The landlord flushed purple, like a plum that wanted popping. A knife would do it, but with his mother holding him, Nick couldn't pull his blade without slicing her, too.

"Listen, you guttersnipe," Bell said. "If I've been patient until now, it's for your mother's sake. But another word from you, and I'll have every building in this parish closed to your likes. You'll sleep beneath a bridge before you're through."

"Please," his mother said. "He didn't mean it!"

"I did!" Nick wrenched free of her, lunging to block the landlord's scurry for the door. The rat changed course, circling, and his boot plunged through a rotten floorboard. For a moment, arms wheeling, he looked for his balance—then lost it, and fell to his arse.

There was justice, all right. Cared more for his rent than the building that supplied it, and now the building had made its opinion known. Though he didn't feel amused, Nick pushed out a laugh. They hated when you mocked them. All these fat pigs disliked nothing worse than getting what they were really owed: disrespect and mockery, and spit in their faces.

Sure enough, Bell's face got darker yet as he clambered to his feet. "It's time someone taught you a lesson." He pulled a dagger from his coat, wickedly curved.

"No!" Ma stepped between them. "Nicky, no! Put it away!" For he himself was no less ready, his knife balanced in hand. "Mr. Bell, I beg you—for my sake—for our child—"

Nick would have flinched, had Bell not been watching with a sneer, ready for shows of weakness. "I'll believe it's mine when angels pay a visit," Bell said, never looking toward Ma. "God knows you've spread your legs for legions."

"But—you said!" Ma forgot about Nick, stepped straight toward Bell. "You promised you'd take me in!"

Nick could not be hearing right. "Ma! Are you loony?" Bell was married. He had a wife and children of his own.

She was too busy babbling to regard him. "He'll beg your forgiveness, I swear it. Bow, Nicky. Bow!" And now she caught hold of him, pushing him by the shoulders, and he could not resist her for fear of cutting her. But as he braced himself, remaining upright, Bell began to laugh.

"What use have I for the bows of a beggar boy? Make

him kiss my boots, and then perhaps I'll think on my offer again."

Offer. What offer? Hands closed on Nick's face, Ma fighting to make him look at her. But he twisted free, repelled. "You would go to him?" he demanded. "Is that why you're on about Whitechapel? You mean to cast me off?"

"Nicky, listen, please!" Her face was awash in tears— she, who had never cried even as they laid Da into the earth. "I'm a burden to you now. You're a big, strong lad. You can make your own way, but not with *me* on your back. Mr. Bell has offered me a place—"

"*Had* offered," Bell said coldly. "But I won't tolerate this boy coming round."

Ma caught hold of his wrist, gripping him hard. "If not for your own sake," she said urgently, "for the child's. Nicky, *think*. Be wise, be smart."

"'Smart,' now, there's a word that'll never apply to this one," Bell said, the words coming dimly through the roar in Nick's head.

Bell controlled Spitalfields. Wasn't a hope of surviving here as his enemy. And the unborn child—why, it was Nick's charge to protect it. Ma would be helpless once she neared her time. And afterward, before the babe could be weaned . . .

He could do it. He could earn enough. He'd find a way, somehow. He'd take care of her and the child, too.

Bell's child. He recoiled from his mother. "Not for his spawn." He'd not bow, much less grovel, for anything that came of Bell's touch.

"Then for me," she whispered.

Bell had paid for Da's casket. Nick remembered now with a shudder. Christ! How long had they been coupling?

"Five seconds," Bell said flatly. "And then my mercy expires—along with my offer to you, Bridget."

"Bow, Nicky." Her great pleading eyes filled his vision. "I love you dearer than my own heart. And if you love me the same, you'll bow to him. Just this once, and never again. For me, dearest. For me, you will bow."

CHAPTER ONE

London, August 1886

*H*is name is William Pilcher," said Catherine's brother. "And it's no wonder if he stares. He has proposed to marry you."

Catherine choked on her champagne. From her vantage point across the crowded room, William Pilcher made a very poor picture. It was not his looks to which she objected; he had a blandly handsome face, square and straight-boned, and a full head of brown hair. But he hunched in his seat with the gangly laxity of a scarecrow leaking its stuffing.

That posture was probably intended to convey a fashionable insouciance. But it looked distinctly foolish on a man in his forties. Indeed, Mr. Pilcher's confidence annoyed her. At the beginning of the musicale, she had noticed how fixedly he gazed at her. That was not unusual; men often stared. But by the third aria, Pilcher's look had grown lecherous. Realizing now that he had finally caught her eye, he offered her a thin, twisting smile. He was congratulating himself, no doubt, on encouraging a spinster's dreams.

Catherine snorted and turned to her brother. At last, she understood his mood tonight—the high color on his face, the poorly restrained excitement. "Peter." She spoke in an undertone, as the soprano launched into Verdi's "O Patria Mia." "For the final time. *You* will not choose my husband."

It was a matter of private regret that she resembled her brother so closely. The cross look that came into his face, and the temper that narrowed his lavender eyes, mirrored her own—as did the fall of blond hair he brusquely hooked behind his ear. "You make no effort to find one," he said. "And Mr. Pilcher is a fine choice. Assistant chairman in the St. Luke's vestry, with no small prospects. Besides, he has agreed to your terms."

Astonished, she opened her mouth—then thought better of it as the soprano descended into a low, soft note that provided no cover for arguments. Instead, she clutched her program very tightly and glared at the small type: "An Evening of Musical Delights from Italy."

For weeks now, ever since Catherine had broken her engagement to Lord Palmer, Peter had been harassing her to find a new suitor. He claimed to think of her happiness. She was nearly twenty-seven, he pointed out. If she did not marry this year, she would remain a spinster. *By the terms of Father's will, you cannot assume equal governance in the company until you are wed. Isn't that your wish?*

But her happiness did not truly concern him—much less the power she might gain, once she married and became his full partner at Everleigh's. What he wanted was to marry her to some man who would forbid her to work at all. Then, Peter would have free rein to loot the place. He was already embezzling from the company to fund his political ambitions. He imagined she didn't notice, that her attention was swallowed wholesale by her duties. But he was wrong.

And now he'd solicited a stranger to accept *her terms*? He could only mean the marriage contract she had drawn up with Lord Palmer. But that had been the product of a different moment: Palmer had needed her aid in drawing out a villain, and she, having just discovered Peter's embezzlement, had felt desperate for a powerful ally who might force her brother into line.

In the end, fate had saved her from the rash plan to marry. Palmer had fallen in love with her assistant, Lilah. Their elopement had left Catherine feeling nothing but relief. She did not want a loveless marriage—or any marriage at all. It was not in her nature to be a wife: to subordinate her own desires and needs to a man's, and to knit patiently by the fire in expectation of his return from the office. She had her own office, her own work, and a gentleman would never allow that. Better to muddle on independently, then, and find some other way to stem Peter's thieving.

But how? Unless she married, she had no authority to challenge him.

The aria soared to a crescendo. Peter took the opportunity to speak into her ear. "Only say the word. The contract is signed, the license easily acquired."

She snorted. "Lovely. I wish him luck in finding a bride."

"Catherine—"

The sharpness of his voice drew several looks from

those nearby. Pasting a smile onto her lips, she rose and walked out of the salon.

In the hallway, Peter caught up to her, his hand closing on her arm. She pulled away and faced him, still careful to smile, mindful of the guests chatting in an adjoining drawing room. "This isn't the place to discuss this."

He raked his fingers through his blond hair, then winced and smoothed it down again. Always the peacock, ever mindful of his appearance. "At least *meet* him."

"No." She should have known something was awry when he pleaded so sweetly for her to accompany him tonight. Like husbands, polite society had little use for women who worked. Nor was this crowd known to her from the auction house, for it represented the second tier of political and social lights in London—those who aspired to bid at Everleigh's but lacked the funds to merit an invitation. The truly rich were summering abroad, or had gone to their country homes for hunting season.

Peter, on the other hand, had every reason to associate with this lot. He nursed dreams of a political career. He had managed to gain a seat on the Municipal Board of Works, but such power meant nothing outside London. Among these minor MPs and political cronies, he hoped to lay the groundwork for his future.

The family business had never held his interest. He was looting it in service of his true ambitions. But for her, Everleigh's was *everything*. Their father's legacy. Her sacred birthright. Everleigh's made her who she was— which was not merely a spinster, the "Ice Queen" that rude wits had dubbed her. She was a person of business.

An expert in the field of fine arts. A learned professional, regardless of her sex.

And she was done looking for common ground with her brother. "I am leaving," she told him. "Fetch my coat, please."

"You *will* meet him."

She started toward the cloakroom. He caught her wrist, his grip bruising now. "Listen carefully, Catherine. I have practiced patience with you. But you have mistaken it for indulgence. I have given my word to Mr. Pilcher that you will—"

"It will not help your prospects to be seen abusing me."

Peter's hand fell away. Far better to quarrel with him in public than in private, in this regard.

"*You* have given your word," she said in a fierce undertone. "Not me. When he asks where I have gone, simply explain to him the arrogance of your presumption—if indeed you *can* explain it. For it is perfectly incredible."

Peter took a breath through clenched teeth. "If you won't think of yourself, then think of Everleigh's. Don't you wish for children to carry forward the company? What is the future of the auction rooms, if not—"

"Stop it." Anger made her hands fist. If Peter had his way, there would be no auction house for her fictional children to inherit. He was trying to tap into the principal now. Did he truly think Mr. Wattier, their chief accountant, would not have informed her of that attempt?

But she could not confront him before she had devised a way to check him. She had sworn Mr. Wattier to secrecy, for surprise was the only advantage she possessed right now. "Think of your own children. Find *yourself* a spouse. But you will leave me be."

"I think of your welfare," he said flatly. "If you do not wish to find yourself homeless and penniless one day, you must marry."

Now he was speaking nonsense. "I am far from penniless. I will remind you that half of Everleigh's belongs to *me*."

His smile made her uneasy, for it smacked of some secret satisfaction. "But you are not a partner in its directorship," he said. "Not until you are married."

That fact never failed to burn her. No doubt Papa had anticipated that she would marry long before the age of twenty-six. But he should have foreseen that Peter would abuse the authority granted to him in the interim.

What she needed, Catherine thought bitterly, was a puppet husband—somebody she could control, or somebody so indifferent that he permitted her to do as she pleased. But Mr. Pilcher would not suit. He was Peter's creature. What she needed was a creature all her own. "Regardless," she said. "Your threats hold no water."

"I have made no threats," Peter said softly. "But I will tell you a fact. If you do not marry, you leave me no choice but to safeguard your future through other means."

She stared at him. "What means that, precisely?"

He shrugged. "I have been thinking of selling the auction rooms."

The breath escaped her in a hoarse gasp.

"Naturally," he went on, "half the profits would go to you."

Had he struck her, here in public, he could not have stunned her more completely. "You . . . you're lying. This is a ruse to make me entertain Mr. Pilcher."

As though her words had summoned him, the scarecrow came into the hall. "Ah!" Pilcher manufactured a look of surprise. "Mr. Everleigh, how good to find you here tonight. And this lovely lady must be—"

"I fear I am no one to you, sir." Catherine kept her eyes on her brother, who *must* be bluffing. But he looked so pleased with himself. Rage roughened her voice. "My brother, however, has an apology to make." She inclined her head the slightest degree to Pilcher—the only courtesy she could bring herself to pay him—then turned on her heel for the cloakroom.

Peter's voice reached her as she rounded the corner. "She is shy," he said. "Only give me a little time to persuade her."

"For such a vision," said the scarecrow, "I will gladly grant as much time as it requires."

A chill went through her, followed by a surge of panic. She needed a method to deter Peter from this mad course. There was no time to waste.

An idea seized her. Perfect madness—but what other recourse did she have? She knew just the man to bring Peter to heel. All it would require of her was a great deal of money . . . and a reckless disregard for decency and the law.

"Sad sight, to see a grown man weep." Nicholas O'Shea lifted away his blade, then motioned to his man by the door.

Johnson hurried over with the flask. Alas, a single

mouthful of ale wasn't going to wash this bitter taste from Nick's mouth. Nasty work, torturing a pig. He tipped back the flagon, drinking long and deep. Would have drained it to the dregs, had a single word not interrupted him.

"Please."

He lowered the flask. "Please, *what*?"

"I'll thell 'oo. Honeshly, I will!"

There was all he'd been wanting: a spot of truth amid the lies. He handed the flask back to Johnson, then crouched down.

The man on the floor was called Dixon. He'd looked much prettier two hours ago, very spiffy with his fine wool trousers flapping at his ankles. Nick had interrupted him in the middle of a poke-and-cuddle with a girl barely old enough to sport a bosom. Why did swine always have a taste for children? It never failed to baffle him, these patterns to which evil so regularly inclined.

But they were handy in their own way. Kept his conscience from troubling him now as he yanked up the bastard's head, and saw what his own fists had wrought. Dixon's face wasn't pretty any longer. No more little girls for him. Now they would spot him at first glance for a monster. "You'll be needing dentures to eat," he said. "I'll spot you the coin, if you make this quick."

Dixon sniveled. There was no other word for the way his face crumpled, nor the sound that came from his bloody, foaming mouth. "Jes' know 'afore I tell you, sir. The buildings, they weren't safe! I was within my rights to condemn them!"

Scoffing, Nick sat back on his heels. Here was the greatest lie yet. "You idiot. You haven't put it together yet. Those properties are in Whitechapel. *I* own them."

"What?" Dixon blinked. "No, you're . . ."

"Tricky things, parish borders. Whitechapel's poke like"—he jammed his finger into Dixon's forehead—"*this* into St. Luke's. Those neighboring lots aren't mine. But the two buildings you condemned, they're out of your jurisdiction. Whitechapel's *mine.*"

Dixon's jaw sagged. He looked properly sick now. "I didn't—"

"Didn't know," Nick finished. He'd imagined as much. For three years, Dixon had been trotting about the edge of Nick's territories, exercising his authority under the Torrens and Cross Acts to condemn hazardous buildings.

Speculators liked nothing better than those acts, for they gave a man a chance to buy property on the cheap. The law required the new owners to replace the condemned buildings with decent housing for the poor. But speculators rarely followed through on *that* part. What buildings they constructed charged rents no ordinary man could afford. Thanks to Dixon, the displaced had been flooding into Nick's territory, placing a mighty strain on the parish of Whitechapel.

Still, Nick might have tolerated it, had Dixon's work remained honest. Recently, however, Dixon had taken to condemning buildings that were perfectly sound. Peculiar business for a surveyor. Downright irritating when the properties he condemned belonged to *Nick.*

"I will ask you one last time," Nick said. "Who paid you to condemn them? And no more rubbish about a corporation. There's a man behind it, and I'll have his name."

"He'll . . ." Dixon swallowed. "Look here, sir—I'll

go to the board. I'll explain the mistake, tell them that I didn't realize—"

"Somebody realized," Nick said flatly. "And I'll have his name."

"He'll kill me for telling you!"

Probably so. "Got to watch who you mix with in the future." He raised his knife again. "Assuming you've got one."

Dixon began to cry, big, fat tears that mixed with his bloody snot. "William Pilcher."

The name rang a bell. "St. Luke's man?"

"Yes," Dixon said. "And . . . he's the vestry representative to the Municipal Board of Works."

Brilliant. The very board that approved petitions under the Torrens and Cross Acts.

Nick snorted as he rose to his full height. Corruption was a rich man's game, with the poor always paying the price for it.

Dixon grabbed his ankles. "Please, sir, I'll do anything. Only protect me from him! I promise, I'll serve you well—"

Nick kicked free. "This is Whitechapel, lad. We've got standards hereabouts." He nodded to Johnson, who pulled open the door.

"What should I do with him?" Johnson asked.

Nick paused. Alas, in this part of town, men kept their word. "Let him go, with a coin for the dentist."

The stairs held steady as Nick descended them by twos. The balustrade felt solid as rock beneath his hand. He'd no objection to the improvement acts, in principle. Once, this building had deserved condemnation, too. A broken skeleton with eight people to a room, it had trembled in the breeze and flooded at each rainfall.

Only the desperate had lived here, knowing it was just a matter of time before the building collapsed and became their grave.

But Nick had fixed that with no interference from meddling lawmen. He'd won the deed in a card game, then rebuilt the place himself. He'd started by knocking down the subdivisions by which the former owner had extracted maximum rent for minimum space. Built new rooms, and allotted two or three to each family. That small trick had turned the male tenants into heads of households, which in turn qualified them as voters. Nick had entered their names in the parish lists. Come the next election, they had voted for him.

He'd controlled the Whitechapel vestry for four years now. Wasn't a single local man who didn't answer to him. Meanwhile, the parish officers would sooner condemn their own houses than one of Nick's.

But those buildings Dixon had condemned were tricky. Whitechapel's western border poked like a sore thumb into the neighboring parish of St. Luke's. No coincidence, Nick supposed, that the plots to left and right, which stood in St. Luke's, had been razed a year ago. Pilcher obviously had plans for that street. But if he thought he could dip into Whitechapel to effect them, he had a hard lesson coming.

On the landing, a tenant stepped aside, bowing. Nick nodded as he passed, sparing a glance for the polished window that looked onto a sea of fine, new roofs. This entire block—and the nine or ten streets around it—would stand till kingdom come, thanks to him. As for how he paid for the constant improvements—whether his coin was earned through fair means or foul—his tenants did not care. As long as the roof kept the rain out and the rent stayed reasonable, they'd bow to him gladly, of their own free will.

That was how he wanted it. What good was respect earned by force? That wasn't respect at all.

In the street, he came to a stop, drawing a long breath of the pungent air. The smell of fried oysters was coming from Neddie's, the pub where he always broke his fast. But today, he lacked the appetite. Irritation had killed it.

Thundering footsteps approached from behind. Nick didn't bother to turn, because a knot of men outside Neddie's had raised their hands in greeting, and in their faces, he saw no alarm. This place, these people, were his. If a threat was coming, they'd be charging to meet it, weapons in hand.

Johnson joined him, breathing heavily. The Englishman wasn't built for speed, but he could slip into places that an Irishman found . . . uncomfortable. Nick had hired him as an experiment. How far did money take you, without the ties of kinship?

So far, it had gone a nice distance. "Shall I make inquiries into Pilcher?" Johnson gasped. "Can't say I know the name, but somebody will. At the docks, maybe."

"No, that's fine." Johnson knew the docks better than almost anyone, for he had been one of the Royals, once—that group of men chosen first for work each morning at the quays. It was there that Nick had first met him, as a boy of ten or eleven.

So perhaps the experiment wasn't so pure, after all. They shared a kind of kinship, even if it wasn't one to cherish. Dock work could be a sight more brutal than torture, depending on the cargo—or the victim.

Today's torture should have brightened his mood. He'd gotten a name, at last. Why, then, did he feel so befouled?

Bloody toffs. They looted and despoiled without a care for the cost. Nick had seventy-six tenants in those condemned buildings. Their fates never troubled a man like Pilcher.

"I could follow him," Johnson offered. "He's heading for the high road."

Nick glanced back, spying Dixon's hobbling retreat. A lick of humor lightened his mood. "Maybe you could even catch him, at that."

Johnson went red. Folks in these parts, now that they'd grown accustomed to him, had taken to calling him Blushes. It was a natural wonder that a giant with a pierced ear and a head as bald as a pirate's could color more brightly than a girl. "I wouldn't let him get away, sir."

"No need." Pilcher's henchman wasn't the problem. A vestry or district could submit petitions under the Torrens and Cross Acts until they ran out of ink, but it took approval from the Municipal Board of Works for a building to be condemned.

Pilcher sat on that board, but a single vote could not do anything. He must have powerful allies—which meant that Nick needed allies there, too.

Nick faced front again, surveying the road. A gaggle of children were playing by Lola's Alley—truants, all. No matter how many times the school board rounded them up, they slipped free. "You see Mrs. Hollister here-abouts of late?"

"No, sir."

It was her job to investigate truancies for the school board, and force children back to school. Should that fail, the new laws gave her the right to summon parents before the board, where they would be fined an amount they could not spare.

"Ho!" Nick yelled. "You lot!" He strode forward, and one of the children, Tommy Ferguson, took note, calling the others' attention in a hurry.

They clustered into a panicked herd at Nick's approach. "Who's keeping you out of school?" he said. Sometimes a newcomer, not grasping the way of Whitechapel, made the mistake of pulling his child from class in order to earn. Then, sure as dominoes toppling, the likely suspects followed suit, bunking with glee.

"It's a holiday," Tommy Ferguson said, brazen as brass.

Nick eyed him. "Does your ma know you for a liar?"

The boy winced. His ma, Mary Ferguson, was as broad-beamed as a ship, and didn't spare a smack for sass. "Don't tell her, sir! I'll go!"

"Take the rest with you. Five minutes, Tommy. If I see a single one of you in the road, it's your mother I'll be speaking with next."

Tommy had a talent for leadership. With gasped apologies, he harried the pack down the road, making them scramble.

"Who's the little one?" Nick asked Johnson. A small girl, more bedraggled than the rest, was barely keeping up, her bare heels kicking as she trailed around the corner.

"New to the street," Johnson said. "Mother's a fur stripper. Don't know the dad."

"She had a beggar's bowl under her arm. And no boots." There was no call for that. He'd seen to it that the Whitechapel vestry covered the school fee for parents who could not pay it, and supplied the boots that the law required schoolchildren to wear. "You speak with her mother. Go gentle, though. She may not know there's help for her."

"Aye. I will."

Satisfied, Nick straightened his hat. Nothing else looked amiss. Brisk business at the cookshop on the corner, women hanging the washing out the windows—he grinned at Peggy Malloy's coy greeting—and men making smart progress toward their destinations, no loitering in sight.

Once this quarter of Whitechapel had looked different—violent, ugly, choked with rubbish. But now it boasted orderly streets, solid tenements, quiet nights, and schools with no seats to spare.

He frowned. He'd been feeling restless of late, uneasy for reasons he couldn't quite place. Everything was going very well—so well, in fact, that he'd left off with petty crime entirely. His legitimate businesses were turning a far handsomer profit, to say nothing of his gambling palace. But contentment too closely resembled carelessness. And carelessness always led to a fall.

Perhaps this was where it started: some upstart toff from St. Luke's.

"Do this," Nick said. "Gather Malloy and the rest of the boys. I'm calling a meeting."

Johnson nodded. "At Neddie's?"

"No, we're done with bloody business for a time. I need a proper meeting." Nick bared his teeth in a smile. The Municipal Board of Works shaped the entire city. One seat was reserved for Whitechapel, but he rarely tasked his man to attend the meetings. Malloy lacked the allies required to sway the board's decisions, and most of the votes didn't interest Nick anyway. He had no care for matters in Southwark or Clerkenwell; the East End was his territory, no farther.

But perhaps it was time he did take an interest. Bring

the board into line, and while he was at it, address the question of water in Whitechapel—these competing companies had been sabotaging their rivals' pipes, making the supply unpredictable.

"Convene the vestry," he said. "I've a proposal to put to the citizens."

CHAPTER TWO

Dear Mr. O'Shea,

Your niece, Lilah, Lady Palmer, speaks highly
of your business acumen. I have a proposition that
promises to profit you handsomely. Please reply at your
earliest convenience.

Catherine Everleigh

———— ❧ ————

Dear Mr. O'Shea,

Your silence suggests that I have given offense. I would
ask you to forgive my forwardness in writing to you
without the precedent of a formal introduction. I had
anticipated that we would be introduced at the wedding
of your niece to Lord Palmer. In consequence of their
elopement, I chose instead to contact you directly. It was
an egregious breach of etiquette, for which I apologize.

*If you would be so good as to overlook my
presumption, I would very much appreciate the chance
to speak with you about a prospect that promises a
handsome revenue for you. Your niece has assured me
that you are a man of fine business sense. I trust you
will not dismiss an opportunity for profit without first
learning of the details.*

*Kind regards,
Miss Catherine Everleigh
Proprietor, Everleigh's Auction House*

—— ⟊⟊⟊ ——

Dear Mr. O'Shea,

    *As a particular friend to your niece, Viscountess
Palmer (whom you once knew as Lily Monroe, but
who served in my employ at Everleigh's under the
name of "Lilah Marshall," for reasons that you will
not require a reminder of), I feel compelled to inquire
after your well-being.*

    *As you may know, your niece has embarked on
an extended honeymoon abroad. It occurs to me that
in her absence, you might have entered into some
difficulty that prevents you from replying to the letters
of her friends.*

    *For her sake, my concern mounts each day that I do
not receive a reply from you. Accordingly, I intend to
request the police to pay a call tomorrow on the public
house in Whitechapel known as Neddie's, where I am
given to understand that your whereabouts would
be known, were you still at liberty to discourse upon*

them. I hope very much to receive happy news from the constables of your continued health.

Again, allow me to extend my apologies for the forwardness of presuming on an acquaintance that has yet to be formally effected.

Sincerely,
Miss Catherine Everleigh

— ⌒⌒⌒ —

Catherine,

Not yet acquainted, are we? I can only assume you've taken a hard knock to your head since we last saw each other. Then again, you and Lily were feeling a mite frisky after escaping that Russian bastard, and you were chugging Neddie's ale by the bucketful—so perhaps the night has slipped right out of your mind.

But sure and certain you seemed sober enough the time before that, when I knocked Lord Palmer on his well-bred arse at one of your auction-house parties. Perhaps it was my mistake to kiss your hand that night, rather than your sweet little mouth—otherwise you would have remembered our meeting. Alas, that's the gentleman's way, more's the pity.

At any rate, I consider us thoroughly introduced. Put your mind at ease on _that_ front.

As for visiting, don't bother to come if it's business that brings you. I've no interest in the sale of glittery bits, or whatever it is that lures toffs to your auction house like chickens toward a cliff.

However, if you'd like another taste of Whitechapel's finest, the door always stands open to a friend of

*Lily's—particularly a girl who can put away so many
pints. This time, however, I won't be picking up the
bill for you—for I am, as you point out, a man of
business, and I know a potential profit when I see one.
(Six pints, did you drink? So Neddie swears. But there's
a legend gathering steam that says you drank ten.)*

*Cheers,
Nick O'Shea*

*P.S. I reckon you'll have remarked that this note was
delivered by the superintendent of the Whitechapel
Division of the Metropolitan Police. Kind of him, ain't
it? Peelers in Whitechapel are tremendously friendly
fellows. I reckon it's because I respect them so. I make
sure Neddie never charges a single one for his pints.
But that's business sense for you!*

"This one's beyond repair, I fear."

"Don't tell me that." Catherine stood at a worktable
in the basement of Everleigh's, where she had spent the
last hour gently chafing mastic resin across a begrimed
canvas—a fine way to work out the frustration she felt.
Or was it panic? The letter from Mr. O'Shea had left her
livid and shaken at once.

What had she been thinking, to correspond with
such a ruffian? She knew him only through his niece,
Lilah, who had served as Catherine's assistant before her
unexpected marriage to Lord Palmer. O'Shea was a notorious figure, a crime lord who controlled the roughest
parts of the East End. What passing fit of lunacy had

compelled her to look to *him* for help? She prayed he had burned her letters. If circulated, they could ruin her.

Then again, ruin was already rushing in upon her. Her brother had dismissed the accounting services of Wattier & Company; there was nobody to watch what he did with the company finances now. He continued to press Mr. Pilcher's suit upon her, and last night, he had been waiting at home with the family solicitor, who had explained that she had no grounds on which to contest Peter's plan of sale unless she married very quickly and thereby came into the directorship.

So, she had looked into Mr. Pilcher. He was a landlord of middling rank, whose family was too undistinguished to promote Peter's political interests. The cause of Peter's fondness must lie elsewhere. If she married Pilcher, she had no doubt that he would oppose her right to work here, and find some way to prevent her from overruling Peter's decisions, as well as his own.

She released a slow breath, then surveyed the painting. The original varnish had crumbled now. She picked up her badger-hair brush, brushing away a spot in the center of the painting to reveal the wonder beneath. It lightened her mood a little. "Look here, Batten. Do you mean to give up on *that*?"

Batten grunted. "Three centuries of being mopped with soap and water—"

"We can fix it." The painting was Italianate in style—not in fashion, at present, but what did she care for fashion? True collectors would recognize genius when they saw it. Her responsibility was to make them look. "Do you see her face?" In the center of the dark tableau, Saint Teresa was being pierced by the angel's spear. She cast her eyes skyward, her expression balanced between the great agony of torture, and the desperate hope of heavenly respite.

Frowning, Batten adjusted his wire spectacles. Some of the other employees, particularly the ignorant girls whom Peter employed as hostesses to flatter the clientele, called him "The Gnome." He was, indeed, unusually squat and boxy, with a tangle of gray curls that resisted even the thickest pomade.

But Catherine had known him since her girlhood. When she looked at him now, she barely noticed the misshapen hump of his shoulders, or the fierce jut of his brow. Instead she beheld a man of great knowledge, able to restore paintings from centuries of abuse—and to answer with endless patience all the silly questions she had posed him as a child, when other employees had only waited until her father's back was turned to roll their eyes and dismiss her.

She held her breath now for his verdict. She must not contaminate it with her own hopes. Business did not allow for foolish romanticism.

"I need more light," he told her.

She went to fetch a candle from the shelf. The basement was a stupid place to have moved Batten's workshop, but Peter had insisted on expanding the public rooms. He did not consider restoration to be a profitable line of investment; too much time expended for too little profit, he claimed. Given his way, he would have rejected any antique or artwork that did not arrive ready for sale.

Before, his attitude had baffled her. If he resented so bitterly being in trade, she had told him, he *might* try to behave less like a shopkeeper and more like a patron of the arts. But now she understood him better. He was done with being a tradesman. He wanted to sell the auction rooms and live like a rich man.

She would not allow it. She would rather marry Pilcher. Or Batten! A pity his wife remained in such good health.

She bit her lip, remorse assailing her as she carried the candle back to the table. Mr. Batten's wife was a dear and friendly creature who did not deserve such ill wishes.

She held the candle steady at an angle that highlighted Saint Teresa's striking expression. Batten rubbed his chin. "Well, you know I don't like to give up," he said. "It's a very rare work . . . or was, once upon a time. But that damage in the upper left quadrant . . ." He sighed. "One almost wishes her face hadn't been spared. Such a taunt, to glimpse what it once was!"

The canvas had undergone some very rough handling. She could not argue that. Nor could she give up on it. "What of Mr. von Pettenkofer's method? Might that work?"

"It might," Batten said hesitantly. "But your brother was very clear, miss. Not above a week on any particular piece. What you're proposing would take much longer."

She grimaced. What a ridiculous policy to impose wholesale! A few of their richest sales had come from items restored by Mr. Batten—and, increasingly, her. She had a talent for spotting the value in damaged things, and thanks to Mr. Batten's tutelage, she sometimes understood how to fix them, too. It gave her a fierce satisfaction to pull beauty from rubbish; to restore the imperfect to its original, unblemished state.

Mr. Batten was gazing at her very sympathetically. "Are you all right?"

She bit her lip. *My brother has gone mad, Batten. He is threatening to sell the place. And I don't know how to stop him.*

But she did know. Marriage was the way. She only needed the right husband. A pity they were not sold at auction!

She managed a thin smile. "I'm fine." As a girl, she had spilled her heart over this worktable with regularity. But a woman could not speak so carelessly of her family. It would put Mr. Batten in a very tenuous position, for Peter was his employer, too. "I simply can't give up on this painting. Go ahead with Mr. von Pettenkofer's method. If my brother complains, tell him that I left you no choice." Not that Peter would. He never bothered to visit the workshop.

She gathered her agenda and made her way back upstairs toward the public rooms. It was half three, but six items remained on her list. She'd not leave Everleigh's till ten o'clock.

The thought made her smile slightly. Her father had rarely made it home for supper, either—though not for want of trying. She, on the other hand, had every reason to linger here. For all she knew, Mr. Pilcher would be at table tonight. Peter made a habit lately of bringing him around.

She emerged into the lobby to discover a group of hostesses—she deplored the common nickname given to them of Everleigh Girls—clustered around a trio of fashionably dressed gentlemen, one of whom she recognized as the heir to a dukedom. The social aspects of the business were Peter's calling, not hers, but she saw no sign of her brother.

Reluctantly, she waved over one of the hostesses, a

fox-faced brunette. "Has someone told Mr. Everleigh of our guests?"

"Oh, he saw them," Miss Snow said breathlessly. Her color was high; like most of the hostesses, she was an incorrigible flirt, and thrived on the attention of men who would never acknowledge her in the street. "He said we were to see to them ourselves, for he has another appointment."

"Is that so?" It was most unlike Peter to lose the opportunity to hobnob with a future duke. Sighing, Catherine girded herself to entertain the guests.

"He couldn't have received them, anyway," Miss Snow continued. "He wasn't dressed for it." Here she lifted one slim, suggestive brow.

"What do you mean, he wasn't dressed for it?" In matters of toilette, Peter was punctilious.

"He was wearing a patched coat." The girl's voice held a sly note of speculation. "And he set out on foot, didn't take the carriage."

"That is none of your concern." But a prickle moved down Catherine's spine, not so much alarm as excitement. "How long ago did he leave?"

"A minute or two, no more."

Her duty compelled her to tour the guests through the collections bound for auction. But this odd behavior on Peter's part might provide a clue to his secret doings—a question on which rested the very future of the auction rooms. For if she could catch him in some unsavory situation, it would give her a weapon against him.

She lifted her voice. "Miss Ames," she called to a red-headed hostess, the most levelheaded of the lot. "Will you see to our guests? I must step out, I fear."

*   *   *

Catherine's life had become an absurdity. She was a woman of business, with an auction house to run. She had a hundred items on her agenda, no inclination toward adventures, and no interest in her brother's private life. At present, her agenda instructed her to be in the receiving room at Everleigh's, supervising the unpacking of the books from the Cranston library.

Instead, she was prowling through the East End, sidestepping stray dogs and weedy cracks in the pavement. On Whitechapel Road, amid the bustle of traffic and the cries of chestnut vendors, she had felt safe enough. But now, as she passed into a narrow lane of tenements, the atmosphere shifted. The buildings leaned together here like tired old pensioners, blocking the sunlight from the rutted lane. In the gutter, a beggar with a scabbed face lay insensate.

She stopped beside him, noting the spittle that dotted his beard. Hadn't her former assistant assured her that Whitechapel was not as dangerous as she imagined? But perhaps Lilah had changed her mind, after what transpired three months ago. Together, they had been kidnapped by a Russian lunatic intent on harming Lord Palmer. The Russian had imprisoned them near this very neighborhood, in such an isolated little shack that had it not been for their combined courage and inspiration in effecting an escape, nobody might ever have found them.

Well. That was not quite true. Eventually, Lilah's uncle would have found them. Nicholas O'Shea ruled the East End like a tyrant of old. He'd been keeping an eye on the Russian, as it transpired. It had simply taken

him and Lord Palmer longer to get there than she and
Lilah had been willing to wait.

Alas that Mr. O'Shea's dominion did not extend to
nurturing beggars. A happy thing that Catherine hailed
from a better part of town, where people took an interest in the troubled. "Sir," she said crisply.

No reply. Was he only drunk, or did he require a
medic? So far, September had proved unseasonably
cold; the newspapers said the chill had caused a wave
of influenza. Nervously, she glanced around. Ahead,
a woman hung out a window, calling incoherently at
somebody only she could see. Not a likely source of aid,
should this man require a doctor.

"*Sir*," she said more sharply.

He loosed a sudden, nasal snore that reeked of gin,
and startled her into hurrying onward.

Half a street ahead, her brother was hurrying, too, his
manner no less furtive than hers. So far, she had managed to keep out of his sight, her hood disguising her
from his backward glances. But it alarmed her that he
seemed to know where he was going. Peter was a man
of fine tastes and lofty ambitions. Whom could he be
meeting here?

Peter drew up at an undistinguished row house,
whose brick face had been handsome once, but now
sported several broken windows. The front door swung
open. An unseen hand admitted him, then closed the
door.

Catherine came to a stop. Somebody had been *expecting* him. Watching for him—here, of all places!

She grew conscious of the curious looks of two girls
strolling by, arm in arm—factory girls, she judged by
their leather-stained hands. To her right, a rutted alley

provided a place of relative concealment. She slipped into it and pressed herself against a damp wall. Her cloak was plain enough, for she had dressed today with the aim of receiving a cargo shipment. But it sported no patches, no rips or stains, and that alone made her stand out in this neighborhood.

Hurry, Peter. She had no wish to be in Whitechapel when twilight fell. Lilah had spoken highly of her uncle's ability to impose law and order—but she had warned Catherine just as volubly about the dangers of prowling here as an outsider.

She sighed, drawing her cloak tighter. She might as well admit it to herself—she missed Lilah. She could not begrudge her a honeymoon, particularly since Lilah had never traveled outside England before. But now, of all times, she could use a friend. And she had only the one, really, if one did not count Mr. Batten. Everleigh's had always kept her too busy to socialize, and even when she had tried, she had little in common with other women of her rank. She had no interest in discussing the latest gossip or fashions, and no time to read novels. Nobody seemed much interested in her thoughts on the art market, or how to tell an old master from a very convincing fraud . . .

Well, she was proud of the business she'd helped to build. Her work gave her purpose; it challenged and sustained her. But . . . it did make for a lonely routine. As a child, she'd longed desperately for a true friend. And secretly, in some corner of her soul, she'd never stopped wishing for that.

An icy drop of rain hit her nose. Alarmed, she looked up into the clouded sky.

"Hiding from somebody?"

She jumped. Around the corner stepped a familiar figure. Astonishment briefly caught her tongue.

She was not good with faces, but it would take a blind woman to forget Lilah's uncle. He was nature's cruel trick on the fairer sex, the perfect picture of dark, charming, masculine wickedness. Shining black hair, high cheekbones, lips as full as a woman's . . . *That* was surely a flaw. But then, he had that brutal jaw and chin to make up for it . . . and the slight bump to his high-bridged nose, suggestive of some violent fracture in his past.

"Mr. O'Shea." She spoke very stiffly, for she had never liked his effect on her. She herself was counted beautiful, and she had seen what power she could wield when she cared to try. She refused to fall prey to a similar spell.

But what a miserable coincidence to meet him here!

He propped his shoulder on the brick wall and looked her over. "Dressed for prowling, I see. Did you steal that cloak from one of your maids?"

She took a strangling hold on her collar. "It is mine, in fact. But I thank you for the insult."

His black brows arched. "Don't think much of your maids, do you?"

She opened her mouth, then thought better of it, and settled instead on a scowl. She had only met him twice, and both times he had looked at her in this smug, infuriating way, as though she were a joke designed for his private amusement. He made her feel . . . judged and ridiculed, found wanting as a woman.

As though *he* were in any position to judge her! He was impertinent, boorish, ill-bred, and criminal. She must never forget that, even if at present he wore a black tailcoat fit for a ball.

She frowned at him. He was in fact dressed with ludicrous elegance, with a diamond stickpin at his neck. "I was unaware that Whitechapel required evening dress of its strollers," she said tartly. "Next time I come, I'll be sure to wear a ball gown."

"You do that, darling. And be sure to keep an eye out for the weather, too."

"I always do." As though in reply, another raindrop hit her chin. "I enjoy the rain."

His laughter had a rich, ringing note to it, unexpectedly beautiful. "Aye, you look as pleased as a wet cat."

"The words of a poet, Mr. O'Shea." She peered around him. No sign of Peter yet.

"Who are you waiting for?"

That purring tone drew her attention back to him. Despite his formal wear, he was lounging against the brick wall with the slouching posture of a dockworker. The sight of such physical perfection, married to such calumny, vexed her in the extreme.

She fixed her attention on the bump in his nose, the single imperfection to which she would direct all her scorn. How rudely he had replied to her letter! What kind of criminal turned down money, anyway? She had thought to hire him to intimidate Peter. It would have made an easy profit for him. "Is it any of your concern what I do, or for whom I wait?"

"In my streets? Yes."

"*Your* streets?" She lifted her brows at this magnificently understated arrogance. "Has Her Majesty been informed of your claim?"

"Oh, I reckon Her Majesty would be glad to cede this piece of London," he said amiably. "Certainly she's never bothered to worry for it."

That smacked of radicalism, which was just what she expected from a man like him. "I cannot say I blame her. There is a man lying in the road nearby, nearly dead from the cold."

"Thomas," he said lightly. "The gin keeps him warm enough."

She scoffed. "How unsurprising, that you should know the names of the local drunkards."

"He's a relation, in fact." His accent had grown abruptly coarser. "Husband to my cousin."

"Note my continued lack of surprise."

"I'll be surprised for both of us," he said. "Didn't figure you for a soft touch. Next time you see a drunkard in the street, best keep moving."

He had seen her stop to speak to the man? "Were you *following* me?"

"The streets have eyes, sweetheart. And they all report to me."

Goodness. She glanced past him, toward the open lane. "You mean to say you employ spies? How . . . peculiar."

"House of Diamonds is just down the way." He waved in the direction of the high road, causing the multiple rings on his long fingers to glitter. His jewelry was as gaudy as a grocery girl's. "Patrons don't like to be disturbed. So I keep track of who's coming down the lane."

She nodded tightly. The House of Diamonds was his gambling palace—thoroughly illegal, although it scraped by on the pretense of a social club. That explained his apparel, then. She recalled having read, in various scathing editorials by upright crusaders, of the dress code enforced there.

If he kept track of passersby, he would certainly know all the tenants in this street. "Do you know who lives in that building?" She pointed toward the tenement into which her brother had vanished.

He did not follow her gesture. "Reckon I do."

"Then—might you share their names with me?"

"No." His gaze met hers squarely, forestalling argument.

He had remarkable eyes, the color of quicksilver, thickly and darkly lashed. She gazed into them a moment too long before remembering herself. She made a noise to signal her disgust—and dismissal. "You may go, then," she said. "I am not in a conversational mood."

He snorted and shoved off the wall, as fast and powerful as a spring uncoiling. "Got a coach standing outside Diamonds. It'll take you back home."

In her amazement, she almost laughed. "Indeed it won't." Decency, and her friendship with his niece, compelled her to add, "But I do thank you for the offer."

He looked at her now as though she'd grown another head. "It wasn't an offer. Something happens to you here, I'll have the entire world poking about to investigate. And that won't suit the business at Diamonds."

She frowned. Sound logic, good strategy. He was a businessman, in his way. If only he paid similar respect to her! *Chickens lured toward a cliff:* that was how he had described her clients. *Glittery bits*—his view of fine arts. "I'll go," she said sourly, "if you tell me who lives in that tenement."

He eyed her. "Thought it was the ale that made you so frisky. But it seems you've got spirit when sober as well."

Boor. "I cannot imagine what you mean. I am always sober."

His answering snort was unjust in the extreme.

"That night at Mr. Neddie's public house," she said sharply, "was an extraordinary occasion, which no *gentleman* would mention. Indeed, had any *gentleman* been nearby, surely he would have intervened in a timely fashion to stop the madman who kidnapped me."

"Wasn't only you who was kidnapped," he said mildly.

She let triumph curve her lips. "Indeed. Your niece was also endangered. Pity we had to save ourselves. At any rate, if either of us did overindulge in the aftermath—which I did *not*—then it was not from any inclination to intemperance, but merely from a natural wish to forget the events that preceded it. To say nothing of the company in which I found myself afterward!" Here, she gave him a pointed look.

His brows climbed. "There's a proper speech. I think I preferred you drunk."

"I told you, I was *not*—" She cut herself off with a hiss. No use in arguing with this ruffian. And, truth be told, she had not been entirely . . . herself that evening.

If only she *could* manage to forget the whole of it. But she remembered saying some very forward things at the end of the night, to do with Mr. O'Shea's face and figure . . . and the amount he might bring at auction, were he a sculpture for sale . . .

Oh, she refused to think on it. She had vowed never to drink again.

She crossed her arms and looked over his shoulder toward the tenement. "Please go."

"In a minute, I'm tossing you over my shoulder."

She recoiled. "You wouldn't dare."

But perhaps he would. His smile looked rakish. "You might enjoy it. I seem to recall a fine compliment to my shoulders, last time we met. I'd put it down to the drink, but you say you were sober. Well, then. Your sober self, Miss Everleigh, adjudged me a handsomely equipped man."

Mortification crawled through her. "You're a churl."

"Maybe. Course, a churl wouldn't drive you home. He might throw you over his shoulder and carry you to his coach, though. Why don't you think on it for a moment." As another spate of rain dampened them, he grimaced and said, "I'll give you five seconds."

She darted another glance at the tenement. Peter might be in that building for hours, yet, and the light was fading now. "Fine. I will allow you to hail me a hackney."

"It's a wonder," he said, "that you ain't been robbed yet. You travel much by cab?"

"I would sooner trust a cabman than you," she said through her teeth.

"You think you've got anything I want?" As his gaze trailed over her, she flushed and crossed her arms again. "Ah," he said, laughter twitching at his lips. "I see. You reckon me a lecher."

"I see the insult gratifies you."

"Oh, I'm gratified by something." His gaze lifted again, but his smile had faded. "You didn't get that idea from my niece," he murmured. "Which means you cooked it up all by yourself. You think of me, Catherine, when you're lying in bed at night? God knows I've thought of you, once or twice."

She gaped at him. Never had any man spoken to her so vulgarly. *You flatter yourself:* it did not seem like a properly sharp retort.

The truth would not serve, either. God help her, how did he see it? Since their first meeting, she had wondered about him. He was so very . . . free . . . in his attitudes and behavior. She had never met anybody like him.

He made some soft noise, then stepped toward her. The alley was not wide. Inches separated them now. She could feel the warmth radiating from his body, so welcome in the damp. She shrank against the brick wall, her pulse drumming in her throat. "What—what are you doing?"

"Wondering," he said softly. He cupped her cheek, his palm warm and rough. She sucked in a breath, and smelled coffee and soap, where she'd expected gin. She could see the fine black grain of his oncoming stubble; his eyes were the shade of mist on a meadow, gray mixing with the faintest hint of green.

She averted her face, appalled by herself. "Let go of me."

His thumb made a soft, lingering stroke down the slope of her jaw. "I'm not holding you," he said. "Seems a pity, don't it?"

She swallowed. "Please."

"Please, what?" He spoke very low into her ear. She felt his nose brush against her hair. He was nuzzling into her, and the knowledge, as much as the sensation, sent a shiver over her skin. "You're blushing," he said, and the surprise in his voice made her blush harder. "Tell me, Catherine. What do you imagine I'll do to you, if I get you alone in a carriage?"

She rolled her lips and bit them. She knew how to handle men like this. She took a steadying breath, then made herself look at him directly.

The devil had given his henchman a face and form

of spectacular charms—and *she* was a woman whose occupation required her to find beauty in unlikely contexts. She would not fault herself for noticing his physical appeal. Perhaps it was educational. Looking at him, she understood the riveting force that drew men to look at *her*.

But a businesswoman could not afford feminine weaknesses. This shivering heat in her—she must crush it. "Were we alone in the carriage," she said, "I imagine you'd clutch your guts and howl."

A frown pinched his brow. "And why is that?"

"Because I would hit you so hard that you'd topple."

With a shout of laughter, he stepped away from her. "Superintendent called you cold as ice," he said, grinning. "I told him he must have delivered that note to the wrong woman. Miss Everleigh, I told him, is the hottest lady you'll ever meet."

A horrified puff of air escaped her. "You did *not* say that!"

His shrug looked lazy and raffish. He would never be mistaken for a man of breeding. Gentlemen moved stiffly, in a disciplined fashion, not with the slinking, prowling laxity of a feline. "Maybe not," he said. "Maybe I hope that you save your hot little temper all for me."

She drew herself to her full height. She was not *little*. And he was a perverse lunatic, if he mistook temper for something to covet. "It was distaste that the superintendent saw on my face," she said sharply. "I have no fondness for corruption. And to see the chief of the Whitechapel police playing lackey for a man such as you—it is loathsome to me."

He lifted one black brow. "A man such as me? What kind of man is that, I'd like to know?"

"A criminal, of course. Surely you don't expect people

to pretend that you're law abiding. Why, you yourself admit that you own a gambling den!"

He made a chiding click with his tongue. "Such horror," he said. "You're clearly an upright soul. Which brings me to wonder again why you're wandering through Whitechapel. Plenty of dirt here, where a proper fly like you is generally drawn to nothing but honey."

She snorted. "So now I am a fly, when earlier, I was a wet cat. Your thinking is disordered, Mr. O'Shea. Pity. It must be for want of a proper education."

"Something is disordered," he said agreeably, "to bring you here. If it was slumming you wanted, you could have gone south of the river; I've no stake in what happens to stupid girls in Southwark. But your idiocy won't become my problem." His tone grew brusque as he held out his hand. "Let's go. Time for you to toddle back to the polite part of town."

Was there anything more galling than male condescension? She sidestepped his reach—and the tenement door opened.

At last! And Peter wasn't coming out alone. She acted without thought, grabbing O'Shea's arm and dragging him behind the cover of the wall.

He was built like an animal, a muscled beast of burden. No gentleman's arm felt so . . . hard.

Peter stepped out. His companion lingered in the darkness of the doorway as they spoke, the shadows concealing his face. "Do you know that man?" she whispered.

O'Shea cut her a sardonic glance. "I believe that's your brother."

"The other one!"

When he shrugged, she realized she was still gripping his arm. Flushing, she pulled her hand away, and locked the errant fingers through their better-behaved twins. "If you do know him, please tell me. I'll make it worth your—"

But she fell silent as the man emerged, for she recognized his face. What on earth was the *scarecrow* doing here?

"Ah," said O'Shea. "Now, that is interesting."

She cut a startled glance at him. "Do *you* know Mr. Pilcher?"

He turned toward her, a predatory ruthlessness in his expression as he took her measure, top to toe. "Seems we've got something to discuss, after all."

CHAPTER THREE

*G*ambling was illegal. But the House of Diamonds made no effort to conceal itself. Tucked away in a cobbled court adjoining the high road, it towered over the surrounding buildings, its facade of pillowed golden stone a sumptuous contrast to the dinginess around it. Through the arched gateway that opened into the court, lacquered carriages waited in orderly queue, discharging gentlemen in evening dress as they reached the red-carpeted walkway. The double doors, painted a brazen scarlet, swung open almost before visitors could lift the brass knocker.

To Catherine's amazement, a bobby loitered on the nearby corner, swinging his baton and looking with perfect indifference on the parade of patrons.

Beside her, Mr. O'Shea was gazing at the building with a look of clear affection. "Handsome, isn't she?"

Handsome was one word for the place. Every bay window was picked out in a shining black frame, the view from within blocked by swags of red velvet that some secret source of illumination caused to glow as lividly as lit coal. "Did you deliberately choose the devil's colors, or was that a happy coincidence?"

O'Shea laughed. "Come," he said. "I'll take you in through the rear."

Relieved, she followed him down a narrow footpath that wound between the shabbier buildings. It would hardly suit her to be seen entering such an infamous place. Indeed, she could scarcely believe she was entering it at all.

But she had wanted a meeting with O'Shea. And now she had managed to win it. Dared she fall back on her earlier plan? The intervening month had not offered other solutions. Her situation had only grown more dire.

After three sharp turns, they arrived at a side door, painted black. O'Shea's knock was answered by a young man in dark livery. A perfect thug, with a shock of disorderly auburn hair, a black eye, and a split lip. "Callan," O'Shea said briefly. "Been brawling?"

"Seems it." The man inclined his head to Mr. O'Shea, but seemed not to see her as he stepped aside. She had the impression, as she passed into a dim, carpeted hallway, that he was practiced in ignoring Mr. O'Shea's female companions.

The notion left her unsettled as she followed O'Shea's swift progress up a narrow stair. It was difficult, with the muffled sounds of carousing and celebration that penetrated the dark stairwell, not to feel as though she were poised on the precipice of disaster. Trawling the innards of London's most notorious club, with its ringmaster as her guide—were she a proper lady, she would be feeling faint.

But she had never aspired to gentility. As they reached

the second landing, O'Shea opened an unmarked door. The raucous laughter and rattle of dice abruptly grew clear, and a strange feeling of pride surged through her. Here was proof, she thought, of her dedication and resolve. Probably she would follow O'Shea into hell itself, if it offered a chance at saving the auction rooms.

They emerged onto a balcony carpeted in the same lurid crimson nap as the street-facing swags. What she saw so amazed her that she drifted to the balcony railing to inspect it more closely.

The balcony overlooked a room three stories high, capped by a frescoed ceiling depicting the heavens. The robed figures were painted in the style of Michelangelo—though these were not saints or angels, but a pantheon of Greek deities, whose vices were graphically depicted.

"Shocked?"

O'Shea's voice came very close to her ear. She shook her head. She had seen far too many paintings in her time to be mortified by the sight of bare breasts and genitals. "Irritated," she said. "I recognize Mr. Taylor's brush." He was a talented rogue. "His forgeries often find their way into our clients' collections. If I knew his address, I would send him a bill for all the time I've wasted weeding out his copies."

"I didn't mean the ceiling."

"Oh." She glanced down into the gambling hall. Between pillars of amber marble, thick swags of cream and scarlet velvet veiled the walls. They provided a theatrical backdrop to deep-cushioned sofas and handsome mahogany end tables, nooks offering a cozy respite for fatigued players. In the center of the hall, chandeliers suspended on bronze chains cast an electric illumination that blazed across champagne glasses, dice, and crystal table lamps. The green baize gaming tables were scattered at well-spaced intervals, each secluded by an encircling stand of potted ferns. But to those above, each table was perfectly visible. With the aid of binoculars, Catherine could have read the hand of every player.

Editorials fulminating against the House of Diamonds painted a seedy picture of dilapidation and decay, the better to evidence the corruption of the man who owned it. But clearly the authors had never set foot in here. The great resorts of Monte Carlo and Nice looked similar.

"I'm not shocked," she said. "Even children play cards." What was shocking, she expected, was the amount gambled and lost here each night. It was not yet five o'clock, but half the tables were full. "It must be crushed in the evenings."

"We've other, more private salons," O'Shea said. "Six hundred can be accommodated, easily."

Six hundred! "Has it ever reached such a number?"

"Come back after supper and see for yourself."

She recognized that easy confidence in his voice. Once she had felt the same way about Everleigh's capacities. How long ago that seemed! Now, as an honorable businesswoman, she would do better to turn away new clients. She could not promise them a fair auction when Peter was looting the accounts—much less planning to sell the place.

O'Shea was her last hope for fixing things. He was the devil's minion, but surely their meeting had been arranged by Providence.

"You have no partners?" she asked him.

O'Shea propped his elbows on the rail beside her,

watching the floor with the calm, narrow-eyed attention of a conscientious proprietor. "Never saw the use."

"But surely you required investors to fund this place." It would have taken a great deal of money to construct and furbish such a palace. She could clear his debts for him.

He slid her an unreadable look. "I had the capital."

She glanced away to hide her surprise. Lilah had told her that O'Shea was well situated, but Catherine had not imagined the degree of it. "How long until you're in the black?" she asked cautiously.

His smile was slow and satisfied. "Broke even in the first year."

"The first year!" How disheartening—and also, she begrudgingly allowed, how impressive. This was clearly a successful enterprise. She recognized some of the players below from their dealings at Everleigh's—men with the deepest pockets in Britain. Why, one of them was a Cabinet member, who had made his reputation in crusades against corruption and crime.

"I'm surprised," she said, "that some of these men would risk being caught here."

"Hence my eyes on the streets," O'Shea said. "My patrons know they can trust me for discretion."

How odd, that a criminal should have what her brother most wanted: the confidence of important people. "Crime pays, it seems."

His mouth briefly quirked. "So it does. Perhaps, instead of billing Taylor, you should hire him to cook up a masterpiece for your auction."

He was shameless, but she'd expected no different. "Perhaps I would do, if money were all I cared about. But there is also the small matter of honor."

"Mm," he said. "Honor, quite right. Not as useful as a ha'penny match, when it comes to keeping the fire lit."

"There are more important things than keeping warm."

"So there are," he said. "Power, for one. Those men below? They know I have them . . . here." He held out his hand, miming, with his long figures, the act of catching and cupping something. His rings glittered in the glare of the chandeliers.

"I suppose that's how you keep this place open," she said slowly. "For it certainly doesn't look like a social club, from this vantage."

He offered her a wink. "Plenty of friendships made over dice. But, aye . . . it helps to hold the markers of men who make the laws." He straightened off the rail and offered his arm. When she pointedly rebuffed it, he shrugged and set a springing pace down the curving balcony.

"It still seems unwise to me," she said as she followed, "to invest so much in a place that could be shut down at any moment."

"Like I said, I make sure to oil the gears."

But superintendents of police retired, and elections changed the composition of Parliament. "If the gears were to change, the new machinery might not prove so amenable to your oil."

He grinned as he opened an unmarked door. "Kind of you to worry for me."

She stepped past him into a spacious office, the walls papered in dark print, the carpet a fine Smyrna facsimile. How odd, that the devil's den should smell faintly of lavender!

As she settled into a wing chair, the leather received

her like a soft embrace. O'Shea took a seat behind the desk, which was magnificent in its own right—carved ornately in walnut, with legs fashioned to look like serpentine sea dragons.

She touched one finely etched claw. "This is not a reproduction," she said with surprise. This desk was three hundred years old, at least.

"Is that so?" O'Shea sounded pleased. "I wasn't certain." He ran the flat of his palm across the smooth surface of the desktop. "I liked it, though."

A fluke. She imagined his taste ran more often toward cheap gilt. Nevertheless . . . "Should you ever wish to sell this, I think it could go for eighty pounds."

He grinned. "A good bargain, then. He only owed fifty."

She pulled her hand back into her lap. Evidently this desk had been looted from some wretch who could not pay his debts. That rather spoiled her appreciation of it. "And if you hadn't liked his desk?"

He met her eyes squarely. "Then we would have had a problem."

She hesitated. If she meant to propose an arrangement between them, she must also know that she could trust him not to . . . abuse her. "Would you have harmed him?"

He tipped his head slightly as he considered her. The thoughtful angle caused a lock of thick black hair to slip over one of his gray eyes. Oddly, her hand itched to wipe that curl away.

"I don't run a charity," he said evenly. "But I've never killed a man over a debt."

A chill ran over her, drawing her skin tight. He had killed men for other things? "I see."

A flicker of dark humor curved his full lips. "If you're feeling faint, I'll remind you that you came here of your own free will—and you're welcome to leave that way, too."

"I never faint." She loosed a long breath. "May I ask, then, what you deem a proper cause for murder?"

He quirked one brow. "Feeling bloodthirsty?"

"Merely curious."

O'Shea studied her, his dark face impassive. She sensed herself being assessed, gauged for anxiety or weakness. But he would find none.

As for his weaknesses . . . She had been trained from a young age to evaluate items for flaws. One might fault his cheekbones for their stark, sharp prominence—but his square jaw balanced them very well. His lips were vulgar, full and shockingly carnal. But the rough line of his nose drew one's attention away before judgment could crystallize.

She had seen no women on the gaming floor. That must be by policy. Otherwise, she'd no doubt that women of low taste would be lining up to play, simply for the chance at glimpsing him.

"Violence is a clumsy way of solving things," he said. "But on rare occasions, it's necessary."

"And you consider yourself a good judge of when it's needed?"

He paused. "You had a proposal for me last month. If it was a killing you wanted, you're looking in the wrong direction."

She felt the blood drain from her face. "It had nothing to do with hurting anybody."

"No?" He laced his hands together atop the desk, flexing them so his rings glittered. "What did it concern, then? Pilcher, I take it."

She hesitated. Did she really mean to do this? Propose an alliance with a . . . ruffian, a gambler, and a crime lord?

"Come now, darling. If it ain't murder, it can't be so bad."

She flushed. Perhaps it was not his face that drew her. Her memory for faces was poor, but she never forgot a voice. His was rich and smooth. Night-dark, resonant.

Suddenly she felt reckless. What did she have to lose? Association with O'Shea might ruin her reputation. But losing the auction house would destroy *her*. "Pilcher isn't the problem. It's my brother, Peter Everleigh. I dislike to say it, but he's not fit to run a business."

"Certainly he's got no talent at cards," Mr. O'Shea said pleasantly.

She stared. "He comes here?"

"Once or twice. Never left but with pockets to let."

She hadn't known that. The news embittered her next words. "What he lost was not his to gamble. He is embezzling profits from our auction rooms. If his corruption were discovered, the scandal would destroy us."

"Pity. And Pilcher? You knew him. Didn't like him, from what I saw. How does he factor?"

"Oh, I . . ." She hesitated, oddly flustered by the need to speak the words aloud. "My brother has taken it into his mind that I will marry him."

He nodded once. "And you don't want to."

"Of course not. I've no intention of marrying anybody. But Peter has threatened to sell the auction house if I don't comply. And Mr. Pilcher, for his part, is oddly persistent."

He sat back, a slight smile working over his mouth. "Not so odd, I'd say. You ever look in a mirror?"

She bit her cheek. It was one thing to play deaf to clients' smooth compliments, but when closeted alone with a rogue, such words felt unnerving. "I—I don't care why he's interested. But with my brother's encouragement, he has made himself quite . . . unwelcome."

His expression hardened. "How?"

"Nothing worth your time."

"I'll be the judge of that."

She frowned. "Very well. There was one evening recently . . . he was waiting for my brother at our home." She had returned home late, and found Pilcher alone in the drawing room. "I had no interest in speaking with him, but he insisted upon it. When I tried to leave, he grabbed my wrist and . . ." It seemed stupid, suddenly, to complain of being touched so, when O'Shea had probably proved far rougher in his time with any number of women. "It was nothing," she muttered. But had the butler not walked past, she did not like to think what would have happened.

O'Shea was staring at her through narrowed eyes. "You make a habit of doubting your instincts, Miss Everleigh?"

"No."

"Good." His smile was swift and sharp, as though she had passed some kind of test.

The approval flustered her. She dropped her eyes, but it seemed there was nowhere safe to look. At some point, he had unknotted his necktie, and his collar fell open to reveal the powerful cording of his neck. The evening coat fit him very closely, emphasizing the heavy musculature of his upper body. He was tall enough that one did not realize at first the power of his build.

She would like to see Pilcher try to manhandle *this* man.

"Never mind that," she said. "I want to hire you, sir. To stop my brother from his depredations. And to . . ." She took a deep breath. "To persuade him not to sell the auction rooms."

"And to discourage Pilcher?"

"A pleasant bonus. But my main concern is Everleigh's."

He nodded, then drummed his fingers once. "Stop your brother, how?"

The show of interest encouraged her. He might have refused outright, after all. "I don't wish him injured. I simply wish him unable to participate in the directorship of Everleigh's."

"Prettily put," he said. "Let's be plainer. You want him kicked out on his arse."

Something in his easy, loose posture made her painfully aware of how rigidly she held herself, and the nerves she was trying hard to conceal. "That is another way to put it, yes."

He grinned. "Not very sisterly, is it? Casting him on the likes of me."

"My feelings do not factor. A businesswoman never acts from spite."

His laughter was short and startled. "Is that so? You hear that in some pastor's homily, or did you make it up yourself?"

She leaned forward. "I believe it," she said heatedly. "The company is my only concern here. My father entrusted Everleigh's to both of us. But Peter cares nothing for it. Politics is all that interests him. Very well, he should be encouraged to direct the *whole* of his interests to the political field. That is what I ask of you."

O'Shea nodded again, his gaze wandering her face. He seemed oddly fascinated by her mouth, studying it a moment too long for her comfort. "Businesswoman, you say."

"Yes." His attention made her feel overwarm and fidgety, as though her blood was rushing too forcefully, or her skin had grown too tight. Her heart was beating faster, suddenly, than the conversation warranted. "Imagine me sexless, if the notion troubles you."

He smiled. "Now, that would be a pity."

"Listen," she said more sharply. "Can you help me, or not?"

"What of the courts? If he's such a criminal, bring him up on charges."

"Naturally I've thought of it." Did he imagine her an idiot? "But the courts would not allow for discretion. I would have to publicly reveal Peter's wrongdoings. *That* scandal would destroy the company, too. Nobody wants to patronize an auction house that cheats and steals from its clients."

"True enough." O'Shea's eyes unfocused as he consulted himself; freed of his unblinking study, she felt like she could breathe again. "So. No courts, no violence. A tricky proposal. And what's in it for me?"

"Money, of course."

"Ah." He glanced down at his hand on the desktop, stretching out his fingers and flexing them slightly, as though to admire the lurid glitter of the gemstones on his long fingers. "Small problem. I don't need money."

What he needed, in fact, was taste. "You surprise me, Mr. O'Shea. Can you ever have enough money?"

He flashed her a swift, startled grin. "A girl after my own heart!"

"No, that's not what I meant." Money was not *her* main concern. "It's only that . . ." He had not struck her as a man to turn down a profit. A recent political cartoon, agitating against crime and corruption, had depicted him outside the House of Diamonds, sitting atop piles of moneybags. Even his niece had once suggested that money would sway his interest. "What do you require, if not money?"

"Well, now." His lashes dropped, veiling his sharp gray eyes as he tilted his hand to make a study of his rings. "Your brother sits on the Municipal Board of Works, I recall."

She frowned. "Yes, he does."

"What's his aim, there?"

"A stepping stone for his political career."

"Suppose so. Your brother wasn't born to a political family. He'll have to claw his way up."

"That's his intention." What did this have to do with Everleigh's?

"No doubt he's using those ill-gotten funds to buy himself friendships." He glanced up. "And he'll need them. To make himself a proper goer, he'll have to ensure those friends are given no cause to shun him, either."

She followed him now. "Blackmail won't work. His reputation is linked to Everleigh's success. He'd never believe I would expose him, if it meant endangering the company."

"Slow down." O'Shea offered her a crooked smile, no doubt intended to charm her. "Lovely lass like you will put my brain into knots."

She snorted. A pity if Mr. O'Shea had not yet heard her nickname. Masculine blandishments were wasted on an ice queen. "Then unknot it," she said, "and hurry up. I have appointments to keep."

His smile faded. "The Municipal Board of Works has become a thorn in my side. I've got two buildings to the west of here, condemned by an inspector that answers to Pilcher. He's got no authority in Whitechapel, but it seems the fine lads at Berkeley House will entertain his petition anyway."

"His petition to . . . ?"

"Knock down my buildings. He calls them hazardous." O'Shea shrugged. "I've put forward my own petition to stop it, but that'll take another vote. When I add up the friends I've got on that board, I'm short by a single man. Your brother's vote would make the difference for me."

Understanding welled up, and with it, disgust. The Municipal Board of Works had undertaken a campaign to raze unsafe buildings and ensure decent housing for the poor. Mr. O'Shea opposed this, as all slumlords did. How low. How *revolting*.

But personal sentiments had no place in business. With difficulty, she checked her distaste. "I'm afraid I have no influence over him. I could not persuade him to spare your buildings."

"I expect not," he said dryly. "You can't even stop him from robbing you."

She bridled. "Yes, thank you for the reminder. I do enjoy this plain speaking, sir."

"Ain't it fun?" He took hold of his fist, cracking his knuckles noisily. "Now, what we require, seems to me, is a proper piece of blackmail. Something to bring your brother to heel for us both. You say the threat can't touch on the auction house, or he'd never believe you meant it. So it must be . . ." He frowned. "Some information which he knows *you* might reveal, at negligible harm to yourself. At the same time, revealing it would ruin *his* hopes for a political career."

"Clever," she said flatly. "Pity I know no such secrets."

"Mind you, it must serve my purposes, too. I want his votes, now and in the future."

"And I would like a world in which Everleigh's belonged only to me," she said. "But I deal in fact, not fiction."

He leaned forward, his weight on his elbows. His full lips canted into a half smile that made her stomach flip. "Then we'll have to make a fiction into fact," he said. "You share a roof, true?"

She nodded, biting her lip very hard as a punishment for the stupid tripping of her pulse.

"You've got all the access we need, then. You'll plant something. Proof of a scandal that he must hide, if he wants to keep himself in the good books of his fancy friends."

She blew out a breath. "Proof of what?" Peter gambled—but who didn't? He was a philanderer—but he never took up with married women. "You must help me," she said. Her mind did not work in such low, corrupt ways.

He sighed. "Well . . . they're not ruling on the buildings for a week or two, yet. Give me some time to think on it."

"I don't have time! I told you, he means to sell the company!"

"Pity," he said, not without sympathy. "And here my niece told me you owned half the place."

"I do, but I can't oppose him unless I'm—"

Married.

Her mouth fell open. He arched a brow, but she felt unable to speak. An idea—a preposterous, astounding, utterly unthinkable idea—exploded through her like a firework.

No. She could not propose it.

But for Everleigh's . . . for the sake of Everleigh's, was there anything she would not do?

God help her. "I know a way," she whispered.

"Oh?" His gaze fixed on her, intense and unwavering. So a man would look, when sighting his pistol. A criminal. A beautiful, dangerous man.

Her only hope.

"He wants a political career." The words felt heavy on her clumsy tongue. Her lips had gone numb, her entire body iced by shock at her own temerity. "I know how to make a secret that would destroy his chances. It would be your secret, and mine, too. He would do anything to prevent us from speaking it."

O'Shea watched her narrowly. "You don't look thrilled by it."

"I'm not," she said. "It's a perfect nightmare. Marriage, Mr. O'Shea." She choked on the next words. "Yours, to me."

"Now, here's a proper spread," said Blushes. "I've not had such a roast since my ma's own passing." As he looked over the spread, table groaning with a dozen savory dishes, a near-religious awe worked over his broad face.

Nick exchanged an amused look with Patrick Malloy,

who sat to his right. Quite a brawl they'd had before sitting down to supper; Malloy's wife, Peggy, had insisted that Nick take the head of the table. When Malloy had muttered about a man's rights, she'd twisted his ear until he squeaked an agreement.

Now Nick presided over a table of fourteen, a solid oak slab that he'd gifted to the oldest Malloy daughter on her wedding day, seven years ago. Peggy and Patrick and Blushes sat nearest, and the Malloys' grown children ranged down the sides, their spouses beside them.

The foot of the table poked out of the room, straight into the public stairwell. But in Nick's service, the Malloys had flourished, and so they owned the upper floor as well. Their brood had grown expert in negotiating the corners of the table as they ran up and down the stairs each day. The youngest generation—grandkids, loud and barefooted and gleeful—barely slowed as they raced in and out, shoving each other to fill their plates fastest.

Peggy was passing a tureen heaped with fried potatoes. "God rest your mother's soul, Mr. Johnson." One would never guess, by her mellow tone, that she'd pitched a fit at having an Englishman to supper. The woman had a soft spot for a man with a stomach, and Blushes was not disappointing her. "She'll have lived to a ripe old age, I hope."

"Oh yes," he said, tipping the potatoes onto his plate in a heaping pile. "Seventy-four years, and each of them sharper than the last."

"You've got brothers and sisters, I expect?"

"Four," said Johnson. He speared a wedge, chewed happily as he went on. "And two nephews and three nieces, now, besides."

"Well, now." Peggy beamed at him. "You'll need to catch up, there. Find a lass of your own."

"A girl of spare appetite," Malloy added sourly. "Else together you'll eat Whitechapel out of house and home. Pass those spuds, boy. The rest of us are waiting."

Johnson hastily complied. For a minute, the only sounds were the clink of forks against stoneware, and murmurs of satisfaction all around.

"Family is a blessing," Peggy Malloy said. Nick felt her gaze fix on him, and braced himself for the usual harangue. "What a man needs, I always say, is a wife, a decent and steady girl to look after him—"

"Like he needs a hole in the head," Malloy muttered.

"Psh." Peggy's hair had turned iron-gray, but her green eyes retained all the force of her girlhood, in which, no doubt, she'd been a proper looker, and had put many men to shame with that fierce glare. "I'll give you a proper hole, Patrick Malloy. Keep it up, and I'll bash you, all right."

"There's care," Malloy said. "You see, lads? Marriage and murder go in hand like meat does with salt."

Blushes had forgotten to chew, his jaw slack with concern. Nick offered a reassuring smile. Was easy, as an outsider, to mistake what the Malloys had. Patrick was a tough old codger, black cold eyes and a flat, mean face; he looked, and growled, like a cur gone rabid. In a pinch, he fought like one, too; woe be to the man who thought his white hair and wrinkles betokened weakness.

But he and Peggy had made a fine life for themselves, and once or twice, when Nick had stepped through a door too quickly, he'd caught them nuzzling like lovebirds.

"We'd all be so lucky," Nick said, "for such a bashing." He lifted his glass, a pint of dark; he always came to supper with a cask from Neddie's. "To good health and good luck."

Tankards lifted. "And to marriage," said Peggy, looking him dead in the eye. "No use dragging your feet on it."

In reply, he busied himself with drinking. Every supper at the Malloys', Peggy started in on him. She couldn't know that today he had nothing but marriage on his mind.

Life had a sweet streak of perversity, didn't it? He'd watched Catherine Everleigh for years, ever since his niece had gone to work at those auction rooms. Hard not to watch her; she was, in face and figure, a living myth. You heard about her kind in stories, fairy tales told to kids: hair like spun gold, eyes like violets, skin without a blotch or stray freckle. Aye, he'd watched her, all right, with idle curiosity, never expecting in his life to come near enough to touch her. His niece had talked of her sometimes, said they called her an "Ice Queen," for she showed no interest in the fine gentlemen who dogged her.

He'd liked her for that. Prettiest woman in London, turning up her nose at the soft swells who cast their caps at her. A woman of rare sense, he'd thought.

But obviously that wasn't true, if she proposed to marry *him*.

It must be a true marriage. So she'd told him, yesterday at Diamonds. At that moment, he'd realized he was dreaming the whole business. A man could lie awake for a thousand nights, his hand on his cock, thinking of a woman. But when she appeared, and told him he'd need to bed her? That was generally a fine sign that he was still in his bed, eyes closed, lost to the waking world.

Only it hadn't been a dream, after all. And he needed to decide what to do about it.

"Mr. O'Shea, Mr. O'Shea!" Small hands tugged at his sleeve.

"Let him be," Peggy said sharply. "Oi, Mary—manage your tyke."

But Nick shook his head at Mary, who was already rising from her seat at the foot of the table. "It's all right," he said. He laid down his fork and turned to the little boy—Garod, he believed, though Mary and her husband were doing their best to confuse him, with a new babe every winter. "What is it?"

Granted full attention, Garod seemed not to know what to do with it. Breathing heavily, he stared up at Nick, his little brows working as he tried to sound out his thoughts. "I want—I want—"

"Spit it out," said Peggy. "Then let the man eat."

"I want to work for you!"

Laughter around the table. Nick grinned and laid his hand atop the little boy's head.

So small. Had he himself ever been so tiny? "Well, that's a fine compliment to me," he said gravely. "But you've got some growing to do, yet. You see Johnson, over there?" He nodded toward Blushes.

The boy looked over. His eyes went round.

"Aye, he's a big one, ain't he? You think you can grow that big?"

Garod licked his lips. "I think so. I *think*."

Malloy snorted. "With that midget of a da?"

"Hey," called Mary sharply down the table.

Nick laughed. "Well, it'll take some work," he told

Garod. "And lots of eating. What say you go eat your supper, and put your mind to growing?"

Garod nodded and raced to fetch his plate.

Peggy was staring. "I won't say a word," she said when she caught his eye. "But what a man needs—"

"God help us," her husband cut in. "Let the lad be."

"He'll make a fine father, is all."

"Thank you," Nick said, to forestall Malloy's defense. But as he applied himself to his food again, his appetite felt peaky.

He'd never given much thought to marriage. Maybe one day, when he was old and gray—maybe then, he'd imagined, he might think about siring a few brats of his own. But he wouldn't do it until he knew, in his bones, that his children would never want for anything. Catherine Everleigh had said it herself: never enough money. He was an Irish bastard in a world of English, and it would take more than two dozen buildings, a minor fortune, to feel ready to bring a child into the world. He'd need . . . he couldn't imagine what he'd need to feel that safe, that certain of the future. A fortress, maybe. A kingdom of his own. But sure and certain, he wouldn't bring a child into the world until he'd found it.

That contract Catherine had sent over to him, it had spoken of offspring. He'd read through it, sounded it out, syllable by halting syllable. *After a period of five years, this contract will be dissolved through a petition for divorce on the grounds of Mr. O'Shea's adultery and desertion, per the requirements stipulated by the law. Or, should both parties freely consent, the marriage will continue, the parties undertaking to produce heirs, of which two will be deemed sufficient . . .*

Such dry language, to frame such fearsome risks.

Fortunes could change in an instant. Two kids? In these parts, two was just the start. Illness, bad water, a moment's carelessness on a rickety stair . . . and then, if you managed to pull 'em through the early years, you took an injury at work or in the street, a carriage cutting too close, a moment's bad luck. Arm broken, you couldn't earn. Then what happened? Nick had seen too many wives, too many widows, starving so their kids could eat. And he was a man with his fair share of enemies, more likely than most to make a widow of his wife.

He'd never wish that fate on any woman. He'd seen it happen to his own mother. Had Da not died, forcing her into desperate measures to earn a coin, she might never have gotten mixed up with Bell. She might be alive right now, sitting at this table beside him.

He exhaled, pushing away that bleak thought. No point in such comparisons, anyway. A woman like Catherine Everleigh wouldn't be helpless when widowed. She had a company of her own, money of her own, and she belonged to a world where danger was always ten streets away. In her part of town, folks went strolling in the evenings to celebrate fine weather. They didn't need to fear the shadows.

"Where's your mind, lad?" Malloy had lowered his fork. "Is it the board meeting that troubles you?"

Peggy looked between them, then turned her back, a pointed announcement that she wouldn't eavesdrop.

Johnson drew his chair closer. "You sure you can't get another vote?" he asked Malloy.

Malloy was the Whitechapel man on the Board of Works. "I've kissed more English arses than a Scotsman after the '45," he snapped. "Not another vote to be squeezed or shat out of them."

"Then it's time to start knocking heads," Johnson said.

Nick thought of Catherine Everleigh, standing in the balcony at Diamonds. He'd no interest in being some rich woman's secret, or in making a marriage in which he would forever fight for the upper hand. He wouldn't tolerate disrespect; he'd worked too hard to endure condescension.

But what came to his mind now wasn't her sneer—though God knew she wielded it handily enough. Instead, he thought of her expression as she'd studied the gaming floor. She'd not looked dazzled, as women usually did when they realized his wealth. Instead, she'd asked how much he owed for it. Nothing, he'd told her. *Then* she'd looked impressed.

A businesswoman, she called herself. Not a lady, after all. And when it came to business, she'd looked to him with respect.

He was madder than a hatter, no doubt of it. But had it not been for a wild gamble or two, he'd be dead now, or half starved, or drunk in a gutter, rather than presiding over this table, with the respect of every man in the parish—or fear, depending.

And so he cleared his throat and stabbed his fork through a potato, for his appetite had suddenly come roaring back. "Good news, lads," he said. "Seems I've got the last vote, after all."

CHAPTER FOUR

Nick's betrothed arrived promptly at half past five on a wet Thursday afternoon. As he unlocked the door, Nick spied her shaking a fist at the cabman, then staring after the hack with an expression of outrage before she seemed to recall herself. With a start, she hurried toward the door.

He pulled it open. She stepped inside, looking sharply around the deserted lobby. "Nobody's about?"

"Had the registrar send home his staff," Nick said. "What was the trouble with the cabman?"

"The rogue thought to overcharge me." She thrust a package at him, the brown wrapping mottled by rain, and smartly untied the knot at her neck. The cloak fell away, revealing a gown of black bombazine, without even a ribbon for trimming.

He made some noise, no doubt, for her violet eyes cut toward his as she folded the cloak over her arm. "What amuses you?"

"Who died?" he asked.

She looked down at herself. "Oh. My father. I wore this to his funeral."

He regretted asking.

She thrust out her black-gloved hands, demanding back her package. "What is this?" he asked as he handed it over. Felt soft, like cloth.

"Something for later. Do you have the license?" she asked as she stripped off her gloves.

She wouldn't make a comfortable wife. Each word she spoke fell like a pearl from her lips, cold and round and perfectly smooth, while all the while she watched him with eyes as sharp as knives.

He pulled the license from his pocket. She seized it for inspection. "It looks real."

"Doesn't it?" he said agreeably.

She looked up at him, suspicion narrowing her gaze. Her brows were a shade darker than her hair, winging at a dramatic angle, like birds in flight. They lent her a look of natural authority, which she no doubt relied upon when bossing the toffs who patronized her auction rooms. "This is no joke, Mr. O'Shea. If you're not certain of the authenticity of this paper—"

"It's a real license," he said. "And I paid a handsome penny to acquire it, from a man who knows better than to cross me. I think you'll find it in order."

"I had better," she muttered. But she took the time to read through it anyway, standing in the rainy light shed from the fanlight over the entry.

Her skin fascinated him. It looked smooth as cream, no sign of smallpox or any of the other countless ailments that had swept through his youth like the regular plague. How could a woman look so newborn?

The paper crackled where she gripped it. She was trying to hide her nerves, he realized. Good to know she had some. Certainly there was nothing womanish about her. She put hard work into diminishing her beauty. Held herself like a weapon, her shoulders braced at a rigid straight angle, her jaw set. Her hands, which once or twice he had seen drifting like poetry through the air, more often stayed locked together at her waist. That perfect mouth, with the dimpled pockets on either side, rarely smiled, while her pointed little chin tilted at an angle better suited to brawlers.

She broke the mold, she did. Then, he was guessing, she strewed the jagged shards in her wake, the better to ward off the nobs who dogged after her, panting.

She handed back the license. "It looks of a piece," she said, with an edge of surprise that lent the acknowledgment the faint whiff of an insult. "Are you certain you trust the superintendent registrar's discretion?"

"I own him," he said.

She rolled her eyes. "This is England, Mr. O'Shea. You do not own anybody, I am happy to say."

He laughed. "Bless you, child. You're like a wee toddler let loose in the big, bad world."

His condescension was an easy way to make her stiffen and scowl. A fine trick, for otherwise he found himself thinking that her mouth wanted smiles, and her sweet little body was wasted, without a man's hands to attend to it. Her very aloofness might be considered a taunt and a challenge—even to him, who practiced restraint as a matter of policy.

But it would take an even greater pervert than he to be lusting after a woman who looked likely to box his ears.

He decided to keep her rattled, for his own sake. "Aye," he said, "you're as tender as a spring lamb, no doubt."

"We will agree to disagree on the degree of my naïveté," she said coldly. What a talent she had for talking in rhymes! "However, if this man of yours breathes so much as a word of this marriage, it will all be for naught."

She thought him thicker than a board. "Also, two and two is four," he said. "Tell me what I don't know."

"I imagine that would take several lifetimes. But how gratifying that you have a grasp of basic arithmetic, at least."

"Oh, I'm a hand at counting. Why, it's only the high numbers that trouble me. Gets tricky after fifty."

She blinked very rapidly. God and his saints, she thought he meant it. He offered her another grin. Let her stew in her preconceptions.

"Well, we might as well get on with it," she said at last, and turned for the stairs.

He lagged a pace behind, not saint enough to resist a free look. Her gown would have suited a widow, but short of sackcloth, she'd not find a way to disguise her curves. Built slim through the waist and arms, and heavy through the bottom—praise God, was there any finer form for a woman? The full swell of her hips would have drawn hoots at a music hall.

She glanced over her shoulder and realized where he was staring. Her face turned pink; she lifted her skirts and walked faster.

He grinned and caught up. "What's got you so red?"

"I do hope," she said in a muffled voice, "that you *understood* that contract you signed. What happens after this ceremony will be a singular event."

"For five years," he said. "Who knows? Perhaps we'll forgo that divorce."

She snorted. "If pigs fly. But at least you paid attention."

"Only to the good parts." At her poisonous look, he laughed. "'Twas twenty-eight pages long," he said. Her solicitors had drawn it up for another man—the viscount who had ended up eloping with Nick's niece. Most of the terms had focused on preserving Catherine's liberty to work. "I'm amazed that Palmer signed it." Nick could admire a woman determined to sweat for her living. But toffs tended to like their women soft and useless.

Good luck to Palmer, if he was hoping the same of Nick's niece!

"The viscount had no objections," she said. "That match, precisely like this one, was designed to be a marriage of convenience."

Funny term, that. You only heard toffs use it. "Marriage of convenience," he said. "*That's* likely. Never heard of a marriage that remained convenient for long."

As she reached the landing, she paused to wait for him. "I take it that you're a cynic in matters of love."

"In every matter, sweetheart."

"Good. So am I."

"Why, we're a perfect match, then."

She stared at him, evidently unsure what to make of his dry tone. Meanwhile, Johnson and Malloy came around the corner. "Got Whitby in his office," Johnson said. He nodded to Catherine. "Miss."

With a brief nod, she swept past the two men, who had come to serve as witnesses today.

Nick followed slowly, wondering how long it would take her to realize she'd no idea where to go.

It took ten paces for her to turn back. In such small moments, lessons were taught. "You passed it," he said pleasantly. "Second door on the right."

Even from this distance, he could see how her jaw squared. She strode back toward them, yanking open the door to Whitby's office with such force that the inset windowpane shuddered.

As she disappeared inside, Malloy muttered, "There's a temper. Sure she ain't Irish?"

Nick laughed. "She'd open her veins to prove otherwise, I expect, if she heard you wondering."

Whitby popped out and waved them forward. He was a scrawny sack of a man, with a bulging belly and spindly legs, and a sandy crown of hair that had thinned at the center, no doubt thanks to his nervous habit of tugging on it.

They crowded into the small office. Whitby shut the door with an air of transparent relief. "As you see, Mr. O'Shea, I had the building cleared and closed. I have also obtained a separate register book, which I will keep under lock and key in my own residence. I hope that satisfies your conditions."

"That's what I paid for," Nick said easily. No use in pretending Whitby was doing him a favor; otherwise, the man might try to collect on it, rather than contenting himself with the bribe.

"Yes, indeed. Well . . . without preliminaries, then." Mr. Whitby crossed to stand behind his desk. "If the bride and groom will stand next to each other, with the witnesses flanking."

Nick stepped up. In the dry heat of the office, he caught scent, for the first time, of his intended's perfume—something faint and not at all flowery. Dark, with notes of exotic spice, like a man's cologne.

That didn't surprise him as much as the fact that she had dabbed it on for this occasion. It reminded him suddenly of his own idiotic impulse earlier.

Well, what the hell. He unbuttoned his jacket, ignoring the faint startled noise from the woman beside him.

"I understand," Whitby was saying, "that the bride is of the Anglican tradition, and the groom—"

"No religion," Catherine cut in. "I do not believe it is required in a register office. Nor, I think, is one meant to *undress* here, Mr. O'Shea."

Nick pulled out the small bouquet. It had looked better an hour ago. He thrust it toward Catherine. She gave him an amazed look, then laid her package on the ground and took the flowers between thumb and forefinger, with all the eagerness of a woman accepting a rodent.

"Thank you," she said, and set the bouquet atop the registrar's desk, where several browning petals promptly detached, showering onto the floor. "Mr. Whitby, if you will get to the point."

"Yes, yes." Whitby placed a pair of spectacles on his uptilted nose, then retrieved a small, leather-bound book with gilt edging. "In such cases, there is a non-denominational ceremony we might—"

"Just cut to the questions," Nick said. "We haven't got all day."

Whitby cast him, and then Catherine, a wondering look. "If you're certain . . ."

"I certainly have better things to do," Catherine said crisply.

"Well, then." Whitby laid down the volume. "Join hands, if you please."

"Must we?" asked Catherine.

Whitby stiffened, as though his spine had suddenly grown. "If this is to be a legitimate marriage—"

"Oh, very well." She turned toward Nick, her magnificent eyes fixing on a space two inches to the right of his ear. She thrust out her hands, palms downward, her fingers braced into boardlike stiffness.

As he took hold of them, a queer surprise jolted through him. Her hands were much smaller than he would have guessed. Much warmer, too. The skin on the backs of her hands was soft and smooth beneath the unthinking stroke of his thumbs. Her fingers flexed slightly within his, a reflex of surprise, and by his own reflex, he steadied them.

Her moist little palms . . .

"You've got calluses," he said.

A tide of color washed through her cheeks. "Yes," she said in a rough voice, almost angry. "I *work,* you see."

In the periphery of his vision, he caught sight of the marveling look exchanged by Johnson and Malloy. But it felt wrong to join in their mockery. Evidently some hidden shred of reverence had survived in him. This might be a sham marriage, but in the eyes of God and state, it would be as true in the particulars as any other.

"Fine thing for a woman to work," he said. "Just thought you would have used gloves, is all."

She met his eyes at last, and her pale brows drew together briefly, as though she were hunting for some buried meaning in his words.

He stared back at her. God's truth, but her eyes were the shade of lavender stalks, a pure, true, uncorrupted color. A weird feeling filled him, a presentiment of some kind, borne of the contrast between her callused palms and the deceptively fragile, fair beauty of her face.

He didn't know this woman in the least. No matter that he'd casually watched her for years, and spent more than one lonely night in his bed, his hand on his cock, thinking of her. Distance hadn't shown him the true shade of her eyes, or the state of her palms. But mere seconds, up close, had proved that he knew no category to describe her.

He didn't like this feeling. Wasn't wise to strike a bargain with an unknown quantity.

"Mr. O'Shea," said Whitby, "do you take this woman to be your wife?"

He hadn't guessed that he would feel discomfort in this moment. Man's laws weren't sacred. But as he replied, the words felt weightier than they needed to be: "I do."

"Miss Everleigh, do you—"

"Yes." She pulled her hands free. "I believe that will serve, Mr. Whitby. Unless you will charge extra for the lack of ceremony."

"Forgot something," Nick said, and caught her by the waist. Her eyes flew wide as she realized his intention, but he stopped her protest with his mouth.

Her hands closed on his upper arms; her fingers, as stiff as steel pins, dug into his biceps, trying to force him off her. But he wouldn't be hurried. His wedding, after all. He kissed those soft, warm lips with deliberate leisure before setting her away from him.

She stared, eyes huge, her breath rasping in her throat. Then, with a strangled sound, she turned on her heel for the door.

"Wait!" Whitby slanted Nick an apologetic look before shoving forward the register book, which was indeed fresh and new, as he'd promised. "I will need your signatures first."

She pivoted back, her pretty mouth compressed into a tight, white line. A lucky thing the pen didn't snap in half, for the jabbing violence with which she wielded it across the page.

"And Mr. O'Shea's," Whitby prompted, "as well as the signatures of the witnesses."

"Can't write," Johnson said.

"Your mark will do."

His new wife made a contemptuous noise, then picked up her package and dashed him a hostile look as she jerked her head toward the door. "Follow me."

Already bossing him. Perhaps she did have a touch of Irish, after all.

Whitby wanted another word—reassurances about compensation, for the lost labor from giving his employees a holiday. By the time Nick stepped into the hall, Catherine was pacing. The click of the door brought her wheeling around.

He'd thought her pale inside, but she was colorless now. "We'll need privacy for the last bit," she said through her teeth. "A hotel? We would need to enter separately."

"I've got a set of rooms at Diamonds," he said.

"You propose to do this in a gambling den?" Her mouth twisted. "How fitting."

Mr. O'Shea's apartment at the House of Diamonds was as ornate as the gaming floor, although the color scheme, thankfully, was a more muted palette of bronzes and browns. Catherine paused in the sitting room, where a healthy fire was blazing, to remove her sodden cloak. The sight of the black bombazine sleeves startled her for a moment; she had forgotten she was wearing mourning. Perhaps it was disrespectful to her father's memory to have worn this gown to such a charade, but she had required the matching veil to avoid notice from passersby on her journey to Whitechapel.

As she laid down the cloak, she caught sight of herself in a mirror across the room. How pale she looked! Like a mourner in truth.

In the distance, a door closed. She waited, listening, but heard no footsteps. Mr. O'Shea had taken himself off on some private mission, and she was grateful for the chance to compose herself. There was no use giving him the satisfaction of finding her pallid and cowering, like some frightened virgin.

She *was* a virgin, though.

She refused, however, to be frightened.

She walked to the mirror, pausing to smooth down her damp hair, then to bite her lips and pinch her cheeks. *There.* Better to look livid than fearful. Last night, lying alone in her bed in Bloomsbury, she had nearly talked herself out of this bit; had almost reasoned herself into believing that consummation was unnecessary.

But Peter had made a remark at dinner that lingered with her afterward. He had been haranguing her again about Mr. Pilcher. "It is only natural to fear husbandly attentions," he'd told her. "But your disinterest in *marriage* is unnatural in the extreme. It suggests some disorder of the brain."

If Peter suspected that she had not consummated this marriage—if he doubted the marriage was true—he might refuse to bow to blackmail. She would have to announce the marriage to the world, then, so she might claim the directorship and prevent him from selling Everleigh's.

That announcement would not profit Mr. O'Shea, however. His buildings would still be imperiled. He might feel tempted to deny the marriage himself.

There must be no legal grounds for him to do so.

She squared her shoulders, staring deeply into her own eyes. That kiss in the register office—it hadn't been so bad. Rude, unnecessary, and unbearably presumptuous, but . . .

His skin had scraped hers. She touched her chin lightly, remembering the sensation. That must have been his stubble—invisible, for he'd arrived freshly shaven. But a man's skin felt very different, regardless.

The rising color on her face made her scowl. She needed to do this only once. Never again. So Mr. O'Shea had agreed, in signing the betrothal contract. What a blessed relief that divorce would be! A pity that caution bade her to wait five years for it. But that span of time would provide ample opportunity for Peter to advance in politics, and lose interest in the auction rooms entirely. By the time the divorce petition was submitted, she hoped, she would have sole ownership of Everleigh's.

The door opened quietly. Mr. O'Shea carried a bottle of wine in one hand, and two glasses in the other. Goodness. She looked away to hide her horrified smile—pray heaven he did not intend to make her *enjoy* this—and her gaze settled on the package she'd been carrying.

"Bottle of red," came O'Shea's voice. "Fresh from France. Will you take a glass?"

Bottle of red? "I don't know that varietal," she said dryly. "At any rate, no, thank you. I no longer drink." She ignored his snort. The last thing they required was another debate on her commitment to temperance. "Let's get to this, shall we?" She picked up the package and walked toward the only other door in the room—relieved, as she opened it, to discover that the bedroom was not nearly as lurid as she'd feared. The walls and bedsheets were brown silk, the pillows tasseled in gold. The dark carpet felt soft and thick beneath her feet. Her muddy boots would ruin it—but that was not her concern.

A single branch of candles lit the small room, lending it a discomfortingly cozy quality.

The creak of the floorboards announced O'Shea's approach. A bolt of anxiety sizzled through her. She took a deep breath, willing the cold resolve to return as she ripped open the package. She had gone halfway across London to fetch it, wearing that bombazine veil, which was so thick that it all but blinded her.

"What's that?"

She flinched. He was speaking nearly at her ear. "A sheet." She snapped it open; it billowed across the counterpane and settled, white as a field of snow.

She frowned. It was not quite as plain as she'd liked. The white embroidery blended into the white cotton backing, but it still looked embarrassingly ornate. Against the dark coverlet, the single hole piercing the center of the sheet became disturbingly conspicuous.

"What in . . ." O'Shea was staring at the sheet, his expression impossible to read.

The blush burned through her like fire. She wanted only to shrink and hide. *No.* She would not give him that satisfaction. A curious anger swam through her, clipping her vowels. "You will make this quick, I trust."

He snorted, his attention still fixed on the sheet. "With that in the way? I hope so. Did you stitch it yourself?"

"Certainly not." She sat on the bed and began to unlace her boots. "I have no gift at domestic arts. There are certain religious communities that sell such paraphernalia."

"Not mine," he said flatly.

She glanced up, startled. "Are you religious, sir?"

He met her eyes, a muscle flexing in his jaw. "Pity if I'm not. I've got the devil at my heels, all right."

She frowned as she pulled off her boots. "I will ask you not to object. It took me a great deal of trouble to procure that item."

"Would it matter if I did object?"

She had enough wisdom not to answer that. But as she rose in her stocking feet to loosen the buttons at her neck, her fingers felt shaky.

The sheet posed a problem. This candlelight, with its soft and flattering quality, seemed to cast a mocking romanticism over the scene. She would prefer darkness. But it would require light for him to locate the opening in the sheet.

She gritted her teeth, then turned the dial in the wall. The lamps blazed to life.

He winced, shielding his eyes with one hand. "Are we to shag in a spotlight, then?"

The word was filthy and unfamiliar to her. She could guess at its meaning, though. "Does it make a difference? Now, please leave so I may undress and place myself beneath the sheet. I'll call out when I'm prepared."

He gaped at her. There was something mildly diverting in the sight of Nicholas O'Shea, so plainly disconcerted. "And here I thought a gently bred virgin might like some pretty words first, if not the wine."

Her stomach pitched nervously. She ignored it. She

was a businesswoman, and this was only another matter of business. Emotion had no place in it. "I am gently bred, and a virgin. But I am not girlish, and I do not require poetry in business transactions."

His brows lifted. "Business transactions? Darling, if this were business, we'd be on the street corner."

She flushed. Why was he making this difficult? It was a comfort to know that he hadn't guessed the great turmoil bubbling inside her, but how much easier it would have been had he simply followed her lead! "I do not mean to give it such a vulgar gloss," she said stiffly. "But I see no need to pretend at deep feeling. Were there some way to avoid this unpleasantness, we would do so. But consummation will mitigate the risk to us. If my brother tries to challenge this marriage, we will speak with a clean and honest conscience to any officer in the land that we are legitimately married."

"And I don't argue with that," he said. "But for my own sake . . ."

"Surely you do not require candlelight in order to perform, Mr. O'Shea?"

His head snapped back. The churning in her stomach intensified. Had she gone too far?

"Fine, then," he purred. "If you're up to it, then certainly I am."

She nodded tersely. "Then please step outside, so I might undress."

"No." He took a seat in the single wing chair, his smile mocking. "If it's the law that concerns you, seems wise to mind all the particulars. I'll need to make certain there's no flaw in you that might invalidate the marriage."

"Flaw?" She stared at him. "What do you mean?"

"I mean, I'll see you naked," he said. "Make sure there's no false pretenses at work. See that you've got all the necessary bits, and such. That sheet, after all, makes it impossible to tell."

She had no words. "I . . ."

"And of course, I'll return the favor." His smile tipped into a roguish slant as he reached for his collar. With leisurely movements, he unknotted his necktie. "Go on," he said pleasantly. "We needn't take turns. Will speed things up if we both work at once."

He began to shrug out of his jacket. She quickly turned her back. "I have no need to watch," she spat at the wall. "I am quite certain that you have the—necessary bits, as you put it."

"Oh?" His voice was muffled, but it grew clearer again as he continued. "I'll take that as a compliment." Muffled thump—from the corner of her eye, she saw his jacket hit the ground, followed by his boots.

"You need some help there?" he asked.

There was a smirk in his voice. He was enjoying himself. No doubt he'd bedded a hundred women in his time. Was it any wonder if innocence, a certain degree of modesty and reserve, struck him as laughable?

But she was not a spectacle for his amusement. She pivoted, facing him, and opened the last button on her bodice.

The pounding of her heart, the rushing of blood in her ears, mercifully deafened her to whatever word slipped from his lips then. But the glare of the lights revealed with stark clarity the surprise on his face—and then, as she let her gown fall to the floor, the infinitesimal tightening of his expression, the new hardness of his mouth, and the fractional drop of his lids, so his gaze suddenly looked slumberous as it trailed down her body.

That look worked some evil magic on her, luring out her own awareness from the safety of her brain—pulling it down into her body, along her own limbs, chasing his glance across her skin, goose bumps rising.

She swallowed. He was a handsome man. She was, despite all rumors, a woman of ordinary flesh and blood. It was a biological effect, nothing more, that caused every inch of her to flush and tighten beneath his regard.

She made herself speak. "Have you seen enough?" Her corset could not contain the uppermost swell of her breasts. Her petticoats were not thick enough to hide any severe deformity, surely.

His laughter was husky. "Darling," he said, "you'll not get off so easy as *that*. Why, you could have three legs beneath those layers."

"Naturally," she snapped. Why had she expected any better of him? She would not give him another chance to laugh at her. She fumbled behind her waist for the knot that held up her petticoats. It yielded suddenly, and the layers dropped to the carpet.

Now she wore only a chemise and bloomers. And her corset, of course. She put her hands to the clasps, then hesitated, her stomach flipping. Once she removed this . . . Her chemise was all but transparent.

"That offer to help," he drawled, "still stands."

She narrowed her eyes. She was a working woman. Her corset fastened at the front. "I can manage," she said. "But perhaps it's *you* who's hiding a flaw." For apart from his jacket, he remained fully clothed.

His grin spread as he rose. "Pardon the delay. I was too busy taking in the sights, I supp—"

"Stop talking," she hissed.

With a soft, infuriating laugh, he reached for his waistcoat. She crossed her arms—there was no need to get so far ahead of him, after all—and stared at the spot directly over his shoulder.

No. She would not let him embarrass her. She fixed her attention on his long fingers, watching as they made a clever dance down the buttons of his waistcoat. The item fell to the floor. He shrugged out of his braces, then pulled his shirt and undervest from the waistband of his trousers and lifted them over his head.

Her mouth went dry. Men wore fewer layers.

"Well?" he asked. He raised his arms, turning a slow circle to display his bare upper body. "Any complaints?"

None, she thought fervently, then recoiled at the thought. But he was built . . . superbly. His broad shoulders and upper arms were powerfully sculpted; his belly was lean and taut, segmented into bands of muscle. A dusting of dark hair framed his flat nipples—and another patch of hair, a narrow, dark line, began below his navel, leading downward into his waistband . . .

"You will do." She meant to say it very flatly. But there was a fracture in her voice, a hitching gulp for air, that she did not recognize. She felt, all at once, acutely aware of how she stood, how she balanced her weight on her feet, how certain parts of her body felt the cool air more keenly, inexperienced as they were to its touch. A shiver skittered over her skin. It felt like . . . excitement.

Get this over with, before . . . Before what? She felt shaken as she unclasped the fastenings of her corset. She could not bear to look up at him now, not even when she heard his breath catch. *Just get through this,* she told herself. *A physical act, the body means nothing, your mind is what matters.* She heard the slither of cloth from his direction, but she focused only on finishing what must be done—the loosening of her bloomers, the clinging fabric of her chemise that seemed to resist the scrabble of her hands . . .

Once naked, she remained staring at the carpet for a moment. She would not blush, nor flinch, nor give him any sign of her nerves. She lifted her chin and looked at him.

He'd caught up to her. He was . . .

"Flawless," he said softly.

She cleared her throat. But no retort, no setdown, supplied itself. No man had ever gazed on her nude form before.

Nor had she seen a man in his natural state.

"Bit pink, though." He lifted his gaze, his smile roguish. "I won't hold it against you."

Was that an attempt at humor? She could not tell, for his expression confused her—his smile so easy, his gaze narrow and fierce, devouring as it swept down her again.

He'd seen enough. She should dive for the sheet— but that would look like fear. She had more pride than that.

She forced herself to look down his body. His thighs were sculpted with muscle, and the appendage between them . . . It was growing and lengthening before her eyes.

God in heaven. If it continued to enlarge, they would face another impediment to this marriage.

"Do I suit?" he murmured.

Flawless. She would not repay him that compliment, even if it lingered on her lips for a moment. He had forced her to this mortifying reckoning, hadn't he? He deserved no praise. "I don't know yet," she said very coolly. "Turn around, and I will judge."

With a shout of laughter, he swept her a low bow. God in heaven, she had not known a man's thighs could flex so.

She would have liked to find some small fault to remark, but his backside offered none. He had not a trace of spare weight on his body, but his bottom was . . . fuller and higher and tighter than she might have expected. Very different from a female bottom. Her palms itched to cup it, to see if it felt as muscular as it looked.

Why, she was an animal, after all, to behold a man's bottom with such interest!

He pivoted back. "Well, mistress?"

"You'll do." She broke for the bed, sliding beneath the cover. "Make haste." His ironical look prompted her to continue, "My brother is attending a dinner this evening, you see." As he came prowling forward, she spoke faster, a nervous babble. "And it seems wise to speak with him before he—" He grabbed the sheet and yanked it off her. "What are you—"

He put one powerful thigh onto the mattress, bringing his member into her field of vision. She turned her head away, scowling at the wall as she scrabbled for the corner of the sheet. "I will remind you, sir, this is a matter of necessity—"

"Agreed." His hot hands cupped her face, his mouth pressing against her ear. "And it will be quick, I fear." His tongue licked into her ear.

She gasped. What was he *doing*? And . . . what was amiss with her ear? For his lips felt . . .

Wonderful. Amazing. She had never known that an

ear could be a source of pleasure, but as his clever lips played over her lobe, she sighed and relaxed.

The full weight of his body came down atop hers. The alien sensation riveted her. He was so much larger. His skin felt so hot. "Here's the thing," he said very softly as he smoothed his knuckles down her throat. She felt the roughness of his palm against her shoulder, then her waist. "Necessity or not, there's no use in making this painful."

"It is . . . always painful the first time. Isn't it?" She knew that much, though *painful* was hardly the word for the strange feeling shivering through her.

He drew back, frowning. "It needn't be."

She looked up into his eyes, so close to her own. His irises were an extraordinary shade, the color of winter frost, the faintest hints of green stippled through bands of silver. His lashes were long, ink-black, curled as extravagantly as a girl's. The bump in his noise looked larger from this proximity.

She watched herself reach up to touch it. Why not? *He* was touching all of her. "You broke it?" she said unsteadily, a little drunk on her temerity. Touching a man; lying naked beneath him.

But he didn't seem to mind it. "More than once," he said, and kissed her neck.

She was not certain what to do. But there had been nothing malicious or unkind in his expression, and his lips were soft. Besides, the consummation had to occur. So she closed her eyes and held still, permitting him to do what he must.

His soft breath warmed her mouth as he raised his head. "By God. Your skin tastes like . . . magic."

She didn't need to be humored. "Soap, you mean." But her voice wrapped very raggedly around the words.

His mouth quirked, an amused little smile. Then he leaned in and kissed her lips. It was very . . . pleasant. His tongue touched the seam of her mouth—rubbing, coaxing. He seemed to . . . want inside of it. Why?

She had envisioned a cold, perfunctory bedding. But with each unexpected touch, each startling moment of pleasure, he was stoking her curiosity, unseating her vow to remain aloof, even here. "Is this necessary?" she whispered.

"A man can't perform on command, Kitty."

Kitty? She scowled. "I do not appreciate vulgar nick—"

He grinned, flashing white teeth, and licked into her mouth.

Her strangled yelp came out like a snort. This indignity kept her occupied for a moment too long—a moment in which his mouth did something wicked to hers, so their tongues tangled. As simply as that, she at last understood the way of kissing. She understood why people favored it.

It was not an assault, after all. Not gross or indelicate, as she had feared. His lips felt . . . incantatory. Patient, persuasive, creating a drugging laxity in her body. Tentatively, she kissed him back. He made an encouraging noise, low and somehow dirty, which made her flush. His chest pressed flat against hers, but he held the majority of his weight on his elbows, keeping their lower halves apart.

That small consideration seemed to be a message: she could kiss him for however long she liked. What lay below—that part of him currently canted off to the side, out of contact—would pose the real problem, but in the meantime . . . she needn't worry.

Not to worry. What a rare and extraordinary indulgence. Eyes closed, she lost herself in this wondrous kiss, which was teaching her so much. No wonder the maids proved so wayward with the footmen. No wonder the hostesses consorted with the clients . . .

His hand closed on her breast. She gasped. "Shh," he said into her mouth, and then, with his thumb, he began to rub her nipple, chafing and then pinching lightly.

Nerves fluttered. But he was allowed to do this, she reminded herself. Just this once, it was not wrong of her to permit it.

With that thought, the tethers of tiresome necessity—rejection; resistance; the need to remain cold and aloof, lest gentlemen misunderstand—fell away. What remained was sensation: the gentle abrasion of his rough skin; the damp heat of his mouth on her neck. This odd, tightening demand inside her. An ache in her breasts and between her legs.

Not weakening, no. Desire felt like a new kind of ambition, a rising awareness of some ineffable goal that demanded her effort. She needed to touch him.

Wondering at herself, she threaded her hands through his thick hair. So soft! The curve of his skull evoked a weird surprise; he, this great strapping man, was just as human as she, made of flesh and sinew and bone, just as mortal. She slid her palms down his broad back, the smooth hot muscled thickness of his upper arms. Had he been made of marble, and two thousand years old, she would have touched him so, feeling for flaws—so she would say—but secretly marveling at the genius of what she felt.

Nature was an artist, too. The sharpness of his elbows, chiseled into such fine points; the prominent veins of his forearms, irony embodied, a delicate tracery that proved his strength . . . What a piece of beauty a man could be!

His mouth tracked down her collarbone, scattering her thoughts. As his hand remained busy at her breast, teasing and pulling, his mouth found her other nipple. He flicked it with his tongue.

She gasped, for it felt divine. Her body wanted to splay open, to yield to him.

Yield.

Her eyes opened. She was staring at a white ceiling trimmed in handsome gilt molding. *Gilt.* Who picked out their molding in gilt? Tacky, a gambling den, God above, he was nudging her thighs apart, he had read her mind. At last, finally, she felt clearheaded—appalled— this stranger, this criminal, was colluding with her body against her, dividing her will from her desire—

She forced her thighs closed. "This isn't necessary!"

He released her nipple with a wet pop as he looked up. "Maybe not for you," he murmured. "But if you need me to perform . . ."

She felt herself turn as red as a flag. "Surely you're ready by now." She darted a look down his body, but he adjusted his hips to conceal the proof.

"Not yet," he said. "I'll let you know when I'm warmed up." With a half smile, he took her nipple into his mouth again—holding her eyes as he sucked her.

The sight undid something in her. Once, while cataloging the library of a country estate, she had flipped through a pornographic book, very quickly, horrified by her own curiosity, and by the feelings the filthy pictures had stirred in her.

But this was even filthier. Yet she could not look away. His long, muscular body stretched over hers, his black hair ruffled, his golden flanks sprawled with unselfconscious disregard, his entire focus now on the breast to which he ministered. He looked content to stay atop her forever, tasting and sucking and teasing her, as with one hand he smoothed over the pale slope of her belly, venturing lower and lower toward the curls between her legs . . .

His fingers slid through her curls, delving through folds that she had barely dared touch herself. And she had no choice but to let him. *No choice,* God be praised! No choice but to accept his touch, to gasp and arch upward voluptuously as he ravished her with small, precise, delicious touches, expertise and skill, the devil's own instinct for how to make her whimper. He touched a spot that seemed to hold all the most sensitive connections of her nerves and sinews, and her entire body tensed like a bow drawn tight. So delicately he touched her, again and again and again, rubbing and stroking and murmuring in a low, hot voice as she gasped, this quaking, unbearable pleasure winding her tighter and tighter, so soon enough, she would snap . . .

"Wet as a river," she heard him say hoarsely, and then his body came fully atop her, and she felt the blunt nudge of his manhood against her sex. Anxiety fractured her daze and made her stiffen.

He kissed her mouth again. "Not like that," he whispered into her ear. "Here, feel me." His hand reached between them, covering her sex completely, his clever finger finding that spot, again. "Feel this."

She bit back a groan. "Just do it."

His tongue curled around her earlobe, making her

shiver. "Don't be bossing me in bed," he said, very low. And then he pushed.

A burning sensation. Discomfort, yes, but also so much more . . . *Here* was what she'd wanted, this animal fullness, this profound possession. But he did not complete his penetration. Half buried inside her, he looked down at her, as little ribbons of sensation radiated out, spilling down the backs of her straining thighs, her shaking knees. "Hurry," she managed.

"Cry out for me," he said, "and I'll finish it."

She bit her lip hard. She would not cry out. She had more dignity than that. "This is—stupid."

"Be that as it may." His voice sounded strained now. "You'll cry out, or I'll go no further."

"Fine. *Ha!*"

For a moment, he went still and silent. And then he ripped himself off her so suddenly that she did cry out, in surprise and confusion.

But he was grinning at her. "All right," he said. "You asked for it." And he dived down, seizing her thighs and opening them wide.

"What are you—ah!" His mouth—he had placed his mouth on her, *there,* that very spot that his finger had found before. "Stop, stop—" It was too much; every muscle in her body was tightening without her direction; she was nothing but need, her bodily awareness focused entirely on his tongue licking and laving her with fierce, single-minded intent—

The tension snapped. Her hips jerked, pleasure crashing through her. Distantly she heard her own sob. Her hands scrabbled over his back, dragging him against her; she opened her mouth on his shoulder, tasting him, biting him as she shuddered beneath him. He tasted like nothing in this world, salt and flesh and wickedness and . . .

"Now there's a proper cry," he said raggedly, and fitted himself to her again, only now, when he pushed, it seemed that his appendage had been fashioned for her, the resistance gone. He seated himself to the hilt, deep inside her body, and began to move.

She wrapped her arms around him and cleaved to him as he thrust. *Yes.* The soles of her feet found the backs of his calves, and she felt them flex; she turned her face into his thick black hair and smelled the essence of him, musky and masculine and beyond anything.

Take me. She could think it; just once, only once. His strong hands gripped her face; he opened her mouth to his tongue, and she accepted it, welcomed it, drinking him in. Here, this natural wonder, this unimagined glorious act—for a few blissful moments, it was all that there was; her mind was quiet, she was only body, nothing else.

At last, he groaned and thrust off her, rolling away to spill his seed safely. It gave her a shock; she realized she had forgotten her plan to speak to him about that again, before unwrapping the sheet. She felt a measure of belated panic at her own carelessness, and deep gratitude for his consideration.

His naked back was pale gold in color, blemishless and broad. When he rolled over, she stared at his body, absorbing his beauty from this novel angle. A long scar slashed over his ribs. His thighs made a sleek and graceful line . . . Panic flickered through her as he reached for the abandoned sheet. No doubt he meant to be courteous as he handed it to her. She covered herself with it, but made no offer to let him share, for there was still so much more of him to see. And she had only this once to look.

But it is already over.

A weird panic swam through her. Never again? After what she had just experienced?

Alarm made her avert her eyes. What ailed her? *Eve with the apple.* Of course. Forbidden knowledge was always sweet—and poisonous. She steeled herself on a long breath.

She felt his gentle touch as he smoothed a lock of hair from her shoulder. "You gave yourself away too cheaply, Kitty." His voice was hoarse. "You should have asked for the moon."

The nickname triggered a different kind of unease. Nobody but her father had ever called her by a diminutive. "I asked for the only thing I want," she said stiffly.

The only thing I knew to want.

No. She rejected that thought. Of course bed sport could be pleasant. Otherwise, there would be no slatterns in the world. That did not mean that this experience would haunt her. She would not permit it.

But she foresaw, even in this raw moment, that it would take effort not to think of what he had done to her.

That was not the worst part, though. The worst part was that when his hand lingered on her shoulder, massaging lightly, she wanted to lean closer, in case he wished to kiss her again.

She inched away. This was no ordinary marriage. She was no ordinary woman. It was not in her to make a proper wife to any man. She depended on her own self-discipline, and she could not allow him to weaken it, for there was no future between them.

She stood, gathering the sheet around her. She sensed him gazing at her, the silence weighted by a sense of expectancy that she could not stand. This was *done*. It must be done.

But a niggling sense of injustice lingered with her as she walked to the mirror to smooth her hair. She was a fair woman, was she not? Committed to honest and transparent dealings.

She made herself turn to look at him. "You are flawless, too."

His swift, flashing smile seemed to snag a hook into her chest. Again, she felt she could not breathe, that this panic would crush her.

She turned back to scowl at her reflection. *The Ice Queen.* That was who she must be. And even if she *had* been a more feminine woman . . . he was a ruffian. Their worlds could never be bridged.

CHAPTER FIVE

Nick was comfortable with silence. As a boy at the docks, he'd found out how much there was to learn by keeping one's mouth shut and letting others talk themselves into carelessness. The misplaced brag or the accidental mention of expected good fortune had led him many times to a windfall that others had lined up for themselves.

As a man, he'd discovered that silence made a weapon, too. Keep quiet long enough, and brave men lost their courage. Wise men lost their discretion. Tongues started to flap, defenses to crumble.

But God save him if the silence in the coach wasn't awkward. Enduring it wore on his last nerve. Didn't help that his new wife sat across from him, swaddled to the throat in a cloak as dark as night, her face emerging like a pearl from velvet, shining in the swinging light of the side lamp.

It aggravated him that she looked untouched, for he himself felt . . . rubbed up against, disordered, all messed and tousled inside. What had happened in that bed today? He was Irish enough to think of witchcraft, and modern enough to dismiss it instantly. But the conviction lingered, unsettling and unwelcome, that something had happened that changed him, knocked him off-kilter the slightest degree, so her face now seemed like the only thing worth looking at.

He couldn't afford that kind of distraction.

Five years till he'd have it again. That term in the contract was looking different, suddenly. No longer just a point of amusement, proof that toffs would legislate anything, right down to the breath drawn by a body. Now it looked like a clever piece of torture. He was ordered, by a point of law, to resist the temptation that had risen right after he'd found his release, when he'd wanted to start touching her all over again.

Ice Queen, they called her. Let them keep on thinking so. He'd made his fortune through opportunities that fools and laggards had missed. He'd spotted her, hadn't he, when his niece had gone to work at Everleigh's? Watching her, he'd come to understand how a good woman might be likened to a rare jewel. With such a lady on his arm, a man would need no flash to show the world that he mattered.

But the world wouldn't be seeing him with Catherine. It would never guess that he'd cracked her wide open, proved the Ice Queen was made of blood and flesh, soft and pale, flawlessly smooth. If he touched that soft skin, now—if he stroked that stray lock of hair from her cheek, and put his lips at that sweet, shadowed crook where her neck met her shoulder—she'd threaten to summon a solicitor.

She couldn't annul the marriage, though. Didn't sit right, how smug he felt about that—or how irritated, at the prospect of five years' wait till he could have her again. He felt rattled by it, in fact, and was glad when the coach slowed and she told him they had arrived.

"You will let me handle this," she said as he opened the door and helped her down.

"Sure." He let go of her as quickly as possible. Cloak or no, he knew that curve of her waist now, and the shape of it made his palms burn. Or maybe what smarted was his pride, for how indifferent she sounded to his touch. He'd made her cry out, all right. But her composure suggested she'd already forgotten it.

He wasn't a man accustomed to being forgotten, though he knew better than to expect anything else from her. Swells, fancy folk, had a talent for dismissing his kind. It hadn't ever bothered him before. He'd taken advantage of their snobbery, or laughed them off as shallow fools.

But she wasn't a fool, this woman he'd married. And he wasn't sure, suddenly, that he could bear her sneers so lightly.

As Catherine walked toward the drawing room, she tried to school herself for the confrontation to come. She should be relishing the moment, savoring the taste of long-awaited victory. Instead, all she could think about was the man beside her.

Was he reliving what they had done in that bed? She felt raw, unsteady on her feet, as acutely, tremulously alive to his presence as a fox to a nearby hound. One accidental touch from him, and she would be undone.

No. She would not let herself dwell on it. She would make herself numb to him.

She shoved open the door with too much force. Peter looked up from his newspaper, his glance flickering to O'Shea behind her.

"What is this?" he asked, frowning as he laid down the newspaper.

"Business," she said crisply.

"You know I receive no tradesmen in the evening—"

"This is no tradesman," Catherine said. "Indeed, I had thought a man like you, who follows the news so closely, would recognize Mr. O'Shea."

Peter rose. "I don't . . ."

"Nicholas O'Shea," said her new husband mildly as he joined her side. The displaced air carried the scent of his skin. She had tasted that skin. She had *bitten* him.

Flushing, she focused on Peter. The first traces of his comprehension registered in the slackness of his expression, his jaw sagging a fraction. "Nicholas . . ." He shot Catherine an astonished look. "What in the *devil* do you mean, to bring such a man—"

"We come to have your congratulations." How sour she sounded. How like a spinster. But she wasn't any longer. "We are married."

Peter reached for the back of his chair. Taking a white-knuckled grip on it, he uttered a short bark, balanced somewhere between laughter and choking. "You *what*?"

O'Shea's broad palm pressed into the small of her back. She swallowed a gasp. Now he'd done it. But she was fine! She was not undone. O'Shea meant only to encourage her—or to provoke her brother. He could not guess how her heart tripped. He would never know.

She inched out of reach. "That's right," she said. "Married, legally and quietly, in the register office in

Whitechapel. So you see, the service entrance would hardly do—for your new brother-in-law."

Peter shook his head slowly. "You're . . . this is . . ."

She darted a sidelong glance at O'Shea. The bright light of the parlor seemed to sharpen his beauty, making him a study in contrasts: sun-bronzed skin; hair gleaming black; and those eyes. *They should call him the Ice King, for those eyes.*

Idiotic! She pinched herself. A devilish smile was tugging at the corner of O'Shea's mouth. Was he privately mocking her? Did he realize how rattled she was?

He caught her look, and winked at her before giving an infinitesimal nod toward her brother.

Frowning, she followed his attention back to Peter, who was gaping like a fish out of water. Why, perhaps O'Shea was laughing at *him.* It was worth some enjoyment. This was bound to be the sweetest discussion she'd had with Peter in years.

She bit back her own swift smile. "Do you find it preposterous?" she asked her brother. "Ludicrous? Both those words have crossed my mind of late—but in regard to *your* doings. I watched in silence as you embezzled from our profits to fund your personal affairs. But did you really imagine that I would let you sell the company? *Our father's company?*"

Peter was turning purple. "This won't stand."

"But it will," she said. "The license was legally acquired. The marriage was entered into the registry. And the union was . . ." She took a deep breath. "Consummated." She rushed onward, blinding herself to Peter's grimace. "There is no court in the land that would contest this marriage. I assume full directorship of the auction rooms now."

"You goddamned—"

As Peter lunged, O'Shea stepped in front of her. As if she could not handle Peter! She had managed well enough on her own, for twenty-six years. She stepped around him. "It is done," she said.

Peter fancied himself athletic. He fenced for pleasure at a local studio, and liked to brag that he could swim the Channel, if only he had the time. But as he sized up O'Shea, he was not fool enough to consider himself equal to what he saw. A curious sneer worked over his features, drawing his mouth into a tight little smile.

He sat heavily on the sofa. "Well," he said flatly. "Congratulations. You have ruined me."

"Your political prospects? No doubt." Sensing O'Shea's surprise, she put a hand on his arm.

Hard as iron. Fearsome strength. But he'd been so gentle with her . . .

She bit hard on her cheek. *Just a moment longer,* she silently begged him with her look. A moment in which to treasure this victory, and to make Peter feel the absolute depths of misery. That would soften him for the bargain she meant to propose.

O'Shea gave a fractional nod, and she returned her attention to her brother, whose expression was murderous.

"You will regret this," Peter said. "You imagine that you will seize control of Everleigh's? Now I will never be away from it. You have left me no choice. I will drive it into the ground to spite you."

Her temper exploded. "How reassuring, that you should finally admit to how little you care for the place!"

He sneered at her. "And you? What care do *you* show, by marrying our name to that of the most infamous criminal in England?"

"Well, now," O'Shea said evenly. "That's a gratifying thought."

Peter's glare snapped to O'Shea's face, then slid away. He slumped, one hand bracketing his brow to shield his expression. "My God," he muttered. "My God, you have *ruined* me."

Here was the despair she'd been awaiting. "In fact, there is still a hope for you."

"It's done," he said, muffled. "You knew it. Why else did you do it?"

"But you spoke rightly, a minute ago. I have no wish to see you without any aim but the auction house. And so Mr. O'Shea and I have discovered a way to preserve your political aims."

Peter loosed a choked snort.

"It is very simple," she said. "You will support Mr. O'Shea's interests at the Municipal Board of Works, and give me full control at Everleigh's."

Peter lifted his head, staring at her with the squinting concentration of a man blinded by the sun.

"Mr. O'Shea's buildings have been wrongly condemned," she said. "They are located in Whitechapel; the inspector from St. Luke's had no right to condemn them. You will persuade the board that the petition of condemnation is null and void. As for Everleigh's—you will continue with your duties as auctioneer and client director. But I will oversee the accounts, and you will confer with me on any matters concerning the general operation of the company. As long as you meet these terms, Mr. O'Shea and I will keep this marriage private. Nobody will learn of it. And *you* may go on glad-handing politicians without any rumors to trouble you. But if you refuse . . ."

He was listening, his attention fixed and unblinking.

"If you refuse to meet our terms," she said, "Mr. O'Shea and I will make a public announcement of our marriage. Per the terms of Father's will, I will immediately assume equal control over Everleigh's in the eyes of the law. The sale will be halted, regardless. Meanwhile, I believe your future hopes will be greatly diminished by the public's knowledge of your new relationship to Mr. O'Shea."

It took Peter a long, stammering moment to find his tongue. "This—this is—this is the most heinous, *ridiculous* blackmail—"

"No more ridiculous, I think, than a thief who wishes to become a member of Parliament." She paused, savoring the moment. "Or—pardon me. That form of corruption seems a perfect qualification for politics. Indeed, perhaps Mr. O'Shea should consider contesting for the Whitechapel borough."

At her side, Mr. O'Shea laughed softly. "Now, there's an idea."

His husky laugh brushed through her like fingertips, stealing her breath. She did not permit herself to glance over. Peter was looking between them as though evaluating two rabid dogs. "You would keep it a secret," he said slowly. "How would you do that? The bloody register book is accessible to anyone who—"

"No fear there," Mr. O'Shea said. "It's tucked away where nobody will find it."

Peter frowned. "But . . . your very association . . ."

"Mr. O'Shea and I do not intend to associate publicly," Catherine said.

Peter blinked. "So . . . it's not to be a true marriage, then? You will never share a household?"

She willed herself to be ice-cold, lest the insinuations—and the memory they evoked, of O'Shea's mouth traveling her body—make her blush. "As I said, it has been made true in every way that pertains to the law. As for our future plans, they are none of your concern."

"But they are." He was staring at her very narrowly now. "Assume I accept your terms. I must do so on the absolute certainty that this marriage will never become public knowledge. For my aim is not merely to be a member of Parliament. That will only be the beginning. I will not be sabotaged by the eventual revelation of this—this grotesquerie!"

"I understand," she said evenly. "We do not intend to live as a married couple."

"Ever?"

"Ever." She would not mention the contractual plan for divorce, which would require a public hearing. *Five years.* What a long time that seemed.

Peter shook his head. "How low you will go to spite me."

"How little choice you left me," she countered.

He took a deep breath, then rose. "Well, then. I suppose I have no choice but to agree to this atrocity."

"I concur," she said. But her brother's composure struck a chord of unease through her, as did the slight smile that flitted over his mouth, gone almost before she could remark it.

"Glad that's settled," O'Shea said. "I'll be needing to speak with you about that meeting next week of the Municipal Board."

"Of course," said Peter.

Of course? "Mr. O'Shea will communicate with you through me," she said slowly. "Nobody will have any cause to suspect your alliance." How odd that Peter had not thought to ask about that himself.

"Very good," her brother said. "I am relieved to hear it. And now, I will thank you to get him out of this house before anybody remarks that he visited."

She watched Peter let himself out of the drawing room. When O'Shea started to speak, she held up a hand and jerked her head toward the door.

Eyes narrowed, he nodded. They stood for a long moment in silence before she whispered, "It's all right, go ahead."

"Bit easier than I'd imagined," O'Shea said quietly.

"Agreed." She hesitated, but her suspicions were nameless. "I suppose he felt he had no choice."

"No doubt. You'd have made a fine lawyer."

The compliment startled her. She allowed herself a small, gratified smile. He smiled as well. His lower lip was very full. If he bent to kiss her right now—

Horrified by herself, she wheeled away. "I'll see you out."

"Perhaps you should stay somewhere else, tonight, just in case."

One hand on the doorknob, she turned back. He had come up hard on her heels; he loomed over her, raw power and protective promise. Another woman would have counted herself fortunate to have such a protector, well capable of defeating danger with his broad, bare palms—

But his handsome hands were quite disfigured by the garish glitter of those rings. He was a criminal, not a gentleman, and she did not require the protection of such a man. She stared at the rings as she spoke. "I've got three locks on the door to my apartment," she said. "But if anything goes awry—"

"Three locks? Why?"

Until she'd had them installed, her brother had liked to burst in to harangue her at all hours. "It doesn't matter." Five rings, he wore. Five too many. "But if something were to . . . well . . . I'll send to the House of Diamonds if I'm in need."

"Look at me."

She lifted her chin, bristling at his scowl. "You'll spend the night at Diamonds," he told her. "There's a guest suite on the second floor—"

"I certainly will not!" She pulled open the door. "Discretion, Mr. O'Shea, is the key to our success. Being seen entering that club again—"

His hand on her arm halted her exit. "You won't be seen." His face, his tone, were implacable. "But you're not staying here. Three locks or no."

His grip caused a wave of small shivers to chase over her skin, percolating into the pit of her belly . . . and lower. But *he* looked wholly unaware that he was touching her.

She yanked free and drew herself to her full height. "We have an agreement, you and I. By the terms of our contract, I am an independent creature."

O'Shea gave her a cutting smile. "Don't mistake me, darling. I'd be glad to let you stumble into trouble. But I need you alive if this blackmail's to work."

She laughed in sheer astonishment, and then to cover her uneasiness. Last spring she had been poisoned by chocolates meant for Lord Palmer. In her delirium, her addled brain had wrongly seized on the suspicions that O'Shea now hinted at.

But Peter was *her brother*. In a sober frame of mind, she could not believe him murderous. "I'm not in *that* kind of danger," she said.

Her temporary husband watched her for a long, level moment. "You sure about that? Your brother's got reasons now."

"I should think I know my brother better than you do." Oh, this was pointless—and it threatened to entangle them further, besides. "You will *not* interfere with me. Regardless of the cause, you have agreed not to do so. If you cannot keep that part of the bargain, then the whole matter is void!"

Narrow-eyed, he blew out a sharp breath. Then he clapped his hat on his head and sketched a mocking bow. "Very well," he said. "I'll bid you good evening. *Wife.*"

"Fifteen-two going once, fifteen-two going twice . . ." Peter paused. "Lot sixty, sold to Mr. Snowden of Sussex for fifteen-two!"

"Rubbish," the man beside Catherine muttered.

She retreated to the back wall, where nobody could see her frown. That lot should have gone for twenty pounds at least. So far, the auction of the Cranston library was proving a wet squib.

At the top of the room, where he presided over the rostrum, Peter looked unconcerned. All this week, ever since he'd learned of her secret marriage, he had seemed unflappable. He visited her office daily to confer on decisions and review accounts. He had even summoned the solicitor to announce, in her presence, that he had abandoned the notion of selling Everleigh's.

But his calm mood had fractured for a moment this morning. "I have done everything you asked," he'd told her at breakfast when she had wondered aloud if she should attend the Cranston auction. "Must you dog my every footstep, too?"

Had he shown a sweeter face, she might have skipped the auction after all. She felt run ragged, exhausted by uneasy dreams. But an instinct had driven her to table her afternoon agenda so she might attend the sale.

She was glad of it. Something was amiss here. This auction had been scheduled for weeks, advertised in all the regular journals and newspapers. The soiree organized to accompany the formal preview had attracted over two hundred bibliophiles. What, then, explained the poor attendance today? Half the seats were empty, and the bidding felt sluggish.

Peter didn't seem to have noticed. It was an auctioneer's duty to broadcast an almost infectious excitement about the lot at hand, the better to spur the bidding. But as he watched the attendants carry out the next lot, Peter slouched against the rostrum like a schoolboy, elbows akimbo, gavel drooping. This lot, a very rare volume on the early history of New York, had survived a century in handsome condition. The olive morocco was richly ornamented by gilt dentelle edging that still shone brightly, despite its age. Its color plates had merited a great deal of interest at the preview, for they had been painted by a famous cartographer.

The clerk intoned the conditions of sale. Almost languidly, Peter waved his gavel to open the bidding.

The reserve was immediately met and raised by Sir Wimple, a crotchety collector who never let a map go by without bidding. "Ten," he called.

"Ten pounds," Peter drawled. "Do I hear fifteen?"

"Fifteen," came the reply, from near the window.

"Fifteen, gentlemen." Peter sounded as though he were battling a yawn. "Twenty?"

"Twenty," said Wimple sharply.

Peter paused briefly, staring at Wimple, then seemed to collect himself with a slight shake of his head. "Twenty-five, then?"

The ensuing pause seemed odd. Unlikely. Patrons exchanged uneasy looks, and no wonder. The volume was exceedingly rare, both in type and condition. It had been expected to fetch fifty pounds at minimum.

"Twenty-five, then," Peter said more pointedly. "Do I hear twenty-five?"

The pause seemed to stretch interminably. The audience looked to Wimple's opponent, a portly blond who stood beneath the great window. As though sensing the general interest, he withdrew a copy of the catalog from his jacket pocket, making a small notation before glancing up at the volume on offer. His slight frown, the faintest shake of his head as he flipped to the next page of his catalog, drew a new round of murmurs. He had the look of a man who was waiting on some upcoming treasure, which quite overshadowed his interest in the current lot.

Others pulled out their catalogs. What did he know that they didn't?

He knew nothing! Catherine did not recognize him; he was no bibliophile of note. Why was Peter not speaking, praising the volume, reminding the audience of its worth? She saw several collectors in the audience who had the knowledge to prize it, if only they were nudged out of their uncertainty—an uncertainty, she privately fumed, that had been fueled by some stranger with a penchant for melodramatic flourishes.

Peter opened his mouth. "Twenty-five, going once . . ." His quick glance toward the man by the window caused a prickle to move down her spine. "Going twice . . ."

The blond man looked up. "Thirty," he said hesitantly, then grimaced, as though already regretting it.

"Thirty," Peter said, with a note of clear surprise. "Do I hear thirty-five?" He looked over the crowd, but did not take special note of Sir Wimple.

He was in on it. He was conspiring with that man by the window to slow the bidding.

No. It couldn't be. A ring, in the saleroom? She looked sharply through the crowd, ignoring the familiar faces for those she did not recognize. Even Peter would not do this, surely. Rings were a plague on country sales, but respectable auction rooms did not tolerate them. *Could* not, if they wished to remain respectable.

"Thirty-five," Sir Wimple said.

But last spring . . . hadn't she wondered about a ring then as well? At an auction of English paintings, she'd sensed collusion at work, strangely sluggish bidding on a portrait by Gainsborough. Rings generally appointed a single man to bid, and agreed not to challenge him. Then they conspired to discourage strangers from mounting a challenge. They spread rumors about the legitimacy of a particular piece; during the sale, they undertook any number of tricks, like that cheap showmanship with the catalog, to convey their indifference to a desirable lot. Once their man had obtained it at a cut-rate price, they reconvened for a new, private auction among themselves, bidding on the item's true worth. The money saved in the first, corrupt sale then went to the ring as a whole.

In corrupt salesrooms, half the profit went straight to the auctioneer.

Not here. Everleigh's was renowned for its honesty. Rumors of a ring at work, supported by the auctioneer himself, would prove disastrous.

"Thirty-five going twice," Peter was saying.

"Forty," said the man by the window.

On cue, Peter rushed through his words. "Forty going once, forty going twice—"

You will continue with your duties as auctioneer. Had she been so stupid, so unforgivably naïve, to imagine that Peter would not find a way to enrich himself despite her?

"Sold," Peter said over Sir Wimple's outcry. "To Mr. Hastings of Haverford, for forty pounds."

He could not be allowed to do this. People would talk afterward. He *must* sell the next lots without any appearance of impropriety. On a deep breath, she started down the aisle.

The clerk stepped forward to announce the next item. "A collection of the *Encyclopedia Britannica,* fourth edition, very rare. Bound in . . ."

Peter caught sight of her as she neared the rostrum. "What is it?"

She climbed the stairs to speak into her brother's ear. "You will stop this ring, now."

"I beg your pardon?" He stared fixedly at the assistants positioning the new set of volumes. "Get off my dais."

"You will have Hastings shown out," she said in a fierce undertone, "and you will smile as you encourage honest bids. I will not disservice Lord Cranston by selling his father's collection at half the price it should fetch."

He turned on her so suddenly that she heard a gasp from below. Perhaps he did, too, for he mustered a sickening facsimile of a smile. "Get out," he said through his teeth. "You are creating a scene."

"Have him removed. *Now.* Or I will stop this auction."

His laughter was low and scornful. "Oh, yes? That will look very good for Everleigh's. Get off this dais, before you turn into a spectacle."

But that, she realized, was her solution. She cast a prayer heavenward, then put her heel backward and screamed as she toppled off the platform.

CHAPTER SIX

Five months ago, the lunatic hunting Lord Palmer had lit a bundle of dynamite in the neighboring building. The explosion had shattered the great window in the saleroom, and driven the patrons to scramble toward the exits, dropping catalogs and canes in their haste.

As Catherine picked herself up off the floor, she remembered that day vividly, for catalogs littered the carpets once more. The saleroom stood silent and empty, the crowd having departed so a doctor might be summoned.

But none was coming. Peter knew she had faked her swoon. He had said as much into her ear as he'd roughly gripped her shoulders. "You will pay for this," he'd muttered before announcing to the crowd that the sale must be halted.

He should have thanked her. Their customers were not blind. Had she not disrupted the sale so spectacularly, they would have left gossiping about corruption in the saleroom. Instead, they would talk of her.

Either way, it did not make for a good day of business.

Her ankle was throbbing. She hobbled toward the exit, using the backs of chairs to brace herself. The double doors were heavy; she caught her balance on one foot as she wrestled with the handle.

It opened abruptly, nearly knocking her off her feet. A familiar figure stepped across the threshold, catching her by the waist. "Here you are," O'Shea said.

Stupefied, she sagged in his grip. For a week she had done her best not to think of him, but with his hands on her, his warmth surrounding her, no time might have elapsed at all. The scent of him kindled a deep, churning need—

Here! She twisted out of his grip, panicked. "What are you doing here?"

"Just happened to be in the neighborhood."

That was a likely story! "If Peter sees you—"

"Is the place on fire?" His luminous gray gaze swept past her, taking a quick survey of the deserted room. "Half London is spilling down the front steps."

Half London, indeed! "You can't be seen here," she said through her teeth. "There are staff—"

He snorted. "Truants, more like. Halls are empty. And your brother went chasing after some bloke. Halfway to the market by now."

Hastings, no doubt. Peter had dropped her back onto the carpet to go hurrying after the man. She blew out a breath. They were working together, no doubt of it.

"What happened?" O'Shea propped one shoulder against the doorjamb, tapping his tall hat against his thigh. "Stampede?"

"I swooned."

His light eyes fixed on her. "Thought you never swooned."

"And *I* thought you didn't frequent the West End."

He shrugged. Clearly he had no intention of accounting for himself. "Hit your head when you fell?" He reached out to touch her cheek, his fingertips surprisingly warm.

She jerked her face aside. His fingers looked brutish. Long and scarred, beringed in Birmingham paste, dramatically thickened around the knuckles—as though brawling had swollen them permanently. A criminal's hands.

Criminals were probably cleverer with their hands than any gentleman.

A flush crawled over her. The bedding had been necessary, contractually. That should not make him entitled to touch her here, in public. "Has everyone truly gone?" she asked. "Nobody saw you as you came inside?"

"Not a soul."

She hesitated. Her boot felt as though it were strangling her ankle. Swelling, she supposed. "Can you help me to my coach, then?"

"Sure," he said, and slipped an arm around her waist. "Lean into me."

God save me. There was no choice for it, was there? She tried to hold her breath, tried to ignore the feel of his strong body as he guided her in a slow, hitching pace down the corridor. He smelled like coffee. Coffee and . . . the faint hint of cigar smoke and . . .

His skin. His naked, bare skin.

She tried to walk faster. Her ankle immediately protested. Wincing, she drew to a stop. "Perhaps I should just stay here tonight."

"Here?" He drew away slightly to look into her face. "You got a bed here?"

There was nothing suggestive in his voice, but her stomach fluttered regardless. "A cot, in my office."

He lifted his brows. "You sleep here often?"

She shrugged. "When work demands it."

"No need for that tonight." He bent and scooped her up; on a soundless gasp, she threw her arms around his neck for balance.

"Put me down," she snapped. "If someone sees us now—"

"I'll say I'm a footman." He grinned at her. Another imperfection! His canine was chipped.

His lips were very close to hers.

She looked quickly away, staring over his shoulder at the rapidly retreating saleroom. "I'll say you're the doctor. Peter was meant to summon one."

"For your swoon?" He started down the stairs at a terrifyingly brisk clip. She gripped him more tightly, convinced he would drop her.

"I won't drop you," he said on a laugh. Before she could register his uncanny knack for reading her mind, he added, "Started hauling cargo at the docks when I was all of nine. Grain bags, that'll teach you to balance properly."

He'd worked as a dockhand? And so young?

Perhaps his early exertions explained his build, then. His dark suit looked like any other gentleman's walking suit. But surely it was cut from a thinner, cheaper cloth. It felt as soft as fine wool, but a suit should not translate so clearly the shifting muscles beneath it. His back, his waist, were whittled lean, and his arms, where they wrapped around her, bulged with power. The feel of them fascinated her palms. Her palms had no discipline.

She was very grateful when they reached the main floor, and she could risk easing her grip on him. "Please hurry," she whispered, looking frantically around. "On the off chance he called an actual doctor—"

"And why didn't he?"

"He knew I wasn't truly sick."

His gray eyes held hers a thoughtful moment. "So you faked it?"

"Yes," she said in a clipped voice. "But—let's not discuss it here."

He grunted acknowledgment, then shouldered open the front door, carrying her into the autumn chill. She took a quick, deep breath. Autumn had always been her favorite time of year—the bite in the air; the scarlet and gold tapestries made by the leaves, and their pleasant crunch underfoot. But tonight, it could not soothe her.

Perhaps henceforth she would remember autumn as the time when everything ended—hopes, dreams, mad conspiracies to save companies. That was only as it ought to be, she supposed; the leaves, after all, only turned because they were dying.

At the curb, he carefully set her on her feet. She looked around and groaned as she saw only the one vehicle—not hers. "He sent away my coach!" Peter was fond of these spiteful little punishments.

"Fine fellow, he. I'll drop you home."

She wrestled with temptation. "That would look very nice. I'm sure nobody at Henton Court would wonder why I accepted a ride from *you*."

He tipped his head. "You think they'd recognize me?"

She hesitated. He had a point. Who would imagine that here stood the king of the East End? The lamplight silhouetted the elegant cut of his suit. It translated his brutal muscle into long and deceptively lean lines, and flattered the breadth of his shoulders, making them appear less . . . conspicuous.

She could hardly hobble to the cabstand. It was several blocks away.

"Very well," she said grudgingly. "You may—" She fell abruptly silent as a group of women approached, market baskets on their arms. She knew none of them, of course, and to her relief, they seemed not much interested in her. Their interest focused firmly on O'Shea, who answered their smiles with a wink.

When they had passed, she said stiffly, "In my company, you might at least *pretend* to be a gentleman."

He lifted his brows. "Who's pretending?"

"Gentlemen do not acknowledge a woman's leering."

"Leering, you say?" He glanced after the women. "And here I thought those ladies were simpering,"

"Ladies, sir, do not *simper*."

He gave her a cat-in-the-cream smile. "But they do leer?"

She cast a dismissive glance after the women, noting the aggression of their strides. No corseting, nor many petticoats, either. "Not if they're well bred."

"It's a cold heart you've got, madam."

From another man, these words might have formed a reproach. But his smile said he was teasing her.

She had no notion of how to reply to such banter, but she knew it should not make her feel so lighthearted and giddy and . . . girlish. Frowning, she opened the door to his carriage herself.

Nick had come by the auction rooms thinking to give Catherine some good news. But his new wife was clearly in no mood to celebrate. She retreated to her side of the coach and curled up there as though he might throw himself atop her.

Not that the thought hadn't crossed his mind. She had a sweet heft to her, she did, all in her bottom half. He'd done his best to keep his mind off that half while carrying her out of the building. But her bottom had a way of announcing itself regardless.

As though she glimpsed his thoughts, her eyes narrowed. "Why did you come to Everleigh's, anyway? You mustn't do so again. Had my brother seen you—"

"Just wanted to tell you," he said. "Your brother kept his end of the bargain. Pilcher's petition got scuttled today."

"What?"

He grinned. "You look surprised. Don't say you thought he'd grow a spine."

"I didn't," she muttered. "No, I'm . . . pleased that he abided by the agreement. Would that he were so amenable in all regards."

"Ah." He settled more comfortably against the cushions. "He gave you trouble today, I take it."

"He was running a ring on the saleroom floor." She made a noise of disgust. "At a book sale, no less! One would think he would save his shenanigans for a richer auction. At any rate, I stopped him."

A note of pride in that statement. "By swooning?"

"Well, yes." She met his eyes. "One can hardly conduct an auction with a woman sprawled on the floor."

He laughed softly. "Clever of you."

She wrestled with her own laugh, and lost. "I thought so."

For a companionable moment, they smiled at each

other. Then she appeared to remember her role, and gave a sour tug of her mouth as she flicked back the window shade. "This coach," she said primly, "looks like a bordello."

He lifted a brow. Scarlet upholstery, gold fringe, black enamel—he'd thought it a grand vehicle. But she had something against the palette, he supposed. Devil's colors, she'd called them when visiting Diamonds. "I'll redo it in blue and white," he said, "just for you. He didn't look happy when I saw him leaving. You expect more trouble from him?"

She shrugged. "I can manage him."

"With those three locks on your door."

"It isn't your concern."

True enough. Yet he felt a lick of temper as he eyed her. She sat a foot away, looking as cool and remote as a stranger. He might still be watching her from a distance, the beautiful, untouchable lady who'd hired his niece.

The difference, of course, was that he'd touched her now. He'd bloody married her. Secret or no, she was his burden to bear.

"You could lodge at Diamonds," he said. "Plenty of locks, and guards as well."

She made a low noise, a sound balanced precisely between amusement and scorn. "Yes, that would be very discreet, indeed. Nobody would guess at our connection when it circulated that I was living at your gambling club."

"Nobody would see you coming and going. There's a tunnel from the high road, entered through a sweet-shop."

"Your offer is kind," she said after a pause. "But there's no cause for it. I am perfectly comfortable at home."

They were circling toward an argument they'd already had. Before she could trot out threats about breach of contract, he said, "I could make it a condition. You stay at Diamonds, where I can keep an eye on you, or the game is up."

She glanced at him sidelong. "Perhaps I don't want you keeping an eye on me," she said evenly. "Why should you? There's no call to pretend that we care for each other. You go your way, Mr. O'Shea, and allow me, please, to go mine."

Had she spat and hissed fire at him, he might have argued back. But she spoke with a calm dignity that he was suddenly loathe to nettle. *Please,* she'd said.

She'd had a rough day. Hid it well, but he saw proof of fatigue. Shadows beneath her eyes, and a sag to her shoulders that put him in mind of discouragement.

She deserved to hold her chin high tonight. She'd showed courage and wit, putting an end to that rotten auction. She'd won a round, and deserved to feel the triumph. But who would share it with her? She'd been all alone in that saleroom, hobbling on her sore ankle. Not even a servant to check on her.

Before he knew what he was doing, he reached across the compartment to catch her hand. "Maybe you need a friend," he said. All those calluses in her damp little palm. Another woman in her shoes would have spent her days eating bonbons and ordering servants to do the lifting. "I'm a good one to have."

She stared at him for a moment, an odd look on her face. Probably a trick of the side lamp—it turned her eyes large and luminous, and made her expression look oddly stricken. "A friend," she said softly.

"That's right."

She took a deep, audible breath. "But . . . why would you bother?"

Good question. It made him uneasy how much he wanted to look after her. Or maybe he just disliked that nobody else cared to do it. He'd been in that position, alone and friendless, nobody worrying where he laid his head. But he'd never imagined that kind of loneliness could afflict people of *her* rank. "Kindness never cost me a penny," he said. "I see no need to hoard it."

She bowed her head, then pulled her hand from his. "Thank you," she said, very low. "But I think friendship would only complicate matters."

Odd to feel a sting in her rejection. A thousand people would be grateful for his interest, but no surprise that a rich, spoiled girl from Bloomsbury wouldn't prize it.

Spoiled. No, that didn't sound right. Nobody was coddling this woman. Nor, did it seem, would she allow someone to do so.

He slid open the window and spoke to the driver. "Bloomsbury," he said. "Henton Court."

When he snapped the window shut, she said, "Thank you." Her sigh sounded relieved. "I had feared you might . . ."

"What?" What did she imagine him capable of doing? To a woman—a woman he'd married, no less, and carried in his arms when her ankle gave way. "What did you think I might do?"

But she only shook her head. "Never mind. The newspapers do you an injustice. You're a decent man, after all."

A note of condescension, there, like she expected him to gobble up the words and wag his tail in gratitude.

Decent, was he? And that surprised her? Whom did she think she'd married?

God above, but if she was surprised to find him decent, she must have been shaking in her boots at that register office. He remembered suddenly the coldness she'd shown in his bedroom, the great effort it had taken to crack her and make her yield to pleasure. No wonder. All the time, she'd imagined herself bedding scum.

"Sure," he said, "I've no interest in complicating matters. But if you ever change your mind, let me know. Wouldn't mind shagging you again."

Her spine snapped straight. "I *beg* your pardon."

He snorted. Clearly she meant to forget that he'd ever touched her—that he'd seen her bare as the day she was born, and made her moan from the pleasure of it. Why, she'd probably scrubbed herself raw afterward, lest his filthy touch leave a mark.

"You're right, the vulgarity don't fit," he said. "What we did in that bed, it was more than the normal fuck. I don't expect you to realize it, being a proper, prissy miss. But I'd be glad to prove it again. Pity this coach is so cramped."

She gazed at him in open-mouthed silence for what seemed like a promisingly long moment. Then she sucked in a sharp breath and averted her face, showing him one rosy cheek. "You're a boor. Stop this vehicle and let me out."

"Don't worry yourself, sweetheart. I'm not going to touch you. You'll just have to take my word for it. Rarely happens that two bodies suit each other, the way ours do."

"*Did,*" she bit out.

"Did, and do, and will do," he said. "It don't change, that kind of chemistry."

"Very good to know." Her voice had stiffened and thinned, a schoolmistress speaking to a hopelessly slow child. "Is there anything else you wish to say, in the hopes of shocking me?"

"Shocking you? No. But here's a promise: if I get you beneath me again, you'll enjoy it even more. It'll only get better, Kitty. Why, the fifth or sixth time, I expect I'll make you come just by kissing your sweet little nipples. I'll suck them slow and soft, and then hard. And when I use my teeth on you, the slightest scrape—"

"Stop." She hissed the word, her face red as she rounded on him. "This is—you are—"

"I'm not telling you this to insult you." Maybe it had started as a jab, but suddenly he felt as bothered as she looked. "I mean it as a promise. God's word, Catherine. You're a gift waiting to be unwrapped. I'll open you up and make you glad to be alive, no matter what the day brings. Because you'll know that come nightfall, I'll be laying you down and spreading your legs and showing you how nature intended you to feel."

Her lips moved around a soundless syllable. She cleared her throat, then said hoarsely, "By the terms of the contract—"

"We'll leave the contract outside the bedroom, I think."

"If you *dare* touch me—"

"Haven't yet," he said mildly. "But you're looking mighty flushed, all the same."

"That is *shock*, Mr. O'Shea. Shock at your shameless-ness—why, you have all the subtlety of an ox—"

"Be shocked at my restraint," he said. "I'm a *decent*

man, after all. Otherwise you'd be under me by now."

The coach slowed. She knocked aside the shade, then gasped in obvious relief before scrambling for the door handle.

He caught her wrist, making her freeze. Lifted it to his mouth, and pressed a close-mouthed kiss to her racing pulse.

"You right that I'm no gentleman," he murmured against her fragrant skin. "I'd make you grateful for it. Give it a thought."

She wrenched free and pushed open the door. "I'd rather—I'd rather sell my company!"

But after she stumbled out, she turned back to him, her lips parting as though she meant to deliver one last retort. Instead, however, she stared up at him, silent, her slack-jawed expression gilded by the mellow glow of the lamp.

"You're awful," she said at last, in a reedy voice.

He laughed. "Seems you've got a taste for it," he said, and pulled shut the door.

Falling asleep always proved difficult for Catherine. She spent the day on her feet; she never laid down but with a sense of exhaustion. But her mind kept ticking onward, cataloging the events of the day, showing her truths that she had not perceived in the frenetic hubbub of routine. This mistake, that oversight . . .

She'd learned a trick for it. Not counting sheep, nothing so juvenile. She simply focused on her breath. One could count on the breath to make a simple rhythm, in and out. Beneath this simple focus, her mind grew quiescent and drowsy.

Tonight, however, the trick failed her. Perhaps she was coming down with something. Each breath, which should have pulled her further toward sleep, only pitched her awareness higher—and of such commonplace things! The sheet, where it lay over her, close and soft as a touch. The braid that lay along her shoulder, heavy and somehow entrapping, like a rope holding her down. She felt restless, hot, though the air held a chill that the dying fire had done nothing to dispel.

If I get you beneath me again . . .

She pressed her palm to her cheek. It didn't feel feverish.

I'll suck them slow and soft, and then hard . . .

Her palm was sweaty, damp. *He* had done this to her. Unsettled her with those vulgar words. He'd known he was doing it. She should not give him the satisfaction of succeeding.

But when she squeezed her eyes shut, what she saw was his bare, tawny body stretched over hers, his head lowered at her breast, mouth pulling like a ravening beast. An incubus.

She cupped her palm over her breast. But that was not where she ached now. She slid her palm lower, to the spot between her legs.

He had put his mouth there . . .

This was why women were cautioned to save their virtue for marriage. She'd never known how a man could make a woman feel. The knowledge had corrupted her.

It will only get better.

She touched herself where he had. A gasp broke from her. It was not entirely *his* power. He was wrong to say that she required a partner. She could make herself feel—not precisely the same. That would take the scent and feel of his skin, the heavy delicious weight of him . . .

No. She did not require those. She could take this power from him, place it in her own control. She *must* do it, for she could not accept his invitation. To do so would be to risk . . . everything.

She touched herself clumsily, frustrated by the comparison to how expertly *he* had done it. He'd touched a thousand women so, no doubt.

Her hand stilled. How curious that the thought should send a dark poisonous feeling through her. This was some trick of the fact of marriage, perhaps. Any decent spouse would dislike the idea of a husband's promiscuity. But hers was no true marriage. He was a criminal, who would never make her a true husband. And she was not fit to be any man's wife. Jealousy had no place in their agreement. He would laugh at her if he ever discovered it.

She shoved him from her mind, rubbing herself harder now. Her body belonged to her, not him. As much as she resented him for it, she must also thank him for showing her so.

But what harm was there in thinking of him in private? She would not allow herself to be alone with him again. With a sigh, she pictured his face . . . the bronzed length of his taut, hard body . . . the feel of his mouth on her skin, the skilled stroke of his hand . . . The pleasure began to build. *It* was coming.

A squeak came from her door. A key turning in the lock!

She sat up, blushing so brightly it was a wonder that the room was not illuminated. "Bodkin?" Only her lady's maid had that key.

No answer.

She threw off the covers and slipped to her feet. The dead bolt turned. "Bodkin, I don't wish to be disturbed tonight."

Now came a scrape. That was the second dead bolt, turning.

God in heaven. Bodkin did not have that key.

Nick lay awake, staring at the ceiling. Fine job he'd done, talking so hot to Catherine. She'd sailed away cool as a breeze, but he just kept burning, visions sparking straight from his brain into his groin.

He should have resisted the urge to needle her, talked straight instead. She'd be safer at Diamonds. Even she should see that. She was valuable to him. One vote down, but who knew when others would come that he'd need her brother to help him with? He had every reason to keep her safe. But to her brother, she was only an obstacle now.

With a curse, he threw off the covers and stood. If she found out he'd wasted a moment's sleep thinking about her, she'd only bridle and remind him that per the terms of that contract, he was beholden not to think on her at all.

So he'd turn his attention elsewhere. Go downstairs and check on business, maybe join a game. He rarely indulged himself so—he was good enough that he almost always won, and clients didn't come here to be trounced by the owner. But a single hand of baccarat, maybe. And a shot of whisky, to take the edge off.

He had dressed and was heading toward the door when the knocking started.

Knew it. Like any full-blooded Irishman, he had a sense for oncoming trouble. He turned the bolt and threw open the door.

His factotum, Callan, looked harried and flushed. "Begging your pardon, but that woman you brought here last week—she's downstairs, demanding to be let in. I would have tossed her out, but she's—"

He brushed past Callan, cutting through the lamp-lit passage into the back stairway, where he took the steps by twos.

She was sitting on a bench in the rear vestibule, wrapped up in a horse blanket. Callan must have lent it to her—it had the insignia of the House of Diamonds stitched into one corner.

She rose, chin high, evidently oblivious to her equine reek. "Do forgive my appearance," she said. "I was forced to leave in some haste."

"Yeah," he said slowly. "I see that." Not much sweetness in this victory. "What happened?"

"Nothing so much." But as she shifted, the blanket slipped, revealing another layer—a cloak, her own— and beneath it, a frilly collar of transparent lace.

She'd fled in her night-robe.

Nick waved Callan off, waiting until he'd rounded the corner to step closer to Catherine. "What happened?"

She took a deep breath. "May I stay here, tonight? I know it—it seems very ironic, given my earlier objections. But I fear no hotel would receive me in such a state."

Half dressed and shivering, she still managed to speechify like the Queen. "Of course," he said. "Come on, let's get you a brandy."

"I don't drink, Mr. O'Shea."

He snorted.

Catherine was trying very hard to remain composed. But shock, to say nothing of the cold, seemed to be sinking into her bones, causing her hard-won control to fray, so at last she began to shiver.

O'Shea noticed, perhaps, as he seated her by the fire in his suite. He made some dark noise and turned away. "Stay there."

As if she had anywhere else to go. She stared fixedly at the handsome Persian carpet, listening to his footsteps retreat into the neighboring room. What a flight she had made. Apparently the dangers of town at night were vastly overstated. She'd had no difficulty hailing a hack, and the cabman had seemed thoroughly unsurprised at her destination. Nobody had even attempted to mug her.

O'Shea returned, carrying the counterpane from his bed, gold threads glimmering in the rich brown satin. "Let's trade," he said. "This blanket will be warmer."

"I'm not c-cold." The fire leapt two feet away. She could feel its heat along her skin, though it did not seem to penetrate to her marrow.

"No matter," he said. "That one reeks."

It did, in fact, have a smell to it. But when the other man had given it to her, it had seemed a veritable luxury. She could not quite bring her grip to ease now. "That's all right."

"Catherine." He went down on one knee. The firelight flattered his angular face. He had remarkable eyes, so light, fastened so attentively to hers. He looked at this moment like a proper gentleman, all consideration and care.

Perhaps he was the first proper gentleman she had met, then. She could not recall much chivalry from the ranks of Everleigh's patrons.

"Give it over," he said gently. But when he tugged at the horse blanket, she resisted, shaking her head.

He frowned. Well, she could not blame him for his puzzlement. The lateness of the hour, and the indignity of her recent experience, had clearly scattered her wits. Certainly it had eroded her discretion, for when she opened her mouth, what came out was the blunt, bizarre truth: "I can't seem to let go."

His hands closed on hers. Large, hot hands, not so different in their feel from any other man's. But no other man had ever touched her like this, massaging the delicate bones of her palms, rubbing the length of her fingers, in a soothing, caressing stroke. "It's all right," he said. "You can let go. Nobody here to see."

That wasn't true. "There's you."

He smiled. "But I don't count, do I?"

Did he? She studied him. What an odd twist her life had taken. She had fled to a gaming hell for safety, and now found herself inclined not to regret it. For he was right. Of all men, she had the least to lose with him— the most notorious man in London.

Did he truly deserve that reputation? He did not strike her as cruel. Indeed, he had shown her far greater kindness than any—

No. She could not afford to indulge such thoughts. The consummation had already opened a Pandora's box of wayward desires. No need to add daydreams about his decency to that mix.

But she did let him pull away the blanket. He settled the coverlet over her. It felt almost as solid, as heavy and reassuring, as his grip.

Almost.

She missed his touch, now that he'd pulled away. God help her.

He sat back on his heels, squatting like a field hand as he said, "Clearly three locks weren't sufficient."

"They held long enough." Perhaps her brother was still fumbling with the third. She'd heard his curses through the door.

"Held against who?"

"Peter, of course. He was trying to break in." A shiver traveled through her. "He said . . . he said it was not too late. That matters could be undone, that I could make a decent match. That Pilcher stood ready; that he—Peter, I mean—could take me to him tonight."

Here was the face O'Shea showed his enemies, she supposed: cold and austere, his mouth a grim slash. "Your brother's got a big mouth," he said quietly, "for a man who wants to keep these matters secret."

She sighed. "I don't think Pilcher knows the whole story. From what Peter was saying through the door . . . I gather he told Pilcher that I was planning to elope." It made no sense. Would he have encouraged bigamy? "I can't imagine what he was thinking. It's done; we are married. I cannot marry again."

O'Shea blew out a breath, his silver gaze trailing down her swathed figure. "You look all right. He didn't lay hands on you?"

"No. I climbed out the window before he made it inside."

His brows shot up. "That's a tall house, Kitty."

She should object to the nickname. She would, next time he used it. "The trellis is sturdy."

"On a twisted ankle?"

Startled, she flexed her foot. "Why . . . it feels much better, in fact." Panic, it seemed, made a fine antidote to pain.

He smiled faintly. "You're a bundle of surprises. You got much practice in climbing out windows?"

"No." She paused, tasting the bitterness of her next words before she spoke them. "Go ahead and say it: you were right, and I was wrong. I was a fool to go back home. I should have known he would want revenge. I embarrassed him by halting that auction."

He frowned. "Here, now. It's not foolish to think yourself safe with your brother."

She did not deserve his generosity. "You said it yourself, Mr. O'Shea. He cares nothing for me. And what I did today—why, if there's anything he won't forgive, it's loss of face." Peter's concern had always been for his image, not the company. How had she forgotten that? "Perhaps I should have let the auction go on," she whispered. "If I've ruined this . . . if he means to call our bluff . . ."

A muscle ticked in his jaw. "It's no bluff, though. It's done."

True. She'd taken pains to ensure that this marriage was legitimate. The memory of how she had done it rippled through her, an echo of the heat she had felt earlier, lying in bed. She took care to keep her gaze from straying toward O'Shea's bedroom.

He rose, light and lean as a cat. What must it feel like, to move through the world in such a tall, lithe, powerful body? Each step must feel weightless, a pleasurable exercise in grace.

The oddness of the thought made her flush. She stared down at her linked hands as he said, "You'll stay here tonight."

"Yes, if you don't mind it. But my brother—"

"I'll speak with him. When does he usually leave the house in the morning?"

"I . . . it varies." On a deep breath, she looked up at him. It put a crick in her neck. He stood almost a head taller than her brother. No fight between them would be fair. "Call me foolish. But I can't countenance you harming him."

His jaw squared. "I said I wouldn't. But at this point, you'd do better not to waste concern on him. Tit for tat, Catherine. Never give more than you get."

A brutal but sensible philosophy. "If that's your belief," she said slowly, "then what do you hope to get from me now? For the contract does not require you to help me in this way."

He stared down at her, his face impossible to read. It came to her that his bedroom was only seven steps away. If he demanded she join him there . . . if that was his price . . .

"It's late," he said, and held out his hand. "Let me show you where you'll sleep."

O'Shea proved far more chivalrous than she'd anticipated. He said he would send someone to the shops in the morning to fetch a readymade gown for her. He opened the door for her, and did not touch her as he escorted her into the adjoining apartment.

He played the gentleman very convincingly. But why? As shock faded, her brain began to click into working order again, and his gentleness began to alarm her.

He had no reason to be kind. He was after something. And she . . . was falling for his trick. This man who had spoken to her so vulgarly in his vehicle earlier—she was softening toward him, surrendering all her native defenses. Longing for him to touch her again as he showed her the points of the suite where she would stay.

She couldn't allow it. She let him bow over her hand before he started for the door, but she made herself call after him. "Don't think I don't know what you're doing," she said. "I'm well aware of your strategy."

He turned back at the door. "What strategy is that?"

"Charm, I believe it's called."

He widened his eyes, japing astonishment as he slouched against the doorframe. "Never say. And here I'd heard I had the charm of an ox."

"I said you had the subtlety of an ox," she said. "But I know these tricks. You're a practiced flirt with a handsome face. No doubt you have good success among certain company. But you won't find it with me. Spare yourself the effort."

"Handsome face." He offered her a lopsided smile. "Are we turning to compliments now?"

"Do you imagine me incapable?"

"I had doubted, once or twice."

"Oh, but I know this game very well. You're not the only handsome face in this room."

"'Handsome' isn't the word for it," he said evenly. "With a face like yours, darling, you could have been a courtesan to princes."

Surprise prickled through her. She squashed the emotion. "Yes," she said. "Perhaps so."

His head tipped as he considered her. "You don't sound pleased about it."

"What is there to be pleased about? Nature worked a fine trick on my features." And that trick grew very inconvenient when it attracted interest from men like Pilcher. "It was none of my doing."

"Well now," he said slowly. "Forgive me for a thick-headed ox, but that's the strangest way to call yourself beautiful that I've ever heard."

"I suppose you would think so. There's the difference between us: I have no interest in my looks. I had rather rely on my brains." She forced a sharp smile. "But then, that choice is reserved for people of actual wit, I suppose."

He laughed! "Be as harsh as you like, Kitty. I'd sooner look to a magistrate for kindness."

"Good," she said. "We understand each other. You will not try to charm me while I'm here. It's a futile gamble, anyway."

"Poor Catherine." She did not like his idle tone. "I'm sure there's many a man who might have charmed you. But they probably lost interest when you opened your mouth."

She swallowed. His words struck at some tender part of her whose existence she had done her best to forget. "You imagine so? I have been admired by many men. Dozens."

"Only dozens?" He offered her a slow smile. "Best not compare us, after all."

"There is no comparison," she said. "I am a woman of honor, whereas you . . . well. There are words for persons who trade on their physical appeal—all of them too vulgar to speak."

His brows lifted. "Why spare me? If you want to call me a whore, say it."

She flinched. "Of course you wouldn't mind that. Lewdness is your native tongue."

"I speak other languages with that tongue," he said darkly. "Once, recently, I made you speak back."

"More lewdness. How unsurprising."

"If you're wanting me to surprise you, you need only ask, darling."

"I doubt you capable of it. Nor is it my desire."

"Is that so?" He came off the doorjamb, prowling toward her. She folded her arms, thrusting her elbows out to prevent him from drawing too near. A smile flitted over his full lips; he laid his hand on the side of her neck, his palm flexing lightly.

"I'd enjoy surprising you," he said softly. "My native tongue, as you call it, has ideas you've never dreamed of in your virginal little bed."

Some strange alchemy was at work, for the threat evoked a hot melting feeling inside her, akin more to excitement than to fear. Heavens—was it possible that she'd provoked him deliberately, to keep his attention a little while longer? "I'm no virgin now," she said unsteadily, rattled by how quickly he made her a stranger to herself. "I have tasted what you offer, and I have no interest in exploring it further."

"You're lying to yourself," he murmured.

But she wasn't. She was lying only to him. For suddenly it was plain to her—his touch made it unbearably clear—that she could not count on her own indifference. Those lips, that mouth, the long warm fingers at her throat, were wicked. They made her thoughts turn dark and heated, swollen with curiosity. "I came tonight from sheer necessity," she managed. "And I am grateful to you for taking me in. But it ends there."

"I know it." He gave her a long, measured look. Then he caught her hand, pried open her fist finger by finger before folding them closed again around a small, cold, sharp-edged object.

A key.

He said, "That's the only key to this room. And there's only one door. You leave it in the lock, nobody will be coming in. Understand?"

She stared at the key. No, she did not understand anything. She understood nothing about him, least of all how he managed to leave her shaken and shamed by her own harsh words to him.

As the door closed behind him, a bitter taste filled her mouth. Again, that haunting question she could not quite dismiss: what if she was wrong about him? What if, despite all evidence to the contrary—his criminal reputation; this gambling den—he was a decent man, who offered his kindness honestly?

The sharp edges of the key cut into her palm. She grimaced and fit the key into the lock. Consideration. Kindness. She didn't want it. *Oh, be truthful.* God help her, but some twisted part of her would have preferred him to ravish her. Between them, *she* seemed the animal.

She distracted herself with a tour of the suite. It was not quite as spacious as his, but the sitting room was handsomely outfitted in neutral tones of cream and bronze. One door opened into a very modern, tiled water closet. The last room housed a bed that looked to be a museum piece. From the doorway, she ogled it. The carved oak canopy—the entire fixture was Jacobean. Were her eyes deceiving her?

She approached, placing one tentative hand against the thick poster. This was no facsimile, she'd wager. It would have fetched a handsome price at auction, for such beds were very rare.

Slowly she turned. The chair in the corner looked to be Chippendale. She hesitated, but there was no point trying to sleep in such a rattled state; she might as well indulge herself. She removed the Trafalgar seat. The outside edges of the front legs looked worn, just as they should. She tipped the chair forward, and found similar marks of heavy use on the back of the rear legs. This was no reproduction.

Amazement prickled through her. What on earth was O'Shea doing with such antiques?

Curious now, she returned to the sitting room. The gilt-mounted clock on the mantelpiece boasted a splendid marquetry of sycamore; it appeared to be a Cromwellian original. She drifted nearer, reaching out to touch the mantel that framed the hearth. Wood overlaid with plaster. Could this be an original Adam? Ceres, goddess of plenty, presided over the central panel, while the friezes displayed wreaths of wheat.

These treasures had been seized from irresponsible gamblers, no doubt. She should not admire them. And yet . . . it took taste to know what to seize in lieu of payment.

She glanced toward the locked door. She had paid little attention to the furnishings in O'Shea's private quarters. Nerves had blinded her. Now she wondered what she had missed. A pity one could not pay a visit at half past two to ask!

A pity one could not *trust* oneself to pay that visit.

Were he some other man . . . The notion shocked her,

but she dared to voice it to herself: were he somebody else, perhaps she would have taken the risk without regard for the shame. After all, hungers could be slaked, fires doused; revisiting his bed might have liberated her from this unsettling fever, allowing her to repossess her once-disciplined state of mind.

But in the eyes of the law, he was her husband. What happened between them in a bedroom would have repercussions outside it. She should not give him any cause to look on her as a true wife, for she had no interest in playing one—nor any ability.

There was another way to douse a fire: feed it no fuel. As she lay down in bed, she forced her thoughts to business, and fell asleep to nightmares of accounts that did not reconcile.

CHAPTER SEVEN

$\mathcal{N}$ick woke before dawn, taking care in his ablutions not to make any noise that might penetrate to the neighboring apartment. This was a task he meant to undertake without interference from innocents, no matter that their tongues were sharp enough to count them armed at all times.

He frightened her. That was clear. He knew the cause, too. Made her feel things she didn't want to feel.

He wouldn't lie to himself. He enjoyed frightening her. He'd never known a pleasure quite as rare and dark, as rattling a creamy girl who thought herself his better, and making her blush against her will.

As he dressed, he felt an old twinge in his left knee, relic of an earlier time when brawls had been dirty and physical. He'd grown hard by necessity, and he wasn't fool enough to miss those days. It had been years since he set out alone on foot, with only his own knife to back him. But when Nick reached the point where he needed friends to take on a single soft-bellied swell, he would be one foot in the grave already, and well past the need for killing.

He woke Johnson for a brief word—Catherine needed a guard, and Johnson would do in a pinch—before stepping out of the club. He walked toward the high road, through alleys still sunk in darkness while dawn grayed overhead. On the omnibus, he stood shoulder to shoulder with dark-suited workers and neatly dressed girls bound for the shops and offices of the West End. Here and there he caught a glance lingering on his face, quickly averted when he remarked it. Some people recognized him, but not most.

This half anonymity suited him. It made it easier to pick out his own people, those with the knowledge to respect or fear him, as their circumstances required. Any better known, and he'd have to send his men to do the dirty work for him—and in this case, particularly, he was looking forward to doing for himself.

Two changes later, and he was in Bloomsbury. Roads swept neat, fat nabobs still slumbering. As he turned into Henton Court, he came across a street sweeper dozing on his feet, chin propped atop his broom handle. The boy opened one eye as Nick passed.

He remembered that kind of sleep. Never easy, never deep. As a child, he'd swept streets for a few months himself. It had taken owning a roof for him to learn to sleep soundly again. Neddie's had been his first purchase; until then, he'd had nothing to show for his ill-gotten coin. Bankers wouldn't touch it. He'd run out of places to hide his cash. When news had traveled of Neddie's plight—rent raised skyward, owner putting the public house to auction—he'd thought hard before making a bid. A man like him owning property? Seemed like painting a target on his back.

Instead, holding the deed in his hand, he'd discovered the intoxication of owning something real. Having a place where nobody could say he didn't belong, had no rights, wasn't good enough. He'd never interfered with Neddie's ways; he let the old man go on as always. But he'd taken to sleeping there for a time—sleeping as deeply and dreamlessly as a babe.

Diamonds was his pride. But Neddie's would always be his first and truest home. Still wasn't anywhere he slept better.

He listened to the sound of his own footsteps echo off the polished stone faces of the townhouses. Nodded politely to a passing bobby, who yawned as he strolled his beat. The curtains were still drawn at the Everleigh house. He passed onward, pausing a few houses away to lean against a scrawny oak and wait.

He'd gambled that the events of last night would pull Everleigh from his bed quite early. Indeed, it didn't take above an hour until a carriage rolled out from the nearby alley, horses pulling up at the curb before the house. The front door opened; Peter went rushing down the stairs toward the coach, a footman at his heels. Nick stole up from the other side, waiting until the other door thumped shut to open the door on his own side and spring in.

"What the—" Peter Everleigh slammed himself backward against his cushions as the coach rocked into motion.

"I wouldn't," Nick said, as the other man's hand rose to rap the ceiling for his driver's attention. "This will be a short discussion."

Slowly, Everleigh lowered his hand. "What in God's name do you want?"

Bastard looked well rested for a man whose sister

had disappeared in the wee hours. Were he smarter, he'd be looking more alarmed by his present company, too. "You're easy to surprise," Nick said. "Should take better care with your safety."

"Some of us live decent lives," Everleigh said tightly. "We see no need to be looking over our shoulders at the crack of dawn."

Nick smiled. "Perhaps that was the case before. Then you gave trouble to my wife."

Everleigh caught on at last. He lunged for the door, but Nick was ready for him. He caught Everleigh around the throat and pulled him onto the bench in a chokehold.

"Stop thrashing," he said, "or I might hurt you."

"Let go of—"

Everleigh's words ended in a sputter as Nick squeezed. "No need for you to talk. Simply nod."

The man struggled harder. Nick seized his hair and forced his neck to an awkward angle. Soon enough, he'd be longing for air. "Nod," he said flatly.

At last, Everleigh nodded. His lips were trembling; he pressed them into a flat line and dragged in a choked breath.

Nick stretched out his legs, making himself comfortable. These cushions were stuffed as plump as a Christmas goose. "Your sister tells me you've got political ambitions," he said amiably. "I tell her she must be wrong. I say, any politician would know better than to break into his sister's room after midnight." The thought tasted foul; he spat onto the floor. "A sister, mind you, who is lawfully married to another, and who was, I expect, only spending the night under your roof as a lark, one final evening in her childhood home. Aye, *there's* a tale. Would play well in the newspapers, all right: the politician who dreams of bigamy."

Everleigh looked white as pasteboard, spit bubbling at the corners of his mouth.

"You'll tell Pilcher to keep his mind off her henceforth. And *you'll* keep away from Pilcher. You'll have him kicked off the municipal board on charges of corruption. Got it?"

Everleigh nodded—then shook his head wildly.

Just as Nick had expected. "Right. What's he got on you, then?"

Everleigh's lips moved soundlessly. Apparently the rat did need to breathe occasionally. Nick let him go.

Everleigh hurled himself onto the opposite bench, drawing his knees up to his chest as an extra defense. "You're a—" He looked frenzied with astonishment. "How dare you! You—"

"Pilcher," Nick said flatly. "What's your connection with him?"

"You're a ruffian, a—"

Slow learner, this one. Nick lunged across the coach, catching Everleigh by the hair. Time to introduce his knife to this discussion. He set it just so at Everleigh's throat.

That got the bastard's attention. He stammered out some frantic, babbling apology.

Nick let the sharp edge of his knife give his reply. A shaving nick, it would look like.

Everleigh's eyes bulged wide. He shut up, finally.

"I'm no nob," Nick said. "Your rules don't apply to me. And your blood won't look blue when I spill it. Ask me how I know."

Everleigh had a shred of intelligence, after all. He didn't ask. Only loosed a little sob.

"Tell me, then, what Pilcher's got on you." He eased the knife away a fraction.

"I . . . oh, God in heaven . . . I can't oust Pilcher from the board. He's got friends, you see, and I won't have the votes—"

"You'll have Whitechapel's vote. The votes of St. George's-in-the-East and Mile End. And your own," Nick added. "That'll give you a fine start for *politicking*."

"No, you don't understand! Your buildings—that inspector had no authority in Whitechapel. Pilcher understood that; he knows that a man of my ambitions must be seen to respect the law. But what you're talking of now—he would never forgive me for it! And I've got investments with him, you see. Land, properties, a great deal of money sunk into his developments. I'd lose it all. I can't afford to make him an enemy!"

So that explained it. Everleigh and Pilcher were partners in land speculation.

Nick weighed his options. Tempting to throw this piece of shit to the wolves. But he'd not come up in the world by indulging his own whims at the expense of good strategy. "How much do you have sunk with him?"

"Three—four thousand pounds."

"Break with Pilcher, then. I'll stand you the sum." He shoved Everleigh onto the floor.

Everleigh scrambled off his knees to the opposite bench, huddling as far from Nick as the vehicle allowed. "But . . . you can't . . . Why on earth would you make such an offer?"

"It's business," Nick said, clipped. "You'll be voting for me, whenever I require it."

"Of course," Everleigh said instantly.

"And you'll hand my wife every account attached to that auction house. You'll put them into her hands, and hers alone."

"I—but the law won't allow that! By the terms of the trust, she cannot assume control unless she is married." Bright color rose to Everleigh's face. "Or are you recanting your offer of silence?"

"No. The accounts will stay in your name, but you'll designate her your legal proxy."

Everleigh gawked. "What on earth do you know of such matters?"

Here was what made the toffs such easy pickings. They imagined, because they'd designed the game, that nobody else could learn the rules. "You'll have that proxy drawn up today. Do you follow?"

"I . . ." Hesitantly, Everleigh uncurled himself. He set one boot on the floor, then another, his posture hunched, clearly braced for another attack.

Nick pointedly sheathed his knife.

Everleigh loosed an audible breath and sat straighter. "Then I accept your proposal."

Nick paused, letting the silence tick out, three long beats. "Wasn't a proposal. It's the only chance you'll get. Understand?"

The other man recoiled. "Yes! Yes, I understand."

Nick studied him a moment, cataloging each twitch. "You sure about that?"

Everleigh offered a flinching attempt at a placating smile. "I do understand," he whispered. "I promise, I won't be any trouble to you." He cleared his throat, then said in a meek tone, "Shall I ask the driver to drop you somewhere?"

"No need." Nick opened the door, then leapt neatly

out into traffic. His last view of Everleigh was the man's pallid, astonished face as he leaned out to pull the door shut.

En route to Everleigh's through a sunny autumn morning, Catherine became aware of how her stomach churned. She fully anticipated a violent quarrel with her brother over the debacle of the Cranston auction. Worse yet, after his bizarre attempt to break into her bedchamber, her own anger felt secondary to nervousness. Peter had made her afraid to return to her own auction rooms! It was outrageous.

As she emerged from O'Shea's unmarked coach, one of his servants descended from the footman's step to escort her inside. A mountain of a man, with a shining bald head and a bashful smile, he introduced himself as Mr. Johnson. "I'm to stick by you today," he told her, "and make sure your brother behaves, miss."

This presumption on O'Shea's part would ordinarily anger her. But today, it seemed like welcome news. "Very well," she said stiffly, and on a deep breath, led the giant inside.

But her brother was nowhere in evidence. In her office, she discovered an infuriated letter from Lord Cranston, the reply to which kept her busy for most of the morning. Cranston felt his pride had been injured by the interruption of the auction, and demanded assurances and recompense.

By the time a knock came at her door, she had all but forgotten her former anxiety, so immersed was she in the tricky politics of soothing an offended peer. "Come," she said absently.

The door opened. Mr. Johnson stepped inside, her brother at his heels.

Her throat tightened, her pulse tripping into a gallop. Peter looked thin-lipped, flushed, and livid. But with Johnson looming behind him, she felt well able to match him in a fight.

She laid down her pen, and rose. "I hope you've come to apologize," she said. "And to account for yourself! Last night—"

Peter threw a stack of papers onto her desk. "There," he said flatly. "That is all you will have from me. Tell him it is done."

"Tell whom?"

Peter grimaced. "Your gutter rat. Who else?" Turning on his heel, he shoved past Johnson and stalked out.

Mystified, she sat back down and broke open the seal on the papers. For a moment, looking them over, she lost her grip on English. The words made no sense.

Peter had made her his legal proxy.

Gaping, she flipped through the pages. Yes, she'd read rightly: she now controlled Everleigh's financial operations. Effectively, she controlled *everything*.

"Are you all right there, miss?"

Had she made a noise? Mr. Johnson, still lingering in the doorway, looked concerned. "I'm . . . very well," she said faintly. She carefully laid down the papers. "Would you mind stepping outside, Mr. Johnson? I require a moment of . . ."

As the door shut, she exhaled—a shuddering, choked breath that brought the sudden pressure of tears to her eyes. She dropped her face into her hands, pressing tightly to stem the urge to weep.

I control the company.

Her mouth was trembling. She was not dreaming. This was real.

She felt her lips curve into a wide, amazed smile.

Saved! No more embezzling; no more thievery; no more threats of selling the business. *She* was the sole effective owner.

Could it really be?

She seized the documents again. The miracle remained unchanged. *I do designate Catherine Everleigh my legal proxy in all matters pertaining to the governance of this company, its assets and properties . . .*

A laugh slipped from her. No wonder Peter looked so pale! He could not touch the principal now—nor any of the client accounts! He would need her permission to avail himself of so much as a penny.

O'Shea had done this.

She shook her head, wonder prickling over her. How had he done it? And why? Nobody, not even the family solicitor who had known her from birth, had taken her complaints about Peter so seriously. But O'Shea had listened to her. He had acted to save Everleigh's, though he had no reason to concern himself with its welfare.

No reason except . . . her.

The thought triggered a curious rush of warmth through her chest. She rose, locking her hands together at her waist, and stared blindly out the window into the little park across the road. He had offered her friendship. Was this how he treated his friends? If so, how fortunate they were!

She swallowed. He had no right to interfere with her business, of course.

But how could she resent him for it?

Turning back, she stroked one finger across the bold, plain print of this legal document, the greatest gift she had ever been given. A curious feeling fluttered through her stomach, soft and unbearably sweet. Surely he had some secret motive. She was a businesswoman; she knew that nothing ever came for free. He was trying to purchase her trust. But to what purpose?

She could not trust a man who offered such extraordinary gifts without declaring his price for them first. But had he told her the cost beforehand . . . oh, whatever it might have been, she probably would have accepted the bargain.

CHAPTER EIGHT

*A*nother bloody note from Pilcher. Callan handed it over, his lean face expressionless. But when he spoke, there was a warning in his voice. "Came himself, this time."

"Did he?" Nick glanced at the letter, snorting. Pilcher had first written on the very evening that the board had overthrown his petition to condemn Nick's buildings. He'd proposed then to meet Nick at Speakers' Corner in Hyde Park—*under cover of darkness,* he'd written, as though plotting a heist.

Now he'd progressed to offering dinner at his club in St. James. Still didn't say what he wanted, though. Perhaps he'd caught on to Everleigh's quiet campaign to unseat him. Or maybe he was still stewing over the lots on Orton Street.

Either way, Nick saw no profit in replying. He reached again for his cards. "You got downstairs in hand?" he asked as he cut the deck. He'd spent most of the evening at Neddie's, settling business with his rent agents. When he'd come back, the crowd had been thick as porridge. Judging by the noise, it was thinning now.

"Locked up tight," said Callan. He rubbed his eyes. "A crowd at the roulette, a handful left at baccarat and poker."

Nick considered him. Lad was sporting fresh bruises on his face. They distorted the line of his jaw, made him look fuller cheeked, younger than his twenty-odd years. Put Nick in mind of the first night he'd shown up at the door, wet to the bone in a pouring rain, barely seventeen, claiming to be a long-lost cousin.

Callan had the height for it, maybe, and the raw-boned strength. But Nick didn't know a single kinsman whose hair had that reddish cast, nor did he recognize the northern lilt of Callan's speech. More likely, the lad had caught wind of the advantage in being related, and invented the kinship while he waited on Diamonds's doorstep to beg for a job.

As long as the fiction served them both, Nick would call him a cousin—and treat him so. "Who hit you?"

"Nobody." Callan had a moody, angular face, and a long mouth that telegraphed sullenness better than a girl's. "He looks worse."

"Sure he does." Boy had a taste for brawling, all right. Made him a fine patroller of the floor—he jumped at the chance to teach cheaters a lesson. "As long as he deserved it. No use in risking your bones for sport."

Callan's jaw tightened. This was an old dispute between them. The lad had used to make a fine income on the side, fighting at Old Joe's in the Nichol for a crowd of wagering swells. "I've not been to Old Joe's in months," he said bitterly. "Not to say I couldn't use the cash."

Nick paid a handsome wage. But he knew that Callan kept little for himself. Sent most of it direct to his siblings in Belfast.

Still, he wouldn't countenance cheek. "You think you can do better, you're welcome to walk out the door," he said as he shuffled the cards.

Callan snapped straight. "No. I didn't mean that."

"Good. Because as long as you work here, you'll keep away from Old Joe's." Nick paused, fixing Callan in a square look. "You're no dog, to risk your throat for toffs' entertainment. No amount of money is worth your pride—or your life."

Callan's mouth curved. "Right."

That smirk right there accounted for most of Callan's bruises, Nick didn't doubt. If he didn't know the lad better, he'd be itching to slap it away himself. Instead, he cast a pointed glance toward the clock on the wall. "Turn 'em out at half three." That was the deal he'd struck with the local precinct. Bobbies liked to know when they could start harassing loiterers in the court, and when to turn a blind eye.

"Will do."

Nick idly riffled the cards as he watched Callan walk off. Distant relation, sure. The O'Sheas, for all their faults, had hearts that burned hot, and the boy was cold to the bone.

A flicker of movement down the balcony caught his eye. Why, if it wasn't his dear wife. He'd expected her to decamp to a hotel after her first night here. But it seemed she'd developed a taste for the place. Last they'd talked at any length, she'd thanked him with a pretty blush for ensuring her brother gave her the proxy, and then she'd announced that he was right—she'd be safer staying under his roof, at least for the time being.

He would have liked a moment to savor that victory. "Right, was I?" he'd drawled, but she'd suddenly remembered some work waiting for her, and had taken herself off before he could properly gloat.

She worked long hours, she did. Sometimes, when he got back at half ten, she was still at the office. Johnson, who had kept tailing her lest her brother cause trouble, complained that he was falling asleep on his feet, thanks to her schedule.

It looked like she'd been interrupted from bed. She wore a pale pink nightdress and matching shawl, and she'd bound her hair back into a golden plait that swung down to the small of her back. She was prowling down the balcony like a thief on a rum catch.

He let the cards fall, watching curiously as she drew up by a hip-high vase that stood against the wall. She bent down, running her palm along the curving lip, and he felt a brief, rueful envy for the cold porcelain. To be looked at with such avid interest, while rubbed like a cat . . . any man would take an interest in the prospect.

He certainly did. He pushed out a long breath. This, right here, was why he'd taken to staying out late in the evenings. He hadn't made it to the ripe old age of thirty-one in order to be ambushed by a constant parade of inconvenient cock-stands.

Wasn't her fault, though. Not by so much as a sigh or a flutter did she encourage him. Each time they had crossed paths on the balcony this week, she'd done her best to look right through him as she'd issued her prim little greeting. "That interest you?" he called now.

She flinched, then wheeled toward him, the fringes of her shawl fluttering around her elbows. "You're here!"

"I own the place," he said agreeably. "You realize we're still open, aye?" For all that her nightdress covered her from chin to toes, she'd probably find some reason to feel shy about it.

But after a visible hesitation, she surprised him by approaching. Pity that he'd had her wardrobe fetched from Bloomsbury. She'd clearly added several layers beneath the pink gown, for he couldn't catch a hint of the roll of her hips. Only the tips of her stockings showed, quick flashes of white lace.

She wore lace stockings to bed. Now, why should that be the best news he'd had all day?

Should have slept at Neddie's, after all.

She drew up at the other side of the table, frowning. He kicked out the other chair in invitation. She glanced at it, but remained standing. "Where do you go each night? You're never here in the evening."

So she'd noticed. Her lace stockings would probably keep him away for five more nights. It wasn't his way to hire companionship—he'd known too many whores in his childhood; even the posh ones rarely enjoyed their work. But at this rate, he'd be wearing out his hand. "I've got business elsewhere," he said. "Why?"

"No reason. I was only curious." She paused, chewing on her lip. That would not help him get to sleep later. "It seems a poor way to run the House of Diamonds, though. I'd imagined . . . when I first visited, you struck me as a more conscientious proprietor."

He grinned. "You've got a talent," he said, "for insults wrapped in compliments."

She gave a curious little grimace. "I didn't mean . . .

I suppose your other businesses demand your attention as well."

An apology! Roundabout, to be sure, but surprising all the same. "Why are you prowling about so late?" Wasn't errant lust, he'd wager. He was trying very hard not to let his pride be injured by that, but damned if he could work out how she didn't feel an ounce of curiosity, after what they'd done together in his bed on the first try.

Her eyes cut toward the vase, then back to his. Shifty look, there. In anybody else, he would have called it guilt, and looked for the reason. "I can't sleep."

He nodded and resumed shuffling the cards.

"What business were you attending to?" she asked after a moment.

Judging by her stiff tone, she was making conversation against her better instincts. "Properties I rent," he said.

"Oh yes. Lilah—that is, your niece mentioned you owned several. She thinks you . . . quite a businessman."

He glanced up at her, amused by the incongruity of Lily befriending this girl. Two more different women he couldn't imagine. Then again, Lily had changed, once she'd started her climb out of Whitechapel into the lap of a swell. A bloody viscount, no less. "You heard from her since she left on that honeymoon?"

She nodded. "A few brief notes. They're in New York now, I think."

"Imagine that." Her gaze had dropped to his hands; he showed off for her a little, cutting the deck single-handedly. "Seems a bit much, don't it? Six months of travel?"

"Lord Palmer asked her what she most wanted, and

she said . . ." Her pale brows drew together as he riffled the cards. "She said she wished to see the world. Where did you learn to do that?"

"What, this?" He made the cards explode from his fingertips, catching them as they fitted back together into a neat pile.

Her lips formed a perfect O. Her amazement was so transparent and childlike, so utterly unlike her usual guarded mien, that he laughed.

Recalling herself, she pulled a face and turned away. "Never mind."

"No, wait." When she looked over her shoulder, he shrugged and said, "It's like asking where you learned to put your hair in that braid. Pretty, aye? But probably comes as second nature to you."

She touched her hair. God's glory, it was, a thick rope the width of a man's wrist, gleaming like a freshly polished guinea. "Plaiting is quite simple, actually."

"And so is this."

She squinted, looking doubtful.

"Honestly. Looks tricky, but it's only a step up from a regular shuffle."

She put her hand on the back of the chair. She had slim fingers, small hands; they looked boneless, her skin opalescent in the low light. A lady's hands, save for her nails, which were trimmed to the quick. Those gratified him, somehow. Calluses and stubbed nails, God love her. Did any other man in London know those details? He hoped not. It was becoming a curious new hobby, a deeply private pleasure, to collect these small secrets about her. He couldn't touch her. But he could learn the quirks of her body, regardless.

"I don't know how to shuffle," she admitted.

"You said you played cards, right? That first night you came here."

Her hand tightened. "I said that children play cards."

"I'm thinking you were one once. Or did you spring out fully grown?"

A smile flitted over her mouth. "Like Athena?"

"Don't know her."

Her smile faded. "The goddess on your ceiling." She waved toward the mural overhead.

"Oh." He shrugged. "Didn't cover the classics in school."

"What did you study, then?"

"I didn't. School wasn't compulsory back then." And the mission schools had rarely spared a seat for a boy like him. Times had changed for the better, that way. Even the nobs admitted now that a grubber should learn to read.

She looked shocked. "You have no education at all?"

"I'm not illiterate," he said. He'd taught himself, painfully, too late to learn any comfort with it. He worked down a page more slowly than Blushes could run.

That look on her face bordered too closely on pity. "I know what I need to," he added. "And if I find I don't, then I put myself to learning it right quickly."

"I'm sure you do," she murmured. "To have accomplished . . ." She glanced toward the railing, in the direction of the gaming floor. "Well. Many men with degrees have not managed as much."

He loosed a low whistle. "Now, that's a proper compliment. You feeling all right?"

She blushed and looked down at her hand, running her thumb along the back of the chair. "It is not a compliment," she said stiltedly, "to remark the obvious. I cannot approve of illegal business operations, but I can certainly admire a profitable enterprise."

Poor Kitty, so desperate to reason herself out of kindness. "I bet you had a fancy education," he said. "Latin, Greek, the whatnot."

Miracle of miracles, she pulled out the chair and sat. "Not really. My brother had a tutor, and then, of course, he was sent to school. But my governess was mostly concerned with teaching manners and deportment. Social charms."

He snorted. "She wasn't so good, I take it."

There was a brief moment in which he could see her weighing whether to take offense or be amused. At last, her mouth curved slightly. "Perhaps not," she said. "I very much doubt she references me when looking for work."

Her dry humor set something at ease in him. He'd seen glimpses, once or twice, of her ability to laugh— but generally only at him. If they could joke together, they would rub along just fine. "Proper terror, you were, I don't doubt."

"She certainly wasn't with us for very long," she said. "But then, it would have been a waste of money. I spent most of my time at Everleigh's, tagging along with my father. That was my true education. He taught me everything he knew—or tried to, at least."

"Ah. Uncommon," he said. "You don't see many men bringing up their daughters to run a business."

Now her smile faded. "He thought I had more promise than Peter."

Sharp tilt to her chin, there. Did she expect him to argue the point? "Sounds like your dad saw things clearly."

"He did." She relaxed a little. "He was very good to me. He took me everywhere—into meetings with clients, even. They could hardly believe their eyes when they saw me sitting in the corner. But when somebody would object to it, my father would challenge them to try to distract me into speaking. I could stay perfectly quiet for hours."

Sounded like a miserable time for a child. But he gathered that she meant to boast. "How old were you?"

She propped her elbow on the table and rested her chin in her hand. "I was seven when he first starting taking me to work with him. But it wasn't until I was nine or ten that I sat in on meetings."

"Nine or ten." With the easy way she was leaning, she couldn't be wearing a corset. He tried to ignore the notion, the memory of what she'd looked like, stretched across his bed in nothing but her skin. He cut the deck again, making a complex bridge to distract himself. Her eyes widened with delight.

He bit down on a smile. This woman was accustomed to gazing on valuable wonders, which men paid fortunes to own. But she watched his small tricks like he was working magic for her. "Nine's young," he said, "to keep so still."

"I should say nine is a fine age for it. Far better suited to study than to heavy labor."

It took him a moment to realize he'd told her about his work at the dockyards. He snorted. "Given the choice, I would have picked the docks any day. Sitting still wasn't for me. What happened if you spoke up, wanted to go play?"

"I didn't. I preferred Papa's company."

"Never once?"

Her voice thinned. "I was good at it. At helping him, I mean. And it interested me."

Telling, how being good was evidently more important than being interested. "No time for cards, then."

"Nobody to play with, either." She shrugged. "That would have made a fine sight for the clients—the staff gambling with a child."

What a contrast to his own youth—brawling in the streets, quipping and conspiring with lads his own age, some of whom he still saw nightly at Neddie's. It hadn't been an easy existence, but he'd rarely wanted for a friend. "Sounds lonely."

Her face went blank. "It wasn't."

"Right."

"I had my father," she said. "And the work."

And now she had only the work. He began to understand why she was so desperate not to lose the auction rooms—and why she might have married a man like him, to keep them.

"What of you?" she asked. "Did you—do you have siblings? Did they work at the docks, too?"

"An older sister," he said. "Much older. Lived here in Whitechapel—Lily's mother, in fact. When my own ma passed, I went to live with her."

"So you grew up with Lilah—Lily, I mean." She offered a smile. "I suppose she was great fun as a girl."

A hellcat, in fact. But Nick wouldn't disillusion her. He looked at her carefully as he reshuffled the deck, noticing the shadows under her eyes, the wan attitude of her pretty mouth. She had nobody to confide in, he supposed. Lily wasn't due back from her honeymoon for a month or two, yet. And Catherine had left her lady's maid in Bloomsbury, for fear she couldn't trust her to keep secrets.

Lonely, indeed. What she needed was to have some fun.

He split the deck and slapped one of the halves in front of her. "Let's play."

She sighed. "I just told you, I don't—"

"This is the easiest game on the planet," he said. "You turn over your top card at the same time as I do. Whoever has the highest card gets to keep both. Winner sticks them into the bottom of his pile, and we both lay down our next card from the top."

"That's all?"

"That's it. Whoever ends up with all the cards, wins."

"But that's too easy. What's the point?"

He laughed. "Now, that's what I like about cards, right there. You learn something about the person you're playing with, regardless of the game."

She stiffened. "Fine. Let's play."

"No, by all means, let's add some savor to it. Five rounds. Best of five wins, and the loser owes a favor."

"A favor," she said slowly. "What kind of favor?"

"That's up to the winner."

"Oh, I think not." Where had she gotten those witchy eyes from? Who had taught her to use them so boldly? Even in Whitechapel, girls batted their lashes. But Catherine Everleigh, Lady of Business, stared him down without so much as a flutter. "I never make a contract without elucidating the terms first," she told him.

There was something deeply fetching about such brisk, mannish words spoken by a rosy, thoroughly feminine mouth—a mouth, if he wasn't mistaken, that was fighting a smile. Her gaze dropped from his, and she ran one finger over the baize tabletop. "Unless," she said, "you're having second thoughts about your chance at winning?"

Now, *that* was saucy, or he was a priest. She had some idea of her effect, then. She simply knew she didn't need to bat her lashes to achieve it.

"All right," he said, smiling himself. "How about—"

"The favor cannot break the terms of any prior contract we have agreed upon." As she met his eyes again, color rose to her face.

Ah. He bit hard on his cheek, delighted. She didn't know it, but she'd just showed her hand. He knew now that her thoughts had been turning toward bed as well. "Fair enough," he said. The contract forbade sexual congress that might beget a child. That left a world of possibilities. "Let's play."

She frowned. "Don't you have any terms of your own?"

"Sweetheart, so long as it doesn't involve killing a man or betraying a friend, I'm game for it."

Her frown deepened as she looked down at her cards. "Very well. But mind you, an oral contract is as binding as any written agreement. You're leaving me a great deal of scope."

"I'll survive, I think."

"Suit yourself." She turned over her first card.

He flipped his in reply. "Look there, you've a talent," he said as she scooped up his six of hearts and tucked it into her pile with a ten of diamonds.

"Don't patronize me," she said pleasantly.

"Don't dawdle, then. This is a game of speed."

She had a competitive streak. He should have guessed that, maybe; couldn't be a woman in business if you lacked ambition. She whipped down the cards faster and faster, until he could barely bother to keep up, much less track who was winning each round. It was better fun to watch her—the ferocious concentration on her face, and the quick glances of annoyance she flicked at him when she realized that he wasn't bothering to look at the results.

"It seems you want to lose," she said as she gathered up the winning pair, leaving him empty-handed.

"That was only the first round," he said. "It's best of five."

She snorted. "A loser's philosophy. The odds have tipped in my favor now. An enterprising man would be concerned."

Was she teasing him? He couldn't tell. "I hate to break the news, sweetheart, but there's no skill to this game. It all comes down to chance."

She arched one slim brow as she handed him the cards to shuffle. "Naturally. But we'll see if your story changes, in the unlikely event you win."

His laugh came out startled. This was banter, all right—pointed and spiky, the kind he'd expect from a bloke. A blunt tongue in an angel's body: it was the devil's own recipe to enamor him. "You've found me out," he said with a grin as he shuffled. "I've no talent whatsoever. Saddest tale you'll ever hear—the man who never won a round, and decided to open a gambling club to make up for it."

The corner of her mouth hitched. She was biting back a smile. "Now you're angling for pity. It's a wasted effort, sir. I don't lose."

"I'll bet you don't." As he dealt out the cards again, he allowed himself the occasional admiring glance. In the lowered light, with her long braid hanging heavy and thick over her shoulder, and her color high from the fun of the game, she looked like a different woman. Tousled. Touchable.

She caught him watching, and held his eyes. "That won't work, either."

He lifted his brows. "What?"

Her gaze broke from his, and her color deepened. That right there was his own little victory. He gathered his hand, and threw down again.

She took the next pair, and showed no grace in gloating about it. "I can't imagine what your patrons would say if they knew of your sad record tonight."

He was thinking that he could have charged admission. A dozen gentlemen would gladly have paid to watch her, lording it over him with such cheeky humor. "You know what they say, Kitty. Pride goeth before the fall."

"They also say the devil cites scripture. How wise they are!"

"So it's the Lord you're fighting for tonight," he said. This run of ill luck certainly began to make him wonder about divine influence. The cards had never broken against him so regularly. "Beat the devil at his game."

Smiling, she opened her mouth—then saw the next card he threw. Her face fell, and she glumly shoved her nine of hearts toward his ace.

"That's more like it," he said. He took the next pair, and the one after that, and she bestirred herself from her sulk to give him a narrow, sharp look.

"You're not cheating, are you?"

"I'd like to know how I'd manage," he said. "A game of luck can't be rigged."

The idea seemed to strike her. "That's why I never depend on luck."

"Is that so?" He was oddly glad when the next round went to her. "You like to plan things out, I take it."

"Always. To do otherwise is base foolishness." She hesitated. "I imagine we're not so dissimilar, in that regard. Surely you can't have managed your . . . rise in the world, were you not a man who planned carefully."

"Planning wasn't the key to it," he said. "I spotted opportunities, I grabbed them. Didn't hesitate, didn't give in to fear. And when I saw a problem brewing, I didn't wait for it to grow; I went to meet it head-on. That's all it took. Throw down, then."

She started and looked down at her half of the deck. "Oh yes." She laid down the top card, a two of clubs. This time the loss did not seem to trouble her. "That's a man's privilege, you know. To go out into the world and face things. A woman doesn't have that luxury."

"Bull—" He caught himself. "Rubbish, and you know it. What do you call your proposal to marry me, if not facing the problem head-on?"

Her head bowed, concealing her expression as she turned over her next card. "That was . . . unplanned," she admitted in a low voice. "Entirely unlike me."

He studied the part in her hair, painfully straight and neat. The precision of it, the tightness with which she'd braided back her hair, seemed suggestive somehow. Here was a woman who liked to imagine herself a tightly buttoned, disciplined creature. But he'd seen another side to her in that bed. It still haunted his dreams. She'd fought against it, but he'd pulled it out of her, regardless.

It had frightened her. He understood that. Maybe he understood it all the better now. Her kind of childhood, the unnatural restraint she'd been trained to show, all for the sake of that company that seemed bound up with her memories of her dad . . .

Well, no wonder if she tried to keep her life tightly laced, planned out, and controlled. She'd never been taught that good things could come of letting loose.

He threw down his last card, and she flicked hers over.

"I win," he said, and took the deck.

"So you do." Her mood seemed to have tipped into somberness; when the grandfather clock chimed, she shifted in her seat. "It's late," she said. "Perhaps we should table this till tomorrow."

"Only a coincidence, I suppose, that you say so after losing a game."

That got her attention. Jaw firming, she said, "Deal, then."

They played the next game quickly, in utter silence. Another victory to him. As he dealt one final time, she leaned forward, watching his hands with searing concentration.

At last, he could not help but chuckle. "You really think I'm cheating."

"I don't, in fact. But it pays to be certain." She paused. "It occurs to me that those rings you wear might be designed to distract the eye from what your hand is really doing."

"Ah, you've caught me out."

She looked up, startled. "Is that really why you wear them?"

He hesitated as he gathered up his hand. "No. They're . . ." A relic of an older time, when the fact of having enough money for three square meals, and plenty besides, had seemed strange and intoxicating and bound not to last. "When I was younger," he said, "I had a taste for flash. And I needed something to spend my coin on." Something that would announce to the world that he had come into money, and was not to be discounted; that he was a man, in fact, to be reckoned with.

Something he could sell, too, if circumstances changed. He'd never admitted that part to himself until he'd finally found a better place to put his coins—into properties and buildings.

She was squinting at the rings. He stretched out his hand. "Have a look."

Hesitantly, she took his hand. The contact seemed to spark straight down into his bones. Her own mouth tightened a fraction, as though she felt it, too, and fought it with everything in her.

He counted the seconds. She wouldn't make it till five, he expected. Two, three—

She dropped his hand. "I don't know much about gemstones." Her voice sounded reedy. "Anyway, I would need my loupe to see them clearly."

"Well, the one on my index finger is a diamond," he said. "There's a ruby on my middle. Sapphire and garnet on the ring finger, and emerald on the pinky."

"I don't believe I've ever seen them all worn together."

He snorted. She'd taken care to say it very neutrally, but it didn't take a soothsayer to guess at the sentiment behind that remark. "It's not for fashion that I got them."

Her gaze lifted to his. In the dim lighting, her eyes were a deep violet. No gem in the world that he knew could match that shade, nor any of the others that her eyes reflected, depending on the hour.

But if there had been one, he'd have worn it. No doubt.

"What are they for," she said, "if not for fashion? I thought you said you'd purchased them when you were cultivating an attitude of . . . flash."

"Well." He allowed himself a slight smile. "I'm Irish, after all. Superstition runs deep in the blood. Diamonds, they're for courage. Hard, unbreakable. Sapphires are generally accounted to bring wisdom to the wearer. The garnet is for good health, the ruby for power."

Her winged brows had drawn together. "You believe in that folklore?"

"Don't know as I believe in it. But I've done well with these rings on my fingers. So I see no harm in letting them be."

She nodded slowly. "What about the emerald? What does it stand for?"

"Not much," he said. "I just like the color." He laid down his top card.

She slowly did the same. "So it means nothing, then? How sad for emeralds. They must feel very lonely, to be left out of the myths."

"Now who's sounding fanciful?" It was her quick, abashed smile that made him unbend enough to go on. "Emeralds are for love."

Her hand paused atop her deck, her gaze breaking from his to wander away into the middle distance. "I thought you didn't believe in that."

"Never said so."

"You did." She looked back at him, scowling. "In the stairwell, at the register office."

"Ah." He remembered now. "I said I was a cynic. I don't expect to find love often. But I don't doubt that it exists. Why, do you?"

"No, but . . ." She bit her lip. "If you hope for love, why did you do it?"

"Do what?" He was winning this game, too, but she didn't seem to notice. She was flipping over cards without looking, her attention focused on him.

"This marriage," she said. "Five years is . . ." She took an audible breath. "A very long time."

Something was upsetting her. He couldn't begin to work it out, so he said the only thing that he knew would put her at ease. "Love needn't only concern a husband and wife, Kitty. You loved your da, aye? Love for a parent, love for a child, love for a friend . . ." Her expression was indeed easing. "The emerald can go to work on those," he said with a smile.

"Of course," she said after a moment. "It was a silly question."

"Not particularly," he said. "What's your fear? Afraid you'll fall in love with some swell before our five years are up?"

She ran a nervous hand down her braid. "I won't."

He didn't much like the idea himself. He pictured some soft-bellied idiot who would like the fact that she'd never played cards before. Probably would count it a virtue, the fool. "Never say never. Fate takes it as a challenge."

"I've already said it. Several times, in fact."

Oh, ho. Bit of arrogance there. "You mean to say you've broken some hearts in your time."

"I have received proposals," she said. "But gentlemen of my rank prefer their wives not to work. I had no interest in taking a husband, only to disappoint him."

"Sounds like you'd be the one disappointed," he said. "It's a right buffoon who would mind a woman able to support herself."

She slanted him a quick, odd look. "It isn't counted feminine."

He shrugged. "Nor is starving, I reckon. But when a bloke bites the dust, there's often a widow who goes hungry afterward, for want of a way to earn."

Her hand hesitated atop her last card. "I suppose . . ." She flipped the card over. "It is good to know I could stand on my own two feet, if necessary."

Her words had the shy flavor of a confession. "*Could* stand? With all the time you spend at those auction rooms, seems like you're already standing. Pity, though—you've just lost."

"What?" She looked down, gaping at her empty hand. "I—"

"And now I'll be asking you my favor."

She looked up warily. "Go on."

He let out a soft laugh. He'd seen street children with more trust. "Nothing so bad," he said. "Just a kiss."

She swallowed. "How unsurprising."

He rose, slowly approaching her. "Is that so? Reckoned it from the start, did you? Yet still you played."

She stood, jostling the table. "Of course, I will not permit it. We agreed at the beginning that the favor could not contravene the terms of the contract."

"Hence a kiss," he said. "The contract, if you'll recall, bars sexual congress that might lead to a child. It says nothing of other pleasures."

"I . . ." Her lips parted; she looked stunned. "The spirit of the term . . ." She cleared her throat. "The *spirit* is very clear."

"Spirit won't win a lawsuit." He slid his hand around her waist, feeling the coolness of the wool, the scratch of the embroidery, the warmth of her body beneath it. The soft line of her waist. "You going to back out?"

Her breath hitched audibly. He felt her stiffen, and then, as she sighed, the tension eased from her shoulders, and she bowed her head.

"Go ahead, then," she mumbled. "But make it quick."

If she wanted it quick, she'd need to make it easier. He tipped her chin up, to take a good view of her pretty pink mouth. She wasn't the classic beauty she first appeared. Pink and gold and white, to be sure, but that upper lip was slightly fuller, slightly longer, than the one beneath. Nature's small quirk, which would have lent her a natural pout if she didn't work so hard, so continuously, to tame her lips into a flat, hard line.

He stroked his thumb over her cheekbone. Like magic, the wash of color that his touch called forth. She smelled clean, skin and the faint lingering scent of soap; no perfume tonight. He lifted his hand to lightly brush the tight cap of her hair against her skull, and felt the smallest tremor communicate itself through her waist, where he gripped her.

"Quickly, I said," she whispered.

"Right." He put his tongue at the seal of her lips, nudging. Trying to rescue that upper lip from its cruel restraint. God, but she smelled good. Some current leapt between them, a lightning flash of information; he sensed with perfect clarity each swell and curve of her body, only inches from his.

He slipped his hand from her waist to the small of her back, drawing her body against his. In the silence, cloth slithered, rustled. The faintest noise came from her. She could feel that he was hardening for her.

With his tongue, he opened her lips. Her mouth

tasted fresh and cool, like a priceless wine that had just been uncorked; untouched, which wasn't right—he'd been here before. He'd been inside her, with his dark hot ways, and he was inside her again now, and he meant to leave a mark this time. He kissed her deeply, angling her back over his arm to show her who was in charge, and her hands caught his shoulders for balance, then hooked in like claws as she kissed him back.

If she was ice, then she was the early spring variety— the thinnest veneer, which cracked at the first nudge. For suddenly, in his arms, she was a hot little wild thing, shoving her hips against him, knocking into the table. He heard distantly the sound of cards falling. He laid her back atop the scattered remains of her defeat, and she accepted him beautifully, letting him fuck her with his tongue as he longed, needed, to do with his cock. Encouraging him by accident, with her desperate grasping hands on his back and waist, his arse, hallelujah; she was making whimpering noises, and it was beyond God's own power to stop him from reaching down and knocking up her skirts, grasping her damp, hot leg behind one knee and lifting it so she could wrap herself around him, and let him put himself against the spot where they both wanted him to be.

She arched beneath him, her eyes flying open—wide, blind, the purplish-blue of sunset over distant mountains, the color of a sky that would draw a man onto the road and keep him there, determined to walk until he found the source of the light. Wasn't a man in the world who had seen her like this, who'd managed to put that look of dazzled, hungered pleasure on her face, and he meant to make sure she didn't sleep well tonight, didn't think of anything but him.

Her inner thigh was plump, sweetly trembling, as he tracked up it. Through the split in her bloomers, he found her. Cupped her as she jerked in his hand. Wet and hot and ready for him. "Shall I kiss you here?" he asked roughly.

Her groan sounded like a yes—and then, abruptly, as he stroked her harder, she cried out and scrabbled at his chest, pushing him off her.

Some part of him had been waiting for it. That part, the only corner of his brain still functioning, made him step backward immediately. The rest of him, instincts and appetite and sheer animal lust, remained locked on her, so when she sat up and met his eyes, whatever she saw caused her to look immediately away and lick her lips.

Christ. Those lips. "Say it," he ground out. "I'll put you to bed properly."

"No." She folded her arms around herself as she stood. "No. The contract . . ." She frowned, as though her own words puzzled her. Then she shook her head, took a long breath, and looked at him.

"No," she said flatly.

His own lungs felt as though he'd run five miles. He pushed out a breath, waiting for his heart to calm. "All right, then." Wonder of wonders, the words came out just fine. Even an easy lilt to them.

She knocked down her skirts, then took a hunted look around, as if expecting a crowd to witness her dishevelment. "Well," she said, then faltered, casting him a sidelong look he couldn't interpret. "Congratulations."

Humor licked through him, unexpected and very welcome. He smiled. "Bet you had a different favor in mind."

"Oh, I . . ." She flushed. "Yes. Of course."

"But this one wasn't so bad, now, was it?"

Her lips pressed together in that schoolmistress line. "It's done. No need to speak of it further."

"What was the favor you wanted?"

She hesitated, then glanced behind her, checking the time. Or, no—it was the vase she was looking at. It had caught her attention earlier tonight, too. "I was going to ask . . ." She shrugged. "If I could have a look through your antiques."

"You mean in the storeroom?"

She wheeled back. "There's an entire storeroom of these things?"

"Sure. Plenty of blokes overextend themselves. If they've got something worth offering, I go easy on them. Let them pay up as they can."

"And all of these furnishings scattered about . . . that vase, and the fixtures in my suite . . . they come from the storeroom?"

"No point in buying what I've already got," he said.

Her eyes widened. "I would *love* to see that storeroom."

"Tell you what." If she would set up the shot so neatly, who was he not to take it? "You can play me again tomorrow night. See if you can win the favor."

CHAPTER NINE

"A full set, you say?" Batten lifted the teacup to the light.

"Yes," said Catherine. The cup was petite and elegant, scrolled porcelain decorated in cobalt blue. Dr. Wall square-marked Worcester, very rare. She had stolen it from her sitting room in the House of Diamonds. "The entire set is in mint condition. I don't think anybody ever used it."

He set down the cup and looked over the rest of her spread—today, a Sèvres figurine and an Elizabethan chalice wrought in silver. Every morning for ten days she had brought him items purloined from the House of Diamonds. Each evening, escorted by Mr. Johnson, she returned to Diamonds and replaced the items before anybody could remark their absence.

"All of these come from the same collection?" Batten asked.

She nodded.

"I know you cannot tell me his name," he said in a leading tone. "But surely, just a hint . . ."

"I've given my word to stay mum." She could hardly tell him the truth: that she was living in a gaming club, and enjoying it far more than she ought.

It was *wondrous* to live independently. For the first time in her life, she could come and go as she pleased. No butler to harass her about dinner menus, or pout at her indifference to domestic chores. No lady's maid to spy on her for Peter. She would never keep a maid again, in fact; she was no grand lady, with complicated corsetry and gowns that required assistance to remove. In the evenings, she took her meals in her sitting room, free to work, with no concern of Peter ambushing her with impromptu guests like Pilcher. And on those rare occasions when tedium struck, she need only walk out to the balcony, and spy on the bizarre antics of the players below.

Even the staff at Diamonds suited her. The footmen took no interest in her, for unlike the players, she gave them no tips. The kitchens, trained in producing feasts for the discerning palates of wealthy gamblers, routinely delivered miracles of French high cuisine. Two maids saw to her baths and laundry—cheerful, plainspoken creatures, without airs or pretensions.

And then there was Mr. O'Shea . . .

Had the room grown hotter suddenly? She blotted her brow with her handkerchief. She had not taken him up on his invitation to play cards again. In fact, she had kept to her rooms for three nights running, to avoid him.

For three nights running, she had dreamed of what would happen should she lose again.

"How mysterious!" Batten exclaimed. He was stroking the rim of the silver chalice, humming his appreciation as he traced the engraving. "One rarely sees such an eclectic collection, so expertly curated. He must have an unusually broad education."

"Unusual, yes," she said faintly. No gentleman had ever managed to tempt her. But she found herself tormented by thoughts of a cardsharp, a criminal, a ruffian . . . A curious, unexpectedly kind, alarmingly fascinating, beautiful man.

She resolved to lock herself in her rooms again tonight.

"Do you think he might be interested in selling his estate?" Batten asked.

"Oh, there's not any question of that," she said hastily. She had brought the first lot from Diamonds out of concern, to make sure she hadn't lost her ability to detect a forgery. Batten's enthusiasm had led her down a dangerous path; now she was stealing—borrowing—these items for the mere pleasure of showing them off. "He was only curious about valuation, you see."

"Perhaps you'll persuade him otherwise." Batten bit his lip. "I could imagine a very interested crowd for the sale."

She gave him a glum look, for no doubt his thoughts strayed down a similar path: such an auction would benefit Everleigh's tremendously, at present. The aftermath of the Cranston debacle had turned uglier than Catherine had foreseen. The new Lord Cranston had not been soothed by her apologies regarding the interruption of his sale. He had insisted on being released from his contract so he might take his collection elsewhere.

Elsewhere, pah. The gentlemen at Christie's must be toasting one another right now.

Alas, Cranston had not been content to break the contract. Viewing the episode as a bruise to his pride, he had complained publicly of gross mismanagement. Letters had arrived now from four different solicitors, seeking to break the contracts of clients whose collections had been slated for winter sales. In each case, the lawyers had cited a "loss of faith" in Everleigh's.

Peter, of course, blamed her for the entire fracas. He claimed she had imagined a ring at work in the Cranston auction. "You're delusional," he'd told her. "Not only this business with the ring, but your bizarre notion that I brought Pilcher to your bedroom door? One almost pities O'Shea for the burden of wedding a madwoman. At any rate, I wash my hands of you. You have the proxy; this mess is on *your* head now. Do as you like, and sleep where you like, so long as you keep your sordid little affairs a secret from the public."

A single flight of stairs separated their offices, but they communicated now only by letter. It made a very comfortable state of affairs, Catherine thought.

"There's a cunning clock I must show you," she told Batten as she gathered up the borrowed wares. "I'll try to bring it tomorrow."

"Are you leaving?" Batten looked startled. "But you haven't yet looked at the painting!"

"Goodness! Is it finished?" She had forgotten it entirely. "I'm terribly sorry, Batten—my mind was elsewhere. Please, do show it to me."

Beaming, he crossed to the easel in the corner. She knew, by the flourish with which he removed the oilcloth, that she would not be disappointed.

"Oh!" She cupped her hands over her mouth. Batten had rescued the angel from centuries of abuse. The great winged warrior loomed over Saint Teresa, his robes resplendently white, his dark mane knocked back by a heavenly wind to reveal a visage of implacable demand. As for the saint, her figure no longer faded into a dark murk. She was writhing in her bed, her agony so vividly rendered that she looked almost in motion as she grasped the angel's spear—

Catherine blinked. Good heavens! How had she not seen it before? That wasn't agony on Teresa's face, but *pleasure*. As the angel's spear pierced her, she writhed in voluptuous delight.

"You don't like it?" Batten asked querulously.

She pressed her palms to her cheeks and felt how they burned. "No," she said in a choked voice. The painting was not at fault. It was she who had changed. She'd been awakened to . . . *this*.

And to the fact that a devil might prove as irresistible as any angel.

"It's lovely," she said quickly. "You've done a marvelous job! Mr. Clarke will be very pleased. *I* am very pleased."

Batten was giving her a very queer look. She tightened her grip around the antiques and croaked out some excuse before hurrying from the room.

A knock came at the door. Startled, Catherine looked up from the writing desk. It was half past four, and she was working in her suite at the House of Diamonds. Since Peter had granted her power of attorney, she had seized every document related to the accounts. Her office at Everleigh's did not seem sufficiently private to review them. "Who is it?" she called. Nobody here ever interrupted her during the day.

Silence. She frowned and rubbed her temple as she glanced back to the papers scattered across the desk.

She sat surrounded by proof of doom. Her eyes had started to cross from tallying sums, but no matter how generously she forecasted, the prediction remained identical: Everleigh's would not turn a profit this year. Combined with the damage Peter had done with his embezzling, the recent cancellations would throw the company into the red.

Despondent, she flipped again through the descriptions of the upcoming sales. Minor estates, furniture of unfashionably recent make, libraries of no real depth and rarity—these were the workaday sales of winter, a far cry from the spectacular events that characterized the height of the social season. What Everleigh's needed was a miracle.

The knock came again, sharper. She stood. "Who is it?"

"Me."

O'Shea's voice. Ignoring the nervous flutter in her belly, she cast down her pen and opened the door.

O'Shea stood flipping his beaver hat against his thigh. He must have just stepped indoors, for he wore a long wool coat and muffler, and cold radiated off him; his hair was windblown and his color looked high. She steeled herself against his effect. That painting of Saint Teresa was a timely warning. If she indulged her curiosity any further, she'd no doubt end up gored for it.

"I need your help," he said. "You got an hour? I'll make it worth your while."

She glanced back toward the desk. "I was working."

"Right. That warehouse down on Wentworth Street—you want into it, right?"

"Warehouse?" She caught her breath. "The storeroom, do you mean?"

"Aye." His glance shifted off down the hall briefly. He sounded uneasy, slightly stiff, as he went on. "I'll give you free run of the place. But I'll be needing a favor first."

A favor! She stepped backward. "I won't play cards with you."

"Not that," he said with a laugh. "A proper good cause. Little girl about to be taken from her sister. No need for it; lass has a proper job in a factory in Back-church-Lane, and it pays well enough to support them both. But her sister's been skipping school, and the board's about to realize there's no adult in the house. They'll remove the little one to a workhouse, unless there's a guardian to speak for them."

She frowned. "A . . . you can't mean *me.*"

"I'm in pinch here," he said. "We need a woman, somebody whose face they don't know." He grimaced. "I just learned of it today. Otherwise I wouldn't be asking."

"I can't lie to a government body!"

"Why not? I'm not asking you to give your true name. Come up with an alias, if you like."

She snorted. "Is that meant to reassure me?"

"You want into that storeroom, don't you? Up to you, I suppose."

She hesitated. Everleigh's needed a spectacular sale. His storeroom, the contents of it, could well be that miracle. "This factory girl. You're certain she's fit to care for her sister?"

"Not a doubt," he said. "Rents a room from me. I talked with my agent just now. Clean and neat, always something cooking on the stove, never a late payment. The little one won't fare so well in a workhouse, I promise you."

But to lie before the authorities! Under a false name, no less.

"It would be a fine thing," he said. "To keep a little girl with her family." He gave her a cynical smile. "And the warehouse, I'll tell you, is stacked to the rafters."

She flushed. It felt very low of her to take that bait. But a businesswoman did not spurn such opportunities. "Would you allow me to put the contents to auction?"

"Oh, ho!" He clapped his hat on his head. "Always business with you."

Her face got hotter. "*You* were the one who suggested—"

"Wasn't an insult," he said with a wink. "You're my kind of woman. Ninety-ten split, you say?"

Now she must be red as a cherry. "Hardly! Sixty-forty is the typical arrangement."

His eyes widened. "Highway robbery, that. I'll take eighty-five percent, and no argument."

"I'll give you seventy-five," she shot back. "Everleigh's will bear all the expenses of restoration and transport, and assuming the collection merits it, we'll pay for advertising, too."

"Eighty," he said, "and it all hinges on you telling a very pretty lie. Call yourself Susie Evans, say you're the girls' cousin."

Lying to the government! But . . . for Everleigh's. "You're certain she would go to the workhouse otherwise?"

"Bastards will take her straight from her sister," he said tersely. "Government can't keep its hands to itself."

"All right." She turned to fetch her wrapper off the back of the wing chair.

"Leave off those pearls," he said. "Susie Evans can't afford 'em."

*   *   *

Catherine clutched her cloak closer to her as O'Shea led her through the tangled streets. An icy wind had shoved the clouds clear out of the sky, and the sunlight fell with sharp clarity over the rutted lane, sparkling off stands of stagnant water in the gutters. "Rotten pipes," O'Shea muttered as they passed a great cloud of stink. "Fix one, the next one breaks. I should put your brother on it, maybe. These water companies won't lift a finger without some swell prodding them."

Catherine covered her nose with her muff, though the men and women sitting on stoops, waiting for children scrambling home from school, seemed indifferent to the stench. O'Shea knew all of them, answering each greeting by name as he passed. As they turned a corner, they encountered a great knot of students celebrating the end of the school day. A line of squabbling boys congregated outside a sweetshop, and two girls slammed a ball against a brick wall with a ferocity that struck Catherine as nearly warlike.

The crowd by the sweetshop fell silent as they spotted O'Shea, then crowed in delight when he dug into his pocket and produced a handful of coins. "Share with the girls," he ordered as the tallest boy snatched up the money. "Molly, Meg!" he yelled to the girls with the ball. "Come over and get your cakes."

At the end of the lane stood a shabby, low building with an arched gateway, letters picked out in rusting relief: The Ragged Mission. A line of men and women stood outside in silence, their bowed heads and exhausted faces a stark contrast to the children's energy. "Notice B Meetings," O'Shea said with disgust. "Always a joy for the parents of the parish. Summon them during work hours, for who needs to earn a wage?"

Catherine tried not to stare as they passed through the crowd. Some of these women looked nearly waxen with exhaustion, and it seemed that half the line was wracked by deep, hoarse coughs that made her long, with a mix of guilt and revulsion, for soap and water with which to scrub herself clean. "Is consumption a common problem?"

His brief, sidelong glance made her feel foolish for having asked. "One of them," he said.

They passed through a dim vestibule into a room covered in pastoral murals. The atmosphere was close and warm, for the crowd was considerable, not a spare seat at any of the five long tables that faced the top of the room. At the head table, placed perpendicular to the others, sat four well-dressed gentlemen and a lady, whose smart brown walking suit made Catherine regret the lack of her pearls, after all.

"That's Mrs. Hollister," said O'Shea, drawing her up with a quick touch on her arm. "She's the one you'll address. Nice and polite, now. Apologetic, like. You didn't know the little one was skipping school."

She nodded, very uneasy. Perjuring herself before the law! "There's a clerk," she whispered. "Taking notes. It will enter the public record."

"Mrs. Susie Evans won't mind that," he said. "Nor will they ask for proof of your name. Hollister plays the battle-ax, but she's on our side."

Our side? Was that the side of the perjurers?

Yet as they stood, waiting their turn, she began to regret her sour view. Each of the parents summoned before the panel offered a more piteous tale than the last.

It took some concentration to understand their variety of accents—for these were country folks, or foreigners, or people who had come of age before public education had become compulsory. Now even the poorest children, through their schooling, learned the rudiments of grammar. But their parents spoke cants that had never been put into print.

"He lost his leg on the factory floor," a woman was mumbling to the board. "Can't walk, can't earn, so's I've got to do it. We've got two wee ones, and . . ." She touched the great swelling mound of her belly, indicating the obvious. "Well, I've got to earn whiles I can, don't I? So Katie, she watches the little 'uns while I'm out."

"That is all very interesting," one of the gentlemen droned. "But it does not change the fact that you are legally obligated to send your child to school."

"I can't . . . What else'm I t'do?" The woman's voice broke. "Three pennies a week for the school fees, and—"

"A trifling sum," the gentleman drawled. "And as I understand it, Mr. O'Shea"—Catherine stiffened as a tide of gazes swept toward the man at her side—"will cover those fees, for those in Whitechapel who can't pay them."

O'Shea nodded to the board man, his face expressionless. But she could sense, in his tense posture, the ferocity of his dislike.

"Aye, Mr. O'Shea's our own angel, I know it." The woman swallowed noisily, then wiped her nose with the edge of her tartan shawl. "But it ain't only fees. Children's got to eat—"

"And once again," the man cut in, "I will point out that Mr. O'Shea provides bread and milk to every student in the hour before school. Perhaps your daughter would not go hungry if you allowed her to attend, as the law requires."

O'Shea spoke in a calm, carrying voice. "You'll make me rethink that generosity if you mean to use it to shame her."

"That was not Mr. Stewart's intention," said Mrs. Hollister, with a sharp look to the gentleman, who scowled and sat back. Catherine nervously studied her opponent. The woman's silver-streaked hair, the deep creases at either side of her pursed lips, lent her a matronly air of authority. Sure enough, the room fell quiet as she leaned forward. "Mrs. Mackle, the law is very clear. We cannot excuse Mary from school in order to care for her siblings. But if you were to find her some respectable form of employment, we might grant her a half-time certificate."

"How?" Mrs. Mackle asked softly. "Hard enough to find work for meself."

Frowning, Mrs. Hollister glanced toward O'Shea. He nodded once. "Speak to Mr. O'Shea about it," she said, and smiled slightly as the woman gasped and pivoted toward O'Shea, hands clasped at her throat as she curtseyed very deeply.

Good heavens. Catherine gave him a wondering look. He *was* the king of these parts—and apparently, his reign was more benevolent than rumor suggested.

An unpleasant embarrassment itched through her. She had cast certain accusations at his head that now seemed unfounded.

But he never defended himself. How was *she* to have known that he played Robin Hood?

"Once she finds employment, we will grant a half-time certificate," Mrs. Hollister was saying. "But she will still need to attend regularly. Otherwise you will be summoned again, and we'll have no choice but to send your case to the magistrate, who will impose a fine. Do you understand?"

The woman nodded.

"Very good," Mrs. Hollister said crisply. "Next?" She glanced down the table, but the clerk with the appointment book appeared to have fallen asleep, chin cupped in hand as he lightly snored.

A titter moved through the crowd as his neighbor elbowed him awake. "Oh, yes, yes—begging your pardon," he said with a sheepish look toward Mrs. Hollister. He consulted the book before him. "Mrs. Tulip Patrick."

"That's us," Nick said softly as a slim, dark girl, no older than sixteen, rose and pushed through the crowd to the spot in front of the head table. She looked clean and neat, her plaid dress without a rip or stain, if slightly too large for her waifish figure.

"Mrs. Patrick." Mrs. Hollister adjusted her spectacles, peering over them doubtfully. "You hardly look old enough to be married, much less stand as your sister's guardian."

"I've been looking after her for years, now." The girl sounded mutinous. "I do a fine job of it. She wants for nothing."

"Very admirable," Mrs. Hollister said evenly. "I am afraid, however, that Mary has not been in school this last month."

"That's not for want of me sending her!"

"Miss . . . Mrs. Patrick." The woman's voice grew gentle. "Have you some proof of your age and marital state? For if there is no adult in the household, custody of the child—"

O'Shea gave Catherine a sharp nudge. She stepped up to the girl and cleared her throat. *God help me.* "I live with them. Their . . . cousin."

For all that the girl looked decent, she showed no hesitation as she glanced over to Catherine and added stridently, "That's right. *This* one looks after us. And she's ever so old."

Catherine lifted her brows. "Nearly ancient, in fact."

Mrs. Hollister dimpled. "And you are, ma'am?"

Goodness, what was the name? "Susie Evans," she said. "Mrs. Susie Evans."

"Mm." Mrs. Hollister's sharp gaze flicked toward O'Shea, who stood behind them. "Well, Mrs. Evans. You serve as these girls' guardian?"

"Yes." God help her, she was as much a criminal now as O'Shea, lying to an officer of the law.

Mrs. Hollister gave her a long, speaking look. "Well, Mrs. Evans, then it is your responsibility to ensure that young Mary attends school. Do you understand that?"

"She does," Tulip Patrick said heatedly. "And Mary won't miss another day."

"Very good, then. Mrs. Evans, you heard my remarks to the last petitioner, I hope. You are aware of the penalties, if Mary continues to play truant?"

Catherine nodded.

"Very good. I hope we do not see each other again, then." Mrs. Hollister turned again to the clerk. "Next?"

Tulip Patrick grabbed her arm and tugged her through the crowd, O'Shea at their heels. Once they were safely back on the street, she said, "God's a mercy! I can't thank you enough, ma'am. Fit to be sick, I was, with them threatening to take Mary." She sucked in a sharp breath, her eyes flashing. "What right have they got, I'd like to know, to separate a girl from her sister?"

"All the rights," O'Shea said flatly. "You bear that in mind, girl. And explain to your sister, too."

"Oh, I mean to. Brattish dolt!" Tulip lifted her fist. "I'll leave her ears ringing tonight. You'll not hear of any more trouble on her account. Thank you, sir! Ma'am." She flashed another smile at Catherine, then turned on her heel and dashed away.

"How old is she?" Catherine asked softly. "Sixteen?"

"If that." O'Shea offered his elbow, and they started back down the road. "Father died last year. She's all her sister's got."

As they retraced their steps, she felt keenly aware of the nods and respectful bows that followed their passage. It raised the itching feeling again, a sense that she had judged him unjustly.

"You support that school," she blurted at last. "Why didn't you tell me?"

"Why would you have wanted to know?"

"Because . . ." She had married him thinking him the lowest species of criminal. "It seems a good thing to know. You're not entirely . . ."

He gave her a bland smile. "The devil?"

She pulled free of him. "You can't blame me for thinking so! You make no effort to advertise your charity. Why, the journalists are always—"

"Those who need to know, know," he said. "I've got no interest in proving myself to pompous bigots."

He probably counted her among that group. "But it's no wonder if they make assumptions," she said helplessly. "You break the law, publicly, every day. Your gambling palace—"

"Is just the start of it," he said. "I've done far worse in my time. It all looks nice and pretty now, but I clawed my way up—and who's to say that a bit of bread and milk make up for it? Rest easy, then; you can keep thinking me the devil, if it helps you to sleep at night. It would sure be fairer than calling me a saint."

She frowned at the broken road ahead of them. If only it were contempt she felt for him—and if only she slept easily! The opposite was the case, but to let him see it would be mortifying—and profoundly dangerous. If he knew that what kept her awake in the darkness was the thought of his touch . . . the hot things he'd told her . . . the prospect of another card game . . . he might press his advantage.

And she no longer knew herself well enough to trust her own will.

She darted a glance at him. Their marriage was a business matter. Curiosity was as pointless as desire— but just as pernicious. How had he clawed his way up? He wore that emerald for love, he said. Whose love had he known, and whose did he hope for?

The thought made her go red. That was none of her business, surely.

But this was her husband. Secret or no, they were married for five years.

"Watch out, there." He put out a hand to help her over a pothole, his grip casual and familiar on her elbow. Her heart skipped a beat.

Did he ever think of the future? Did he despair of the bargain he'd been forced to make, to keep those buildings? Surely he must think her a cold, unfeeling woman. The Ice Queen, men called her. He had better reason than most to do so.

"Miss Patrick's situation," she said haltingly. "I wouldn't have—that is, if you had explained it in full, I would have done it for nothing."

"Lied for her?" He cocked a wry brow. "To an officer of the law?"

She bit her lip. "Yes. I think so."

"And missed the chance to get into that storeroom?"

His plain skepticism made her laugh. "Well, no," she admitted sheepishly. "Not when you'd already made the offer. On the chance you've got a collection worth auctioning? I would have been remiss to turn it down."

"Especially when the profit could prove so rich." He tipped his head. "Forty percent of the profit. Is that truly your usual bargain?"

She fought her smile, and lost. "Heavens. You actually believed that?"

His eyes widened. Then he threw back his head and laughed, a rich ringing shout that drew the notice of the entire block. "Kitty," he said, grinning, "for all your fine airs, I'd say you've got a bit of devil in you, too."

CHAPTER TEN

"This is foul work." Catherine's voice came from deep within the cavernous gloom. Outside, a cold rain was falling, turning the streets to mud. The small line of windows shed a swampy light over jumbled piles of bric-a-brac, furniture jammed together like ill-fitting jigsaw pieces, piles of books threatening to topple.

Nick maneuvered carefully down the makeshift aisle, following the mineral glow of Catherine's naphtha lamp. She'd been working in the storeroom for five days, a punishing schedule that saw her leaving Diamonds before dawn. Johnson went with her, kept guard at the door. But today, he'd tracked down Nick at Neddie's to complain. "A man occasionally needs to piss," he'd grumbled. "But when I tries it in the corner, she knows somehow. Barks from the far side of the room, *Don't be a savage!*"

Nick found her crouched low to the ground, her skirts hiked carelessly over her knees. Now, here was a sight: she wore lace stockings to work as well. Perhaps he'd been wrong to give Johnson the oversight. He would gladly stand in himself.

She was scowling at a chest of drawers, pulling at the wooden knobs with fretful fingers. As the floorboards creaked beneath his heel, she snapped, "Do you see this? Some butcher used glasspaper to scrape off the patina! And this French vice!"

"French vice?" That sounded promising.

She turned, one hand to her chest. "Oh! I thought you were Mr. Johnson. Yes, French polish—though I suppose it's more properly an English vice, since I can't recall any Frenchman fool enough to use it." She wiped a stray lock of hair from her eyes, smearing dust across her cheek. She looked rumpled, sweaty, thoroughly begrimed. Nick had seen beggars in the rain who kept cleaner.

He grinned. A woman willing to get dirty for her work. He'd never have guessed it. "You need to eat," he said. "Johnson says you skipped luncheon."

"There was no time for it." As she started to rise, a wince crimped her mouth. He took her elbow to help her up. The feel of her arm startled him. She had proper little biceps. No doubt she'd earned them through labor—Johnson said she was stubborn at shifting furniture on her own, fearful that he might break something.

"Thank you," she said breathlessly. "I've been down there since . . . why, since Mr. Johnson left, I suppose. The mind proves willing, but sometimes the knees don't." She drew away to smooth down her skirts. Then she kicked out her legs, wiggling each foot, and pulled each of her elbows across her body in a long, unselfconscious stretch.

Cats moved like that. He'd never imagined Catherine capable of it. The sight riveted him. Made his voice slightly husky as he said, "Find anything good?"

"Oh, goodness—where to start? It's like Ali Baba's cave of wonders." She beamed up at him, and in the sodium light, she looked like a wonder herself, her hair incandescently pale, her large eyes glittering. He reached out and wiped away a smudge with his thumb. It was a mark of her single-mindedness that she did not even protest. "Remind me," she said, "to tell you about the tambour-topped table tonight. The most extraordinary specimen!"

Her skin seemed to leave a mark on his, his thumb feeling branded as he tucked it back into his pockct. They had made a practice of dining together this week. Seemed she felt it was professional to keep him apprised of his possessions. In truth, he had no use for the information; this stuff had been rotting in here. That she would turn it into coin was a favor to him—another, after her fine work at the B Meeting on Tulip Patrick's behalf.

That piece of mercy hadn't gone unnoticed in the neighborhood. *Who was Tulip's angel, then?* Mrs. Sheahen had stopped him in the street to ask. *I hear she spoke like a poet.*

Catherine hadn't said much that he could recall. But she'd committed to it, all right, in spite of her reservations. No doubt it was the first time she'd lied to the law, but she'd done it in smooth, steady tones that rubbed like balm across a man's sore ears. Tulip had looked at her in amazement, and half the room had gaped. She had that kind of power, though thank God she didn't know it. She had no idea that she could light up a room like a lamp at midnight.

He liked their dinners together. He liked her company, for all that he didn't understand half of her interests. Surprising deal of pleasure in listening to her speechify about furniture. The enthusiasm that animated her face, the fervent appreciation in her voice, put him in mind of a girl discussing her lover. No ice queen, here. Aye, he was learning a good deal about the lies she told—to herself, as well as others. *Business,* ha. Wasn't business that made her spring out of bed each morning, and kept her vibrating well through supper. What she called business, he called passion—and she had it in spades, albeit for dusty relics of the past.

But passion, it seemed to him, was a native resource. You had it or you didn't—and if you had it, it made a moveable talent, durable and directable. No man alive would watch her grow flushed and rosy as she praised a walnut stool, and not think of how it would feel to be the focus of that flushed intensity.

He put his hand on her waist now, nudging her down the aisle. She came willingly, lamp swinging at her side, her attention darting back and forth as she tracked the shifting beam of light—hunting, no doubt, for what she might have overlooked. She would have made a fine thief. She had the steel for it, the discipline, the constant watchful attention. But he wouldn't have risked her on it.

The thought made him frown. He'd risked himself, and his family, and any number of other people whom he cared for.

Still. It didn't sit right, thinking of Catherine chased by the law.

"It will take another few days to make certain I've combed through everything," she was telling him in a cheerful, chattering voice. "Then two days, at least, to crate and transport the items to Everleigh's. I mean to rush this lot to auction. We'll hold it in early December. Does that sound acceptable?"

"Fine," he said brusquely. Wasn't that she was too good for danger. He didn't think her better than himself or his kin. But for all the luxury of her upbringing, she'd known little joy, it seemed to him. Treated ill by the very people who should have cared for her best. Her brother, sure, but her dad, too. What kind of father asked his little girl to prove herself by sitting silent for hours at a time? Nick's own da had been no example of fatherhood. But one imagined that gents who had no need for a child's income might indulge their kids a bit, rather than . . . train them like circus dogs.

She'd kept quiet, though. She'd told Nick as much, with pride in her voice. Aye, she'd have made a fine thief, too, if her dad had asked it of her. She'd have obeyed, no doubt, without a word of challenge. Maybe there was the difference. Nick had put his nieces to thieving when they were still girls, believing family stuck together. Training them in the only way he could. But he'd always trusted them to speak up for themselves, to challenge him and break away once they found their footing.

Catherine, in their place, would have become the best thief in England, and never broken free of it. *That* was the difference. That was why Nick wouldn't have put her to it.

It was also why he wouldn't listen to her again should her brother cause trouble. If Peter Everleigh menaced her once more, Nick would draw blood.

"Are you listening?" she demanded.

"Sorry, lost track, there. What was that?"

"December won't draw the best crowd, of course. I wish we could wait. This collection deserves a spring auction, when the ton is in town for—"

He snorted. "If it's money you want, you should look outside that lot. They're up to their eyeballs in debt. Otherwise, I'd have no collection to auction, would I?"

She paused. "A fine point. With land prices falling . . . Whom, do you think, has the money?"

"Tycoons. Industrialists." He offered her a sideways smile. "Criminals."

She bit her lip to stop her own smile. "I don't think the criminals have postal addresses. But perhaps you're right. We should expand the invitation list to include—"

"Why bother with invitations at all? Throw open the doors. Come one, come all."

She shook her head. "Exclusivity is what distinguishes us. Otherwise, why not go to Christie's or Sotheby's?"

He drew up by the door. "Your goods might distinguish you. Try trading on them."

"Of course we trade on goods. But . . ." She handed him the lamp and reached for the cloak hanging on a nearby hook—then turned back, laughing. "One thing I'll say for it: it would enrage Peter. Worth considering, simply for that."

"There you go," he said. *There* was the devilry in her. Just took a nudge.

"At any rate, I'll certainly take out a grand advertisement—full page, illustrated. Heaven knows that some of these pieces would draw a crowd all the way from China." She set to buttoning her cloak. "How did you manage to acquire them? I can't imagine that your debtors would offer their finest wares straightaway."

"Generally not." She was having trouble with her

buttons, he noticed. Hands tired from her work. "But I know how to read a face. How to tell what a man doesn't want to part with, and what he wouldn't mind losing."

Her hands paused. She tipped her head, looking struck. "Very clever. So you don't pay attention to the antiques, but to the demeanor of the man who offers them?"

"That's right." And her demeanor right now was warm, interested, engaged. He gently knocked aside her hands, fastening the rest of the buttons himself.

He could feel the way her breath hitched in the rise and suspended fall of her breasts. Could hear her noisy swallow, and sense the agitation behind her rush of color. "I . . . am very bad, I think, at reading faces."

"Oh, I think you've got a fine eye," he murmured, and smoothed her hair back with his knuckles. Very fine eyes. Impossibly lovely. "I expect you don't need to bother with faces, though. The tables and cabinets keep you occupied."

Her lips curved in a hitching, hesitant smile. His knuckles still pressed against her cheekbone. But she didn't step away. She was looking directly at him. "My brother once said that I'd rather sleep with a cabinet than . . ."

He leaned forward, lips brushing her ear. "Than what?"

"A husband," she whispered.

He pressed his mouth to her neck. That tender skin just beneath her ear.

A small gasp escaped her. "You . . . shouldn't."

He lifted his brows, intrigued. *Shouldn't* was a far cry from *couldn't.* He opened his mouth and tasted her skin. Was rewarded by the shudder that moved through her—and then punished, as she stepped backward, out of reach.

Her lips parted, plump and rosy; she looked dazed. "You . . ." She cleared her throat. "I will remind you. You aren't a cabinet."

He grinned, delighted by the banter. "I call that a blessing, in fact." But when he reached for her again, she sidestepped and hauled open the door. He followed her into the street.

The rain had died off, but the air was cold and moist, piercing his nostrils like needles. She tugged her cloak tighter around her and yanked her hood over her hair before striking a brisk pace down the road. "A cabinet," she said over her shoulder, "doesn't care if a lady spends her days at the office and works late into the night."

He caught up to her. "And a husband would?

She snorted. "A husband generally wishes his wife to be at home knitting doilies and waiting like a loyal dog for his return—thence to strip off his boots and rub his feet, and murmur sympathetically while he complains of *his* work."

"The foot rub sounds nice," he says. "But doilies go cheap at market. Seems a doltish man indeed who minds a wife with ambitions, and has the guts to pursue them, besides."

With one finger, she hooked back her hood to dart him a sidelong glance. "Most gentlemen don't feel so."

He shrugged. "Well, but I'm no gentleman."

She faced ahead again, but after a moment, she said, "Perhaps your tastes will change, now that you have come into money."

"I didn't come into money," he said evenly. "I *made* it. And no, I don't think my tastes will change, since I never gave the matter much thought before a few weeks ago."

"A few . . ."

He waited, but she seemed unwilling to finish that sentence. They drew up before the side door at Diamonds; he rapped his knuckles against it. "A few weeks ago," he repeated. "When I married you, Kitty."

She looked up at him, something troubled working across her brow. "I wish you wouldn't . . ."

He seized her hand and delivered it a smacking kiss. "Don't lie," he said.

She snatched back her hand, but before she could argue, the door opened, and Callan was bowing them inside.

Was the candlelight more diffuse tonight than usual? Were the lights turned lower? As O'Shea busied himself at the sideboard, filling Catherine's plate from a variety of dishes sent up from the kitchens, she took her accustomed seat by the fire and looked for the cause of her uneasiness. His sitting room felt . . . smaller. Or he seemed larger. She could not take her eyes off him.

Like a solvent applied to varnish, these dinners had begun to erode her defenses. His casual touches, his genuine, disarming interest . . .

She made a fist in her lap. *Ladies hold their hands in elegant postures. You must have a care with your hands, Catherine: they look so mannish and ragged!*

Odd that her mother's voice was so strong in her memory tonight. She had spent long minutes in her bath, scrubbing at her palms with a pumice stone. But the calluses were all but permanent now.

The maid had added sprigs of lavender to her bath-water. The scent still clung to her skin. If O'Shea noticed it, he might think she had perfumed herself for him.

The notion left her unsettled as he carried over two heaping plates. "Outdone himself again," he said as he placed hers on the table before the fire. "One of these days, we'll get snails, I'll lay a wager on it."

She managed a smile. They had developed a small joke about his chef, whose name was Thomas but who preferred to be called "Pierre." Thomas, it seemed, felt himself sorely mistreated by fate; he was convinced that he'd been designed a Frenchman. "Have you ever had escargot?"

"God be praised," O'Shea said fervently as he sat. "I've been spared thus far."

"They're actually quite tasty."

"That's what old Wilson at the cookshop once told me of squirrel," he said with a grimace. "But I found a new source of mince pies the next day, I promise you." As she laughed, he came to his feet again. "Forgot the wine."

This, too, was becoming a tradition of sorts. "I won't drink it," she said serenely as she picked up her fork. Thomas had indeed outdone himself. Lobster salad, roasted lamb, plover eggs, and butter-drenched artichoke hearts crowded her plate. She glanced to the sideboard to weigh her strategy: dessert looked to be a platter of chocolate profiteroles, cream custards, and a variety of hothouse fruit. She would go lightly on the lamb, then. In heaven, every course would include profiteroles.

O'Shea returned, carrying a bottle in one hand and

two glasses in the other. "You'll only need one," she said, per the usual routine.

He lifted the bottle to display the label. She squinted: Painted Pipe Madeira, 1790.

1790? She choked on a mouthful of lobster. "You can't mean to open that!"

He gave her a cat-in-the-cream smile as he pulled a jack-knife from his pocket. In a showy, one-handed move, he flipped open the knife. She rolled her eyes. She would not encourage his penchant for thuggish talents. "Why not?" he asked.

She sighed. "Do you remember the Sheraton dresser in the storeroom?"

"French vices," he said, a purr in his voice. "How could I forget?"

She bit hard on her cheek, a punishment for blushing. He made everything sound so . . . suggestive. "At auction, that bottle would go for more than the dresser."

"Oh?" He turned the bottle in his hand, examining it with new interest. "Seems a sight less useful than a sturdy chest of drawers. You're running quite a con at that auction house."

"A con? I beg your . . ." But he was grinning, so she abandoned her dudgeon. "It's not a con," she said mildly. "That madeira is very rare. I should be surprised if ten bottles still existed."

"It's a con," he said. "For one madeira's much like another. Only you say it isn't, and somehow you cozen the sheep into believing you and spending a small fortune on a single bottle."

It was impossible to take offense at his words—not when he spoke them so amiably, with that teasing hitch to his mouth. "Those sheep are men of good taste," she said dryly. "I can understand how you might mistake them as a foreign species."

He laughed. "So, tell me, then: what would be the reserve for this bottle at auction?"

"I'd have to consult previous sales. But at a guess? Fifty pounds."

He loosed a low whistle. "And then what?"

"What do you mean? And then it would sell for seventy, perhaps, and you'd be"—she quickly calculated their agreed percentage—"fifty-six pounds the richer."

"Highway robbery, that split." He flashed her a wolfish grin. "You're a thief as well as a swindler, with a pretty face to cover for it. And the man who won the bottle—what do you think he'd do with it?"

"Add it to his collection. A great many men"—she narrowed her eyes—"men of taste, that is—collect madeira."

"Wouldn't drink it, then?"

"Of course not! A bottle so rare? Why, I expect one would open it only for a—a state dinner, an evening with the royal family—"

"Well, then." He stabbed his knife into the cork, then yanked it out with a loud pop. "No sense leaving all the good stuff to those who take it for granted."

Her fork clattered to the plate. She sat back in her chair, aghast as he splashed the straw-colored wine into a glass.

He held it out to her. "Feel like making an exception tonight?"

Temptation battled against caution. It was a *very* rare wine. And perhaps, to broaden her professional knowledge, it would be wise to sample it . . .

He took her hand and wrapped it around the glass,

then guided it to her lips. His gray gaze caught hers over the rim of the glass, his long black lashes a dramatic frame for the devilish light glinting in his eyes. "Tell me if it's any good," he murmured, then dropped his glance to her mouth.

Awareness fluttered through her, soft and ticklish as moths' wings. If he was the devil, then she was his willing victim. She breathed deeply of the sweet fumes, then opened her mouth as he tilted the cup, pouring a small bit into her mouth.

Heaven. She pushed the glass away and closed her eyes, rolling the liquid over her tongue. A mild, nutty sweetness, almonds and maple, yielded to the faint, surprising tang of citrus peel. When she swallowed, a creamy, lingering note of toffee spread across her tongue, a hook that demanded another sip for certainty.

"Oh yes," she said. "It's . . ." The words fell away as she opened her eyes. He was watching her, a tense cast to his face, his eyes narrowed and his mouth hard.

He recovered himself instantly, offering her a quick, curious smile before sitting down and slinging back a mouthful from his own cup. His broad, tanned throat rippled as he swallowed. The way he sat, with his long legs stretched out and crossed at the ankles, drew his trousers into tight definition across his brawny thighs.

She had seen those thighs naked. She knew the shape of the muscle that gripped his bones; the way that muscle narrowed, so dramatically and elegantly, into his neat, square knees. Awareness, full-bodied and almost painful, surged through her. She felt breathless.

"Not as bold as I expected," he said.

She made herself look away from him, into the

depths of her cup. "They call it a rainwater madeira. It's generally milder than the other types."

"Ah. Didn't know."

She tried for a smile. He was sitting four feet away, behaving with perfect courtesy. She should encourage such behavior. "Let me guess. This came from the cellars of another hapless gambler?"

"Had it from a client, aye, but he wasn't in debt. Needed some quick cash, he said." He was silent for a moment. "I favor ale, myself. But every year, I open a bottle of madeira. This is my sister's birthday today. And she favored it." He lifted his glass. "To Oona."

She lifted her glass as well. "Will she join us?"

He looked briefly startled. "Oona was Lily's mother. Lilah's," he corrected, with a wry tug of his mouth. "Guess she prefers that name, and now she's a proper lady, I suppose she can have it. She never told you about her ma? It's been years since Oona passed. Cholera took her."

"No." Catherine paused, troubled that she hadn't known. "She told me of you, of course, but . . . not much about her childhood." *And I never thought to ask.* It spoke ill of her, didn't it? It was one thing to be professional, another to be callous to those she counted as friends. How selfish she'd become, wrapped up in her concerns about the company. "Was Lilah very young when her mother died?"

"Eight," he said. "Or—no, nine." He frowned. "I was . . . sixteen, just. Had been living with them for five years by then. Raising hell." His smile was faint and fleeting. "It's a wonder Oona put up with me. I'm sure I did no favors to her marriage. Lily's da called me the devil's spawn, said I must have worn out my welcome with Lucifer."

He sounded amused, but it didn't seem safe to smile. "That couldn't have been comfortable, to be so judged by your brother-in-law."

"Oh, he meant nothing by it. Simply joshing me. He was a good man, Lily's dad." He turned his wineglass in his hand, his gaze distant. "Ruled these parts before me—not with any discipline, mind you. Ran a ragtag band of thieves and swindlers, and had no plan for the future, no interest in investing his coin. But he was a good man, and a kind one. Much loved. Much . . . missed, afterward."

Something dark had roughened his voice, there. She sensed an unhappy history. She could pass by it, turn the conversation to lighter topics—the Sheraton dresser; the tambour-topped writing desk she'd found. But with her ignorance of Lilah's past still fresh in her mind, she took a deep breath and surrendered to her curiosity. Her desire, God help her, to know more about this man. "How did he die, then?"

"Killed." The syllable was curt. "Rival gang decided to sink its claws into Whitechapel. Jonathan tried to stop them. Got ambushed one night, by cowards who knifed him from behind."

"Goodness." This was the history Lilah had overcome? Catherine felt dizzied. Lilah looked, moved, and spoke like a genteel lady. She had remade herself entirely, and showed no signs of having survived such tragedy. "What happened to his killers? Did the police catch them?"

He lifted his glass, took a long swallow. "I caught them."

She opened her mouth, but no words came out.

His smile looked cold. "Police weren't lifting a finger.

They'd got better things to do, they said, than interfere in a street brawl between a pack of rabid dogs."

He sounded as if he were quoting them. "How unjust," she whispered.

He gave a single sharp shake of his head. "Justice was done, all right." He met her eyes. "I told you once: violence is clumsy. But sometimes it's called for. And when me and mine are at stake, I'll do what I must. Show no weakness, accept no insult, allow no advantage: that's the law of the street."

She stared at him. He looked brutal in this moment, his face dark and lean, stripped of all softness. As though the smiling charm he more often showed was simply a mask, which he had momentarily set aside to allow her to see him clearly.

Perhaps there was a secret blackness in her soul, for as she stared back at him, she felt no repulsion. No distaste. She could respect a man who fought for his own. Who allowed nobody to cross him or his.

Why, *respect* was the lie here. She *envied* his own. How differently her life would have developed, had she been able to rely on Peter's loyalty and aid, rather than always needing to guard against him.

"Good," she said roughly. She raised her glass again, another toast, before draining it. "I am glad you got justice, whatever it took."

He blinked, a curious expression on his face. She had surprised him, maybe. As he refilled their glasses, he cut her a look through his lashes, a speculative glance that she did not know how to answer.

Now that she had decided to indulge her curiosity, her brain buzzed with a dozen questions for him. "What's your aim, then?" she asked as she reclaimed her glass.

"What do you mean?"

"You say Lilah's father had no plan. But you do, I take it?"

"Ah." He leaned back, kicking one leg over the other, his ankle atop one thigh. At some point he had un-buttoned his jacket; where it gaped open, she caught a glimpse of his waistcoat, stretched tightly across his lean, flat belly. "Well, I'm a rich man now—so a poor man would say. But I've been studying up on your kind. The creamy lot. And I know that what a poor man calls rich, a wealthy man calls middling. What I aim for is wealth that grows itself, without any tending from me."

"Investments," she said. "Do you have a man in the City?"

"Acquired a broker a year or two ago." He shrugged. "I'm on my way now. I'll give it another couple years. And in the meantime, I'll keep building the walls."

"The walls? Are you in property development as well?"

He smiled. "Not real walls. Walls to keep the world out, is what I mean— should I decide that I'm better off apart from it. At present, I've got—let's see." He held up one finger, sapphire and garnet sparking in the fire-light. "Whitechapel." Another two fingers, the diamond and ruby. "Bethnal Green, St. George's-in-the-East." A fourth finger, emerald. "Mile End." He snapped his fin-gers into a fist. "Limehouse, soon enough. Docks are mine, but the vestry there's a bit touchy, I fear."

She realized what he meant. "You control *four ves-tries*?"

He laughed. "Just said so, didn't I?"

"But that's . . ." It was a very large swath of east-ern London. "If you control so much of the local government . . ." Why, he was more powerful than some London MPs. And he answered to no sponsors, no patrons—which made him more powerful by far. "To what end? Do you mean to go into politics?"

He snorted. "Rich man's game. No time for that."

"Then why bother with the vestries?"

"They're my walls," he said coolly. "Not a law nor a lawman can operate in four parishes without my approval. You try to put the police on me, you'd best hope they come from the City, because no bobby east of the square mile will cross me. You want to open a shop, a public house, even a church, you'd best hope you ran it by me, or you'll find no joy from the local authorities."

"That sounds like a kingship," she said softly.

"No. I'm no tyrant. I stopped taking graft years ago. I don't demand a protection fee. All I ask for is respect."

It sounded very seductive. She resisted the urge to approve. Law had its place; civilization had not been built by men who defied a central authority. "What you ask sounds less like respect than allegiance."

"Well . . . maybe. I prefer to call it . . . a sense of being at home." He hesitated, his gaze oddly thoughtful as he looked at her. "A stretch of territory where I don't need to be looking over my shoulder when I walk down the streets at night. Where nobody needs look, so long as they're one of mine. That's a . . . fine thing, for folks raised in these streets." He gave a tug of his mouth. "For a lad who slept in 'em, when the coin was short." He reached out, running a finger around the rim of his glass. "Whose ma worked in them," he said quietly. "Sometimes. When the coin was short. To feed me, she did what she must, I think."

Her breath caught. She pressed her lips together, terrified of having to loose that breath, for fear that he might interpret the sigh as disgust or contempt.

But . . . to her mild amazement, she felt only sorrow for him. After what she had seen at the B Meeting, the raggedness and the tales of piteous want, she could imagine that many women in these parts sometimes lacked the coin to feed their children. Of course a mother in dire straits would do anything to prevent her child from starving. Even if it meant selling her body or soul.

"So you want to be . . . immune," she said hesitantly. "Immune from uncertainty. From danger and risk."

His gaze lifted to hers. "No," he said after a moment. "That comes when you're dead, Kitty."

"Then . . . what do you want?"

He laid down his glass, a soft click of glass against wood. "I want the freedom to live as I please," he said quietly. "By my own rules, nobody else's. How does that sound to you?"

He had not moved off the chair. But the intensity of his look suddenly made her flush, as though he had crossed to stand before her, close enough to touch. Her own reaction confused her, made her stammer. "I think it—it sounds very grand. But surely most people have that privilege. I do."

"Do you?" He hadn't looked away. Hadn't even blinked. "Seems like you could have it. If you paid attention to what you really wanted."

A frown pulled at her brow. "I don't know what you mean." But her mouth felt dry, and her pulse was suddenly thrumming, as though part of her did understand. "I've gotten what I want. Thanks—thanks to you. Everleigh's, safe. The accounts in my hands—"

He did rise off the chair then. Her heart skipped as he prowled toward her. He went down on his knees in front of her, so their eyes were level; he took the wineglass out of her slack hand, then lifted her palm to his mouth, pressing his lips against her racing pulse.

"I'm not talking of your company," he said. "I'm talking of you. Look at me."

She had averted her face. She squared her shoulders and lifted her chin, glaring at him. "I came in here to tell you of what I found in the storeroom, not to be—"

"Business," he said. "You hide behind it. You hide from yourself. What were you thinking earlier, when you were staring at me? Wasn't business that made you blush. Be honest with yourself now. I'll wait. No need to speak it aloud."

She took a sharp breath through her nose. Was she so transparent? The possibility mortified her. She tried to pull her hand free. His grip tightened.

"What keeps you so afraid?" His words were low, hoarse. "That you'll like it too much? For if so, you're right. I'll make sure of that."

Her voice wasn't good for more than a whisper now. "I don't know what you mean."

"Liar," he said. "Who are you lying to? The door's closed. Not a soul in the world to hear you. Nobody to know what happens here. Nobody to judge."

"There's you," she said shakily.

He cupped her face, his thumb soothing the corner of her mouth. "And what of it? You imagine I'll think less of you, for wanting the same thing I do?"

She bit her lip hard. This wasn't fair of him. "It's not you who would stand to pay for it!"

"And if I promised to make sure you didn't pay," he

said. "If I had that power. What then? What would you do?"

She closed her eyes. That was not a question she dared ask herself. She believed he had the skill to prevent a child. But if she went forward with touching him . . .

She might pay anyway. Suddenly the truth was plain to her: already she was drawn to him. She craved his company. She longed to make him laugh. She felt grateful to him. And she believed him, despite his history and his sins, a good and decent soul.

There was more at risk here than the possibility of a child. At risk was something she could not afford to lose. She could not afford to love him. She could not be a wife.

He spoke, again with that uncanny way of reading her mind. "You've got an ironclad ticket to freedom," he murmured. "I signed that contract. You'll have your divorce, one day. But what of the meantime? We could enjoy each other. *Live,* Kitty. I could cut this gown off you. Lick my way from your mouth to your breasts, put my tongue between your legs and kiss you until you screamed. But not unless you admit you want it. What you'll permit me to do, how far you'll let me go—it's up to you, Catherine. Only you."

With her eyes closed, those torrid images were too vivid. She opened her eyes, and the sight of his dark, wicked face was no easier to bear, no less of an aching temptation.

"You ever really felt free?" he whispered. "Because here it is: here, you're free. My territory. And yours, if you want it."

The breath exploded from her in a gasp. He took note. A dangerous smile curved his lips. "I'll take that as a yes," he said, and rose on his knees, coming over her as soundlessly as a thief. His fingers speared through her hair, causing a pinching pain as her pins stabbed her scalp.

She braced herself against the brutality of his grip—and was undone by the gentle touch of his mouth. Small, fleeting touches. His lips on her earlobe. Her cheek, her neck. Light as a whisper, he scattered his kisses, while his hand at her hair plucked out pins, soothing now, his fingers skilled, clever. Her hair came tumbling down, a heavy cool mass, and he smoothed it away from her shoulders as his mouth closed on hers.

The kiss felt familiar. Wildly startling, but also . . . not surprising. She had kissed him too many times now for shock to blind her mind to the details: the slight roughness of his lips. The hot lick of his tongue as he chased hers into her mouth. The firm, steady grip of his hand around her throat—a gesture that might have menaced her, had it not been for the gentle brush of his thumb across her skin, settling at last over the spot where her pulse hammered, pressing there as though to remind her: *you want this.*

He tilted his head, angling for a deeper intrusion; his mouth searched hers, ravishing. She was being devoured . . . but she was devouring him, too; she did want this. She *did.*

An odd sob escaped her. He fell still, then started to ease away. She caught his upper arms to hold him to her; to feel for the solid strapping breadth of his shoulders, to prove to herself that she had not embroidered the memory by a single degree. He felt forged of something tougher, finer, and hotter than mere flesh. He was a long, lethal blade of a man, a weapon that she could touch, that she could stroke now without any fear of being injured. Nobody to see; nobody to judge. Freedom, indeed.

He coaxed her to lean back against the chair. His expression was rapt, almost reverent, as he molded his hands down her body, feeling the shape of her breasts through the thick impediments of silk and cotton and corseted canvas. She arched upward, and his hands slid around to her back, disarming with impossible economy all the devices by which a woman was bound up in herself: buttons and hooks, laces and clasps, detestable obstacles, falling away beneath his fingers like vanquished enemies.

He slid her sleeves from her shoulders, then ripped her chemise apart. He parted the layers like the petals of a flower, baring her to the waist before taking her breast in his mouth. The door closed. Nobody to see. Only this man, whose judgments didn't matter; whose judgments would be sweet, regardless.

She clasped his head and held him to her breast, desire like greed, not satisfied by his suckling, wanting ever more. She fumbled blindly for his hand, gripped it firmly, strongly enough to grind his bones. She wanted this hand employed elsewhere.

He met her eyes, his mouth glistening, his gaze adamant. "Put it where you want it," he said.

She squeezed her eyes shut. She could not do it. She would die of embarrassment.

He closed his teeth around her nipple very lightly, then blew.

She gasped, then shoved his hand into the depths of her skirts. "There." The syllable was threadbare. She could not bear to look.

But oh, the sweet sensation of his palm on her ankle—she held her breath, seeing in the darkness behind her lids the path his hand traveled. The tender curve of her calf. The damp cove behind her knee. She choked back a noise as he hooked his fingers beneath her drawers, as he flexed his grip on the soft flesh of her inner thigh. And then . . .

"Here," he whispered, as he found her quim. The delicate touch of his fingers, the unbearable nudging exploration, made her squirm—and then he found where she'd wanted him, after all.

His thumb toyed with the seat of her desire, while his fingers—she gasped. His fingers slowly penetrated her, a slow, stretching pressure that made her feel fuller and heavier and ripe for him. She forgot to keep her eyes shut.

He watched her as he petted her, his gaze slumberous, heavy-lidded, his mouth full and loose. She stared at his mouth, remembering his promise. He would put it there, below. All she need do was ask . . .

The thought magnified her pleasure. She put her fist to her mouth to stop a sound as his fingers quickened their rhythm. He seized her hand, pulling it to his own mouth, running his tongue between her tightly knotted fingers, sucking her fingertips, making low murmurs now, shameless words. "Tell me," he said. "After you come, what next? How will I make you come, the second time?"

The words shot through her like an electric current. They laid the truth bare: the first time wouldn't be enough. Perhaps the second wouldn't be, either.

Women were not meant to enjoy such things—her mother had warned her of the pain of the marriage

bed. But it was possible that her desire was like her
ambition—limitless, unnatural for a woman. In which
case . . . indulging it would only be a torment, once she
lost the means to satisfy herself.

Once she lost *him*.

The pleasure was coming now, like a torrent building, building toward the lip of a dam. It would break—
overflow—and she tensed against it. Her lips formed
the syllable once—twice. The third time, she managed
to say, "*Stop.*"

He did not pretend to mishear her. His hand stilled.
Some low sound came from him—a curse she did not
know. She braced herself, still shaking, for his anger. But
after a moment, he sank his forehead against her bosom,
breathing raggedly against her as his hand slipped away,
down her leg. His breath sent a hot whispering pleasure
along the tops of her breasts, raising a shiver she could
not repress.

She felt empty, nothing but an unsatisfied ache. Had
she saved herself? Or was this punishment wasted?

His soft, broken laugh tattooed her skin. "Christ," he
said. "You've got some restraint."

Her hands seized the opportunity to thread through
his hair, holding him against her as he breathed her in.
They made a silent apology to him, stroking the curve
of his skull.

At last, he eased back by slow degrees, then fell onto
his heels with the ease of a cat, with that loose limber
grace that no gentleman possessed.

"You want it," he said, the words ragged. "And God
knows I will give it to you. But for God's sake, Kitty.
Make up your mind."

CHAPTER ELEVEN

*I*t was William Pilcher's habit every Saturday at half
three to attend the washhouse. By rumor, he came
to clear his head and dwell on great matters of local government in the silence and restorative heat.

No doubt he spared a few thoughts, too, for women
he'd like to harass.

As Nick took a seat on the bench beside the man, his
fists fairly itched with the urge to meet Pilcher's face.
"Fine situation you've got here," he said.

Pilcher frowned and shifted away, evidently dis-
pleased by the interruption of his peace. "Do you know
me, sir?"

Man had a well-fed look to him. Wasn't just the hairy
roll of gut hanging over his towel. Certain folks, generally those who had been born into comfort but had
persuaded themselves that they'd earned it, carried this
gloating, well-satisfied air, as though the entire world
existed to give them opportunities to sneer.

Pilcher was sneering now. "Oh," Nick said, "I should
imagine everybody knows Mr. William Pilcher." But

not for the crime of bigamy, thank God. Then again, had Peter Everleigh managed to talk Pilcher into forcing Catherine to the altar, the man would no longer look so satisfied. He'd be rotting at the bottom of the Thames. "Vice-chairman of St. Luke's Vestry, aren't you?"

Pilcher's glance passed over Nick's shoulder toward the door, which stood shut to keep in the steam. "I do not talk business here. Make an appointment with my secretary, should you desire a word."

The closed door also blocked the sight of Pilcher's brawny guard, otherwise known as St. Luke's chief sanitary inspector. Little inspection, much bribery. The vestry of St. Luke's was rotted through.

"I've got no interest in your vestry," Nick said. His ambitions did sharpen, though, as he eyed the man's skull. Looked ripe for crushing. "You've been leaving notes at my doorstep, begging for a word." It had started to annoy him that the bloke had the presumption to call himself to Nick's attention. "We'll speak here."

Pilcher stared hard. His lizard's brain at last provided the answer; he sat up a little. "You—you're Nicholas O'Shea?" He slid an incredulous glance down Nick's form. God knew what he'd expected. Somebody toothless, with the devil's brand on his cheek.

Nick settled more comfortably on the bench, as the crowd on the other side of the room gawked. "That's me," he said. Those other men knew their places better than they should. They squeezed ten to a bench, so their vestryman might spread his bulk in comfort, alone. "Fine windows in this washhouse." The gray light lit the audience's astonished faces with sharp clarity. This was the only washhouse in St. Luke's, and for all that it was funded by parish taxes, Nick had needed to bribe the man outside to win entry. "My compliments to the vestry."

Frowning, Pilcher scrubbed his brown head. "I had hoped to have this conversation in privacy. It concerns a matter of some delicacy—"

"Orton Street, I suppose." Pilcher had sent his first note right after the board meeting in which his inspector's petition had been overturned. Nick offered a slight smile. "You should give your men a map. Those parish borders prove tricky."

"Indeed." Pilcher hadn't blinked. "On behalf of the St. Luke's vestry, I do apologize for the confusion. One of the oddities of our fair London, I'm sure you'll agree, that areas of such . . . different character can abut each other."

In short, the good people of St. Luke's fancied themselves too fine to be neighbors to Whitechapel. Nick shrugged.

Pilcher cast another glance over the witnesses on the opposite bench before taking a deep breath and hitching his towel higher. "Those vacant lots on either side of your properties—they must make a terrible eyesore for your tenants."

Nick snorted. Wasn't the view that his tenants cared about. Reasonable rents and a solid roof were what they asked. "What of them?"

"Naturally . . . as a representative of this parish, that is . . . I can't like them, either." Pilcher mustered a thoughtful look. "How familiar are you with the Torrens Act, sir?"

Nick had certainly gotten an education recently. "Passing familiar, I'd say."

"The law has created a terrible tangle for St. Luke's.

When a property is condemned, as were the three lots neighboring yours on Orton Street, the Board of Works seizes ownership, and hires an appraiser to value the property. The man who valuated the lots on Orton Street . . ." Pilcher grimaced. "Idiot. He assigned a price far higher than the market will fetch. In consequence, nobody has offered to buy them from the board."

"Pity," Nick said. "I've yet to see how the problem concerns me."

Pilcher's mouth tightened. "Well, I am coming to it. The law requires the parish to compensate the former owner for the full sum named in the appraisal. The promise, of course, is that the land will eventually sell, and thereby will the parish be recompensed. But no one will pay such a ridiculous sum for those vacant lots. In consequence, St. Luke's is teetering on bankruptcy." He cleared his throat. "Those properties *must* be sold—quickly, and for not a penny less than the previous owner was compensated. That would be far easier if we could offer the entire street for sale—all five lots at once."

Including Nick's own lots. He saw the way of it now. "Shame, then, that half that street belongs to me."

"Indeed." Pilcher leaned in, lowering his voice. "Mr. O'Shea, I am interested in purchasing those two buildings from you."

"They're not for sale."

Pilcher's smile looked strained now. "I will pay you a very fair price. More than fair—I will match the valuation of the adjoining properties."

"Now, why would you do that? You just said the appraiser named an ungodly sum."

Pilcher's smile faded. He sat back, eyeing Nick—

reevaluating his approach, no doubt, now that his mark had proved less easy than he'd anticipated. "I will take the loss. For the welfare of my parish, I am willing to suffer."

Rare day that one got a front-row seat to such a self-righteous performance. Nick bared his teeth in a nice, friendly smile. "And to think you're only vice-chairman. What does the chairman do? Give St. Luke's poor the bread from his own kids' mouths?"

Pilcher's palm slammed onto the bench. Against the opposite wall, several men flinched. "I will not be mocked by you," he said.

"That's what you call mockery? I'll spare you my next thought, then."

"I am sure it would be vulgar in the extreme," Pilcher snapped. "Much like the crowds teeming in those buildings of yours. Keeping chickens in their flats—stabling donkeys and pigs in the yard! They are an affront to every decent person in this parish, and I will not allow their likes to fester among us. For the sake of the women and children of St. Luke's—"

"But a music hall will elevate the tone. That right?"

Pilcher's jaw sagged. "I have no idea—"

"Liquor loosens lips," Nick said flatly. "And your nephew's a drinker. Seems he favors a pub in Spitalfields, where he was boasting of an uncle who means to set him up handsomely, in a new development planned for Orton Street. Sounds flash, all right—public house, theater, couple of dining rooms. Little Joe says the builders have been throwing money at you for the chance to develop those lots. Pity you don't own them yet. You want to talk about chickens? Never count them before they're hatched."

Pilcher lurched to his feet. The slip of his towel raised

a single startled snicker from the other side of the room, quickly quashed. No doubt that man had expected more from his local crook.

Pilcher yanked the towel up, doing himself no favors. His scrawny legs couldn't have kicked a chicken from the road. "Lies," he hissed. "Base slander, which nobody will credit from *you*—"

"Doesn't matter if they do. For you'll have to tell the builders yourself, soon enough: you're lacking the plots. I'm not selling."

Pilcher's eyes bulged. "If you know what's good for you—"

Nick made a chiding click of his tongue as he stood. "Now, here I thought you wanted to speak to *me*. But you must have me confused for somebody else, if you think I'm a man you can threaten."

Pilcher's throat bobbed in a swallow. He shot a glance toward the door, then began to inch backward toward it, Nick matching him step for hobbling step. "Do you— do you truly imagine you have any power, outside that squalid pit where you live? You think you're the only one who knows secrets? I know all about your plot to force me off the Board of Works!"

Bloody Peter Everleigh. Nick shrugged. "One way or another, you're going."

Spittle flew as Pilcher laughed. "Never say you're banking on *Everleigh*. He knows which side his bread is buttered." As he slammed squarely into the door, he transferred his grip from the towel to wrestle desperately with the handle. The steam had made it slippery. Nick reached to assist.

Pilcher shrank into himself, cringing like a dog from a boot.

"Aye, you're a proper man, all right," Nick said softly. "So worried for your parish. Say what: I'll save it for you. Buy those lots to either side of mine. See what the builders offer *me*."

Pilcher glared up at him. "Try it. See if the board will sell them to you. I *own* that board. And no gutter rat will—"

Nick yanked open the door, knocking Pilcher onto his knees. The towel fell to the ground. Pilcher scrambled to retrieve it, then shot a livid look toward the onlookers. "If any of you *dare* speak of what you saw here—"

Nick snorted. "Not much to speak of, is it? Get out."

Flushing a violent purple, Pilcher left.

Nick shut the door, then turned to the audience gawping from their bench like a bunch of brainless sheep. "What say you, lads? Has your vestry served your interests as handsomely as they have Mr. Pilcher's?"

The first man to shake his head showed courage that quickly infected the others. But Nick was not interested in the followers. It was the first man to whom he looked as he spoke.

"Then do something about it," he said. "Be a man. Stand up for yourself. In this world, nobody else is going to do it."

No reply. He shrugged and let himself out.

Catherine put down the crowbar and brushed splinters from her palms before seizing the corner of the canvas. Her stomach was jumping from excitement; she had anticipated this moment for days now. "Hold your nose. It's still a bit dusty."

Batten turned back from his inspection of the French-polished Sheraton dresser, a mournful crimp to his mouth. "Whatever it is, I pray it hasn't been *restored*."

She yanked the canvas off the writing cabinet. "Voilà!" Over three hundred years old, the cedar still perfumed the air. "Look at the initials. *Look* at them!"

Batten squinted through the bars of light that fell through the receiving-room windows. "Praises be," he whispered. His knobby hand shook as he brushed the scratch-carved initials. "E.R. 1590." His fingertips trailed up the drawers to the central cupboard, where a cunning image of a palace was worked in marquetry. "Is this . . ."

"Yes!" She pressed her hands to her cheeks; smiling, she'd discovered, could cause a delightful ache. "I spent yesterday combing through illustrations at the British Museum. This is Nonsuch Palace." One of Queen Elizabeth's favorite abodes. "I've booked an appointment in the archives. *Batten.*" She dropped her voice to a whisper; the words were too wondrous to speak casually. "If we can document that Elizabeth was there in 1590 . . ."

"Goodness." He traced one wrought-iron handle. "The furor this will cause!"

"I know. And added to the rest . . ." She cast her gaze again over the spread of treasures; they had spent all morning unpacking the contents of O'Shea's storeroom. Queen Anne cabinetry, china plate, Sheffield candelabra, Lambeth pottery . . . That warehouse had proved richer than a palace. And now it was all at Everleigh's. "What do you say? Shall we invite the Prince of Wales?"

He grinned. "With the cabinet as our centerpiece, I'd say we should invite the Queen."

She laughed just as a door slammed nearby. Her

brother's curse followed; a crate rocked precariously as he came into view. "What is all this rubbish?" He yanked down his jacket. "If this is the Mandeley estate, we're not slated—"

"A new estate," Catherine said. "The last sale of the autumn. I mean to announce it in the *Times*, with a full page of illustrations."

"For an autumn sale?" He gave an impatient pull of his mouth. "What nonsense."

"Look around you," she said serenely.

Scowling, Peter turned full circle. He had never applied himself to the studies required of an appraiser; between a Rembrandt and a copy by Mr. Taylor, he was helpless to spot the differences.

But even he knew a proper Sheraton when he saw one. As he faced her again, he looked puzzled. "Whose estate is this? Surely they insisted we hold it till the season."

"No. I contracted for the first week of December."

"December?" His glance strayed to a group of Chippendale chairs, the original patina intact. "Catherine," he said slowly, "this collection should be saved for the spring."

"Batten, will you give us a moment?" She held Peter's eyes, waiting until the other man had left to go on. "In the normal course, I would agree. This collection is well worth the spring. Unfortunately, our finances don't allow for delay. Curious, don't you think? It seems someone embezzled over five thousand pounds from our accounts. And then, the aftermath of the ring at the Cranston auction—"

"Enough," he snapped. "I won't hear of that again."

"And I won't argue," she said, too cheerful to do anything but shrug. "I have power of attorney now. Full authority to do as I please. Unless you mean to sue for it back, you have no business telling me when to hold this auction."

He laid a hand on the Sheraton dresser, rubbing the horrid French polish with a thoughtful frown. "Who is the client?"

"He prefers to remain anonymous."

He cast her a sour look. "Fine," he said. "Do as you please. Forego the handsome profit we might have fetched in May. I was coming to speak to you on a different matter."

"Oh?" She pulled her handkerchief from her pocket to dust off the writing cabinet. To imagine that Queen Bess herself had stored papers in this chest! There was a proper businesswoman. She'd run the country single-handedly, free of meddling brothers.

"O'Shea is out of hand. He challenged Pilcher's bid on the Orton Street properties. Did you know that?"

Mention of his name shot through her like a current of electricity. She carefully wiped the iron handles. "I don't know anything of Mr. O'Shea's private affairs," she said. What a lie! She knew more now that she had ever imagined she would wish to know. She knew the ways he could kiss a woman—softly, and then savagely, with a roughness that somehow translated as the greatest compliment a woman could hope for. She willed her brain away from that line of reflection, for it was bound to make her blush. "You must speak with him directly on such matters."

"We had an agreement," Peter said sharply. "Brokered by *you*. I fulfilled my end of that bargain. But now he is persecuting me."

She looked up from the desk. Her brother was flushed, nearly shaking. "What do you mean?"

"I mean, he has tendered an offer to the board for the properties that neighbor his. Properties in *St. Luke*. And the price he offers is ludicrous! It is an act of aggression, I tell you. Pilcher will have those properties!"

She frowned. "Do you mean his bid is very low?"

"Absurdly high," he burst out. "And so the fools on the board wish to entertain it! But I won't allow that. Do you hear me, Catherine? I'll quash it flat. The tender period should have closed weeks ago—it was an oversight on some idiotic clerk's part to even accept O'Shea's bid. He's *mad* if he thinks I'll oppose Pilcher so openly. That was never our agreement!"

She hesitated, then nodded. "Is that all?"

"All?" He uttered an outraged laugh. "Yes, by God. Only your brother's future. Perhaps you can spare a thought for that, in between polishing the furniture!" He paused, breathing heavily, his expression bullish. "Catherine, I have tolerated your shenanigans. I have met your terms. But I warn you—if you back me into a corner, I will have no choice but to fight."

"I understand," she said slowly.

His grim nod alarmed her more than his threat. She felt a sinking in her stomach as the door slammed behind him. It was not like her brother to depart without having the last word.

Catherine stepped up to the railing that overlooked the gaming floor. Dinner had come and gone without a visit from O'Shea. Did he not wonder how his treasures had fared during their transport to Everleigh's?

Did he not wonder if she'd made a decision?

Make up your mind, he'd instructed her last week—and every day since, in a silent monologue just beneath her conscious thoughts, she had been battling to do so. He made no move to assist her. He had not touched her again. He didn't need to. The way he watched her . . . Even the act of breaking open the crates today had come to seem strangely portentous. Wood snapping, restraints shattering . . .

She leaned out, searching the crowd. Where was he? Had he gone out for the evening? The possibility sank through her as sharply as a blade.

She clung tighter to the rail, amazed by herself. How had her life been so unseated from its steady, disciplined course? The future of Everleigh's remained precarious. One could never count on a single auction, no matter how promising. Failing to turn a profit this year might be the start of a pattern; failure, in the art world, had a way of compounding. *That* was what required her attention. So she had told him, stiffly, the day after their confrontation in his rooms. He seemed to have heeded those words.

Apparently she hadn't.

She spotted O'Shea at last, at the table directly below. He sat looking over his hand of cards as a *woman* hung over his shoulder.

Catherine recoiled from the railing, her face stinging as though she'd been slapped. For a moment, the chandeliers, the brilliantly painted ceiling, seemed to spin around her.

A woman. *What* woman?

She forced herself back to the railing. *That* kind of woman. Indeed. Not a natural redhead, no. Her head-dress, a vulgar disarrangement of badly dyed feathers, protruded from hair the livid shade of an overripe rose. For some awful reason—not merely from a lack of taste, but from an absolute well of depravity—she had chosen to wear a gown that matched her hair, trimmed in lurid silver lace.

People of similarly depraved tastes would probably count her pretty. Her face was delicately featured and dramatically heart shaped, broad at the temples and cheekbones, narrowing to a small, sharp chin. Her nose looked like somebody had taken a scoop out of it, then patted it upward, the better to display her neat little nostrils, which flared as she laughed.

Catherine could hear her laughter from two stories above: rich, robust, ringing. Ladies did not throw back their heads and shout out their mirth. But the gentlemen at her table did not seem to mind her lack of decorum. To a man, they were grinning at her. And no wonder! Her neckline was cut low enough to display a good portion of her bosom.

Catherine supposed she could feel a grudging admiration. Yes, why not? Most women were not encouraged to cultivate talents apart from feminine wiles. At least this one was plying hers with dedication.

A gentleman does not admire a woman for her mind, Catherine.

So her mother had told her, time and again. But it had been years since she felt this bitter sense of insufficiency. What did she care if O'Shea found her wanting? Theirs was no true marriage. His hot words were lies, of course. Any woman would do for him. It made her an idiot to have imagined differently.

Still, what poor business sense on O'Shea's part! Such

a . . . spectacle . . . posed a distraction to the players, turning them away from their game. Look at them now—their attention was not for their wagers.

Had she actually ventured to the railing in the hopes of drawing his attention? She took a step backward. As least she knew now why he had not joined her for dinner. He'd already found companionship for the night— somebody far better equipped to flatter, admire, and cosset him.

But how dare he flaunt her here? This marriage might be a sham, but must he rub his debauchery in her face?

Why, that contravened the terms of the contract! In public situations, he was legally obliged to accord her all due measures of respect! Furious, Catherine resolved to confront him.

CHAPTER TWELVE

*H*alfway down the back stairs, just as Catherine began to doubt the wisdom of her course, O'Shea came around the corner, halting a few steps below. "There you are," he said, one hand on the banister as he smiled up at her. "I was coming to have a word with you. Did everything arrive to Everleigh's in one piece?"

Very relaxed, he looked. Very *windblown,* as though somebody had been dragging her fingers through his thick, black hair. "Kind of you to come ask," she said stiffly. "Particularly when you looked so very content downstairs."

He eyed her as he came up the steps. "What's got you so sour?"

She turned and preceded him up to the balcony. "Lemons are sour," she said. "*I* am—uncomfortable, irritated, offended—when I must watch you consort with harlots."

"Harlots?" He caught her arm, turning her back toward him.

His frown annoyed her. "Don't pretend to be confused. That woman with the cheap red hair, who was hanging over you at the card table."

He let go, sweeping a marveling look from her head to her toes. "Jesus, Mary, and Joseph. Looks like we're married, after all. Will you be dragging me off to the priest now for my penance?"

Blood rushed into her face. "Don't mock me."

A grin tugged at his lips, infuriatingly smug. "Deirdre Mahoney's no whore, although I'll grant you that she flirts like one. And aye, I'll admit it—she wasn't a redhead as a child."

She would not be distracted by his charm. "So you admit that you were flirting with her, in plain view."

He lifted a brow. "You'd rather I flirt with her in private?"

She gritted her teeth. "I have no interest in what you do in private. Nor, I imagine, do you care what *I* do behind closed doors. But the contract was very clear: in public, we will accord each other all due—"

"Here, now," he interrupted in a dangerous tone. "I'll be damned if you're doing anything behind closed doors that doesn't involve me."

"I . . ." The shiver that ran through her felt oddly delicious. She crossed her arms tightly. "We're not speaking of me."

"Now we are," he said grimly. "You won't be consorting with other men. We're married in the eyes of the law, and I won't be raising another man's bastard."

She gasped. "How dare you imply—well, and *I* won't be touching a man who consorts with other women!"

"All right, then."

His easy tone disconcerted her. "All right, what?"

"I said, all right, then. We've revised our agreement."

She hesitated, hunting through their last remarks for clarity. "What do you mean? I didn't revise—"

"Binding oral contract." His smile looked wolfish. "Just as good as written. Looks like you're stuck with me until that divorce."

"I didn't . . ." She bit her lip. What had just happened, here? Why did he look so pleased about it?

He gave her no chance to work it out, taking her arm as he started toward her apartment. "I'll be needing a meeting with your brother. Shall I arrange it, or will you?"

She should pull away, but his hand made a pleasant warmth on her elbow. She hadn't realized she was cold until now. "Is this about the buildings on Orton Street?" she asked as she opened her door.

"He mentioned it, did he?" He followed her into the sitting room, releasing her to take a seat by the dying fire. "Well, Pilcher did make an offer for my buildings. The ones on the St. Luke's border."

Confused, she sat down across from him. "Did you accept?"

"Of course not. I don't need his money. But those other properties, which surround my lots. I've sent an offer to the board for them."

She nodded. "Why?"

His brows drew together, two inky slashes. He rose and walked to the sideboard, uncapping a bottle of brandy. "Because I can."

"But . . . those buildings aren't in Whitechapel."

He carried the drink back to his seat. "Brilliant," he said flatly. "Just what I need—another swell telling me to know my place. Only this time, it's my own wife."

"That wasn't what I meant! I simply don't understand. This will only anger Mr. Pilcher."

He lifted his brows. "And do I give a good goddamn whether Pilcher's in a snit?"

"There is no need to curse," she said stiffly. "I simply don't understand how you mean to profit by this purchase. The lots are empty. You're a landlord, not a developer."

His jaw set in a hard line. "I'll profit by teaching that bastard a lesson. Thinks his precious parish is too good for the likes of me? Well, he'll have to change his mind." He took a large swallow of his drink.

"So you *want* to provoke him." What idiocy! "Why not ask a fortune for your buildings? That would hit him where it hurts."

He slammed down his glass. "And the seventy-odd people who live in those buildings?"

"What of them?"

"Pilcher would toss them out like—" He snapped his fingers.

"There are other buildings," she said. "They can find somewhere else to live."

His mouth twisted. "Aye, you *would* think it that easy. Never had to worry for finding a roof in your life, have you? When your brother's got too hot, you came straight to mine."

She recoiled. "*You* invited me. And—what has it do with me, anyway? This is a business matter—"

"Fuck business. They're my people," he said darkly. "And I take care of mine."

She bit her tongue. He glared into his drink. The fire crackled; a log collapsed, throwing sparks.

"Very well," she said. "Go to war with Pilcher, then."

He speared her with a hard look. "It would be war, if Pilcher had his way. The moment I was seen to roll over for him, let him throw my own into the street—why, every other man I've crossed would think I'd gone soft. Wolves at my throat: *that* should mean something to you, even if seventy-six innocents don't."

Why was he speaking to her as though *she* were the enemy? "You're being unfair. I never said that your tenants don't matter—"

"Unfair, sweetheart, is being tossed out on your ear because some silver-suit has a crooked deal with his vestry. But you're right, aye, why bother with the seventy-six who would pay most dearly for it? Poor wretches. Factory workers and dockhands. I doubt their fate would keep you up at night, for all that their hands don't look so different than yours."

She took a sharp breath. "I am no snob—"

His harsh crack of laughter silenced her. "You? That's rich."

"When have I ever said—"

He rose, the drink clenched in his hand. "You say it in a hundred ways, Catherine. You think I didn't see your face, when we walked through that crowd at the B Meeting? You asked about consumption. That sideways look, the lift of your brow—you think I don't speak that language? I learned it as a lad. I learned it in the street, sweeping the path so the likes of *you* could cross without dirtying your skirts."

He'd been a crossing sweep?

"Pennies," he said. He set his glass on the table without making a sound, and somehow the care he took to do so was more unnerving than his anger had been. "Folks crossing the road, they tossed their coins at my feet, because they didn't want to risk touching my hand, lest I carry some sickness. And did I blame them for it? Not once. I knew there was a better world, where babes didn't cough in their cradles, and sickness didn't come regular as church on Sunday. I didn't blame you for asking about the consumption. Why would I? It's a wonder you came with me at all. In your shoes, I would never have done it. Never would have left the West End. For I know what it's like. I saw it as a boy. Peeked into your windows, when the street was empty. Made a fine sight for a boy like me. Chairs for everyone. Piano in the corner. Always a fire in the hearth—real wood, no coal to fume up the place. You ever stayed up all night, Catherine, struggling to breathe? Choking on the smoke that keeps you warm?"

"No," she whispered. "I don't . . . why are you angry with *me*?"

He ran a hand up his face, clawed through his hair. "I'm not," he said on a sigh. "It's not your fault. Nor your brother's, either." He pulled a quick grimace. "Not even Pilcher's. You think I blame your kind for tossing their pennies? No. Why risk what you've got? Why risk that little piece of heaven?"

She shook her head. Whatever heaven he referred to, it did not encompass her experience. A wood fire and sufficient chairs could not make a paradise. She'd grown up taking for granted the roof over her head— she couldn't argue that. But there had never been peace beneath it. The only peace she'd ever found was at Everleigh's.

He misread her silence, perhaps. A curious smile twisted his lips. "And now you've got no words," he said. "That look on your face—it's pity, I expect."

She recoiled. "No," she said. "Not for you."

"Not for me." His tone was sarcastic. "I'm not poor enough, I reckon. Or deserving. It's the fashion, ain't it, to save your pity for the *deserving* poor."

She felt the first lick of temper. She would not be chided by *him*. "If so, then you're right, you certainly don't deserve a trace of sympathy on either account."

"Good," he said coolly. "And don't bother with the people you see in the streets here, either. They don't want your pity, and they don't care that you won't touch them. They don't want your respect, either. What they want is what you've *got*. And that's what scares you the most, ain't it? Because you know you've got more than your fair share. You know it's not right. The Bible tells you so."

"I have earned my keep," she said, very low.

He snorted. "Sure, you lot will say that, won't you? Sit around your fine wood fires at night, come up with reasons for why you deserve what you have. And *that,* Catherine, is what burned me as a lad. I never wanted your respect. I never cared for your pity. But with God as my witness, I wanted you to know that the only thing separating us was luck. When I swept the road, I wasn't scrambling to do it out of respect. I was only doing it for money. *That* was what I wanted the toffs to realize, just for a *second*."

He took a deep breath, then issued a curt laugh as he sat down again. "Of course, then I grew up." He pressed his palms together against his lips for a long moment, his rings glittering in the firelight. "I grew up and realized it ain't so simple. Manners and family and what-not—bloody aristocracy, breeding—the lies are piled thick as hail. And I saw I was never going to prove them wrong. The con had been going on too long. Fighting it would take a greater man than I."

He lowered his hands and fixed her in a cold, steady gaze. "So I decided not to play that game. I made a game of my own instead. And I decided no man was going to beat me at it. Pilcher wants to try? Good luck to him. He's not the first. And he sure as hell won't win." He paused. "So. Your brother says he won't help me? Then I'll find another way. A way to make him, maybe. You understand?"

Her hands, knotted together at her waist, were trembling. She tightened them, willing them to steady.

He noticed. His gaze dropped to her lap, and his expression gentled. He reached out, laid his palm over her knuckles. "Catherine," he said. "You're one of mine now, too. So there's no call to shake."

"I'm not shaking," she lied.

He studied her a long, silent moment. Then he eased out of the chair, kneeling with lithe grace in front of her chair. "You're safe here," he said. His thumb stroked lightly over her knuckles. "You believe that?"

"Yes." She felt no hesitation in saying so. After his heated, radical speech, that seemed a proper wonder. But she did not shake for fear.

His pale eyes were steady and unfathomably beautiful. He lifted her hands, pressing his lips softly against them. Perhaps he felt her breath catch, for as he glanced up, the taut line of his mouth eased. He slipped his hand through the heavy mass of her chignon. "No dye for this color," he said huskily.

"No," she whispered.

Very slowly, he pulled her toward him. Their lips met. The kiss was slow, impossibly strange—him kneeling before her, her heart still thudding from shock. Her eyes drifted shut. His mouth was soft, almost tender. She felt herself sag, tension melting from her back as he nuzzled her.

At last, she made herself avert her face. "What poor taste you have," she said very softly. "To kiss one of the lot whom you damned as unchristian."

His laugh was soundless, a soft puff of air. "Maybe I think there's hope for you."

She looked at him. "Or maybe you're the hypocrite. *You're* the snob."

A curious look came over his face. "You think so?"

"Yes. Or a coward. I'm not sure which."

He sat back from her, his expression impenetrable. "Now, there's something I've never been called."

"I'm sure no one dared to say it. That doesn't make it untrue."

He made a low, sharp noise that probably wanted to sound like amusement. "You care to explain yourself?"

"Certainly. You're glad to talk of the injustices you see. But rather than doing anything about them, you use them to justify your own abuses of the law—your own enrichment. What would you call that? Certainly not courage."

His eyes narrowed. Now, at last, she saw true temper in his face. He shoved to his feet. "Politics is for those who think they can make a difference for strangers. I never cared about anything but mine."

"That's not true," she said steadily. "Just look what you did for Tulip Patrick, and all those students—"

"For Whitechapel," he spat. "Whitechapel is mine."

"Very well. But you *choose* to sell yourself short. Your ambitions, your abilities."

"No. I simply confine them to what matters."

"I don't believe you," she said with a shrug. "I think you're afraid."

He offered her a disbelieving smile. "Is that right?"

She ignored the scorn in his voice. "You're afraid to aim higher. You call it a rich man's game, but that's only an excuse. You're afraid to try—and fail. And I think you *did* want the passersby to look you in the eye, as a boy. Otherwise, why would you be so angry at me now?"

He stared at her. "That's a fine question. Maybe I'm a fool, after all. Maybe I imagined that marrying you meant something. That we could treat each other like humans, for all that I swept your dad's streets as a boy."

She clambered to her feet. "Indeed? You mean that you could see me as more than some spoiled doll from the West End? Tell me. How many of my letters did you ignore before you brought me here? Would you have ever bothered to speak to me, if you thought I couldn't help you save those precious buildings?"

"Two buildings," he said softly. "If that's all you'll profit me, you're the poorest gamble I ever took."

"What . . ." She pushed out a sharp laugh. "Come now. Am I— Surely you're not suggesting you wanted something else all along. From me? I won't believe it."

His smile was brief and dark. "Why not? You think a man can't covet what he's told he doesn't deserve? A boy can look into a window and covet a wood fire. You think a man can't look into your auction rooms and covet a woman?"

Stunned, she fumbled for words. "I . . . You never met me. We barely spoke—"

"I watched you," he said quietly. "From the moment

Lily first showed up on your doorstep. I always had my eye on you."

She crossed her arms against a strange feeling, tremulous and unbalancing. "You . . . worried for her, I suppose."

"I watched *you*."

"No." She shook her head, panic bolting through her. She didn't want to hear such things. This was business! This arrangement had not been borne of anything to do with feeling, with curiosity, with . . . desire . . .

But it did. His face showed her so. He didn't look pleased to have made his admission. His expression was stark, the look of a man beholding a fatal mistake.

And suddenly she could not bear to be his mistake. "Why did you watch me?" she whispered. And how foolish was she, to feel this momentary, fragile hope? She'd caught a hundred men gawping at her. Her face . . . *my beauty,* her father had called her. *You have your mother's face.* But she'd always wished to be so much more than that—not only to her father but also, perhaps, to someone else . . .

"I can't say." He spoke in a low, rough voice. "Maybe because I'd never seen a woman like you. Out of place in that world. *Owning* it, regardless. Maybe I admired that. Or maybe you simply looked like the next rung on the ladder. Or it was even simpler—and you're right; I wanted what I'd never had as a boy. For a woman like you—for *you,* Catherine—to look at me, and see . . . not a crook. Not a gutter rat raised high. But a man." He stepped toward her. "A man who could do more for you than that bloody auction house ever could. Simple, sure. Simple as what we shared in a bed together. Maybe that's what I wanted all along."

He called that simple? "I'm . . . I can't give that to you. I've told you, I'm not fit, that way."

A shadow crossed his face, tightened his mouth, and it stung her like the lash of a whip. She had warned him of this. How *dare* he look disappointed in her! "Bollocks," he said flatly. "What does that mean?"

"That auction house may seem like nothing to you, but it's all I ever wanted—"

He gripped her cheek. "Now you're lying," he said softly, "and here I thought we were being so honest. I saw you want it. I *heard* you want it, the other night. If you're afraid, then say so. But don't you bloody lie to me."

She lifted her chin. He would not bully her. "It has nothing to do with fear—or our stations, either." As cynicism sharpened his mouth, she cast caution to the wind and spoke in a rush. "It's me. I would disappoint you." And she could not bear that thought. She, Catherine Everleigh, did not fail. She did nothing by half measures. She would not allow herself to aim for what she could never hope to do well.

"What nonsense is that?" When she shook her head, he turned her face back toward him. "Look at me," he said. "How are you unfit? Who put that idea into your head? Your goddamned brother?"

"He has nothing to do with it," she said bitterly. "Some things one knows from a young age. My mother . . ." So unhappy with her life. Squandering her energies on gossip and backbiting, silly feuds among her friends. Taking to her bed at any sign of Papa's wrath. Quarreling, always quarreling with him. She had warned Catherine that a woman's lot was to be dependent on the pleasure of a man. *Marriage, Catherine, is the most perilous risk a woman ever takes. Take care whom you choose. Make sure you can keep him happy.*

But the only man whom Catherine had known how to keep happy was her father—for she excelled at her work. And what other man would be content with that?

"I don't want that life," she said fiercely. "I don't want to be . . . beholden . . . to an ideal I can't achieve. And yes, I enjoy your touch. I *want* it. I will admit that. I . . . think of you, at night, and too often during the day, and I . . . But it means nothing! You said it yourself, once—it happens on street corners!"

"Like hell this does," he growled, and caught her by the waist.

Had she resisted, he would have let go. But as Nick drew her toward him, something changed. Her face, so taut from her inward struggle, suddenly relaxed. She closed her eyes and took a deep, audible breath, then threw her arms around him, like a child leaping from the edge of a high wall, aiming for the unknown.

He held her tight, gripped her waist as she buried her face against his neck. Some powerful emotion rocked through him, a ferocious need leavened by deep relief. Even as a boy, he had never begged but once. He'd swept streets, blacked boots, ducked the occasional swing of a ganger's fist at the docks—but begging, no. There, he'd drawn the line. And had Catherine pushed him away just now, he might never have reached for her again. For it had come to that, hadn't it? He wouldn't take what she didn't give freely, and by God, he wouldn't beg.

But she had come to him. *Hallelujah.* She stood

pressed against him, her breath warming his throat in unsteady puffs, some lingering effect of the fears that wracked her.

Nick didn't hope to understand those fears. Didn't expect he could reason them away for her, either. That was her battle. But he could sure as hell give her a reason to fight.

He kissed the crown of her hair, soft and silken. The kiss seemed to jar her from her trance. Her hands scrabbled on his waist, tightening as though to keep him against her. He swallowed a ragged laugh. As though, even with a gun at his head, he would step away. Given practice, she'd come to understand that.

He meant to give her a great deal of practice now.

He smoothed a path down her arms, pulling her hands free of their grip on him, lacing his fingers through hers. He eased down to kiss her neck. Her pulse was still drumming. She turned her face away, either from shyness or to give him a better angle.

He tracked his mouth slowly down her throat, right to the edge of her gown, high-necked, unadorned blue wool. Dozens of buttons fastened it closed; he had noticed them as he'd followed her up the stairs earlier.

God help her if she liked the dress. He reached into his pocket and pulled out his knife. Felt her tense as she saw it.

"Hold still," he said.

She did better. She turned for him, bowing her head as she presented her back.

Wealth had given him a thousand pleasures he'd never anticipated. But he'd never known any sweeter than this: to cut Catherine free of her clothing, without regard for the cost.

To feel her trust, her unflinching faith, as she held still beneath his knife.

The dress split and fell away easily enough. The corset laces were no trick to cut. But as he threw it across the room, the sight of her underlinens struck a flint deep in his belly, an impatience that made his hand shake. He cast down the knife and used his hands on the rest. The way of a savage, no doubt. He felt so. *Desire* was too pretty a word. She'd held herself away too long. His entire life, she'd been held away. But she was here, now.

Naked, before him.

She turned back, the shredded layers mounded at her feet, God's own glory emerging from the ruins of what had separated them. Straight-spined, every inch of her skin gilded by the candlelight. The slope of her shoulders, like water flowing. Her waist dipping, then swelling into her full hips, like a crescendo of song. He laid his palm along that curve, touched her bare skin, and felt the shock of rightness sing through his bones.

How could she not know? How could she doubt, even for a moment? He looked up into her face for the answer. She was watching him. Not blushing. Not bashful, nor defiant, either. Her eyes were wide and awake to him, her lips trembling at the edge of a smile.

They looked at each other in the silence. Elsewhere, penetrating dimly through the walls, were the sounds of the ordinary world—muffled laughter, gleeful cries from the gaming floor, the rattle of dishes, mundane routine. Here, inside her rooms, as she stood naked before him, an enchanted silence enclosed them, profound and deep, like the hush in a church during prayer.

He trailed his hand up her body, skating over the

weight of her breast, the delicate winged line of her collarbone, the graceful column of her neck.

He touched her face very gently. "How can you
know what you might be? Without trying, how can you
know?"

A sheen filled her eyes. "I . . . suppose I can't." And
then she stepped forward and kissed him.

His eyes closed. He'd been no virgin when he'd taken
her to his bed. But it came to him now, as he kissed
her back—as her arms wrapped around him like vines,
and she moaned and tilted her head, to encourage him
to go deeper—that he'd been innocent all the same. A
blessed kind of innocence: he'd not known a kiss could
take him like a hard blow to his chest. All the breath
went from him as he kissed her. All his ambitions, they
seemed to spiral through him, to concentrate into one
aim: to make her never let go. For she tasted . . . like all
the money in the city. Walls that reached to the heavens.
A view that spanned the world.

He picked her up, swung her into his arms, and carried her into the bedroom. Laid her on the bed and
stood another moment to look at her, sprawled across
the sheets like Christmas morning. Here was the view.
He would sear it into his brain, each detail: the sunlight
spill of her unraveling braid; the gentle curves of her
bent legs; the heavy sway of her breasts; the shadow between her thighs, calling to him, calling . . .

She started to sit up. He put one knee on the mattress, holding her down by the shoulder. "Let me look,"
he said.

"Look while you undress," she said softly.

A faint sound escaped him. Maybe the beginning of
a laugh, for he meant to encourage such brazenness. But

the sound broke apart as she reached for his shirt, fumbling with the first button.

"No." He had no patience for this, either. He stood, quickly shedding his own layers. Dropping them without regard, so he could join her on that bed.

She opened her arms for him. He wanted to go slow. Some distant corner of his mind, canny and conspiring, urged him to take care. To take her so thoroughly, leave her so limp and satisfied, that she would never again question that she belonged beneath him, with nothing to keep them apart.

But for once in his life, his discipline failed him. When her hands—cool, small, rough—touched his bare chest, something snapped.

He fell on her mouth. Drank her in as he swept her body with long, firm strokes. Greedy, he felt greedy; panicked in the old way, the desperation of a boy who didn't know when the next feast would come. If it would ever come again. He'd grown up with want, need, as his main companion. He felt it now, deep in his gut, as he broke from her mouth to suckle her breast. *Take all you can, now. For you may never have this again.*

She seemed to catch his mood. She reached down his body, her palm sliding over his chest, his belly. He caught her hand before she could find his cock; he had no faith in his restraint; he refused to spill himself before he'd been inside her. He placed her hand beside her head, holding it firmly there, and then felt her teeth: she had turned her head, caught hold of his thumb. He groaned as she sucked his finger into her mouth; their eyes met, hers heavy lidded, frank and unashamed.

He stared at her, riveted. Here, this, her face now—that look would be his aim, God willing, every night henceforth.

Until five years is up.

He pushed the thought away too late; it made him snarl. He pulled his hand free, stroking her nipple as he slid down her body. Took hold of her thighs and pushed them open. Blond curls, soft to the touch; he brushed them with his hand and felt her hips shudder.

He lowered his head, kissing the plumpness of her inner thigh. She smelled like the ocean; she whimpered once as he splayed her wider, ignoring the token resistance of her thighs.

Here, the other beating heart of her. He laid his tongue against her, and felt her jerk. Slid his hands up her belly, the gently rounded satin-soft flesh, this miraculous work of God that was her womanly flesh, and with a choked noise, she subsided, her thighs relaxing for him.

It was a gift. He felt, for the briefest moment, overwhelmed by it—the feel of her, the smell, the taste of the heart of her, the surrender, laying herself open for him, vulnerable and trusting.

And then he licked into her, and the sound she made, the way her thighs clutched around him, made him groan deep in his throat. He tongued her again and again, listening hard, waiting for the stroke that made her body jerk most sharply—*there,* that was what she wanted.

He gave it to her, ignoring the clutch of her hands in his hair, the broken murmur she made. It wasn't too much. He'd see to that. He'd see her through it, and when she was broken, when she could not shudder again, he would fit himself into her softness, hard as a bloody rock he would sink himself into her so deeply that she'd cry out anew—

She gasped and keened, her hips shuddering beneath his. He felt through her folds, pushed a finger inside her as he blew on her, a violent satisfaction at the feel of her contractions. He could give her that. He would give it to her again.

He rose over her, aching and swollen, sucking in his breath as the head of his cock brushed her slippery quim. She was flushed, frantic, as she scattered kisses over his face. "Please," she whispered.

He pressed into her, filled her to the hilt. She pushed her tongue into his mouth, gripped him against her as he began to move. It was ancient. It felt ancient, with her. It felt like something begun in a dream, long ago, and resumed now by the force of inevitable fate, that he should strain now against the fierceness of his own need, that he should kiss her deeply, and stroke her cheek, and focus on the shape of her ear beneath his hand, the tender flex of her lobe beneath his thumb, as he fought against his own climax. He rotated his hips, and she gasped. She liked it. He did it again, and she clutched onto his shoulders, nails digging hard.

A laugh ghosted from him, hoarse soundless triumphant delight. He reached between them, finding her spot as he twisted his hips again.

"Oh—" She gaped up at him, then her lashes fluttered shut as she arched to meet him. "Oh . . . I think . . ."

Not yet. He slammed his palm into the headboard, sharp carved edge digging into his skin, focusing on that, on giving her what she needed, stroking her steadily, deeply. God but she was the most beautiful sight on this earth as she writhed beneath him, struggling to find it—

"Ah . . ." The breath burst from her as he felt her

clutching, deep inside, around him. And as simply as that—he was done for.

Ripping free of her then was the hardest, the sweetest bloody punishment he'd ever taken. With one hard stroke of his hand, he brought himself to completion. Then he turned back to kiss her.

Her lips felt lazy on his. Her hand brushed over his face, her thumb stroking his cheekbone. For a long minute they lay together. And then, with a rueful smile, he rose to find his discarded shirt.

When he'd cleaned himself off, he turned back to her—and saw the remoteness that had gathered in her face like a shadow as she watched him.

He took a hard breath, preparing himself for what came next—her withdrawal. A resumption of the quarrel.

But when she spoke, she sounded thoughtful. "I know how you must do it."

He didn't follow. "Do what?"

"How to get those lands from Pilcher." She sat up, her hair a shimmering fall down her back. "My brother means to argue that your bid came too late. You must go before the board, insist that the tender period was not adequately advertised. That the board should put the lots to public auction, in order to ensure the process is fair. Make an argument about the politics of it. How the board will made to appear in the press, if they deny you the chance to bid."

He sat down on the edge of the bed, a bit rattled by how quickly she had moved on to business. "That gives him a chance to outbid me," he said slowly.

"He may try, but we won't allow it." She swallowed, then reached out and laid her hand over his.

Such a small thing, such an ordinary sight, to seem so . . . important. When he looked up, he caught her own gaze lifting from the same spot. "If you truly want those lands," she said, "we'll run a ring. We'll ensure nobody can outbid you."

He turned his hand in hers, threading their fingers together. "A ring." But there was a more surprising word yet, in that sentence she'd just spoken. "*We.*"

"Yes," she said softly. "I'll show you how. I'll help. But first, you must persuade the board to hold the auction."

He smiled. But she did not smile back. Her expression looked very sober now. Very pale.

Ah. It might have been a victory, this offer of aid. But he sensed suddenly that it was the opposite. A woman so fierce—unique in all his experience—in her commitment to honorable business, would not make this offer lightly.

But she would do it for him. Her gift, to make up for everything she felt she lacked the ability to give.

He considered her. Lovely, proud, stubborn, infuriatingly deluded woman. He was too much the businessman to turn down the opportunity she offered. But he was also a crook. He knew how to steal what wasn't on offer. He wouldn't lose those lands. But between those lots and her, he knew the better investment. The one more likely to yield a lifetime of riches.

"All right," he said. "Whatever it takes, I mean to do it."

She gave him a relieved smile. He smiled back at her, no effort required.

Her naïveté was his best advantage. *You're one of my own,* he'd told her. And he didn't let go of what was his.

CHAPTER THIRTEEN

*N*ick squinted at the page. "In closing, then, I tender my petition—" He broke off, irritated as somebody in the far corner, old Burke maybe, yowled for another pint. "I can't do this here. Too many distractions."

Catherine sat in front of him, her own pint of ale untouched, looking serenely oblivious to the squawking, boozy men at the tables around her. "Neddie's is the perfect setting in which to practice. If you can remain unshaken by all the noise here, you can certainly—"

"That boardroom won't be full of men three sheets to the wind, will it?"

"Of course not. Instead your audience will be full of quarrelsome *swells* who think you're wasting their time."

He smiled. "Swells, is it?"

"That is the word you use, I believe." He saw her catch herself smiling at him; she sat straighter and fixed a serious look on her face, every inch the schoolmistress now. "Perhaps we should take you to Speakers' Corner. Nothing like the threat of a shower of rotten fruit to focus one's mind."

"God forbid." He sat down, sheepishly aware of the disappointed hoots that went up.

"Was just getting good!" called Nate Hooley.

"Couldn't understand the half of it, but sounded very fancy," Nate's cousin Kip Hooley agreed.

"Bugger yourself," Nick muttered as the arses toasted each other and cackled.

"Mr. O'Shea," his wife said coolly. "Such language—"

"One day you'll call me Nick."

"One day I might call you Beelzebub. What of it? The Municipal Board of Works does not allow ladies into its meetings. Take heart, then: I won't be there to harass you."

"Or to prompt me," he muttered. He looked over the speech, three pages written in her finely flowing script. It might as well have been gibberish, though her hand was clear. "I'll need to memorize this."

"You don't have time for that."

She didn't understand. He took a breath to school his frustration, but the words still came out sharp: "Don't got a choice, do I? If I don't mean to make an ass of myself—"

Her hand closed on his, startling him. When he looked up into her face, he realized that she'd seen more than he intended to show. Sympathy softened her features.

"The marriage contract," she said. "Twenty-eight pages. You seemed to know it well enough."

"Aye." His pulse was drumming, a sick feeling in his stomach. Curious. He wasn't ashamed of anything. Had vowed as a boy to carry his head high, and until now, he'd always succeeded. "I don't sign a contract without knowing what's in it."

"Someone read it to you?"

No judgment in her voice. Only that steady, unwavering pressure of her grip around his hand.

He loosed a breath. The admission came out easier than he'd feared. "Had Callan read most of it. Otherwise it would have taken me days."

She nodded. "Then reading this speech will not work," she said brusquely. "We must find another way." She withdrew her hand, but it didn't feel like a rejection; he knew her well enough now to understand that frown on her face betokened the spinning of wheels in her brain.

She turned her frown on the various oglers around them. "Have you nothing better to do?" she said in a raised voice. "Talk among yourselves." And then, as a hubbub of chatter hastily broke out, she glanced back to him, her frown deepening. "What are *you* laughing at?"

"You," he said. "Queen o' Neddie's. Tell 'em to doff their hats and take their boots off the benches, while you're at it. Neddie'll thank you; he's been trying for years."

She folded her lips together, her typical trick for hiding a smile. But her eyes gave her away, turning into half-moons over the crests of her rosy cheeks. She had more laughter in her than she knew how to manage. The real sin was that she'd been taught to trammel it. And wasn't it a wonder, he thought, that they could sit across the table from one another, easy and friendly as you please, as though he hadn't had her naked and moaning beneath him just this morning, with plans to do so again tonight?

For she wasn't a coward. Once she admitted her desires, she didn't disown them—not even when he'd shown up with the breakfast tray and found her only in her shift.

She'd dropped her robe as she'd stood to receive him. "As long as we're clear," she'd said unsteadily, "that it doesn't mean . . . anything more."

Tonight seemed awfully far away. Why wait? He folded the speech and slipped it into his jacket. "Let's go back to Diamonds," he said. "Clear our . . . heads."

Her eyes narrowed; she averted her face a fraction of an inch, the better to give him one of those skeptical, sidelong glances. But the rising color on her face showed that she'd followed his thoughts well enough. "Not just yet. You don't require any practice at *that*."

He grinned, delighted. "Nice to have it confirmed," he said. "But if you don't mean to drink, or to take these hooligans to task, then—"

"That's it!" She slapped the table. "Why, we've gone about this all wrong. I'm not the one whom these hooligans will listen to. But you've ages of experience in bringing them to heel. Forget a scripted speech; you don't need one. You shall fly impromptu, relying on the powers of your oratory."

"The powers of . . . No," he said flatly. "I need a script. I'm not going into that meeting with nothing."

"But you won't," she said. "Your wit, the talents of your brain, are all you require. You've a magnificent way with words, Mr. O'Shea. You will simply speak to the board as though they're the men here at Neddie's, in need of a lesson in fairness and decency."

He snorted. "Look around you. You think I've ever lectured these lads on decency?"

As she took a survey of the shabby, noisome groups around them, her smile briefly faltered. But it brightened again as she met his eyes, and God save him, he wasn't cold enough to resist it, all that confidence and glee directed solely at him. "You'll prove it for me," she said. "Stand, and discourse to them on the need to doff their hats and remove their boots from the table."

"I will not."

"Do it!" She rose, coming to his side of the table to tug on his arm, so after a second, he was forced to get to his feet, lest the crowd get a fine show for free.

But once standing, he realized that the crowd had already punched its tickets anyway. For the noise dimmed immediately, and every eye in the place fixed on him.

"Go ahead," she urged him quietly. "You've the gift of—of blarney, sir. Use it! Or your Irish forebears will no doubt disown you from their graves."

He cut her a wry look. "And you've the English gift for scheming."

With a serene smile, she retook her seat—leaving him alone, beneath the press of a hundred expectant eyes.

He took a deep breath, feeling foolish. What did it matter if Neddie's benches got a heel-scuffing? But she was watching him expectantly now, her pointed little chin cupped in one hand, her eyes bright and wide.

Very well. He'd ordered men to far more dangerous pursuits than this.

"Lads," he began—then paused at her slight frown. "Gentlemen," he amended, and a chorus of hoots went up from the far corner.

"Gen'lman, are we? Y'hear that, boys?"

He paused, scowling.

"Don't permit that," Catherine whispered. "Pilcher's men will try to mock you, too."

He fixed his glare on the Hooleys, who knew on

which side their bread was buttered. They quieted abruptly.

Aye, he'd given speeches before, and they'd concerned uglier things by far. He'd persuaded men to risk their throats for him, fighting by his side against the McGowans after that crew had slain Lily's dad. And he'd put the fear of God into men with flapping lips—men who would go to their graves now without breathing a single word of what he'd asked of them.

Beside that, boots and land parcels were small fry.

"Gentlemen," he said, "it has come to my attention that we live in grim times. This fine, fair city, which you'll know from the newspapers has got more wealth than any other place in the world—which you'll have seen, with your own two eyes, has got more swells, more toffs, more nobs living in high-flying style than any kingdom from the books of history—in these same streets, where nabobs and silver suits rent an inch of space to your loved ones for half their weekly pay, people are dying for want. They're dying for want of bread. They're dying for want of space and air. Dying for a drop of milk to give to an infant who cries for his mother's breast, when she perished five days ago on the factory floor."

Silence now. From the corner of his eye, he could see Catherine's pallor. Aye, he'd take her on a few twists before he got to the straightaway.

"You step outside this pub," he said, "you walk south toward Clerkenwell. You walk farther, till Southwark. Or you walk west, to St. Giles. And what do you see? Darkness, gen'lmen. Beggars dead in the lane. Rubbish and foulness and water too brackish to drink—but they drink it, don't they?"

"Poor souls," someone muttered, to a muted round of agreement.

"They drink it 'cause they've got no choice," Nick said fiercely. "'Cause the water pipes don't work. A dying man, dying of thirst, he lifts that pump and what comes out but flakes of rust. While in Mayfair, they're too good for water. It's all champagne and fancy French wines, and the water collects in their bathtubs larger than six men around."

Catherine shifted uneasily. He caught a whisper from her: "Don't start a revolution, please."

He bit his cheek and pressed onward. "Aye, lads, there's darkness all around. Misery and suffering. Grievous injustice, children born only to pass in their cradles. Thirst and hunger, endless want. Dying like animals—like the animals the toffs call us, as they walk down gold-paved lanes."

Scowls, angry grumbles. George Flaherty wiped his eyes.

"But not here," Nick said. "Not here in Whitechapel. Not here."

"Not here," someone called.

Nick lifted his voice. "Not here in Whitechapel!"

"Not bloody here," came another voice.

"Here in Whitechapel," Nick thundered, "we look after our own!"

Somebody slammed a table. Stamping of boots, a thunderous wave of applause. Nick paused to let it draw out. In such a world as this, men looked for reasons to celebrate.

When the applause began to fade, Nick continued. "Here," he said in a speaking voice, "here the streets are swept clean. Here, when the water stops running, we raise our shouts, and neighbors come running with a pitcher to spare! Here, when our children clutch their stomachs and call for bread, we tell them, 'Get to school, and find out how many rolls you can eat!' Here, when women fall in the street, men stop to help."

"Praise God."

"Damned right."

"And here," he said, his voice falling to a hush, "when we come to Neddie's after a hard day of work, we know we've *earned* the right to sit back, to let the sweat of honest labor cool, to lift our pints and look our fellow men in the eye—for we ain't animals, no matter what they say!"

"Fuck them!"

"Fuck the lot of them!"

"And as we ain't animals," Nick shouted, "as we know what decency is, as we understand it far better than any of them ever will, so I ask you, lads—why the bloody hell are you all still wearing your hats?"

In the sudden silence, he could hear Catherine's slow, shaking breath.

"No, you heard me right," he said to George Flaherty, who was scratching his ear and looking puzzled. "We've got a precious place of peace and decency here, lads. So take your goddamned boots off the benches and put your hats aside. Do it!"

Across the room, hands slowly lifted to heads. Boots hesitantly lifted from benches, hitting the floorboards with dull thuds.

"'Cause we didn't come by this decency by accident," Nick said. "And you don't get respect for free. So prize what you've got here, lads. Nod to your neighbor, and hold his eye like the proud man you are. Don't show him less respect than you'd show a bloody toff. When you come into Neddie's to drink with your neighbors—sit straight, and take off your goddamned hats."

That did it. All the hats came flying off now. Nick cast another narrow look around the room, nodded to a few men here and there, before retaking his seat.

"Well," said his wife, looking very pale indeed. "That was . . . a bit too much foul language, but . . ."

Maybe he'd have made a fine schoolboy after all. His bloody heart was in his goddamned throat as he waited for the conclusion of her judgment.

"All the same, it was very effective." She smiled at him, and his spirit burst loose, soared straight up into the rafters. "I almost pity the Board of Works."

Catherine snorted as she glanced down the page. " 'Straw colored'? Why not call it hay colored? Indeed, why not praise the chest's alfalfa-like sheen?"

Silence from the group ranged before her. Catherine sighed. The sun had been pouring through the office windows when she had arrived to review the catalog for O'Shea's treasures. But the scarlet light of sunset now spilled through the long window that overlooked the street, and her copywriters—two of them so young as to barely sport whiskers—slumped in a variety of glum postures behind their desks, their pens abandoned, their ink-stained hands tucked sheepishly into their pockets.

"Gentlemen," she said more gently as she laid the draft onto a nearby desk. "I don't require poetry. But if *you* were looking to acquire a chest of drawers, would these descriptions light a fire in your pockets? There is no need to abuse your thesauruses. 'Golden' and 'amber' will serve nicely, even if they appear twice on the same page."

A rustle of movement: the men's shoulders abruptly straightened; chins lifted and spines stiffened. For a moment, Catherine fancied that she had inspired them. Then the sound of a cleared throat drew her attention toward the door.

The redheaded hostess—Miss Ames—blushed prettily at finding herself the center of so much masculine attention. "Miss Everleigh," she said in a soft, apologetic voice. "Your brother requires a word with you."

Catherine took a careful breath. O'Shea had intended to interrupt the board meeting this afternoon. No doubt Peter had come straight from Berkeley House—fuming, she hoped, over the results. But he might as easily have come to gloat.

"Very well," she said, and reached for her wrap. "Gentlemen, I will return tomorrow. I hope to see all *agricultural* similes stripped from this text."

She stepped out into the hallway, but Miss Ames stopped her from walking onward.

"You should know," the hostess said tentatively, before trailing off, her color deepening.

Nobody blushed as violently as a redhead. But Catherine had never seen Miss Ames lose her composure quite so vividly. She frowned. "What is it? Go on."

Miss Ames ducked her head. "Miss, I know you don't appreciate us to speculate on what doesn't concern us. But . . ." She looked up, hooking a curl away from her elfin face. "Lilah, she asked me to watch after you while she was gone—"

"Did she?" Catherine's first instinct was to bridle. Before her promotion to assistant, Lilah had worked as a

hostess—a position that had left Catherine very skeptical, at first, of her capacity to make herself useful in any
meaningful regard.

But Lilah had proved her wholly wrong. Mindful
suddenly of the prejudice that had blinded her for so
long, Catherine softened her tone.

"Speak frankly, Miss Ames. What troubles you?"

"Your brother isn't waiting in his office alone," Miss
Ames said in a low, rapid voice. "And the two men with
him—they don't look like clients to me."

Catherine studied her for a moment. Among the
hostesses, Lavender Ames stood out for her elegant composure. Granted, she took every opportunity to accept
money from advertisers; her face was plastered across any
number of cheap advertisements for soap and whatnot.
But in her demeanor with the clients, she displayed a
tasteful reserve that quite contrasted with the other girls'
silly flirtations and chatter. Catherine suspected she
came from a different sort of background than the other
girls; that her position here represented a fall, rather
than a rise. Moreover, she was sharp, often making savvy
suggestions about where a collector's interests might
be steered—and whether or not a client's claims about
provenance might be trusted.

"Miss Ames," she said, "tell me plainly. What is your
concern?"

"It . . . perhaps I should accompany you into the office, miss."

Alarm goaded Catherine to a quick calculation. She
walked to the broad window and glanced out at the
street.

Several coaches loitered on the curb. One stood out:
unmarked, peculiarly boxy. Windowless.

"That's the one they came in," Miss Ames said, touching her finger to the glass to indicate the windowless vehicle.

Catherine took a deep breath. This panic was baseless, of course. But Miss Ames had never carried such concerns to her before. She frowned down at the coach. There were three exits from this building. It grated unbearably to slip away like a thief from her own building on some half-formulated suspicion, but perhaps . . .

Miss Ames caught her arm, gripping very tightly. "Don't turn around," she whispered. "But they've just come into the hall. They're walking toward us."

Catherine laid her hand over the woman's. "Listen," she said very quietly. "If something seems odd to you— send word to Mr. O'Shea at the House of Diamonds in Whitechapel."

Miss Ames knew the name. She gave Catherine a slack-jawed, marveling look. But she nodded once, to show she understood.

Catherine wheeled. Her brother was indeed coming down the hall, flanked by two men of such burly proportions that they made Peter appear a child.

She understood, in one glance, Miss Ames's concern. The men wore sober gray suits of identical cuts and fabric. They had bowler hats tucked beneath their arms.

They came to a stop. The stairwell, and her path to the exits, lay beyond them.

"Catherine," her brother called. "There you are. Come, speak with me a moment. I have a most interesting proposition for you."

Catherine squared her shoulders and walked forward. "I am busy," she said, acutely aware of Miss Ames behind her, stepping into the office to remove herself from the men's notice. "The catalog for the December auction—"

"It's urgent," Peter said. He came forward, smiling blandly, but the grip he took on her arm was firm enough to give her cause to pull away.

He did not let her. His grip tightened. "Come to my office," he said. "We'll walk together."

She gave a sharp yank. "Let go of me."

"It's urgent," he said mildly. "These gentlemen, you see—"

She did see. She saw the impersonal way they compassed Peter's grip on her, and the lack of surprise, the absence of discomfort, which any client would surely evince, at the sight of the proprietors wrestling each other in the hall.

That was all she needed. She threw her weight into Peter, causing him to stumble and let go. She whirled for the copywriters' office, desperate to reach the safety of onlookers—

And a new grip caught her, a brutal arm around her waist, while a hand shoved a rag against her nose, a sickly sweet odor invading her nostrils.

She choked in a breath, and the world began to soften at the edges, dimming . . .

Her last glimpse was the wide eyes of Lavender Ames as the girl peered out in horror at her.

CHAPTER FOURTEEN

*H*er tongue felt like cotton. Parched. Swallowing hurt.

Dim sounds nattered at the edge of her awareness. She lay in darkness, spinning, odd visions flashing through her brain. The jolting noise of a carriage on unpaved road. Some liquid, sharp and noxious, forced down her throat, choking her.

Fear. Why had she been afraid? What had the dream concerned? She couldn't recall.

Gradually, the murmuring sounds clarified into voices. That was her brother, speaking: "The delusions worsened recently. She accused me of trying to break into her bedroom. I say *break,* for she had three dead bolts installed, quite without my knowledge."

"Paranoia," a stranger said in concerned tones.

"I suppose so, yes. She claimed that I was conspiring with one of my business partners—I'm not sure what reason she invented for it. But she felt convinced that I would force her to marry him."

It came to her that she should be alarmed. That this

was no dream; that she was lying, trapped in her body, unable to open her eyes. Her limbs did not respond. She could feel them like dead weights, pinning her down.

"A common brand of fantasy," said the other voice. "Particularly in unmarried women of an advanced age."

"Perhaps. But it makes no sense. Were I such a villain, I would never wish her to marry! She has no rights over the company, you see, as long as she remains a spinster."

"Delusions of this kind rarely make sense. Hysteria has its own logics, which we can only begin to glimpse."

Memory sharpened, slicing cleanly out of the murk of her brain: Peter striding down the hall. Ruffians flanking him. A cloth at her face, some drug . . .

Her heart began to hammer. She managed to open her eyes a crack—was blinded by light before they fell shut again.

"I did not want to write to you," Peter said quietly. "I thought I could manage her on my own. But then she fled the house. I've no idea where she's living, now. She refuses to tell me. I'm concerned for her safety. She is a danger to herself."

"Your concern does you justice, sir. Now, you mentioned in your letter that her health has been failing?"

"Yes, that was the most recent development. These fainting fits come on without warning. Why, she passed out in public, recently—at one of our auctions, no less. Quite a scene, as you can imagine."

"I'm not surprised it should have happened in the workplace. The feminine temperament is not suited to such exertions."

"So I told her. But it seemed a breaking point. She has gone beyond reason now. Imagine this: she has invented a husband for herself."

"A husband? Not your business associate, I take it?"

She wrenched open her eyes. The ceiling above her was plastered smooth, painted a sunny yellow.

Oh, God. This was not Everleigh's. This was not the house in Henton Court, either.

That carriage ride had been no dream. Where was she?

"No, no," Peter was saying. "Far wilder than that. Some common criminal, whose name she glimpsed once in a newspaper, no doubt. Some East End thug. She swears she is married to him. Can you credit it?"

The other man chuckled. "Very inventive."

"Of course, if I thought marriage would cure her, I would gladly try to arrange a suitable match, but in her current state . . ."

"Oh no, Mr. Everleigh. From everything you've told me, she has gone well beyond such simple cures. For that matter, I doubt any magistrate would recognize the legality of such a union. A woman must be of sound mind, you know, to properly consent to wed."

Horror burned away the vestigial paralysis of the drug. She managed to bend her fingers. To turn her head.

She lay on a cot in a small, bare-walled room. A single stool. A sturdy writing desk. A window that showed a darkening sky, stars already emerging.

Those stars shone too clearly to overlook the bright city of London.

She tried to push to her feet. Fell back heavily, with a gasp she swallowed lest the men overhear. They must be standing just outside the door, which was ajar. "I had wondered as much," Peter was saying. "So—if she were to be married, the union would not stand? Due to her . . . mental instability?"

Everything became clear to her in one single, ice-cold moment. He had brought her to an asylum. He had found a way, after all, to overturn her marriage.

"In her current state, certainly not." That man must be a doctor. "Based on what you've told me, I can't imagine any officer of the court would judge her compos mentis. Any marriage contracted in such a state is deemed invalid, and rightly so." He chuckled again. "Even an imaginary species of it."

"Well, thank God for that," Peter said with a great warmth that triggered a flood of hatred through her, hatred so black that it gave her the strength, at last, to push to her feet.

She lurched toward the door, catching her balance on the doorjamb. "He's lying," she said hoarsely. The two men turned toward her, Peter with his hands hooked casually in his pockets, his smile sharpening as he caught sight of her. But it was the other man to whom she spoke, placing faith in his professional, kindly face, with its well-groomed mustache and wire-rimmed spectacles. "Don't believe him," she said. "He has every cause to wish to invalidate my marriage. He is manipulating you. I am perfectly"—she paused for breath, clutched the doorframe against a wave of dizziness—"perfectly sane, and he—"

Tsking, Peter stepped forward to brace her by the waist. "Again with that nonsense?" he said gently. She jerked her face away as he stroked her hair behind her ear; the violent movement unbalanced her, caused her stomach to lurch with nausea, and she sagged into Peter's arms.

"You see," she heard him say over her head, "she is quite invested in this story."

"I do see." The doctor gazed at her sympathetically. "Would you like another rest, Miss Everleigh? A sound night of sleep, before your treatment begins tomorrow?"

She swallowed bile, clawing at Peter's loathsome grip. "He is *lying* to you! I don't require treatment! Send to my husband—he'll bring the register book to prove it! By law, my brother has no right—"

"Yes," Peter cut in, his grip tightening around her rib cage, causing her to wheeze. "By all means, Mr. Denbury, send to the gambling palace where she imagines her husband to live."

"A gambling palace!" Mr. Denbury stared at her now as though she had sprouted another head.

In that moment, she realized that nothing she said would persuade him. He did not see her as a reasoning person. He saw her as a woman—a feebleminded, wayward girl in the grip of feminine madness. Whatever she said now, it would only fortify that opinion.

Nevertheless, she had to try. "Please," she gasped, "at least make sure of the facts! Sir, I beg you, as a man of science—"

Peter hauled her back inside the room. She shoved him away—but not hard enough to account for how he stumbled backward and crashed into the desk.

"She'll grow violent now," he said urgently, edging away from her toward the door.

She lunged—too late. The door slammed and bolted. "Peter!" She would not beg. But her voice did break as she said, "For our father's sake, please—"

"Let us move away," Peter said loudly. "It pains me to hear her in this sad state."

"I'll see to it that she is calmed," came Mr. Denbury's reply. "In the meantime, take heart: we've had excellent results with electrotherapy. Why, by this time next month, she might seem like a new woman to you."

She trapped her sob with one hand, straining to hear Peter's fading voice:

"No need to rush through the treatment," he told Denbury. "Money is no object. For my sister, I am willing to take all the time in the world."

"Can you hear me?"

Catherine stirred, hastily wiping tears from her face. That was not the coarse slur of the male nurse who had assaulted her earlier, but the lilting, well-modulated voice of a lady, speaking through the bolted door. "Yes. Heavens, yes." She clambered to her feet, battling with rash desperation, and lost. "Oh, please—can you help me?"

"It depends."

The breath exploded from her. "On *what*?"

"One moment." Something scratched across the door. The knob rattled. It came to Catherine, as she waited, that she had no idea who stood on the other side. This was a madhouse, after all.

She took a step backward as the door swung open. Her visitor was a blond woman swathed in a white lace wrapper that made her appear ghostly. She had deep, large, shadowed eyes of indeterminate color. She hesitated in the doorway, looking Catherine over as though she felt doubtful, too. "You mustn't try to get past me," she said. "If I scream, they'll be on you in a moment."

Catherine slowly nodded.

"I heard you crying out before," the woman said.

In the sane, civilized world, Catherine would have

been mortified by this news. But tonight, she had been strapped to a bed and forced, by a giant brute with clumsy hands, to drink a poison that had paralyzed her body but not her brain.

She had feared she would suffocate. When she had finally regained the ability to twitch her fingers, it had not seemed so important to muffle her sobs.

The woman seemed to compass all of this in one sympathetic glance. "They gave you a treatment, did they?" When Catherine nodded, she sighed and stepped inside, softly shutting the door. "Ever since Denbury took over from Mr. Collins, he has grown more brutal than I would wish. He was a soldier, you know—not a medic. His notions of healing are . . . unpleasant."

"Not for you, apparently." For the woman carried with her the scents of orange water and roses, and an air, moreover, of perfect serenity. Her pale hair was neatly dressed, threaded through with white silk ribbons.

"He would never cross *me*," the woman said. "He knows better."

In the opening silence, Catherine weighed her strategies. Was this woman allowed to wander freely, or did she have a way with locks, as Lilah did? Moreover, did she know how to slip out of this place?

As though sensing these thoughts, the woman shifted squarely in front of the door. "All the main doors are locked," she said, not unkindly. "And I do not have the keys to those."

Catherine swallowed and opened her mouth—but did not trust her voice. After a moment, she put a hand over her eyes. *Don't cry again. It won't help.*

"My name is Stella," the woman went on. "And yours

is Catherine, I believe? I heard the nurses speaking of you, earlier. May I sit, Catherine?"

On a deep breath, Catherine lowered her hand and nodded toward the stool. The woman eased onto it with the grace of a dancer, perching there with an impeccably straight posture. "The key," she told Catherine, "is to remain calm. Resistance is seen as proof of illness. If you don't wish the treatment, you must give them no reason to use it."

Easier said than done! "He intends to use an electro-shock device on me," Catherine burst out. "And I rather prefer my brain as it is!"

"Do you? How lovely for you." The woman looked up at her. "Won't you sit, too?"

That was the last thing she wished to do. When Denbury or his nurses came through that door again, she wished to be ready to meet them. The room offered no weapons—the stool and even the chamber pot were locked in place by bolts in the floor. But she had her nails. And her teeth.

Just like a proper madwoman, in fact.

"None of the men will come back tonight," Stella said. "They like their sleep too much. A nurse might come, but she won't abuse you. Simply drink the medicine, if she insists."

That serene tone was beginning to grate on Catherine's nerves. She grudgingly sat on her cot. "Do you know where we are?"

"The hospital is called Kenhurst."

"Hospital!" Catherine felt her mouth twist. "Prison, you mean."

Stella sighed. "Well, once it was a hospital. But I agree with you; it has changed since Mr. Collins left."

Catherine had no interest in the golden days of yore. "Where are we?" From the great silence outside, and the crystalline clarity of the stars, Catherine judged them to be in the countryside.

"Five miles from the railway station at Kedston."

Five miles. She could get there by foot.

"Even if you made it into the entry hall, you would go no farther," Stella said gently.

How resigned she seemed to the situation! "What brought *you* here? Let me guess: some man took a disliking to you, too?"

The woman smiled slightly. "Rather, I took a disliking to him. The courts sent me here for killing him."

Horror snapped through Catherine's chest. A strong wind rattled the windows, and she found herself grabbing for the rough bedspread, drawing it over her lap as though it might serve as armor to protect her from a murderess.

"I hate to see you afraid." Stella sounded ruefully amused. "There's no cause for it—not with me, at least. My husband, you see, liked to use his fists on me. And so one day when he lifted his hand, I pushed him down the stairs." She leaned forward, bringing her face into the wash of moonlight. "The result was not by my design."

She was younger than Catherine had first realized—thirty at the most. Her eyes were a bright, vibrant blue, her heavy lids lending them a sensual look, quite at odds with the delicate cupid's-bow of her mouth. Here was a face that would cause men to stare. She was not pretty, precisely, but she was certainly striking.

She also looked familiar, somehow. "Who are you?" Catherine whispered.

The woman frowned. "Never mind that. You don't want to be here, do you? That troubles me."

"Who would want to be here?"

"Most of the residents. But as I've said, times have changed. You're not the first woman brought in recently to be mistreated."

"I'm sane," Catherine said fiercely. "And Denbury means to torture me. To shock me, in the morning."

Stella studied her. "I gather it was not a magistrate who dispatched you here."

"It was my brother. He wants to steal my company."

"Oh dear." The woman pressed her palms together at her lips. "One expects it from a husband—but a brother? How terribly distressing."

This conversation was beginning to feel ludicrous. To sit commiserating politely about who had landed them in the madhouse! "Listen," Catherine said through her teeth. "You seem to have full liberties here." If only she had asked Lilah to teach her how to pick locks! Instead, she would make do with secondhand hopes. "Can you post a letter for me? I must let someone know what my brother has done."

Stella shook her head. "I could have done it, before. But I fear Denbury is reading my letters now before he posts them."

Catherine swallowed hard. "Then I am doomed."

Stella seemed to sense her fight against tears. She came off her stool and settled beside Catherine in a fragrant floral cloud. Catherine breathed deeply of the civilized scent as Stella closed one soft hand over hers. "Take heart," Stella said. "I have a brother, too—a far kinder one that yours. I'll write to him, ask him to come visit. Denbury shan't oppose that. James will be here within hours of receiving my letter. And once he's here, I'll tell him to carry a message for you. Whom would you like him to contact?"

Catherine opened her mouth—then hesitated as the pieces clicked together. Stella and James. James, Viscount Sanburne. Stella, Lady Boland. This was the notorious murderess, daughter of the Earl of Moreland, whose trial had been in all the newspapers years ago.

Catherine stared at her, unable to square it. Lady Boland hardly struck her as a vicious madwoman.

"You must tell me now," said Stella with a soft squeeze. "I have seen what electrotherapy can do. It's possible you won't remember the name or address afterward."

Fear passed like an icy draft through her bones. She had never known such terror. God above, who would she be without her mind? Without her learning, her knowledge?

"Nicholas," she said as her tears spilled over. The very feel of his name seared her; she had never gotten a chance to speak it aloud to him. And she might never do so now. Heavens, how had she taken his attentions for granted? And how had she imagined that his touch was his greatest allure? He listened to her; he respected her opinions; he consulted with her as an equal. He would never look askance on her for working; never imagine that labor might imbalance her mind. He was . . . a miracle, and she had squandered him. "Nicholas O'Shea," she managed. "Write to him at the House of Diamonds, Whitechapel, London."

"I will ask James to carry the message himself." Stella's grip tightened. "Look at me, Catherine." Her gaze was steady and resolute. "You are stronger than you think. You can bear this."

Footsteps sounded in the hall, heavy from the weight of clogs. Stella rose, tightening the knot on her wrapper. "I will do my best," she whispered rapidly, "to keep Denbury distracted, tomorrow. The electrotherapy cannot be undertaken without his—"

The door flew open. "Lady Boland!" The nurse in her white smock looked shocked. "You can't be mixing with these likes. This one's dangerous!"

"She seems very composed to me," Stella said. "I believe you might skip her medicine tonight."

"Mr. Denbury's orders, m'lady. I can't cross him. You know how he's gotten."

Stella cast her an apologetic glance before brushing past the nurse.

Catherine rose. "Lady Boland is correct," she told the woman. "I don't require—"

But the nurse's deference had disappeared with Stella's departure. "Your choice," she said with a sour twitch of her mouth. "You take it, or I call the men to hold you down while I pour it into your gullet." She lifted her brows. "And it gets hard to measure that way, mind you."

Catherine's glance fell to the bottle in the woman's hand. Laudanum, perhaps. Or chloral. Too much could kill a person.

She tried twice before managing the words. "I will take it," she said numbly. "No need to call anyone."

The gates had posed no challenge. Spike-topped wrought iron, they were for show. The doors, too, yielded after a round of brute force from Johnson's crowbar.

But now that they were inside, finding her would

be the trick. For this was no ordinary madhouse, but a granite palace, three stories high, sixty rooms across. Nick had counted the windows earlier as they had tied up the horses and planned their attack. As he prowled down the dark hall, Johnson at his heels, the tick of a nearby grandfather clock seemed to amplify his urgency. The moon had already set. Three hours till dawn—less than that, before the servants stirred.

It had taken too long to get here. Johnson had staggered into Diamonds with a nasty gash on his head, and no memory of how he'd acquired it. Amy, the domestic Nick had been bribing to keep an eye on Everleigh's ever since Lilah had gone to work there, had married last month and was no longer in his employ. His only clue had come from the red-haired lass who'd burst into Diamonds in a panic, babbling of brutes and a kidnapping. "Kenhurst," she'd said. "I heard them mention a place called Kenhurst."

He wasn't a man given to nerves. At knifepoint and gunpoint, he'd never felt his heart skip a beat. But as that girl had spoken, his vision had grayed, a buzzing filling his ears as the world tilted underfoot.

He'd reached out to the wall to catch his balance. *So this is terror,* he'd thought.

His fear didn't matter. Only her safety. That single moment of weakness was all he'd allowed himself before launching into action.

Kenhurst. Nick had never heard mention of such a place. The name didn't appear in any of the railway schedules. Nobody at Neddie's knew of it. And so he'd convened a meeting in Malloy's flat to plan a kidnapping of his own. Ambush Everleigh and make him talk, before Nick ensured he'd never talk again.

Everleigh would be prepared for such an attack. Had he any interest in survival, he would not return home. He'd be far from London right now, hiding like a rat.

But the land auction was slated in two days' time. And Nick had seen enough in that board meeting he'd interrupted—had seen Everleigh pale as the members voted to endorse the auction. Had seen him scurry over to Pilcher, whispering frantically before excusing himself. He was a man beholden. He dared not skip that auction, for fear of displeasing his master. Pilcher would expect his support.

Everleigh would return to town, all right. And Nick would be waiting, armed to the teeth.

They had been planning their respective roles when Peggy Malloy had passed through the kitchen. Catching wind of their conversation, she'd stopped dead. "Kenhurst, did you say?" Peggy had always been an avid one for tales of murder, particularly when a woman was the villain. Kenhurst, it transpired, was home to the most famous murderess of the decade. "Locked her up in Kenhurst, they did. Madhouse up Kedston way. Four hours in the saddle—no farther."

It had taken three. Nobody was stirring. The hallways were empty. Once, distant footsteps called them to a halt where two corridors crossed; Johnson drew his knife, and Nick tightened his grip on his garrote.

But the footsteps faded, mounting the stairs.

And so they continued their prowl. Place tried to look fancy, with tapestries on the walls and a thick carpet underfoot. But each door bore a padlock and an inset panel, which could be unlatched to spy on the inmate within. At odd moments, curious moans floated through the walls, causing Johnson to flinch, and Nick to walk faster, teeth gritted.

The first corridor held only men, slumbering in nightcaps on their cots. But the next hall proved more promising. Women. Nick opened shutters in rapid succession—then startled backward after he pulled one open to discover a woman peering back at him.

He wheeled toward Johnson to warn him—but it proved unnecessary. The door began to open.

Damn it. He'd missed a detail: this door had no padlock on it. These quarters didn't belong to a patient.

He caught Johnson's eye, laid a finger to his lips, and stepped aside.

The woman leaned out into the hall. He hooked his arm around her throat, pulled her back against his body, and muffled her gasp with his palm.

"Stay quiet," he said, "and you won't be hurt."

"All right." Her voice, muffled by his hand, sounded surprisingly steady. "I've no interest in troubling you."

He caught Johnson's wide-eyed look. The woman's composure seemed odd, given the circumstances. Perhaps working here had prepared her for this kind of surprise.

He didn't trust her promise, though. He kept her locked in his grip as he said, "I'm looking for someone. Catherine—" *Catherine O'Shea.* That was her name, by all rights. He silently cursed this bloody charade they'd undertaken. "Catherine Everleigh."

"Oh." He felt her relax, and realized she'd not felt as calm as she'd appeared after all. "Are you Nicholas O'Shea?"

He exchanged a frown with Johnson. If Peter Everleigh was trying to blot out this marriage, he was going about it the wrong way, bandying Nick's name about.

"Doesn't matter," he said flatly. "You're going to show me where she is. Nod if you understand."

She nodded readily. "Around the corner," she said. "In the . . . receiving wing, they call it. It's not quite as nice as the ladies' department, I'll warn you."

He nudged her forward, into a shuffling half step as he held her tight against him. But at the corner, she suddenly balked, twisting in his arms and dragging at his hand. "Stop it. Stop it!"

Her sudden panic baffled him. He tightened his grip, heedless now of whether or not he hurt her. "Be—"

"I won't be manhandled!"

From the corner of his eye, he saw Johnson raise his knife, a silent offer to do the dirty work. But after a moment, he shook his head. Instinct, maybe, nudging him.

"Make a shout," he said into her ear, "and you'll regret it." Slowly he released her.

She took a long, shaking breath before facing him. Tall and pale, with hair a shade darker than Catherine's. Didn't look like a prisoner, in her fine lace nightgown. Nor did she look like some humbly paid nurse.

"You *are* Mr. O'Shea, I think. Catherine was trying to get word to you. I promised to help her."

"Did you, now?" He had no interest in whether it was true or not. All he cared for was finding her. "Then I'll spare you that effort. Show me where she is."

"She won't be awake. They drugged her again."

He gritted his teeth against a red haze of rage. He could not afford to indulge it. He blinked until he got a clear view of her again. She mattered not a whit. Nurse, madwoman, innocent, she mattered nothing. He'd never hurt a woman, but in the place where his scruples should be, he felt nothing at all. "Show me," he said, very low, and saw her realize that he was done with talking.

Her gaze dropped to the wire wrapped around his knuckles. "All right," she whispered, and lifted the hem of her robe to walk quickly down the hall.

Around the corner, flagstones changed to creaking wooden boards; handsomely carpeted walls gave way to rough plaster. She drew up beside the third door, grasping the padlock for a moment before turning to him, an apologetic twist to her mouth. "I can't open this. The nurse took away my skeleton key, after she caught me visiting."

He opened the shutter, peered in. Impossible to tell if that huddled figure was Catherine. The woman looked too small, curled up like a child on her side . . .

His breath caught. He glimpsed her braid, peeking out beneath the blanket.

He snapped at Johnson, who stepped up, slamming the crowbar down on the padlock with a smashing bang.

The woman jumped. "Quiet! If they hear you—"

"Give me that." Nick seized the iron bar, fitted it into the door, and threw his weight into it. Wood began to splinter. He eased off, breathing raggedly for a moment, before throwing himself against it again.

The door groaned, but wouldn't budge.

"Don't," the woman said, as he raised the crowbar over his head. "I'm telling you—the guards are armed."

"So are we," Johnson told her, and lifted his pistol.

Nick brought the bar down—once, and then again, allowing himself to imagine, for a sweet black moment, that the lock was Peter Everleigh's skull.

*　　　*　　　*

They were coming for her. Coming to shock her, to wipe her mind clean, to destroy her. She pushed them away, but her hands flopped, lax as damp rags. "No," she managed. "No—"

"Catherine. Shh. It's me."

She was dreaming. That was O'Shea's voice. Maybe she had dreamed the whole thing, and she was safe in his bed at the House of Diamonds—

She managed to open her eyes. Saw the loathsome bare wall, the chair bolted to the floor.

She'd dreamed *him*.

Her eyes fell shut. Tears came too easily. She felt . . . exhausted, hollowed out, heavy and . . . so dizzy. The world was falling away—

She was being lifted. She summoned her will, all the power that remained to her, and managed to hook her nails into skin, this time. To *claw*.

"Bloody— Kitty!" His voice came at her ear now, urgent. "I am taking you out of here. Keep *quiet*."

Features swam before her. Eyes rippling, crossing, a nose swimming by a mouth . . . She took a shallow breath and blinked, and the features reassembled.

His face.

He was here.

"You came," she whispered.

He gathered her tighter, his hand cradling her skull, pushing her face into his shoulder. Wool, soft and fine. He smelled like horses. Like smoke and a cold night.

"Quiet," he said, but she felt his hand stroke over her hair once and a great wave of relief moved through her, and she sobbed into his shoulder.

She was dizzy because he was carrying her. He was carrying her out of this prison, to safety.

She lost consciousness for a moment—or a minute, or several. When she regained awareness, he had ceased to walk; he grasped her tightly as he spoke in low tones to somebody else.

"All right," he said, "there's a man in the entry hall. Do you know another way out?"

"Through the back," came a cool feminine voice. Stella's. "But it leads past the guardroom. The front is our best chance."

"*Our* best chance?"

"Yes, I'm coming with you. This place once seemed safer than the world outside. But clearly that has changed."

O'Shea swore softly. "Lady, you've got me confused with someone else. I've got no time for—"

"Wait." The words were so hard to shape. She was drooling, and could not care. "Let . . . her."

Catherine felt him tense, the minute adjustments of his posture as he leaned to look into her face. She could not manage to keep her eyes open to meet his, but she managed to speak again. "Let her . . . come." Stella had been kind. She was owed this.

She felt his hand frame her cheek, a brief firm pressure. Then he said, "Fine. Quietly. Johnson, you'll—"

"Got it. One clean shot."

"Don't kill him," Stella said. "Let me speak with him first."

"Bloody—" O'Shea was squeezing her very tightly. She was coming fully awake, now, alert enough to register that his grip was iron hard. "Like hell I will."

"You want his blood on your hands?" Stella asked. "Have you ever killed someone, sir?"

"I have," he said flatly. "And I'll not hesitate to put a bullet through you, if you betray us."

Catherine's eyes came open. Stella was staring at O'Shea, the wall sconce behind her shining through her dark blond hair, creating a frowsy halo around her pale, resolute face. "I invite you to shoot me," she said. "I'm sure I wouldn't mind. But then you would have to deal with my brother, who would." She turned on her heel and walked into the entry hall.

"Wait," O'Shea snapped—not at Stella. Catherine caught sight of Johnson lowering his pistol, his mouth pressed into a furious line.

"She'll . . . keep her word," Catherine whispered.

He glanced down at her. His expression briefly eased, the faintest smile ghosting over his mouth. "Hey." He rubbed his thumb over her cheek and gently said, "Shut your eyes again, Kitty." And then he looked back toward the entry hall. On a deep breath, he shifted her weight in his arms. She felt his hand make a fist at her back.

He was carrying a weapon. He intended now to use it.

A strange feeling swept through her. She closed her eyes, surrendering to this queer, curious peace. This sudden, intense certainty that all would be well.

His heart drummed beneath her ear. A solid, pounding beat. She felt enfolded. She felt . . . *protected*.

For the first time in her life, here, in this awful place, she felt safe.

"All right." Stella sounded breathless. "He's gone to the water closet. We've got five minutes, no more. Hurry, now."

Catherine tightened her arms around O'Shea. Her husband. Who carried her now in long strides, one hand on his weapon, the other holding her to him. They crossed the entry hall and exited into the cool night air.

She heard the whicker of horses, and smiled into his shoulder.

CHAPTER FIFTEEN

*S*ome noise woke Catherine from slumber. She opened her eyes. O'Shea sat on a chair drawn up beside her bed, his face grave, shadows beneath his beautiful eyes. He was watching her, and the moment she smiled at him, he leaned over to cup her face.

"How are you?" he asked.

She put her fists over her head in a long stretch, then yawned. "Much better. My head feels clearer now." She glanced toward the drawn curtains. "What time is it?"

"Seven thirty, eight o'clock."

"In the evening?" When he nodded, she pushed herself upright. They had arrived back at Diamonds after sunrise. It was very odd to have slept the entire day away. "Where is Stella?"

"Her brother came to fetch her."

Concern pricked her. "He won't send her back, will he?"

O'Shea laughed. "From what he said? I'd wager he'd sooner blow that asylum to kingdom come. Didn't seem half bad, for a toff."

"Oh." As she relaxed again, his hand smoothed down her braid, tracing the path of her spine. She had a vague recollection of his hands at her nape, fumbling . . . She reached behind her for her plait, and laughed at the straggling mess she uncovered. "You're better at shuffling cards."

"Hair's a sight trickier than cards." He was smiling, too. "You seemed quite fed up with me, this morning. I thought you were going to give me a proper smack."

She pulled an apologetic face. "I was so tired. I'm sorry, I hope I didn't—"

"Catherine." He nudged her face toward his, meeting her eyes. "Stop." He drew a hard breath. "It's I who must apologize. I should have foreseen that Everleigh would—"

"Don't." She caught his hand, holding it hard against her cheek. Then, with a daring that she hadn't known she possessed, she kissed his fingers. "You came for me. Thank you."

He sat back slowly, withdrawing his hand. A flicker of hurt moved through her. She frowned down at the counterpane, stroking the silk, feeling suddenly, oddly shy. That moment, in the asylum . . . the absolute certainty she had felt, the sense of elated conviction . . . She couldn't quite recall the nature of it. But it had centered on him. She was certain of it.

"There's a doctor outside," he said quietly. "He said . . ." He paused, cleared his throat. "He said if you woke, you'd be in the clear. But just in case, I think he'll have a look at you. All right?"

She nodded, then watched him rise and cross to the door. He looked . . . travel worn. Dust on the cuffs of his trousers.

Why, he hadn't changed his clothing since their mad dash from Kenhurst. Had he sat by her bed the entire time?

The doctor entered. A slight, rabbit-faced man with a courtly manner and a faint stammer, he listened to her lungs, then looked into her eyes and asked her to follow his finger as he moved it around her field of vision. He tested her reflexes, and judged them satisfactory. Did her head hurt? No, but she was profoundly thirsty.

"Fluids," he said decisively as he snapped his bag closed. "And rest. But as I said, she is well out of danger, Mr. O'Shea. She may have some lingering moments of confusion—depending on the dosage, opiates can be felt for several days thereafter. But I will be glad to proclaim her in fine health."

Catherine wanted to protest that she felt quite clear-headed now. But as she lay back against the pillows, she found herself dreamily content to consider the pattern on the ceiling—only it was, after all, not a pattern, but the random stippling of shadows cast by the candlelight.

Still, it made for fine entertainment. It kept her quite ensorcelled until O'Shea returned, this time bearing a tray full of several bowls.

"Fluids," he said in disgust as he retook his seat by the bed. "I told Thomas that you wanted fluids, and what do I get? French soups."

She took a deep breath. A moment ago, she would have denied that she was hungry. But Thomas had a rare talent. The smell of something rich and savory awoke a beast in her stomach, which growled loudly enough to catch O'Shea's attention.

"Well, now," he said, one dark eyebrow rising. "Seems my wife fancies a French broth."

"Yes, she does." She reached for the spoon, but he *tsked* and took it from her.

"Lie back," he said, and carefully ladled soup into the spoon.

Perhaps she was dreaming again. "You're going to . . . feed me?"

She *certainly* was dreaming. In real life, O'Shea was incapable of blushing. "It's a fine counterpane," he muttered. "And in your state, you're likely to spill."

"Oh." That made sense. She nestled happily into the pillows and opened her mouth. He carried the spoon to her lips, tipping carefully. Ah, but Thomas had outdone himself. The broth was light and perfectly seasoned, a medley of greens with the slight savor of a poultry base.

"Give him a raise," she said once she'd swallowed.

He smiled. "Another?"

She nodded. But as she watched him spoon up another mouthful, that strange shyness came over her again. Had anybody ever fed her? Not since she was very young. There was a peculiar vulnerability in allowing him to fit the spoon to her lips; to feel his eyes on her, monitoring her so closely, waiting for her to swallow. It made her feel . . . fragile. Quite unlike herself.

It made her feel . . . loved.

But he didn't love her. Her brain was muzzy. She was inventing fantasies. Worse, she was persuading herself to believe them.

When he carried the spoon toward her again, she caught his wrist, gripping it as a way to trammel the panic that wanted to bubble up within her. She should tell him not to help her. She could do for herself; she always had done.

"What is it?" he asked gently.

She looked into his eyes, his beautiful dark face, which she had once imagined the product of the devil's own genius, designed to ensnare her. She'd been partly right. God help her. She was ensnared.

He tilted his head slightly. "Have you had enough?"

"No," she said softly. "Not yet."

She would blame this foolish contentment on the opiates. With any luck, she might not think clearly for days yet. A doctor had said so.

"Like hell you're going out."

This belligerent declaration came from the doorway, which O'Shea was currently blocking. Catherine continued to wrestle with the buttons on her glove. She had fallen asleep beside him, but this morning, she had woken alone. He'd intended to leave without a word to her; that much was clear. "I'm feeling much better," she said calmly. "Quite myself now. And I understand that there is an auction to attend. A *public* auction."

He stepped into the room and pulled the door shut on a bang. "God as my witness, you're not going. You're going nowhere near your brother. Give me a week, and I'll make sure you have free run of this city. But until then—"

"You don't command me," she said gently.

He leaned back against the door, pinning her in a fierce glare. What a contrast to the tender solicitousness he'd shown her yesterday! No doubt he was vexed that she'd found out about the land auction. Alas, he had forgotten to inform Johnson of his secrecy, and that man had popped by to ask Catherine a quick question about the manner in which a bid was signaled.

"I am going," she said now, aiming for a calm, reasonable tone. "The plot is my design. Surely I deserve a taste of the victory. And yes," she added as O'Shea scowled and opened his mouth to speak. "I know my brother will be there. Hasn't it occurred to you that that's part of my reason for attending?" To her own amazement, she felt curiously at peace with what Peter had done to her. At last, he had behaved in a manner that left no room for lingering doubts about his motives. He had revealed his true nature so plainly that she would never hope for better from him again. It was freeing, somehow, to be liberated from any lingering sense of familial obligation. He was her opponent, nothing more. "I want to see his face when he spies me. When he realizes he hasn't managed to cow me an inch. And I trust you to keep me safe," she said more softly. "I won't feel a moment's unease, beside you."

He frowned, slouching a little as he turned his beaver hat round and round, his beringed hands squeezing. "This isn't your battle to fight."

She looked directly at him, letting the silence draw on a moment too long. "Isn't it?"

He loosed a long breath. "Catherine, I . . . need my head about me, today. And if you're there—"

"Stop." She abandoned her gloves and crossed to him, taking his face in her hands. "Surely you have the discipline to resist my lures." She went on tiptoe to kiss his lips, and felt his surprise in his momentary stillness.

Then he caught her by the waist and swung her around, setting her against the door as he took control of the kiss. His tongue plunged deep, and she opened her mouth for him, pulling him as hard against her as their bodies allowed.

It was as though she had touched a match to a fuse. His mouth ravaged hers, his hands moving feverishly down her body, smoothing hard down her ribs and waist and hips, palming the shape of her as though to persuade himself of her solidity, that she was here with him.

For a moment, his ravening intensity frightened her. There was no courtesy, no tentativeness, in the way he felt for her breast through the thick layers of her gown. He gave no warning, asked no permission, as he grabbed her skirts, hauled them upward past her knees, then thrust his hand beneath, reaching between her legs. He found the split in her drawers, delved unerringly through her folds, and cupped her hard as he kissed her more deeply yet. It was predatory. It was . . . overwhelming. She broke free to catch her breath in a gasp, and he seemed to sense her confusion; he grasped her chin and pulled her face around so he looked into her eyes as he stroked between her legs, his gaze adamant, bright and fierce, his mouth a grim, hard line.

She kept her gaze steady on his, lifted one hand to his cheek, bit back the gasp that his touches pulled from her, the groan of pleasure as his fingers breached her and penetrated, widening.

He leaned forward and licked her mouth. "Let me in," he said in a low, fierce voice.

Yes. She nodded—a brief, strained jerk of her head that drew a low noise from him, something between a groan and a snarl. He gathered her skirts in great wads, crushing the wool, shoving it away as with his other hand he unbuttoned his trousers and freed himself.

She caught her breath as she felt the swollen head of his member nudging against her. His hands dropped to her hips, grasped her hard as he entered her.

In silence, holding her in place against the door, he thrust into her, deep, steady strokes that made her head tip back; made her eyes roll and her lashes flutter shut. So many sensations, all of them suffused with this growing, building physical hunger—even the unyielding press of the door, cool against her bare upper arms, seemed sensual . . . the crush of clothing between them, the way it whispered . . . the heat of his mouth on her throat, his tongue stroking her . . . and below, this unyielding, rhythmic invasion . . .

He whispered something in her ear, garbled, unintelligible. Then he pushed down on her hips, forcing her to bend her knees the slightest fraction, and the new angle—

She moaned. He was hitting that spot now, somehow—every stroke brushed against it, teased and then tormented her; she felt herself swell, grow hotter and wetter and needier . . . He showed no signs of flagging; he seemed to go deeper, to hit something inside as well, and her thighs loosened; her knees gave way. He gripped her now to hold her on her feet as the pleasure broke through her, washed down the backs of her knees, prickled down her spine, her inner muscles contracting around him.

The noise he made burned her ears. He sank into her, trapping her against the door with the weight of his body, remaining there a long moment before he stepped back.

When he let go of her, she sagged. Would have fallen, had he not caught her again, lifted her, and swung her into a nearby chair.

Only minutes had passed. Or maybe not even a minute. She had no sense of time. She felt . . . boneless, as she sat watching him. He leaned back against the door, his face dark as he studied her. His expression, paired with the rigid set of his shoulders, gradually made her frown. Made her cast her thoughts back.

She caught her breath. "You didn't . . . withdraw, did you?"

"No."

"I'm sure . . ." She swallowed, bestirred herself to sit upright. "I'm sure nothing will come of it. There are couples, married couples who have lived together in a regular fashion for years, who still don't conceive—"

"And some that conceive on their wedding night," he said curtly.

She stiffened. Was that anger in his voice? "You can't blame *me* for this."

He sighed. "I don't." He came toward her, kneeling down to look into her face. "I don't," he said very softly. "It was my own damned carelessness. That's what angers me, Kitty. Not you."

She let him gather her hands, confused by her own reaction. It would indeed be ruinous to conceive a child in this situation. She should be horrified. She should be angry, even—not only at him, but at herself. Such inexcusable recklessness, to continue to take this risk again and again.

But the horror that should have assailed her was curiously difficult to locate. Instead, as she looked at his broad hands enfolding hers, curiosity wisped through her, stealing her breath.

He was not her kind. Born in the gutter, raised with a knife between his teeth. When angered or amazed, he lost hold of his grammar, and spoke like a common thug. A criminal—reformed, mostly, but while he still owned this gambling den, he could never be counted on the right side of the law. He was no fit match for a woman.

And yet . . . he was keenly intelligent. Honorable, in his own peculiar style. Wise in ways she wasn't. Ambitious, disciplined—save when it came to her.

A flush warmed her face. She bowed her head to hide it, amazed that she should feel such gratification at this revelation: she alone had the power to undo him.

For what good could come of that? This marriage had been forged as a dark secret, to wield like a weapon. She must be mad to entertain, even for a second, what a child of theirs would look like—act like—what talents it might inherit, in the curious combination of her reserve and restraint and savvy, and his more daring, roguish cunning.

"What's got you so pink?" he asked softly. "You know, if it came to that, we'd make do, Catherine. And God save the world from any child of ours. God save the Queen, for no doubt the tyke would have ambitions for a crown, ere long."

Her smile startled her. It felt so easy to hold. She felt peculiarly vulnerable; she folded her lips together, made herself stand. "We should go."

"You're not going."

"Yes, I am."

"I said it, Catherine. I won't have you there. Especially not now," he added in a mutter as he turned away to fasten his fly.

She stared at his broad back, struck dumb by that statement. "Not now? Now, you mean, that you might have . . ."

"Yes," he snapped over his shoulder.

Her teeth clamped together. Now that he might have seeded a child in her, he would bully her for it? "No," she said, her voice ragged. "That does not give you rights over me. If I wish to go, I am going."

He faced her, looked down at her from his great height, his face impassive. Remote and cold. She felt, as he stared at her, the difference between their sizes—and, in a horrible prickle of awareness, the fact that he stood between her and the door.

"I'd rather bear your anger than the risk to you," he said.

"That isn't your choice to make!" She started for the door, and he stepped sideways, blocking her.

"Don't make me do this," he said. "Wait here. I'll—"

"Make you do *what*? Keep me locked here against my will?" A wild laugh ripped from her. "Don't you see? This is exactly what I told you I wouldn't allow. I am not your ward, your property, to boss as you see fit—I am not your *wife*, O'Shea!"

"Today you are," he said grimly, and reached for the doorknob.

"No!" She lunged for the door, but it was too late—he had already stepped out.

The lock turned.

He had taken the key with him.

She should have raged. He had rescued her from a prison yesterday, only to make another for her. Instead, after shock had subsided, she felt only a weird, numb grief, too deep for tears.

Did he know what he had done? She felt as though some light inside her, briefly flickering, had been crushed by a careless boot heel. He had used her desires to trick her. He had shown he did not respect her judgment. Or, even worse, he had shown that his judgments would trump hers, regardless of his esteem for her.

By trapping her here, he had all but admitted that he wanted doilies after all. A woman who waited by the fire like a lapdog, eager for the sound of her master's footsteps after a day spent tending the hearth.

By the time footsteps came at the door two hours later, she had packed up her things. She was waiting, primly erect, in the wing chair, her hands locked tightly in her lap. She would not weep. She would not raise her voice. She would simply go. The moment he opened the door, she would walk through it—and if he stopped her this time, she would make him pay for it.

The knob rattled. But it did not immediately turn. She frowned. Now came a scratching at the keyhole.

She rose, uneasy. "Who's there?"

"God in heaven," a familiar, feminine voice said. "Catherine?"

That voice! She gasped, then hurried over to the door, tugging angrily at the knob. "Lilah?" She sank to her knees, peering through the keyhole. "Can that really be you? I thought . . ."

Darkness filled the keyhole—Lilah kneeling, too. "So Callan wasn't lying," she said in marveling tones. "Let me in, then!"

"He took the key."

"He *what*?" A brief pause. "All right, stand back, then. I'll pick it open."

*　　*　　*

"And then we visited Boston, which was the coldest place this side of the North Pole, and if you thought *London* was bad for snobbery—"

"Oh, I can't imagine anybody was rude to you," Catherine murmured. They sat in the Palmers' drawing room, chairs drawn together by the fire, knees nearly brushing, a discarded tea tray shoved off to one side. The room was very grand, a vaulted ceiling painted in rococo style, cherubs gamboling in the heavens; the furniture was powder blue and white, the carpet pale as a newborn's cheek, not a stain upon it. That shade spoke of extravagant wealth, no care whatsoever for the cost of replacement, once mud was tracked in, or soot, or the mere dust of everyday life. Yet Lilah looked perfectly at home amid the splendor, dressed in a bronze silk gown tailored expertly to her curving body. French, Catherine guessed. Pingat, the very newest style; she herself had never worn anything so fashionable or rare.

"You're a proper lady now," Catherine said. Nobody would mistake Lilah for anything else. She wore a necklace of emeralds at her throat, French lace at her cuffs and collar. The bronze gown flattered her rosy complexion, and contrasted with the deep, inky shine of her hair, coiled so elegantly at the crown of her head. "Surely the Bostonians bowed."

"Well, of course they did." When Lilah smiled, her full cheeks turned her azure eyes into laughing half-moons. "Doesn't mean I felt like bowing back. Sourpusses, the lot of them. At any rate, we were meant to go on to Philadelphia, but when somebody mentioned they expected snow, that did it for me. I said to Christian that summer was a fine time to travel, but in the autumn, I liked nothing better than a proper scone. He went looking for one, and came back with some wretched biscuit that a baker had conned him into buying. We took one bite and booked our passage back home."

Catherine smiled. Marriage had not diminished Lilah in the least; if anything, it seemed to have amplified her cheeky, laughing charm. She seemed . . . easier in her skin, more relaxed. That slight wariness which Catherine remembered in her was nowhere in evidence now.

Perhaps love did that. It made one feel at home, at last—even with oneself.

The velvet nap of her armchair was very fine. She drew a pattern into it, a chain of diamonds. The auction would be concluded by now. O'Shea would have discovered her absence. She should have left a note. What if he imagined that Peter had found her again? But no, Callan would tell him of Lilah's visit, surely.

She scowled. Why should she trouble herself for *his* feelings, when he had shown his complete disregard for hers?

Silence intruded into her thoughts. She looked up and discovered herself the object of intense scrutiny.

"I'm not the only one here with a tale to tell," Lilah said.

She cleared her throat. "But first, you must finish yours. How was the voyage back? Smooth, I hope?"

Lilah pulled a face. "Lovely, I ate myself sick, we made record time. Enough with the honeymoon. Explain why I had to spring you out of my uncle's gaming den." She arched one dark brow. "Callan said you'd been staying there. Wouldn't tell me why."

"Oh, I . . ." Catherine blew out a breath, then locked her hands together in her lap, hunting for a neat sum-mary. But the challenge overwhelmed her. Had Lilah appeared a day ago, how much simpler the tale would have been! She felt a pang of loss for the possibility she had glimpsed—the sweetness of a simpler conclusion. A . . . happy ever after, even.

The opiates must have accounted for that wild hope. They had invested her with a foreign optimism, spinning a fledgling dream that now seemed bizarre and embarrassingly foolish. But yesterday, she might have said . . .

She might have said that for the first time in her life, she had done something wild, and she had no regrets. None.

"I married your uncle to save Everleigh's." That was a fine place to start.

"Married him!" Lilah pressed herself back in her chair, as though to physically distance herself from these tidings. "You *married* him?"

"Yes, that's what I said." Asperity seemed to open a road for her, show her how to advance. "Peter, you see, was planning to sell the auction rooms. And unless I was married, I had no authority to oppose him."

"And you thought Nick was the best choice?" Lilah covered her mouth with one slim hand, a diamond band glinting on her wedding finger. But her snort sounded suspiciously like a laugh.

Catherine scowled. "It seemed a very fine choice. He promised not to interfere with me. He signed the very contract that—" She hesitated, suddenly conscious of the delicacy of this tangent.

With her usual bluntness, Lilah pushed right through the pause. "The same contract my husband signed for you. It's all right, Catherine; that was a strange time, back in the spring."

"So it was." She offered a grateful smile. "And I rather thought the arrangement was . . . perfect, after all. Peter, you see, had everything to lose from such a marriage. We told him we'd keep it a secret from the public, provided he . . . behaved himself."

"Blackmail!" As Lilah arched her dark brows, she looked, briefly and powerfully, like her uncle, and the resemblance raised such a strong wave of feeling that Catherine turned away from it, fumbling for her teacup.

It would be lukewarm by now. She blew on it anyway. "I hope . . ." She took a sip and winced. Oolong did not profit by cooling. "I hope we can remain friends."

"What?" Lilah leaned over to touch her arm. "What's this? Why wouldn't we be friends?"

She turned the cup in her hands. No handle, floral motif in cobalt blue against white. Deep saucers, too. Dresden, eighteenth century. Five pounds at auction for this cup alone.

Lilah was waiting. Catherine returned the cup to its saucer. "I know your uncle has not always been a friend to you." Indeed, he had demanded certain favors of Lilah during her employment at Everleigh's that might well have cost her position. Catherine swallowed, surprised by herself. How had she forgotten that? O'Shea had cast a spell on her, maybe, but now that she was free of the enchanted atmosphere of Diamonds, she remembered again. She clung to the facts. "He forced you to thieve for him. Had anyone discovered it—why, I would have sacked you." The thought amazed her. "Had I learned of it before I knew you, you would have been thrown onto the street. You never would have met Lord Palmer, and . . ."

Lilah's face had darkened. "I don't like to think on

it," she said slowly. "Of course, Nick's the reason I made it to Everleigh's in the first place. He funded my education. He took me in after my dad died. So . . . I've made my peace with him. He's the only family I've got." She blinked, then brought her hands together in a clap. "Why, but that's not true, now. If you're married to him—*we're* family."

Catherine smiled. "Aunt to a viscountess? How I've come up in the world," she said dryly, with a wave around the grand chamber.

Lilah followed her gesture, and burst into a laugh. "Isn't it ridiculous? A cream carpet! I can't imagine where Christian found it."

But after a moment of shared laughter, Catherine sobered again. "You remember the betrothal contract, I think. There was a provision in it. You and I shan't stay family forever. I only wish . . . your uncle remembered the terms."

"All right, then." Lilah looked grim suddenly. "What's he done?" Chair legs thumped as she dragged her seat closer. "Why were you locked in that room?"

Catherine hesitated. "He has never abused me—"

"No, of course not. It's not in him to abuse a woman," Lilah said readily. "But it isn't like him to lock her up, either."

Catherine sighed. "I think I must tell you the whole story."

And so she did—omitting nothing, not even the fact they had been intimate, though she mentioned this in a delicate euphemism, which Lilah showed she understood only by the slight widening of her eyes. By the time Catherine finished, the light had faded from the long windows overlooking the park across the street, and Lilah sat in slack-jawed silence, her astonishment so clear that it almost embarrassed Catherine to look on her.

"I've made a hash of things," she admitted softly. "Our . . . entanglement was never meant to be so . . . profound."

"Catherine." Lilah shook her head. "I've never . . . the way you speak of him. You sure it's just about a contract now?"

She took a deep breath and reached for her courage. "Perhaps it . . . might not have been. But the terms of that contract are not incidental. Lilah, I won't have my will suborned, my freedom compromised. And he has shown now that he will do so. That he will override my judgment when he sees fit." She bit her lip, frustrated by how flimsy her objection seemed when spoken aloud. After all he had done for her, it would be no wonder if an onlooker faulted her for taking exception to his attempt to keep her safe.

But . . . "You know me, Lilah. How can I trust a man who would do that? For nothing about my life seems safe and civil to an ordinary man. I deal with strangers constantly at my work. Sometimes I speak with gentlemen in private, without chaperonage. I travel the streets without escort. Everything else I hold dear depends on my independence—"

"Everything *else*?" Lilah asked softly.

She grimaced. "A slip of the tongue."

But perhaps a telling one.

"Catherine." Lilah was gazing at her with transparent sympathy. "I can't tell you that my uncle will be bound by a contract. He's got a code, all right, but it was never one and the same with the law's."

"I know that," she said quietly.

"And he's stubborn as a mule. If he decides something is the right thing to do—if he sees a way to make things work out as he wants them to—he'll take it. He won't pause to ask your feelings about it."

"That is very clear to me now." How bitter those words tasted!

"But it will always be in your favor," Lilah added. "He talks a hard business. But for all that he's twisted my arm in his time, he's never done me wrong in the end. Why . . . he even helped Christian, when it came to it, though there's no love lost between them. He did that for me. He'd do anything for the people he loves."

Catherine crossed her arms. The room suddenly felt very cold. "He hasn't spoken that word. I'm not sure it's in his vocabulary."

"Is it in yours?"

She closed her eyes. It was there. It sat in her throat like a hard knot she could not swallow. She had no practice in speaking it anymore. In her childhood home, that word had been measured out like toxic medicine, used only in moments of direst necessity—save with her father.

But she had known how to earn his love. She'd been well equipped for that. And she'd asked nothing in return for it. A child had no right to do so.

But if a woman had any respect for herself, she *must* make such demands.

"You look tired," Lilah murmured. "You'll stay here, won't you? For as long as you like. It's safe here. Your brother won't guess it."

"I'll have to confront him. I need back into Everleigh's. I have an auction to arrange." She opened her eyes. "Unless your uncle withdraws his estate to punish me."

Lilah's face softened. "That's not his way, Catherine. And I think you know it."

"Yes," she said after a moment. "I do."

"I'll talk to Christian about arranging a guard for you." Lilah rose, taking Catherine by the hand to draw her up. "But what should I say if Nick comes knocking?"

The thought caused a thousand butterflies to flutter through Catherine's stomach. "You think he will?"

Lilah rolled her eyes. "With what you've told me? I give him another two hours at most."

The butterflies, this solid lump in her throat . . . she needed time to digest them. "I'll speak to him when I'm ready," she said. "But it will be my own decision, not his. And it won't be tonight."

CHAPTER SIXTEEN

*F*ive days in a row, Nick went knocking on the door at Palmer's townhouse in Grosvenor Square. Five days in a row, hat under his arm, clothes brushed, collar starched, every button fastened, like a goddamned idiot he walked up those steps and let Lily's bloody butler turn him away like trash.

On the sixth day, he kept himself in Whitechapel. A man's pride could only endure so much. It didn't stretch to sending her the letter he'd tried to write—half a ream of paper in the rubbish, his chicken-scratch scrawl growing more illegible at each pass.

He wouldn't apologize for what he'd done. He'd done enough, damn it, to prove himself to her. He'd broken her out of a madhouse. He'd made love to her until she couldn't stand. He'd lain awake long nights beforehand, keeping his hands to himself while her eyes all but begged him to take her, but her lips still said *no*.

And he was restraining himself from killing her brother, to the wonder of every man in his service, all of them rotating by lots through the watch they kept on

Everleigh's comings and goings, making clear to him, through their very presence at his heels, that he wasn't to approach the auction rooms. Aye, Nick was keeping his finger off the trigger for her sake alone, though God knew the dog needed to be put down, because if locking her in a room for a couple of hours was enough to cast her into a cold, distant silence, then no doubt of it, putting her brother into the grave would drive her away forever.

He distracted himself. He met again with Pilcher, this time at a gentleman's club in St. James, a snooty place where you could hear a pin drop, or, for that matter, a man's stifled belch—and by God, but these toffs were a bean-eating lot, by the sound of them.

He'd outbid Pilcher by five hundred pounds in the end, and had been prepared to take it to the streets afterward if that was what Pilcher required. But the swell had surprised him. He'd written to Nick the next day.

> *You have no reason to take mercy on me. I only lay out the facts for you now: I have rashly committed myself to a certain group of builders, accepting money from them that I cannot repay. They expect those parcels to be made available for development. I am ruined; very well. But they threaten my family now, and this is not something I know how to face.*
>
> *They have expressed an interest in dealing with you. Accordingly, and only with your permission, I would offer to make your acquaintance with these builders, so you might consider their offer. I believe they would be willing to revise their plans for Orton Street in a way that accommodated the two buildings you currently offer on lease.*

*The arrangement would profit you handsomely.
In full honesty, while I no longer bear any hope of
repairing my own finances, I would also stand to
profit, by the alleviation of the dangers currently posed
to my family.*

In short, Pilcher wanted protection.

At his club, they dined on an overdone roast that Nick's own cook would have tossed into the rubbish. Pilcher, it was clear from the start, wanted to pretend that they were gentlemen, dining together as a matter of course.

Nick had no use for the pretense. "A few things first," he said flatly. "Catherine Everleigh."

"Catherine . . ." Pilcher blinked. "Peter's sister, do you mean?"

"Aye. You had designs on her. I want those scrubbed from your brain."

"Designs?" Pilcher's fork sagged; he looked honestly baffled. "Peter did speak of . . . That is, for a time, I considered courting her. But that was when it seemed that her brother would make a profitable partner in business. Of course, if he pushes through the sale of that auction house, he may have the money—"

"He won't," Nick said. "That's been off the table for a while."

"Indeed?" Pilcher's eyes narrowed. "Typical that I did not know it. Well, then." He shrugged. "She'd be of no use to me now. Money is the thing, old fellow."

It was the coldness of his assessment that persuaded Nick. Just like a toff to evaluate a woman the way he would a stock. "All right, then. These builders. Who are they?"

Gradually they worked out a deal. Nick knew the

corporation; St. Giles men, who had built a music hall in Seven Dials that was doing brisk business. Pilcher was right to feel out of his depths, but Nick understood their kind. He proposed to cut a deal that spared Pilcher their threats; even offered to stand Pilcher the money to repay them, though his rate of interest caused Pilcher to choke. Or perhaps that was only the fault of the over-cooked roast.

In return, he wanted one thing. "You put Peter Everleigh off the Board of Works."

Pilcher considered this for a moment as he took up his brandy. "I might be able to arrange it," he said slowly, swirling the glass. "He's not popular; I believe I could muster the votes. But he will fight, of course. He'll cling to his position like a cat to a wall." He smirked. "He nurses *political* ambitions, you see."

Nick did see. Suddenly he saw a solution for the whole mess. "Then you take him this proposal," he said. "Can you get a pen and paper around here?"

Pilcher snapped at a passing server, who fetched over a sheet. Then, in slow, methodical detail, Nick explained what he required if Pilcher wished to be spared the further attentions of the St. Giles crew.

He'd always preferred strategy to bloodshed. In the past, finding that kind of solution would have left Nick well satisfied with his day's work. But his mood was oddly bleak as he returned to Diamonds. Never count chickens before they hatched. He wouldn't celebrate triumph, just yet.

And maybe it would ring empty anyway.

He hung over the railing as he waited for his supper, but the usual comforts—the resplendent luxury of the interior; the sight of the crowds, jammed shoulder to shoulder on the floor below—left him unmoved. He didn't try to kid himself about the reason for it. He was a fool, but countless men before him had been struck down by the same idiocy. He might have stood there all night, staring at nothing, had Callan not interrupted him.

"Note came," Callan said.

"Put it on my desk."

"Note from Mayfair."

Nick turned. "What's that?"

Callan passed over the envelope, handsomely stamped in wax. "Lily's footman. Wore livery, if you can credit it. She's risen high, ain't she? Makes one wonder—"

But Nick didn't hear the rest. He was already making for the exit.

Nick had never stepped beyond Palmer's entry hall. No interest in it. If Lily wanted to see him, he'd thought, they could meet at Diamonds or Neddie's. Mayfair wore on his nerves. Wasn't that he felt out of place here—he'd belong anywhere he cared to set foot, damn it. But the house felt lifeless. Too much marble, carpets threadbare. The rich in these parts liked to flaunt the age of their money. Nothing new, nothing bright. This house felt dead to him, cold and joyless, a testament to power with no care for comfort.

But Lily seemed not to mind it. As she guided him down the hall, she even pointed out things to like. "That was Christian's grandfather," she said, gesturing to an oversized painting of a beady-eyed bloke perched stiffly on a horse. "He was a great racing man. Six wins at Ascot."

He grunted. "Palmer's done a lot of bragging, I see."

She looked over her shoulder to show him the twist of her mouth. "It's called *conversation,* Nick. Some people speak openly of their family's history, having nothing to hide."

"That right?" He caught up with her as she rounded a corner, disliking the feel of dogging her heels. "So what do you say when Palmer's fine friends ask after yours?"

She drew up by a set of folding-doors, facing him. "I tell them I don't have much family to speak of," she said. "But I have an uncle, who raised me as best he knew how. And then I throw in a joke about hopeless bachelors, and everyone laughs, and the subject passes onward."

He allowed himself a faint smile. That was a kinder reply than he deserved. "Hopeless, am I?"

"Until recently." She hesitated, searching his face. "But maybe you'll surprise me. You told me once, Nick—I remember it like yesterday—that life will always give you a reason to look away from opportunities. But courage means grabbing them, no matter the circumstances. Do you remember that?"

He did. She'd been seventeen, stricken with grief for her late sister. He'd been mourning, himself—battling with guilt over not having done more. Not having noticed Fiona's pain earlier, when the surgeon might have made a difference.

He'd been at a loss as to how to help Lily. Finally, he'd reenrolled her at that typing school that she and Fiona had favored. But she'd turned it down, saying there was no point in aiming higher, now that Fiona was gone.

"You took that advice," he said. By God, had she ever. "You took it further than I ever guessed you would."

He looked beyond her, at the marble walls, the statuary. In the distance, somewhere, a fountain made a musical splashing. "This place suits you, I guess. It's what you deserved."

She smiled, the kind of soft, secretive, satisfied smile that belonged to a lady without any sharp edges. She'd been nothing but, once upon a time. If Palmer had smoothed those edges away, then Nick would find a way to rub along with him, no matter what it took.

"This house is nothing," she said. "Christian is what I deserve. I hope you'll give Catherine a reason to feel the same about you." She opened the door before he could reply, then turned away, her heels tapping off down the hall.

His wife sat across the room, swaddled in a thick blanket that she dropped as she rose. "Congratulations," she said. "You won the land auction." She tossed the newspaper onto the chiffonier, pages fluttering before they settled.

He eyed her as he approached. She looked cool, tightly buttoned, hair scraped back, expression impenetrable. She was wearing armor, all right. She wasn't intending a reconciliation.

He glanced down at the newspaper. Caught sight of the small article on the sale of the lots on Orton Street. But one of the pages peeking out interested him more. He flipped to it. "You took out the advertisement." A full-page spread, featuring illustrations of pieces he recognized from her rhapsodic descriptions during their dinners at Diamonds. The tambour-topped writing table. Clocks and chairs and whatnot.

"Yes. Come Friday, we'll see how effective it was."

He frowned down at the print. He trusted her judgment; if she said these things were valuable, then no doubt they'd fetch a fine profit. And it certainly wasn't the artist's fault that they looked so ordinary, now, to his eyes. But he couldn't square them, these workaday things, with the way she'd spoken of them in his sitting room at Diamonds. Listening to her, he'd imagined fantastical treasures. Her words, her voice, her attitude had conjured visions to which mere objects could never match up.

She did that. She made him think outside himself. Not a small thing, for a man without formal learning. When reading was a struggle, when books were impenetrable, you got your knowledge from firsthand experience, mainly. You learned through trial and error. You focused on what lay around you, visible, tangible, real.

But she had a way of leading him into dreaming. She made him imagine, hope for, ideas and realities he'd never himself known.

She'd done it before she even knew him. He'd started to dream the first time he'd seen her, but at least, back then, he'd known it was impossible. Somewhere along the line, he'd lost track of that fact. Once he'd touched her, he'd begun to persuade himself that maybe impossible, fantastic outcomes could happen.

He wrestled with himself, still staring at the advertisement, seeing nothing. He didn't beg. He wouldn't. Nothing was worth that. Nobody worth it would ever demand it of him.

The air shifted, took on the faint scent of bergamot

as she joined his side. She'd perfumed herself like a man again, for the first time that he could recall since their wedding day.

Strapping her armor back on.

"Look," she said. She drew a line with her finger beneath the bold type at the bottom of the page:

Open to Public—

First Time in Company History—

All Are Invited to This Historic Auction

"Well, now." A foolish sense of pleasure suffused him. "So you took my advice."

"I did." He heard her deep breath. "It seemed sensible. The regular crowd would be thinner at this time of year. Christie's opens its doors to all and sundry. And . . . I thought I would take this chance to tweak Peter's nose. The only one I might have."

He caught the accusation in her voice. Slid a sidelong look at her. "I won't apologize for leaving you behind that day."

"No." She was still gazing in the direction of the advertisement, but perhaps she was seeing something else, too. Her expression was very distant, her hands locked tightly at her waist. "I didn't expect you would apologize. But at least you admit that it would be . . . appropriate, were you able."

He didn't like the sound of those words. The resignation in them. He faced her. "Look. He threw you into a madhouse—"

"Yes."

"And the fact he's still breathing is my gift to you, for it's God's own truth that I would slit his throat in a second if I didn't think you'd feel the guilt for it."

She lifted her chin. Looked directly into his eyes. "That's true. He means nothing to me now. But I draw the line at murder."

"Well, then."

"He's suing for his proxy back."

It took him a moment to follow. "Christ. He—"

"He has petitioned the court to give him sole custody of the auction rooms. He alleges me to be of unsound mind. Mr. Denbury, from the asylum, has written a letter in support of his bid. He further claims that he is being menaced and forced into hiding by thugs in my employ. Is that true?"

He gauged his reply carefully. "I've put some men to watch his comings and goings."

"Have they threatened him?"

"I don't see how. He hasn't come back to Henton Court."

"That's not an answer," she said evenly.

"Catherine." He hadn't intended to mention this, not until he felt certain it would work. "I may have found a way to get him out of your hair for good. But until I can be certain—"

"The contract," she cut in, "laid out the terms by which you and I were to rub along. You have overstepped those bounds again and again."

"Overstepped." She was no solicitor, and he was no schoolboy to be lectured by her.

But words were her weapons. He wouldn't bother fighting on that ground. Instead he grasped her face, felt her flinch at the touch of skin to skin. He held her in place, watching the color bloom in her cheeks, registering the way her breath hitched, waiting in silence until she found the spine to look into his eyes again.

"You want to pretend like that contract guided us for a *moment*? If you were honest," he said, "you would have ceased speaking of it right after you rose from my bed that day we were married. Because you knew then—I saw it in your face—you knew it wasn't going to be simple. You knew you were already in over your head."

She licked her lips, then spoke very rapidly. "If I lose Everleigh's to him—"

"What?" Here was the main fear, which she kept circling back to, which she held before her like a flaming sword to keep him at bay. "What if you did lose it? God's name, Catherine—what if you stopped fighting for it? Imagine this: what if you simply let it go?"

Her jaw sagged. For a moment, she gaped at him, struck speechless. Then she twisted out of his grip, writhing like a snapping cat. "How *dare* you—"

"I asked you a question," he said. "Answer it, for once. What would you lose? Apart from a company?"

"You—you can't imagine," she whispered. "You . . . I thought you knew. It isn't simply a company. It's . . . *me*."

At least she had said it now. Put it into words. He saw, by the way her gaze broke from his, darted to the side, that she heard the foolishness of her own words.

And that alone killed his temper, and stirred compassion in its place. "I do know you feel so," he said. "It's how you made sense of the world, and your place in it.

And it's so deep a part of you that you're not sure you can lose it and still remain whole."

She nodded once, then bit her knuckle and bowed her head. "Then . . . how can you ask?" she said raggedly.

"Because I'm telling you that you're wrong. You're stronger than you know."

Her voice emerged muffled. "I know how strong I am."

"Then you should know that you're bigger than the company. Everleigh's isn't you, Catherine. *You* are Everleigh's. And far more besides. If you can't keep hold of this version, then you'll make another. A new Everleigh's, grander and greater than the one that came before it." He hesitated. "I could help you do it. I've got the funds."

The offer caught her off guard. For a wild, staggered moment, Catherine dared to envision it. An auction house like none other, specializing in artwork that no other house would touch. A center of restoration and rare curation, for the most select and knowledgeable patrons.

But at the next moment, the very prospect made her feel dizzy and disoriented and exhausted, as though staring up an endless cliff that she must scale without a map. "I couldn't, though. It would never be the same. I couldn't make it the same."

He loosed a long breath. "I never thought to see you doubt yourself."

She flinched. "I don't." It was the world she doubted. "Don't you see? Without Everleigh's behind me . . . I would be nobody." Without the respectability of a

known institution as her calling card—a credential that
evidenced, even to skeptics, her claims of professional-
ism—she would be nothing but an ordinary woman,
subject to the typical condescension of the male-
governed world.

"You'd be somebody to me," he said.

The tender note in his voice, the somberness in his
thickly lashed gray eyes, struck her like an arrow to the
heart. It made her chest feel full, and choked her breath.
"As your wife, you mean."

He stepped toward her. "Yes," he said in a fierce
voice. "Catherine O'Shea."

She put her hand to the back of her chair, clawed into
the silk fabric, searching for her will. "Your wife, whom
you will overrule whenever you deem it fit. Your wife,
whom you will lock away when her desires strike you as
inconvenient."

"To hell with that," he snarled. "If I think you in
danger, *yes*. That's what a man does—for his wife, for
his friends, for anyone he loves. You think I give a damn
if you're angry now, so long as you're safe tonight?"

She barely heard the rest of his words, after he'd spoken the one. *Loves.* She blinked at him, but it did not
bring him into clearer focus. Her vision seemed to have
clouded over. He'd not confessed anything just then.
He'd said just enough to knock her off her balance, to
unsettle her from the tight, swaddling layers of indigna-
tion . . .

"You promised," she whispered. "You promised to
respect me."

He stared at her. "And you think I don't."

"I . . ." Her gut, her instinct, had never been so at
odds with her clamoring brain. *You showed you didn't,*

her brain nattered, when all she wished to do was reach out and brush away that single black curl falling across his cheek. To trace the rough line of his nose. These battling influences held her motionless, mute and agonized with indecision.

Marriage, Catherine, is the most perilous risk a woman ever takes.

He gave a sharp tug of his mouth. Turned away, clawing his fingers through his hair as he stared at the mantel. "Maybe I'm the fool here," he muttered. "Swallowing your nonsense, hook, line, and sinker." He pivoted back, his face harder, his voice implacable. "Well, I won't bite. I'm done listening to you. Because what matters is what I see, and that's a coward, hiding behind lies."

She sucked in a breath, stung beyond measure. "If you refer to *me*—"

"That's right. A businesswoman, you call yourself." His voice drilled, cold as iron. "But a businesswoman wouldn't turn away from opportunities. She wouldn't shrink from risk. You can't trust me to respect you? You can't build a new company? *Bollocks.* Bloody excuses. You said it to me once—afraid to try and fail. Well, that's you. It's got nothing to do with me. You say you don't believe in me? You don't believe in *yourself.* That's what ails you, Catherine—in the end, it's *you* whom you lack faith in. Your own ability. Your judgment. What you actually *want.*"

She opened her mouth, but nothing came out. Fear. He was accusing her of fear. And God above, but . . . it could be no coincidence that her heart was pounding; that she felt unable to defend herself.

He made some noise. It sounded like contempt. He turned on his heel for the door.

Suddenly she was lunging for him, catching his elbow and dragging him around. "You want to talk of fear?" She glared up at him, at his stony face, that space of safe remove he'd created for himself. "Then tell me. Who sits on the Board of Works for Whitechapel? Is it you?"

He shrugged out of her hold. "You'll not duck this matter with accusations—"

"I'm not accusing you. I'm only speaking the facts. You spoke before that board—you brought them to heel, you made them hold that auction. What else could you do, if you made them listen to your voice every day? Perhaps you could get the sewers fixed. You once said that you would tell my brother to argue for it. But why should a man from Bloomsbury care for your streets? Why would you force others to fight your battles, when you've proved you could do it better? What's stopping *you*? It's not lack of care. Would you call it fear? For if I'm afraid, so are you! And if I'm a coward—are you less of one?"

A muscle in his jaw ticked as he stared at her. "Fine," he said at last. "Fine. A fine pair we make. I'll not argue it."

His reply frustrated her. It provided her no inroad, no grounds on which to argue with him further.

And she saw, in the way he shifted his weight and glanced toward the door, that in a moment, he would leave anyway.

So she looked for her courage and gave him what she could. "I want to be able to trust you," she said roughly. "I want . . . to be the woman who would take that risk. And I want you to be the man who deserves it. Who deserves *me*. But I . . . I must know, in my head as well as my heart, that the risk is worth it. That it's wise."

His mouth softened. Not quite a smile. "You idiot," he said gently. "This . . . between us . . . it isn't supposed to feel *wise*. Even I know that. And nobody ever called me a romantic."

He leaned down. His lips brushed hers softly—too softly; he didn't try to open her mouth, to clasp her against him or deepen the kiss, even when she caught his shoulders and squeezed in a silent petition.

And when he pulled away from her, she could not work out the grounds by which she might pull him back. She was the one, after all, who had left him.

He still stood before her, but the distance seemed unbridgeable, widening with each second that she wrestled for what to say. When she did speak, the words emerged unbearably stiff, all wrong. "You'll come to the auction, I hope."

And by the shadow that passed over his face, she realized that she had proved, at last, that she had no feminine wiles in her. No tricks by which to keep him, no art that might make her face and body communicate a message contrary to her words.

Never had she regretted that deficiency so keenly.

"Do you want me there?" he said.

She floundered. "Yes, I . . . it's important that it go off well, for . . . Everleigh's sake."

His smile was brief and humorless. "For yours, you mean."

"Well—yes. It would go far to proving I'm in full possession of my faculties," she said hesitantly. "If I am seen to coordinate a successful sale."

He clapped his hat onto his head and said, "I'll come, then."

She stood there watching as he walked out. Such cold words on which to part.

CHAPTER SEVENTEEN

*W*as she afraid? Could it be that he was right? Catherine asked herself this as she stood before the little mirror in her office the morning of the auction. The thick door, hewn of Berkshire walnut—her father had been so proud of that; he'd always insisted that no place in the world could rival Berkshire for walnut—usually proved stalwart against the noises in the hall. Today, however, the tumult seeped through. Downstairs, the doors had been thrown open, and for the first time in the company's history, the footmen were not taking names to check against a list that had been pruned to an elite and exclusive number. She had already looked out the window once and felt at first sick, and then thrilled, and then sick again at the crush in the road.

The advertisements had worked. All of London, it seemed, had turned out to attend the auction. Whether any of them had money to spend was another question.

She looked at her face now, so pale and tight in the mirror. What had she done, inviting the public? If the auction failed, if the sales were meager, Peter would no doubt use this as evidence against her. She had no doubt he was plotting in some hidey-hole. That they were locked in a battle now that would not end until one of them had won sole control of Everleigh's.

Let it go, O'Shea had suggested.

And then, as though to show her how it was done, he had left her. Not a backward glance. Not a visit in the intervening days. Lilah, noting her wan mood, had offered to visit him, to inquire after his health.

But Catherine had refused the offer. She knew he was hale. She had no fear for his well-being. She had full faith in him to look after himself.

She thought of him every waking moment.

She also thought of her father. What would he have thought of Nicholas O'Shea? Too easily, she could imagine his horror. A man who put himself above the law. Who ran an illegal club, and boldly owned his crimes.

But . . . she could also imagine a different story, in which her father saw his ambitions. His accomplishments. Her father had made a wish for her, once, which she had never forgotten. *A man of discerning tastes, who knows brilliance when he sees it, and knows to treasure it, too.*

A man. He had not said a *gentleman.*

A knock came at the door. She opened it. Mr. Hastings stood before her, attired smartly in his formal blacks. "I believe we are ready, miss."

She blew out a breath. "Have you taken a glimpse of the crowd?"

He shifted his weight, his leather shoes creaking. "A . . . mixed lot, miss. But I think I see some goers. Lord Hambly and Lord Monteford are among them. And Sir Wimple. Also, I believe, some new faces, very promising. Come, see for yourself."

She followed him down the stairs, her heart drumming harder with each step. Her father seemed to be walking beside her. He had urged her never to forget the auction rooms. Would he have approved this innovation? *Art is our calling. You will be the soul of this place.*

They entered the saleroom through a private door. She lost her breath at the crowd jammed inside it. The crush spilled out into the hall. The balcony, so rarely used, had been opened, the screens thrown back. People leaned over, some only to gawk, others to examine the first lot, the tambour-topped writing table, which two assistants were arranging on the dais beside the rostrum.

A seat had been kept for her, on the other side of the podium. But she found herself standing behind it, gripping the chair tightly as she scanned the crowd.

There. At the back wall, standing beside Lilah and Lord Palmer. She met O'Shea's eyes.

He nodded to her.

"Good morning," said Hastings from the lectern. "My thanks to you, ladies and gentlemen, for attending this historic occasion, the first public auction to be held in this establishment. The collection today is a rare and varied one, spanning centuries and continents in its excellence . . ."

His words faded as she stared at O'Shea. He did not look away from her. The crowd, the noise, might not have existed.

He smiled slightly. She smiled back, a trembling smile that seemed to dislodge some piece of her heart. It plummeted straight into her stomach as Hastings opened the bidding.

The reserve was met and instantly raised. A buzz rose—she recognized the edge of titillation; the excitement at such rich figures. It had no place in a saleroom, properly; some of the crowd had clearly come only to ogle the wealthy. For a moment, the bidding paused, and the buzz seemed to assume a sour, snide tone.

"Fifty going once," Hastings intoned. "Fifty for this rare specimen, this eighteenth-century tambour-topped writing table, fine mahogany, the best workmanship you'll find, fifty going twice—"

It should go for eighty at least. She squeezed the back of the chair, anxious. If the first lot went low, the rest would be sure to follow that sad suit. It was no way to open; that was why she'd slotted the table first, hoping, counting, on it to start the auction briskly—

"Sixty," came a coarse male voice—one suspiciously familiar to her. She frowned, hunting through the crowd, and barely mastered her reaction as she caught sight of Johnson, boldly lifting his hand.

"I have sixty," said Hastings, "sixty, very good, sir. Do I hear—"

"Sixty-five." And that was Malloy!

"Seventy," Johnson barked, scowling.

She bowed her head and rubbed her brow, masking her expression lest it betray her. O'Shea was running a ring in her auction—a ring in reverse, to drive up the bidding!

It certainly wasn't ethical.

Her swelling heart did not care.

"Seventy-five." That was Lilah's voice, cool, feminine. Another first: a former hostess, bidding in the saleroom!

"Eighty," someone else called—a stranger, whom Catherine did not recognize. At last!

"Eighty-five," Lilah shot back.

From there, the figure mounted with dizzying speed.

Amid the mounting clamor, the shifting of the throng, it was impossible to tell who was bidding, but none of the voices were familiar to her. Above, Hastings had a clear view, and was glancing about the room, pointing and nodding, beckoning with his hand.

"Hundred twenty-five going once," he said. "Going twice—sold, to Lord Monteford in the corner!"

The crowd burst into applause, and Catherine's knees seemed to weaken. It had taken off now. The crowd was warmed up; bids were flowing.

The next lot was brought out—the Sheraton dresser, looking, thanks to Batten, far more elegant than when she'd first glimpsed it in O'Shea's storeroom. Hastings had barely finished describing it before the first bid was called—and the second and third followed in swift succession.

Only then did she feel able to take her seat. This time, when she bowed her head, it was to hide a smile.

"Success, was it?"

Startled, she turned. O'Shea stood in the doorway to her office, a parcel beneath his arm. He was not dressed to linger; he already wore his hat and gloves, and a gray muffler around his neck that made his eyes flash like silver.

She cleared her throat. "A smashing success. Beyond my wildest hope, even." How stilted she sounded. She tried for humor. "Congratulations, sir. You've just made a great deal of money."

He shook his head. "For once, I didn't make it. I came into it, like a proper gentleman."

Her smile kept slipping away. "I'm not sure money

has anything to do with gentlemanliness," she said quietly. "Either way, you fit the part."

He gave her an odd look, as though unsure of what to make of the compliment. His reaction made her feel all the more miserable and tongue-tied.

I was afraid, she wanted to say. *You were right.*

But before she could shape the words, he had pulled the parcel from beneath his arm, offering it to her. "I brought this for you."

She took it hesitantly. It felt like a book, a very heavy one. She could feel the ridge of the spine through the brown paper wrapping. "Should I . . . Do you wish me to open it?"

"No need. You've seen it before. Ours are the only signatures in it."

It took a moment to understand. There was only one book they had signed together. "The register book?"

"One and the same, with the certificate tucked inside." He held her gaze. "There's no other proof, mind you. I made sure of that."

"But . . . why are you giving this to me?"

He took a deep breath and retreated a pace toward the door. "Here's the thing, Catherine. You asked me once if my nose had been broken. You remember?"

Jarred, she cast her mind back. She located the moment, found it embedded amid some of the most startling, heated minutes of her life.

Their wedding day. His bed.

The very first time she had dared to touch him.

Her gaze fell to the parcel in her hands, the edges so crisply folded, so neatly tucked. Somebody had taken great care with this. They had bound it in twine several more times than necessary. "Yes," she said. "I remember."

"I'd hope so." There was a smile in his voice, but when she glanced up, hoping to see it, she found him looking at her with a curiously sober concentration. "I never told you how it happened," he said. "The first time, I mean. No wonder there. I've never spoken of it to a soul. Nor have I thought on it, I'm glad to say, for a very long time—not until today, when I was wrapping up that book for you."

She clutched the parcel tightly. *He* had wrapped this. He had taken care with it, had spent more time than required on creasing the folds, tying it up in twine.

Suddenly the book seemed to weigh fifty pounds. It came to her to lean against something—or to sit down; such was the silence settling between them, a brooding, heavy weight that foretold a blow to come.

Instead, she straightened her shoulders, braced herself against it. That strained look on his face was so unfamiliar. Whatever he meant to tell her obviously came at a cost to him. She could bear the hearing, if he could bear the telling.

"Tell me," she whispered.

He brushed his fingers along the bridge of his nose, then lowered his hand to his side—trying, perhaps, to hide the fist it made. "It was a man who broke it." He spoke evenly. "A landlord, though the title is too kind. A slumlord, let's say. He owned most of the buildings in Spitalfields back then—that's where my ma raised me. She'd never married, of course—but there was a fondness between her and my father. He dropped by every now and then. Spared coin when he had it, to make sure I was well kept. And my ma, she did her best, too. This room we'd landed in, the floorboards were rotting, the roof leaked in the rain, but it was a step up. The rent, she said, was wondrous. She could afford it, barely. With the help from my da, she could pay for it. Sometimes we even ate meat on a Sunday."

His speech had fallen into a different rhythm, chopped and coarse. She doubted he knew it. His gaze shifted away from hers, fixed somewhere in the middle distance as he went on.

"Now, when my da died, it got rougher to pay the rent. I guess she took up with Bell—that was the name of the man who owned the place. Traded what she could to him, in lieu of coin. Only then it happened again—she found herself belly full, I mean. I reckon she despaired when she found out—another mouth to feed, when she could barely fill mine." He focused on her then, an unblinking stare. "I do understand, Kitty, why a woman might fear to be trapped. There are all sorts of traps in life. And women, they face more than their fair share."

She sucked in a sharp breath. She had no idea what to say.

But he seemed not to require a reply. After a second, he shrugged and said, "So one day, Bell comes knocking, looking for his rent. Only this time, she doesn't have it—not enough, at any rate. So they have it out, while I'm on the other side of the curtain. I hear something that tips me off—realize she's breeding, and Bell is the dad. And being a proper young hothead, I decide to confront him." An ugly smile twisted his mouth. "Defend her honor, I suppose. Stupid. So young."

She did not like the contempt in his voice. That young boy he'd been did not deserve his scorn. "Don't say that. Of course you wished to defend her."

He sighed. "See, that's a fine aim for lads raised in

your world. But in mine, it's sheer foolishness. Honor means nothing once you're starving. And my mother knew that. She knew I was ruining her chances. For it seemed Bell had made her an offer. He'd a hankering for another son, didn't matter whereby he got it. So they'd struck a deal; he'd support her until the babe came, and set her up nicely if it happened to be a boy. Only then I went at him like a cur gone rabid, and knocked him on his arse, and he threatened to leave Ma flat. Said the deal was off, until I kissed his boots and begged. Otherwise, he was done with her."

God in heaven. She set the package down very slowly on the desk, for fear she would drop it. "What did you do?"

His face looked bleak, but his voice leveled, recovering the usual polish of his vowels. "I did it. For her sake, I did it. Took some persuasion, of course. Some tears. But for her sake, I went down on my knees and I kissed that bastard's boot." His mouth curved. "And he lost not a moment in kicking me straight in the face. Broke my nose, chipped off a nice piece of one tooth."

Her hands were over her mouth. How they'd gotten there, she didn't know. She felt the ragged rush of her breath, shockingly hot in the chill of the room.

He shrugged. "He took her in, though. Not that it made a difference. Babe came too early. Took her along to the grave."

It was too much. She found herself stepping toward him, reaching for him, her hands closing on the soft wool of his sleeve. "Mr. O'Shea—" But no, that was not right. It was profane. "*Nicholas.* I'm so—"

"Don't say you're sorry," he cut in softly. "Like I said, I haven't dwelled on it in years. But the lesson it taught me, I'll never forget. You don't beg for anyone. For it never comes to good. Nothing's worth that price. And I don't mean the price is honor or pride. I mean, it's got to do with knowing your own worth. The world will crush you, if you let it. So you don't. You stand tall. And you never stoop, because there's nothing worth having that requires you to grovel."

For a brief, blessed moment, he cupped her cheek in his gloved hand. And then he stepped backward, removing himself from her touch, so her own hands closed on empty air. He nodded toward the desk, the register book she'd left there.

"I won't keep you trapped," he said. "Not even for five years. You burn that book, and nobody can say this marriage ever happened. You're free as a bird, Kitty. And I won't beg you to come back to me, even if I want to." He exhaled. "And I do. There's the hell of it. You almost made me beg. Instead, I'll speak plainly: I want you. I love you. But you'll come freely, of your own choice. Or you won't."

"I . . ." *Say it.* "I'll come," she said hoarsely. "I think . . . I will come."

He made a convulsive move, as though to grab her—but then he decided against it.

Instead, hands fisting at his sides, he withdrew another pace. "I don't want you to *think,*" he said quietly. "I want you to *know.* I won't have you uncertain. And I won't have you in secret, either. I'll have you in front of the world, and you'll hold your head high beside me. Or I'll not have you at all."

He turned on his heel. Her heart leapt into her throat, choking her, uncontainable. She opened her mouth—and he turned back.

"One more thing," he said gruffly. "I'm taking over the seat for Whitechapel on the Board of Works. You were right, I guess. It was time."

The breath left her. "You were right, too," she whispered.

But he did not hear her. Or he pretended not to. Without another word, he left.

It was one of those rare mornings that rightfully belonged to October, but had somehow found its way into December by mistake. The sun shone brightly through the bare-branched trees, and the park was full of nannies in black gowns, overseeing the games of children in neatly starched pinafores and smartly-pressed trousers.

Catherine paused to watch the scene. To draw another deep lungful of the bracing air. Winter was upon them. She would long soon enough for the days when she had walked down the pavement without regard for the chill. This moment in particular would come to mind—one of the rarest in her life, for she never acted rashly, without first feeling certain of the outcome.

She had only done it twice before, in fact. The public auction. And the day she had wed Nicholas.

The sound of children's laughter followed her up the short flight of stairs. A uniformed servant opened the door for her, bowing smartly.

The lobby was mostly empty. One desk sat vacant; at the other, a single gentleman waited to speak with the clerk. The sight baffled her, brought her to a stop. She had counted on a longer queue. She had counted on a few more minutes, at least.

She found herself turning back toward the door, the sunlit scene without. The false promise of autumn, when winter was already here.

She caught herself with one hand on the door. Waved off the doorman and turned back into the room. She could not be sure of the outcome. The waiting would be painful. The result might shatter her. It might be too late.

But no part of her doubted her course.

"Madam?"

A new clerk had entered the lobby, was taking his seat at the desk. "May I help you?" he asked.

He looked very young, though she noticed a ring shining on his finger as she approached, which might have been a wedding band. Some men had taken to wearing them of late. But he looked too young to be a husband. She saw no sign of whiskers, and his cheeks looked plump, as though he still sat at his mother's table every night, cosseted and urged to eat more.

But maybe it was his wife who cosseted him. Maybe he was wiser than his years, and he had met a rare girl, and leapt to marry her, before he lost his chance to somebody quicker, bolder. More courageous. Rare chances, wondrous chances, did not come often.

"Ma'am?" He was frowning up at her, his sandy brows knitted. "Are you quite all right?"

"I am very well," she said, and she sounded well; she sounded bold, decisive, a woman who knew how to seize an opportunity before it got away. "I would like to take out an announcement in your newspaper."

"What kind of announcement?" he asked.

She smiled. "An announcement of marriage," she said. "Mine, to Mr. Nicholas O'Shea."

*   *   *

"You'll wear out the carpet," Lilah drawled. "And I rather like it, for all that it's the most impractical color."

Catherine wheeled. Lilah looked intolerably comfortable, stretched across the chaise longue beneath a cashmere throw, a book in her hand. She did not seem at all alarmed by the fact that the marriage announcement had been published to the world eight hours ago, plain as day, in stark black and white, albeit tucked in abominably small print in the very last page of the *Times*. Regardless, it was public knowledge now. Anyone might read of it.

Yet no visitors had called. Not a single rap at the door. Nicholas O'Shea was nowhere in evidence.

"He's not coming." For hours she had battled this awful suspicion, and now it came rushing out, acidic like bile. Like fear, fear such as she'd never known. "He's changed his mind. He gave me that register book *hoping* I'd burn it."

"I very much doubt that." Lilah cast aside her book and stretched, arms over her head, lolling with shameless abandon. Was she even wearing a corset? Her posture made Catherine very suspicious suddenly. "He's canny, I'll give you that much. But if he wanted it burned, he'd have burned it himself."

"How can you be so calm?"

Lilah shoved herself up on one elbow. "Men can be very stubborn," she said. "Perhaps you should call on him."

"What? I can't!" The notion left her aghast. "Don't you see? He walked away from me. He said—he said I must prove myself. Well, I've done it. Must I do all the rest as well?"

Lilah sighed, then sat up fully. "Catherine," she said. "You've lived at Diamonds. You've been to Neddie's. Have you ever seen a man in *either* of those locales making a study of marriage announcements in the *Times*?"

Spoken aloud, the idea seemed ludicrous. Mouth agape, she shook her head. "You can't . . . Do you think he hasn't seen it?"

"I think it possible that he has no idea what you've done. So perhaps you should go make it clear to him."

She stood indecisively for a moment. Going to him was not at all what she'd imagined. Going to him meant . . . possibly facing his rejection in person. If the announcement wasn't enough—if he was not persuaded, if he *had* changed his mind—why, she did not think she could bear to witness the look on his face when he told her so.

"Consider this," Lilah said. "Do you want to remain here, waiting, another day? Or possibly five, or ten?"

"You could write to him," Catherine whispered.

"No," Lilah said gently. "That would be wrong, and I think you know it."

She pushed out a breath, then nodded. "May I borrow your coach?"

"Of course." Lilah lay back again, smiling. "Oh, and if you pass Christian in the hall on your way out, tell him I have . . . something to show him."

Catherine snorted. No doubt, then—Lilah was certainly not wearing a corset.

Without Johnson's key, she had no way to use the secret passage through the shop. For that matter, she needn't bother with secrecy, did she? Not when the rest of the world now knew of her marriage—even if, so she prayed, the other party had yet to realize it.

All the same, it was very odd to approach the front door of Diamonds and bear the mystified looks of two young swells waiting to be admitted. They gawked outright when Callan opened the door and admitted her straightaway, while leaving them to cool their heels on the grounds that the establishment did not open till half three.

"Is he upstairs?" she asked tensely as Callan led her past the empty baize tables.

"His office," he said. "I don't think he's expecting you."

The words scored her like claws. She bit her lip hard and summoned her courage. "That's all right," she said. "I'll show myself up."

His door stood ajar. She did not bother to knock, throwing it open and speaking at the same time. "Do you not read the newspaper?"

Nicholas was seated at his desk, working through a thick sheaf of papers. At the sound of her voice, he cast down his pen, but she saw his shoulders square before he looked up at her.

"No," he said evenly. "Not on regular occasion."

Her throat filled. Some knot she could not quite swallow. Nerves, maybe; hopes and fears and anxiety all tangled up in one lump. How well he looked. Not yet in his evening wear, not even fully dressed; his waistcoat was unbuttoned, but shirtsleeves became his broad shoulders very well. "Perhaps you should," she whispered.

His jaw tightened. "Reading is not my strong suit."

She pressed a hand to her mouth. Lilah had been right. What an idiot she was! "Does *nobody* around here read the newspapers? Have a care for the state of the country? The stocks, the gossip, the . . . fashions?"

His brow lifted. "Is there a reason they should?"

His tone was all wrong. So polite, so distant, when in her dreams he was rushing toward her, wrapping her in his arms, putting her against a door the way he had done once, showing her with language deeper than words how much he wanted her. The disjuncture between fantasy and reality left her strangely off-balance, confused and dizzy. She felt trapped inside some poorly scripted farce, while he was following a different script, cold and refined. "I would imagine one of your—your customers might have mentioned it," she said. But—of course; the club did not open until half three. Perhaps he'd met no customers yet today.

He rose from his desk, frowning. "Was there some story printed about the auction, then? Did word get out that the collection was mine?"

A disbelieving laugh spilled from her. "No! That is—yes! The *Times* did mention the sale. But there was also *this*." She tossed her newspaper onto the desk and crossed her arms to hold her heart in her chest, for it was knocking hard enough to break free.

He looked down at it. Back up at her. "You might as well tell me," he said flatly.

"No." Suddenly she felt mutinous. He'd obviously had a very calm, collected morning. Meanwhile, she had been stewing in that house, stretched on a private rack of nerves, straining for the sound of a knock that had not come, agonizing—

She huffed out a breath. "Look for yourself. I don't care how long it takes you. I'll wait." She dropped into a chair. "Go on. I have all day."

"All day?" He lifted a brow as he came around the desk. "Work doesn't keep you?"

"Forget the auction rooms," she snapped. "Read."

"Forget the . . ." He gave her a marveling look, which narrowed as he reached for the newspaper. He leaned back against the desktop, looking down the front page.

"Not that page," she blurted. "The very back."

He flipped it over. She saw the effort he took, squinting as he scanned the print. For a man not easy with reading, it was no small task to look over the crowded columns, the crammed typeset, for a single unknown item.

She saw the moment when he reached her wedding announcement. The paper abruptly crumpled beneath the clench of his fist. He looked up at her, mouth agape. For one moment, she thought she saw a world of emotion in his face. She thought she saw a happy ending, after all.

And then he clawed a hand through his hair and burst into laughter. "By God," he said, choking out the syllables. "He's done for, after all. Killed in one sentence."

"What?" She sprang to her feet. "Who?"

"Your brother. You've finished him."

He would talk now of her *brother*? "Is that all you have to say?" She felt unaccountably furious, suddenly. For she had showed courage—she had proved that she had no doubts; that, rather than hiding, she would trumpet their marriage to the world. And he was *laughing* at her for it?

He shook his head, struggling for composure; put his fist against his mouth and dragged in a hoarse breath. "I was going to send word to you," he said, his voice oddly rough. "Your brother—I had Pilcher broker the deal.

Peter keeps his seat on the board, in exchange for selling his half of the auction rooms. But Pilcher and I mean to keep him useless, as far as the board goes. It's all done, Catherine." He groped behind him, not taking his eyes off her as he found and held out the stack of papers he'd been looking through. "Everleigh's is yours. I had a solicitor draw up the transfer of sale."

She stared at him. Then at the contract. Hers? Everleigh's, entirely hers?

No. This wasn't right. She didn't want this gift now, of all times. The auction rooms, overshadowing what she'd done today—what that newspaper announced—

"Forget that," she said very softly. "Forget Everleigh's."

He stared at her for a silent moment, shock tightening his features. Then he opened his hand. The contract thudded to the floor.

"What did you just say?" he asked.

She cleared her throat. Said it louder. "Forget Everleigh's."

"Did you . . ." Now *he* cleared his throat. "Did you take out that announcement for *my* sake?"

Her stomach jumped. "Yes, of course. Why else would I have done it?"

"To . . . check your brother." He blinked, then straightened off the desk. "You took out that announcement for me," he said, but this time there was no question in his words, only wonder. And *there*, at last, was what she had wanted to see in his face—the look she had been envisioning, willing, praying to behold. He stepped toward her, a prowling movement, full of design. Seized her hands, then lifted each to his mouth, kissing them in turn. "For me," he whispered.

"Yes, yes, yes." She pulled her hands free of his only so she could grasp his face. "I took it out. I wanted the world to know."

"That we're married," he said huskily. He turned his face, kissed her palm.

"That we're married," she agreed. "That you're my husband. That I . . . do believe I love you."

"Believe?" He fixed her in a narrow gaze.

"Know," she whispered. "But perhaps . . . perhaps you had better make sure of it now. Against . . ." She swallowed, feeling the blush steal over her. He noticed it. His gaze dropped to her mouth, and the heat in his look loosened her next words, brought them out in a rush: "Against the door."

"Against the . . ." A smile slowly widened his mouth. "You liked that, did you?"

"I seem"—her voice was breathless, ragged—"I seem to be more wanton than I knew."

"Oh, you don't know the half of it yet." He lifted her beneath her arms, carried her up against the door, held her there as he buried his face in her neck. "You've got . . ." By her hand on his back, she felt the deep breath he took of her. "A lot to learn," he said, lips brushing over her skin. "Happily, seems we've got the time."

"All the time," she said. "All the time in the world." But after a long moment, in which his grip tightened, but he seemed content only to hold her, she frowned. "I wouldn't mind hurrying up with this lesson, though."

He lifted his head, laughing, his dark face impossibly beautiful, more beautiful than she had ever realized, for there were no shadows in it now, nothing in his look but the kind of wonder, the open unveiled adoration, that she had seen only in dreams—and never dared envision for herself.

"I hate to disappoint my wife," he murmured, "but I don't mean to hurry this time."

She almost argued. But as he kissed her, a deep, leisurely kiss that made pleasure purl down her spine, she changed her mind and threaded her hands through his hair. No need to rush, after all. She was exactly where she wished to be. He could take as long as he liked.

More sizzling and sensual historical romance from Pocket Books!

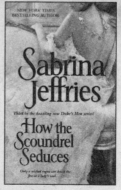